I stared at the lofty, square-shaped structure with its towers on each corner. "Welcome to Castle Paling," Colum said softly.

I turned to him sharply. "I understood you were taking me to the inn."

"Nay," he said. "This is better."

I looked at him and I felt a sudden fear possess me. A faint moaning sounded in the trees and I seemed to hear a warning in the air: "Get away from here. Go back where you will be safe."

Fawcett Crest Books
by Philippa Carr:

THE LION TRIUMPHANT   23233-6 $1.95

THE WITCH FROM THE SEA   22837-1 $1.95

The Witch
from the Sea

Philippa Carr

FAWCETT CREST • NEW YORK

THE WITCH FROM THE SEA

THIS BOOK CONTAINS THE COMPLETE TEXT OF THE
ORIGINAL HARDCOVER EDITION

Published by Fawcett Crest Books, a unit of CBS Publications,
the Consumer Publishing Division of CBS Inc., by arrangement
with G. P. Putnam's Sons

ISBN: 0-449-22837-1

Printed in the United States of America

3 4 5 6 7 8 9 10

Contents

The Witch
from the Sea

Part One

LINNET

Trade Winds

It is the custom for the women of our family to keep a journal. My grandmother did, and my mother must have learned the habit from her. I remember my mother's saying once that by doing so one lived one's life more fully. So much is lost if one cannot remember it, and even memory is apt to distort so that what actually happened, when looked back on, often takes on an entirely different aspect from the truth. But if it is set down with the emotion of the moment—exactly as it appeared then—it can be recalled in detail. It can be assessed and perhaps better understood, so that not only does one preserve a clear picture of some event which is important to one, but with it acquire a greater understanding of oneself.

So I will begin my journal in the months which followed our glorious victory over the Spaniards, which seems appropriate because it was a turning point in my life. At this time we were all living in a state of what I suppose can only be called euphoria. We had discovered how close we had come to disaster. We had never believed that it was possible for us to be beaten, and perhaps this supreme and superb confidence was one of the factors which carried us through to victory—but at the same time we could soberly contemplate

what defeat would have meant. We had heard stories of the
terrible things which had happened in the Netherlands where
men had stood out against the might of Spain. We knew
that when the Armada sailed from its native land, it came
not only with the weapons of war but with instruments of
torture. We knew that those who would not accept their
doctrines of religion were tortured and burned alive; we had
heard that men had been buried with only their heads protruding from the earth and there left to perish. There was
no end to the tales of suffering, and that would have been
our fate . . . had they come. But we had defeated them.
All along the coasts were the wrecks of their ships; some
drifted on the high seas; perhaps a few returned to Spain.
And here we were in a green and beautiful land, with our
good Queen Elizabeth safe on her throne. It was a time
for all Englishmen to rejoice, and who more so than the
men and women of Devon? We were of the sea, and it was
our own Francis Drake, whoever else might claim the credit,
who had saved our country.

Captain Jake Pennlyon, my father, was in the greatest of
good spirits. Lusty, strong, adventurous, determined to drive
the Spaniards from the seas, despising weakness, assured of
the rightness of his own opinions, arrogant, outspoken, bowing to no man, he was characteristic of an Englishman of
our age. I had hated him when I was young because I could
never understand the relationship between him and my
mother. I loved her devotedly, in a protective way, and I
did not realize until this time how much she loved him too.
In my youthful inexperience I misjudged their behavior
toward each other; they seemed constantly to be in conflict,
but now that I was growing up I understood that these battles
gave savor to their lives, and although at times it seemed
as though they delighted in taunting each other and that it
was impossible for them to live in harmony, they were
certainly deeply unhappy apart.

One could not feel mildly in any way toward my father,
so now that I had ceased to hate and despise him I had
to love him and be fiercely proud of him. As for him, he
had resented me because I was not a boy, but now he had
made up his mind that his daughter was better than any
boy, and I sensed that he was rather pleased that I was a
girl. My three-year-old sister Damask was too young to
interest him much, but he no longer wished for boys because
he knew there could be none. He was content with his
illegitimate sons. My mother used to say that he had scattered

them throughout the world, and he did not deny this. The three I knew were Carlos, Jacko and Penn. Carlos had married Edwina, who owned Trewynd Grange, the nearby mansion which she had inherited from her father. She was in a way already related to the family because her mother had been adopted by my grandmother. Jacko and Penn lived with us when they were not at sea. Jacko had captained one of my father's ships, and Penn who was seventeen years old—a year younger than I—was already going to sea.

We had lived so long with the fear of the Spaniards that without it our lives seemed suddenly empty, and although I had planned to start my journal, there seemed little to record. All through those weeks reports were coming in about what had happened to the Armada. Ships were constantly being washed up on the coasts, their crews starving; many were drowned; some reached the coasts of Scotland and Ireland, and it was said that their reception there was so inhospitable that the lucky ones were those who were drowned. My father roared his approval. "By God," he would cry, "if any of the plaguey dons see fit to land on Devon soil, I'll slit their throats from ear to ear."

My mother retorted, "You've defeated them. Is that not enough?"

"Nay, madam," he cried. "It is not enough and there is no fate too bad for these Spaniards who would dare attempt to subdue us!"

And so it went on. People came to the house, and we entertained them, and over the table the talk would all be of Spaniards—of the wretched man in the Escorial who had sought to be master of the world and was now defeated in such a way that he could never rise again. And how they laughed when they heard tales of the anger of those Spaniards who had stayed at home and who were demanding why the Armada, which had cost them so dear to build, did not return. Why did the Duke of Medina-Sidonia, who had boasted of the victory he would win over the English, not come home to be honored? What had happened to the mighty Armada? Was it so pure and holy that it was too good for this earth and had wafted to heaven?

"Wafted to the devil!" cried my father, banging his great fist on the table.

Then he would recount the action in which he had taken part, and all would listen eagerly, and Carlos and Jacko would nod and agree, and so it went on.

I did not wish to write of this in my journal. It was

common knowledge. It was what was happening in thousands of homes all over England.

"How is your journal getting on?" asked my mother.

"Nothing happens," I said. "There is nothing to record. So many things happened to you," I added enviously. "That was different."

Her face clouded, and I knew she was looking back to the days when she was young.

She said, "My darling Linnet, I hope you will never have anything but happiness to record."

"Wouldn't that be rather dull?" I asked.

Then she laughed and put her arm about me.

"If so, I hope your journal will be a very dull one."

It seemed it would be, and because of this, I forgot it. It was only when the ship *Trade Winds* came sailing into the Sound that I remembered it and began to write regularly.

The *Trade Winds* was built in the style of the great Venetians with four masts, fore, main and mizzen and a small one on the poop—the bonaventure.

My father, who was always restive on land and nowadays did not seem so eager to go to sea, was constantly on the look out for the ships that came and went. I was on the Hoe with him when the ship was sighted. There was a shout, and all eyes were on this one.

My father said, "She's a carrack. Looks as if she's a trader."

He spoke contemptuously. He had been a trader of sorts, for in his heyday he had brought home many a cargo which he had taken from a Spaniard. My mother often told him he was nothing more than a pirate.

"What sort of trader?" I asked him.

"Following the Dutch," he said. "Carrying goods and trading them and bringing back a cargo. Fishing in the Baltic and bringing back the catch. Trading!" he added disparagingly.

Then he stood legs wide apart watching, and when the little boats brought her captain ashore, my father roared. "By God, if it's not Fennimore Landor. Welcome to you, man. How fares your father?"

That was the first time I saw Fennimore—with his fair bronzed skin and his hair bleached with sun and his light-blue eyes crinkled as though they had faced miles of wind and sunshine; he was tall and strong, a man of the sea.

"This is my girl Linnet," said my father, and he laid his

hand on my shoulder in a way that lately had begun to thrill me. It meant he was proud of me, and although he was often intolerant and often crude, it was wonderful to please Captain Jake Pennlyon. "And this is Fennimore Landor, my girl. I knew his father well. A better captain never sailed the seas. Welcome! What brings you to Plymouth?"

"The hope of seeing you," said Fennimore.

"To see *me*. Well met then. You must come to the Court. You'll be welcome. That's so, eh, Linnet?"

I said he would be very welcome.

We looked at each other rather searchingly, and I wondered whether he liked my looks as much as I liked his.

I hoped so.

"The Court" was Lyon Court—the house which had been built by my great-grandfather when he began to amass his fortune. It was a little ostentatious compared with older houses like Trewynd, the home of Edwina and Carlos. I heard my mother say once to my father when they were battling together that the Pennlyons, not being used to money for long, had to make sure everyone knew they had acquired it. The center of the house was its Gothic hall as high as the roof, and its grand staircase led to the gallery where we had a few family portraits—the founder, my great-grandfather, my grandfather and my father. If I had been a boy, I daresay I should have been beside them. Our living quarters were in the east and west wings. There was plenty of room for entertaining, and the house was often filled with guests.

As we walked up to the Court from the Hoe, Fennimore Landor and my father talked of seafaring matters. I glanced sideways at the newcomer, and once or twice I caught him doing the same to me. When the house was in sight with the stone lions guarding the doors, I said I would go and tell my mother we had a visitor.

She was coming down the staircase to the hall. She was very spritely and had a wonderful vitality which was more attractive than beauty. She must have been about forty-eight years old, but because she had had an adventurous life, this had somehow preserved her youth.

"Father is bringing a guest," I cried. "His name is Fennimore Landor. A captain I think. Oh, here they are."

Fennimore Landor bowed to my mother, and when the introductions had been made, she led the way to the small winter parlor which was more intimate than the hall.

They drank malmsey and talked mostly of the sea and Fennimore was to join us for supper before he was rowed out to his ship. He mentioned that *Trade Winds* would be staying in the Sound for a few days. My mother and I left them drinking together; then she went to the kitchen and I to my room to make an entry in my journal.

Later, when we were at the great table in the hall, Fennimore sat beside my father, and I could see that he was trying to arouse his enthusiasm for some new venture in which he believed wholeheartedly. I liked his enthusiasm. It shone in his eyes, and it was in the lilt of his voice too. I thought he was an idealist, and if he cared about something, he would do everything of which he was capable to make it succeed. This matter in which he was trying to interest my father was trading to various parts of the world. I enjoyed listening to him, and I was a little angry with my father because he sat there with his head on one side looking, I thought, faintly skeptical.

Fennimore was saying, "From now on the Spaniards will offer little rivalry. They're crippled."

My father nodded. "Crippled by God and blasted off the seas." He was launching out on the well-worn theme of how we had defeated them, how they had boasted they would vanquish us in a day or so. Fennimore was faintly exasperated. He did not want to talk of the past but of the future.

He interrupted. "They can no longer have their galleys going out from Barcelona and Cádiz. Where are their galleys?"

"At the bottom of the ocean." My father chuckled.

"Of course, there are the Dutch."

"The Dutch!" spat out my father.

"Worthy seamen," put in Fennimore.

My father puffed his lips impatiently. "There's no seaman like an English one and preferably a West Countryman at that."

My mother laughed with that touch of tender derision she so often showed toward my father. "You will find Captain Pennlyon a little prejudiced," she said.

I looked around the table. We must have seemed a strange family to Fennimore—if his own was a conventional one, which I imagined it was. There was my father with his wife and daughter and his three illegitimate sons and Romilly, the mother of one of them. Of course it was clear that my father was no ordinary man, and for that matter, my mother was no ordinary woman. We were a small party because no one had known that we would have any special guest, but there had been time to ask Carlos and Edwina to join us. In any case they often did.

Carlos' mother had been Spanish, but he had inherited scarcely anything of hers. He was clearly my father's son. His hair was darkish brown and his eyes were light hazel color; he swaggered when he walked in a manner similar to that of our parent. He had been brought up under my father's influence from an early age, and the great aim of his life seemed to have been to grow up as exactly like him as possible. He was a great favorite with Jake. So was Jacko, the son of Jennet, my mother's maid, who had been with her for years and had shared many of my mother's adventures. She was a lusty irrepressible woman and had had a succession of lovers. At the time it was one of the gardeners. We all knew because for Jennet lovemaking was so natural that she made no secret of it. She was enormously proud of Jacko and delighted that he had been brought up in the household to follow his father's profession. She thought there was no one quite like the Captain and was very proud that Jacko provided living evidence that he had once glanced her way. Then there was Penn—also with a look of the Captain—and his presence at the table with his mother was perhaps the most difficult to understand. Romilly Girling had come to the house when she had been destitute after her father had been killed in one of my father's ships, and during one of those periods of dissatisfaction with each other which occurred in the past between my parents, my father out of pique or lust had got Romilly with child. Penn was born and was brought up in the house as Romilly had nowhere else to go. It was only later that my mother had discovered who the boy's father was, and it was inconceivable that she would turn them out of the house then. My father would never have allowed it in any case, and I think my mother liked to remind him now and then of his infidelities.

However there we were on this day when Fennimore came to Lyon Court, all assembled at the table. The only absent one being my little sister, Damask, who was too young to be of the party. I think it was after her birth that my father realized that my mother would never have a boy and became reconciled to me.

Fennimore, I am sure, was too full of his own project to waste much time thinking about our household. It was clear that he wanted my father's backing for his project. It seems from what I could gather that he was hoping for some sort of partnership.

I listened to him with pleasure. He had an unusually soft musical voice for a sailor. I could not imagine his shouting to sailors on the deck. There could not have been a man less like my father. It was amazing how I compared them all with him.

"If we had entirely neglected trading," Fennimore was saying, "we could never have beaten the Armada. We shouldn't have had the ships."

"Traders!" cried my father. "Nothing to do with it. We beat the dons because we were better seamen and we were determined not to let them set foot on our land."

"Yes, yes, Captain Pennlyon, that's true of course. But we had to have the ships, and by good fortune we had them."

"Now, young man, don't you make the mistake of thinking this victory was due to luck. Good fortune you say. Good seamanship say I."

"It was that, but we did have the ships," insisted Fennimore. "Did you know that in 1560 we had but seventy-one ships trading on the seas and in 1582 we'd increased that number to one hundred and fifty. Why, in 1560, sir, our merchant navy was almost nothing . . . we weren't among the maritime nations. What were we doing? Our coastal trade was insignificant. We did a little with the Baltic ports— just with the Low Countries and perhaps a little with Spain, Portugal and France . . . a few Mediterranean calls. That will not be so anymore. We, Captain, are going to be not *one* of the foremost trading nations in the world but *the* foremost. There's coal to be carried . . . coal and fish. This has been done in the past, but now that we have driven the Spaniards off the seas we have to take advantage of it."

My father was listening now. Any method of worsting the Spaniards appealed to him.

I found it fascinating to listen to Fennimore. It was obvious that he had studied the matter; he believed in it wholeheartedly. Carlos was inclined to support him, while waiting for the cue from my father of course. Jacko watched with bright eyes so like his mother's; if the family was going into trade, he wanted to be in it too. Penn's eyes never left our father's face. And watching him there, his startling blue eyes fierce at the mention of Spaniards, I was never more conscious of his intolerance, and there was a great yearning in me for him to like and approve of Fennimore Landor. I realized that Fennimore in his way was as determined as my father was in his, but while one was noisily vociferous, the other achieved as much impact by his quiet insistence.

I sat listening to his voice, and it was as though he created before my eyes the fulfillment of a dream. He was going to make our country great. To ply peacefully throughout the world practicing legitimate trading would prove more profitable, Fennimore was implying, than riding the high seas armed with guns and cannon, boarding, robbing, fighting, killing—sometimes acquiring a prize of great worth and as often suffering loss as well as death.

"The time has come," he cried. "The troubles between the Low Countries and the Spaniards have crippled them both. At one time Antwerp was a center of great wealth—one of the greatest in the world. The closing of the Scheldt three years ago finished that. We have still to contend with Amsterdam. They'll be our rivals for a while. That is good. Rivalry is necessary. It is the spur."

He leaned his elbows on the table and contemplated my father earnestly.

"I prophesy that in the next decade we in this country will build a merchant fleet which will be the envy of the world. We have come through a great ordeal victorious. It is not for us now to gloat over our enemies but to go on to greatness. Our derision cannot hurt them—our trading ships will. We have to beat the argosies of Venice, the tartans of Marseilles. God and our seamen have taken care of the galleys of Barcelona."

I clapped my hands together, and then I flushed because everyone was looking at me.

"Congratulations, Captain Landor," I stammered. "I . . . was quite carried away."

He smiled at me then, and it seemed a very long moment that we looked at each other.

"The trading ships would have to be equipped with guns," my father said.

"There is no doubt of that," replied Fennimore warmly, "for there will always be pirates. We must be ready. Our shipyards should now be working at full strength. We need ships, ships, ships."

"England has always had need of ships," said Carlos.

"But rarely as urgently as now. We have this breathing space. I doubt the Spaniards will ever recover from the trouncing they've had. Our rivals will be the Dutch. We must be prepared to meet the challenge."

"And this," said my father, "is what you wish to speak to me about."

"Captain Pennlyon, your praises are sung all along these coasts and farther. The Queen herself has spoken of you as one of the guardians of the realm."

"God bless her," said my father. He lifted his glass, and we all drank to Queen Elizabeth.

"May this be the beginning of a new era," said Fennimore earnestly. "The great age of peace and prosperity because of these great blessings."

"Amen," said my mother.

My father looked at her, and I saw the faint smile which passed between them; I knew then that she would persuade him to consider Fennimore's proposal whatever it was going to be and that he would.

After that the conversation became more general.

Jacko had two of the new medals which had been struck to commemorate the victory. We all laughed over the one on which was engraved *"Venit, vidit, fugit,"* a play on Julius Caesar's "I came, I saw, I conquered." The Spaniards had come, seen and fled.

My father kept gazing at it and chuckling over it.

My mother said, "The Captain has suffered a great bereavement. He has lost his Spaniards. What shall you do, Jake, with no one to curse, no throats to cut, none to run through with your sword?"

"I doubt not," he said, his eyes flashing fire at her, "that there are some lurking in that poxy land who will yet feel the steel of my sword."

Edwina commented that she had heard that Robert Dudley's death had caused the Queen great sorrow. "She truly loved him," she said. "What a pity she could not have married him. I believe she would have been happy to do so."

"She was too wise for that," said Fennimore. "She is a great Queen. England comes first with her. She would let no man come between her and her duty to her country."

"I like the medal," said my mother, "which stresses the fact that she is a woman and that a woman was at the heart of our victory. *'Dux femina facti.'* It is a heartening thought . . . for us women."

"She is an unusual woman, don't forget, and she wears a crown," said Jake. "It would be a sorry state of affairs if all women thought they could govern men."

"It would be worth a try," retorted my mother. "You have all been saying—and my husband in particular—

that we have just had the most resounding victory ever known. A woman was at the heart of it."

"There were men who served her well," pointed out Fenni-more. "But perhaps they did so because she was a woman."

Edwina said that in her opinion men and women should work together. There should be no rivalry between them. They should be complementary one to the other.

"If men would remember that, there would be complete understanding between the sexes," said my mother.

Penn said, "Is it true that Robert Dudley was poisoned?"

There was a brief silence at the table. It was not usually wise to discuss such matters freely, but over the last weeks we had all grown a little less careful.

Court affairs were always of the utmost interest to us, nonetheless so because being so far from London, we usually heard of them some time after they had taken place. This distance may well have made us perhaps more reckless than we would have dared be had we lived closer to the court.

My mother said she had heard that Robert Dudley's countess was enamored of her Master of Horse, Christopher Blount, and there were rumors that Dudley had been mur-dered by her that she might change husbands.

"Well, he had his first wife thrown down the stairs," said Penn, "so he can't complain if his second poisons him."

Everyone laughed, and Romilly said, "Hush, Penn. You must not say such things."

"Why not, if they're true?" He was looking at Jake for approval, but Jake said nothing. I believed he was still think-ing about those trading ships.

"There is no proof that they are," my mother said firmly. "Now," she went on, turning to Edwina, "tell us of the recent rumors."

Edwina's stepfather, Lord Remus, had a post at court, and this meant that visitors from London called now and then at Trewynd Grange. Also, Edwina's mother wrote to her regularly, and she consequently had the latest court gossip and scandal.

"There has, it seems, always been gossip about Robert, Earl of Leicester," she said. "Naturally there would be because of his closeness to the Queen. It is said that she was heartbroken when he died. She will miss him. But I don't think she ever forgave him for marrying, and it is true that at court they are saying that the poisoner has died of a dose of his own medicine."

It was an irresistible subject—the amours of the court—

and one of the most amorous of court gentlemen had been Robert Dudley, Earl of Leicester. We talked of poison then. How it was being used more and more effectively. There were so many secrets of the poisoner's art, and many people died mysteriously. Leicester had had a reputation of being an expert in the field.

We all knew the story of the Queen's passion for him and how his first wife, Amy Robsart, had died mysteriously. The general verdict was that he had had her put out of the way and because the Queen was known to be passionately in love with him at that time, she dared not marry him. When Mary Queen of Scots lost her head at Fotheringay— and that was not much more than a year before—there had been a great deal of talk about the Queen, Amy Robsart and the Earl of Leicester because Mary had been in a similar position. Her husband Lord Darnley had been murdered, and she, Mary, had married the Earl of Bothwell, his murderer. It was said that was the fatal step that led to Fotheringay. Our own Queen was admired for her astuteness. She had not married Leicester but had kept him hoping and dancing attendance on her. When he, realizing the Queen would never marry him, had married someone else, the Queen had hated Lettice, his wife. Rumor had it that Leicester had never married before that and in secret to Lady Sheffield and that he had poisoned her husband that he might do so. Then later, when he had wished to be rid of her, he attempted to poison her too.

"Her nails began to wither, and her hair fell out," said Edwina. "The Queen suspected there was some sort of liaison between them and had them watched. It's strange how she still remained faithful to Leicester in spite of everything."

"Our Queen is a faithful woman," said Jake. "An example to you all."

"Yes indeed," said my mother. "For she was sorely tried. Leicester hoped for years that she would change her mind and marry him, but she never would. That old scandal would have been revived! How hard it is to live down a scandal!"

"But he did marry the Countess of Essex," I said.

"And when the Queen heard," put in my mother, "they say she was furious with him."

"She all but sent him to the Tower," said Edwina. "But she relented and she has hated Lettice ever since."

"And now he is dead. Do you really think it was poison that killed him?" I asked.

"With poison one can never be sure," said Edwina. "If

it is true that Lettice was in love with Christopher Blount and that Leicester was trying to poison him and was given one of his own concoctions by his wife. . . ."

"Would that be possible?" I asked.

"Yes, indeed it would."

Edwina should know. She was descended from a witch. I was never quite sure how far back, but her mother was the great-granddaughter of one, I believe. My mother told me she used to tease her adopted sister about it.

Edwina talked of herbs then, for she had built up a big herb garden at Trewynd. She was very interested in the uses of the plants, and whenever we were not well, we always first asked Edwina if she knew of a cure before consulting apothecaries or doctors.

She had just learned that woodruff was good for the liver, and she was working a cure on one of the grooms at Trewynd. Fennimore became quite interested then—far more than he had over the chatter of Leicester's affairs. In fact, I feared he was a little bored by all that.

He said, "You must find something that will cure sailors of their ills on long voyages. They suffer from terrible diseases—scurvy is one of them. If you could grow an herb that would cure that, you would be performing a great service."

Then he began to talk again of sea and the prosperity he hoped would come to England.

I watched from my window the rowing boat take Fennimore Landor out to his ship. As I stood there, I heard someone come into my room and, turning, saw that it was my mother.

She came over to the window, and together we looked at the carrack out there on the faintly moonlit waters.

"A fine ship," said my mother. "What did you think of her captain?"

"I thought he was a man with a purpose."

"There was no doubt of that. It sounded very sensible to me."

I was pleased and showed it; she looked at me intently.

"I liked him," she said. "I liked his earnestness. He's an idealist. And that's a good thing for a young man to be."

"This idea of trading," I said, "how much better than fighting!"

"There will doubtless be fighting involved in it," replied

my mother grimly. "Men never seem to be able to get along without that."

"Do you think he wants some sort of partnership?"

"I gathered he wanted your father's help."

"Do you think he will give it?"

My mother was thoughtful. Then she said, "He might. As a captain who has been accustomed to see a prize and take it he will find it a little difficult to adjust himself to legitimate trading. I doubt not. But I fancied he was less skeptical as the hours passed than he had been in the beginning."

"Shall you persuade him?"

"My dear Linnet, do you think anyone could do that?"

"I think you could."

"Why, the very fact that I thought it a good idea would make him try to prove it wasn't. So you liked the captain, Linnet?"

"I thought as you did that he was earnest . . . serious and dedicated to his plan."

"If your father joined him in some enterprise, doubtless we should see a good deal of him. I discovered where he comes from. Farther along the coast toward Falmouth."

"Not so very far from here then."

"No." There was a slight pause. Then she said, "Edwina had some good news she whispered to me. What do you think? She is going to have a child."

"I'm so glad. She has long wanted that to happen. I thought there was something different about her tonight. Now I come to think of it she seemed to be hugging some secret."

"It won't be a secret for long. Of course it's early days yet. But I'm so happy for her. She and Carlos have been married . . . why, it must be seven years."

"It's a long time," I agreed.

"I know exactly how they feel." Her eyes had that look which they had when she looked back into the past. Then she was right back in the present looking straight at me. "The greatest happiness, Linnet, is to hold your own child in your arms. I remember. . . ."

Suddenly she put her arms about me and held me close to her for a few moments. I knew she was thinking that I should marry soon and have children of my own.

And the thought had been put into her head by the arrival of Captain Fennimore Landor. It meant that she liked him, that she would persuade my father to help him in his venture and that from now on the young man might well be a frequent visitor at Lyon Court.

By the time *Trade Winds* sailed out of the Sound my father had arranged that there should be a further meeting with the Landors. Whether my mother had persuaded him or whether he had been impressed by Fennimore's earnestness, I was not sure, but the fact remained that he was interested in his ideas and had said in a few weeks' time he would visit them for further talks.

I was delighted, and I believe my mother was too when an invitation came for us to join the party.

"What women have to do with commerce, I fail to see," growled my father.

My mother retorted, "Of course a woman should know what kind of business her husband is involved in. In any case the invitation is for me, and I shall accept it on behalf of Linnet and myself."

My father had gone off on a short trip and Jacko was with him, so it was arranged that my mother and I, accompanied by her maid, Jennet, and two grooms, should make the journey to Trystan Priory, the Landors' home.

It was early November when we set out, warm, damp and misty; the hedgerows were festooned with glistening cobwebs, and the bare branches of trees made a lacy pattern against a gray sky. A touch of color was supplied here and there by patches of golden gorse which was always with us. I remember my father's once saying that the only time a man should not make love to a woman was when the gorse was not in bloom, the implication being that the gorse bloomed all the year round.

I was excited. I was sure there was something in the air that day which told me that I was on the verge of adventure. It must have something to do with Fennimore whom I was looking forward to seeing again.

"What a gloomy day," said my mother as we rode along side by side.

"Do you find it so?" I replied, and she laughed suddenly. She seemed very happy. I read her thoughts. I was eighteen years old. Every mother wants to see her daughter married; she dreams of grandchildren. My mother wanted that for me, and she had decided that Fennimore was a good choice. She had been impressed by his sincerity; perhaps too she thought that he did not live very far away and she would see me frequently if I married him. It was a sad point with her that she was so far from her own mother, whom she adored.

Yes, I was in high spirits that morning. Adventure was in the air, discoveries, marriage, children, the right of every woman to love and reproduce. There might have been some warning in the mist, but I could not sense it. Nor did my mother, for she was as eager for what was awaiting us as I.

The road took us through country lanes with high green banks and hedges in which a few wild flowers lived on as a reminder of the riot of colors they had offered at different times of the year—some campion, dead nettle and shepherd's purse—and every now and then we would have a glimpse of the sea, grayish, silent on this still, windless day. We met few people, only a party on horseback like ourselves who called a greeting, a peddler whose pack we stopped to examine, a farmer at work on his land. We had made good progress on that first day, and before darkness fell, we reached an inn where we spent the night. The landlord had a good roasted ox and ale, which we ate and drank in the parlor before retiring to our room. My mother and I slept in the big bed and Jennet on a pallet on the floor. The grooms lay in the stables, and as soon as it was light, we were off, our horses rested and ready for the day's journey. There would be one more inn stop, and then we should arrive at Trystan Priory.

In spite of the excitement which possessed me, I slept soundly and so did my mother, and we were up early and ready to continue at dawn.

The second day was like the first. The country changed a little, though. The coast was more rocky, the countryside stark; it lacked the lush greenery of our Devon scenery; and on that night we came to the Traveler's Rest.

The host came to the door to welcome us, bowing low, recognizing us, I suppose, as what he would call "the quality." Yes, he had a room for us, and he would have a fire lighted in the fireplace and a warming pan put in the bed. He rubbed his hands together. He had a suckling pig on the spit; he had beef and mutton and great pies. In fact, he had everything to tempt hungry travelers. If we would sit awhile in the inn parlor, he would have our room made ready. It was the best in the house. He whispered conspiratorially that it was called the Oak Room on account of the very fine paneling on the walls and some of his guests had told him that it was fit for the Queen herself.

We sat in the inn parlor and drank wine and ate little

cakes which were quite pleasant, for it would take some time before the meat was cooked. Meanwhile, a fire was lighted in the room allotted to us, and we mounted the stairs to it. It looked rather charming in the light of two candles, for it was now dark. The fire in the grate threw its pleasant flickering light about the room. I touched the oak paneling of which the landlord was so proud, and I said, "It is a pleasant place. And the landlord, although a little too unctuous, seems determined to look after us."

My mother said, "We will tell him we will stay here on our return, which will be in a week or so, for I doubt we should overstay our welcome at Trystan Priory."

Jennet unpacked what we should need for the night, and by that time a maid came to tell us that the food was ready.

"We will come down at once," said my mother, "for I must confess I am ready for it."

It was then that I was aware of the noise below. Someone was shouting in a loud and imperious voice, "Don't tell me that, man. Take me there. I tell you this, no matter who has the Oak Room they must vacate it. Do you think I'd take one of your poxy little rooms?"

I heard the landlord, all unctuous pleasure departed: "But my lord . . . if I had known. . . . It is not more than an hour or so. . . . A party of travelers. . . ."

"It matters not," came the shout. "They can take another room. By God's life, host, have I not slept these many times in your Oak Room, and what other room have you to suit me? Tell me that!"

"None worthy of your lordship 'tis true, but. . . ."

"Stand aside."

I stood there, holding a candle in my hand. I heard the heavy tread on the stairs.

Then he came into sight and saw me standing on the threshold of the room. He stopped short, looking up at me. I was surprised to see that he was young, by which I meant he was reaching up to thirty. His eyes were dark, large and lustrous; his hair looked blackish in the candlelight. What struck me most was the size of him. He must have been all of six feet six inches tall. I had rarely seen such a tall man. His shoulders were broad, and his padded jerkin made of satin and velvet with its puffed slashed sleeves made him look even broader. His bombasted breeches were of fine material, and his jornet, a loose traveling cloak, was thrown back over his shoulders. This arrogant man, who,

I gathered, was demanding the room already let to us, was
a dandy.

"By God, madam," he said, "so 'tis you who have taken
my room."

"Is it yours, sir?" I answered. "I had thought it was one
the landlord had set aside for guests, and my mother and I
have already taken it."

"Is that so?" he said and his smile was sardonic. He
started to mount the stairs. "I am a frequent patron of this
inn. There are times when I pass and wish to rest for a
night. This room is always at my disposal."

"Then," I said, "this is an occasion when it is not."

My mother came forward. I realized—though no one
else would—that she was a little nervous. But she was not
the sort to give up her rights without a fight.

She said, "What is this trouble, sir?"

He bowed to her. "Whether it be trouble or not, madam,
depends on you. You are occupying my room. Vacate it,
and you may have a pleasant night, though perhaps a less
luxurious one."

"We had already taken the room," said my mother.

"Ah, but that was before I arrived. Nessie," he shouted.
Then: "God's eyes, man, where's your daughter?"

The innkeeper was at the bottom of the stairs. "I will
call her, my lord, and send her to you."

"Tell her quick. I like not to be kept waiting."

His eyes were on me. "Do not think," he said, "that it
pleases me to turn a beautiful lady from her bed."

"I am sure it does not," I retorted, "and I am equally
sure that our good host will find you a comfortable lodging
somewhere in his inn."

He had stepped into the room. My mother watched him
coldly. Jennet was frankly staring, her mouth a little slack.
I knew what she was thinking. This was the kind of man
she adored. But he seemed unaware of her. He touched the
wall and murmured, "This paneling is beautiful, is it not?
Worthy of a mansion. I always admired it. 'Tis a good bed
too. You'll not find a better in any inn in the country."

"I am sure I shall agree with you when I have used it,"
I said.

"Ah, but we shall have to come to an agreement earlier
than that. I wish to sleep in this bed tonight."

"As I shall be sleeping there, that is out of the question."

"It is not an impossibility," he said insolently.

I flushed, and my mother said, "I must ask you, sir, to

leave us. If you continue to insult us, my husband will hear of this."

"Pray who is the gentleman? Our host has been most remiss in making introductions."

"He is Captain Jake Pennlyon," said my mother firmly, "and he is a man who will not allow his wife and daughter to be insulted."

"His repute has reached my ears. Who would be ignorant of his existence? Ha, here is Nessie. It takes you a long time to come, my girl. Did you not hear of my arrival?"

Nessie bobbed a curtsy. She was a plump, pretty girl with rosy cheeks and abundant, fair, curly hair; her gown was low-cut, and the thought occurred to me that she knew this man very well. He caught her by the ear and pinched it. She gave a little yell and put up her hands to his. He laughed and let his hand drop to her breast, which he patted, caressing, as he said, "Now, Nessie, clear the room. This baggage comes out, and mine goes in."

"I will not allow this," cried my mother.

"My dear lady," he said, "how will you prevent it?"

"I wish to see the landlord immediately."

"Come," I said to my mother, "we will go to him now. Come, Jennet," I said.

She left our bags where they were and followed us.

The landlord was in the hall; he was visibly trembling.

"This is a fine way to treat your guests," began my mother.

"My lady, it is no fault of mine. I did not know he would be here this night. It is only last week that he came. He does not usually come so often. I have a very nice room . . ."

"No," said my mother, but she was very uneasy. Outside, it was dark. If we left the inn where could we go? There would not be another for some miles. The horses were tired. We would have to stay, and yet she was in revolt against the arrogant, churlish behavior of this man.

"My lady," said the innkeeper, "you do not know Squire Colum Casvellyn."

"If that is the name of that oaf, I do not wish to."

"Ah, my lady, we cannot always help these things. I can prepare a good room for you. It is not our best room, but it is a good room, and there you can spend the night in peace."

"You have forgotten that you gave us the Oak Room."

"I do not forget, madam, but Squire Casvellyn can make great trouble. He is a man who must be obeyed. I could not say what would happen to us all if I refused to allow him to have the Oak Room."

"I will speak of this with my daughter," said my mother.

He nodded. We went into the inn parlor, which mercifully was deserted.

"The wise thing to do would be to take the smaller room," said my mother. "I wish your father were here. He would make short work of him."

I was not so sure. I saw in this man something akin to my father, and he was many years younger.

"But my father is not here. How I hate giving way to him!"

"I also. But what would happen if we refused to leave that room. He would be there too. He might throw us out. What sort of night should we have then? No, 'tis better to accept the other room and behave with dignity. But when your father hears of this, he will not allow it to pass."

I could see that she was right. We were not in a position to fight against him, and his remark that he might share the room with us had upset me.

"Let us then tell the landlord to give us his next best room. We deplore the ill manners of his guest, but as he will do nothing about it, we must needs accept this insult."

My mother sent Jennet for the landlord. He came, his hands under his apron trembling, I'm sure. I felt sorry for the man.

"We have decided we can do nothing but accept your offer of another room."

Relief flooded the poor man's face. "You are wise, madam," he said. "I promise you that everything shall be done. . . ."

"I can see," said my mother, "that this is no fault of yours. Tell me who is this man who strikes such terror into you and your servants."

"He is the lord of Castle Paling—a man greatly feared in these parts. He is the lord of the neighborhood. It has always been so with the Casvellyns. They own much of the land hereabouts. He could turn us out of our homes if we displeased him. He would have no mercy. His father was lord of us all, but he was but a shadow of his son."

"You live in terror of him?"

"He does not come this way so often. That is why since he was here last week I did not think he would come again. He pays well for his lodging here. He is not one to stint.

There is grandeur at Castle Paling, I have heard. My daughter once went there."

"Your daughter . . . Nessie," I said sharply.

The landlord looked embarrassed, and the thought came into my head that the landlord's daughter would doubtless sleep in the bed which had been taken from us.

"Yes, he . . . noticed her. He is good to people who please him."

I felt disgusted. "Let us be shown the humbler room," I said, and to my mother: "It is unimportant. Tomorrow we shall be on our way."

"I am grateful, ladies, for your good consideration. Believe me, I am deeply grieved that this should have happened."

"Think no more of it," my mother told him. "Let our bags be taken to another room."

"It shall be done while you eat," said the landlord, fast regaining his equilibrium. "I trust the flavor of the sucking pig—which I know will be the tenderest you have ever partaken of—will make up for this unfortunate upset."

Fresh rushes had been laid in the dining room, and the smell of the herbs was clean and fresh. I was hungry, and the sucking pig, which was already on the table, looked as succulent and appetizing as could be wished. There was a great pie and several tarts besides roast beef and mutton, wild fowl and spiced tarts, marchpane and gingerbread. No wonder the host was proud of his table.

We were sampling the sucking pig when Colum Casvellyn entered the dining room. I kept my eyes averted, and my mother and I talked of the journey we had had as though he were not there.

He was not the sort to allow himself to be ignored.

He demanded the host's attention; he would have the prime cut of the beef and the largest of the pies. Nessie waited on him, ignoring everyone else to obey his command immediately.

"It has been a fine day," he said, addressing me.

"It has," I agreed.

"You have come far?"

"A day's ride."

"How long is that?"

"It would depend on the riders, I doubt not."

"I was referring to these riders." He nodded toward my mother and me.

"We left Plymouth two days since."

"Plymouth. But of course. Captain Jake Pennlyon! One of the nation's heroes."

"I doubt not you were at sea with the fleet, sir."

"Aye," he said. "And gave a good account of myself."

"I doubt not that either," I said. "Mother, have you finished?"

She said she had.

"Then," I said, "let us go to see how this room in which we are to spend the night compares with the one this *gentleman* has taken from us."

He laughed loudly.

We rose, but unfortunately we had to pass close to him on our way out, and as we did so, he caught at my gown so that I was pulled up short.

I looked down at his fingers which held my skirt but had no alternative but to meet his gaze. He was looking straight up at me, with mischief in his bright dark eyes—and more. He disturbed me; I tried to tweak my dress out of his fingers, but he held on firmly.

"Sir?" I said with fury and indignation.

My mother was pulling at my arm, not aware that he was holding me.

I said, "You will take your hands from my gown."

"I but wish to be civil," he said.

"Civil. I do not understand your manner," I retorted.

My mother was getting very angry. "How dare you lay hands on my daughter," she said. "If you do not. . . ."

He waited for her to go on, his brow slightly cocked, the insolent smile on his lips. He wanted to hear what she would do, knowing full well it could amount to nothing. He was the master here. The landlord lived in terror of him. What could two helpless females do against such a man?

He said, "I was about to say, madam, that I have no wish that you should think hardly of me. Therefore, I shall tell the landlord that I shall occupy the inferior room, for I shall give up the Oak Room to you ladies."

We were silent, completely taken off our guard.

My mother recovered herself first. She said coldly, "There is no need. We are quite prepared to take the other room."

He was vehement. He had released my skirt and rapped his fist on the table. "You shall have the Oak Room. I will sleep happily in the inferior one. Nessie, call your father. At once, girl. Don't stand there gaping."

As we were about to leave the room, the landlord appeared. "These ladies are to have the Oak Room," roared

Colum Casvellyn. "Take their baggage and put it back. I relinquish it. Now, Nessie, fill my goblet."

My mother said to the landlord, "This is a ridiculous matter, and I would see an end of it. We will not go back to the Oak Room. We shall leave it for that . . . that . . . ill-mannered oaf. . . ."

The landlord shook his head, beginning to tremble. "He has said it shall be, my lady, and so it must."

He looked so terrified that my mother shrugged her shoulders. Our bags were brought back to the Oak Room, Jennet unpacked, and we decided we would settle down for the night.

My mother locked the door. "With such people in the inn one could never be sure," she said.

It was a long time before I could sleep although the bed was comfortable. I kept thinking of Colum Casvellyn and imagining his being in this bed with Nessie, for I was sure the girl was spending the night with him. I felt excited in a rather unpleasant way; something had been aroused in me of which until this time I had been unaware.

My mother was wide awake too. We talked a little and then were silent, and finally she did sleep. Jennet on her pallet was asleep, breathing with the deepness of complete and undisturbed repose. I tried not to toss and turn for fear of disturbing my mother and lay rather stiffly and uncomfortably.

And as I lay there, I heard a faint thud on the windowpane. At first I thought I had imagined it and lay still listening. It came again. Swiftly and silently I got out of bed and went to the window. I pushed it open and looked out. The half-moon threw a white light on the trees and hedges. It was beautiful out there, and the air was mild and sweet-smelling. Then I saw the shadow emerge from among the trees, and he was standing there, legs apart, looking up at the window.

I drew back; I heard him laugh. He put his hand to his lips, kissed it and threw the hand toward me. I was so astonished that for a few seconds I just stood there looking at him. He threw out his arms as though inviting me to come down.

I shut the window hurriedly and went back to bed. I lay there trembling a little, terrified that I would awaken my mother. I kept my eye on the window, half expecting to see him appear there. I lay listening for a sound at the door. Nothing happened. It was a long time before I slept, and then I was disturbed by vague, shapeless dreams, but he was there dominating them.

Before it was light, we were awake. The landlord gave us a hot breakfast, and we left soon after dawn, before the inn was fully astir.

I was glad to get away, but I knew I should remember Colum Casvellyn with a kind of fascinated horror for a long time to come.

That day we came to Trystan Priory. It was a lovely house some five miles inland. My father had not yet arrived, and we were warmly welcomed by Fennimore and his parents. The house had been recently built on the site of an old priory which had been demolished during the dissolution of the monasteries in the reign of the Queen's father. There was a little of the old priory left, and Fennimore during that day and the next while we awaited the arrival of my father took great pleasure in pointing these remains out to us.

His parents were charming. His father was a sea captain, and that gave us much in common, and I liked Fennimore as well in his own home as I had in my own. I liked his quiet earnestness, his purposefulness; against my will I found myself comparing him with the man whom we had met at the inn. There was one who would take what he wanted; so was Fennimore in a way, but how different his methods would be. I fancied Fennimore would be one always to consider other people. I was looking forward to my father's arrival and hoped that he would come to some agreement with the Landors.

There were a large number of rooms in the west wing, for the house, like so many, was built in the shape of a letter *E*, and my mother and I were given rooms side by side, and there was a small one for Jennet close by. Our grooms were accommodated near the stables with those of the household, and I was immediately struck by the absolute peace of the place. That night I slept soundly, no doubt because of the previous disturbed night, and I found the atmosphere of Trystan Priory decidedly pleasant.

My mother liked our host and hostess very much, and there seemed to be a tacit agreement that Fennimore should look after me. That first morning he said he would first show me the house, and as after three days' riding I must be in need of a rest from the saddle, he would take me for a walk around the estate so that I could really become acquainted with the place.

The great staircase which led up from the hall to the gallery was very fine indeed, with exquisitely carved banisters; in the gallery were the portraits. I paused before that of Fennimore. He looked from the canvas out with unruffled gaze on the world; it was the look of a man who would know exactly what he wanted.

"An excellent likeness," I said.

There was a space on the wall next to his picture, and I knew that another had hung there once. I wondered vaguely why it had been removed.

It was a homely house. Less ostentatious than Lyon Court and so modern when compared with ancient Trewynd Grange. It had its buttery, pastry bolting house, where flour was bolted or sifted, and the winter parlor which was much used during the cold weather. The kitchen was large with its great range and spits and ovens. Fennimore pointed out to me how convenient it was being so near the winter parlor and the main hall. That hall was the center of the house, as it was in Lyon Court and Trewynd, and in it dinner was eaten when there was a large gathering. The family frequently used the winter parlor.

We walked in the gardens, which were beautifully laid out. There were fountains and shady walks and several marble statues; the flower beds were numerous and charmingly bordered with rosemary, lavender and marjoram. He showed me the enclosed garden with the pond in the center. Most houses had them, and they were planned on the style of the famous one made by Henry VIII at Hampton Court. Secluded, surrounded by a tall hedge, here members of the family could come in summer, the ladies to sit and embroider or paint pleasant little pictures; the men to talk with them, to relax, to enjoy the sunshine.

Fennimore and I sat by the pond, and he talked to me of his dreams of the future. I liked to listen to him, and I encouraged him to talk. There was prosperity as yet not dreamed of, he told me. He had been visiting shipyards in Britain and trying to impress their owners with the need to build ships, bigger ships, ships capable of carrying heavy cargoes and holding their own on the high seas.

"They will have to carry armaments, I suppose," I said.

"Alas, such is the way of the world. There will be battles on the high seas, doubt it not. Where there is prosperity, where there is profit, there will always be those who envy it and seek to take possession of it through force. Rivalry there must be and I would welcome that . . . good honest rivalry, but it can hardly be hoped that men will suddenly become reasonable. They will still seek to take what is not theirs and to believe that there is more to be gained by robbery than by hard work. There are some who must be grander, bolder, richer than all others. There are some who must exert their power over others. . . ."

· I immediately thought then of the man at the inn, and I was on the verge of telling Fennimore what had happened. I changed my mind. The garden was so pleasant; I was enjoying our conversation so much I did not want to introduce a discordant note. The more I thought of that man—and I had to admit I had thought of him a great deal—the more unpleasant the encounter seemed. He was crude, he was bold, and he had dared awaken me and bring me to the window. Had he really thrown a kiss to me, or had I imagined that? Had he really been suggesting that I come down to him? Surely he must have known that was impossible. No, he had merely wished to disturb me. He had certainly done that.

Fennimore went on talking about the boom in shipbuilding which must follow the defeat of the Armada. "The Spaniards were only half aware of what prospects there were," he was saying. "They were obsessed by making the people of the world conform to their religious doctrines. Therein lay their weakness. Their King is a fanatic. What misery he must be enduring now. I could almost feel it in my heart to be sorry for him."

"Do not let my father hear you say that."

"Nor shall I," said Fennimore. "He would not understand, but I believe it to be a fact that even the most cruel, the most misguided of mankind have some spark of humanity in them and if we could but ignite it . . . who knows?"

I realized then that he was a very different man from my father. He was gentle and tolerant. A faint misgiving came to me then, and I wondered whether the quality needed to succeed in this rough world was that ruthlessness which men like my father possessed, that single-mindedness which could only see one side of a problem. I was aware that Fennimore's nature made him see many.

But he certainly talked like a man with a vision. He made me see our ports alive with peaceful merchant vessels. I could picture the unloading on the Hoe—spices, gold and ivory—because he planned that his ships should travel not only in the Baltic and Mediterranean ports but right out to the East Indies.

It was very pleasant on that damp November day to walk through the gardens with Fennimore, to listen to his plans, to learn about the estate on which he lived when he was not at sea.

I found his parents delightful, and so did my mother. His father was undoubtedly a man of the sea, and that meant that he shared certain characteristics with my own father. He was not the roaring, ranting man that Jake Pennlyon was. In any case there could only be one Jake Pennlyon; but he had clearly had bloodthirsty adventures on the high seas, and they must have left their mark on him. Fennimore had inherited something of his mother's more gentle nature.

I suppose when two families are of a similar kind and each has a young member of it and these are of the opposite sex, there must inevitably be some speculation as to whether or not they might marry. I knew this was in the minds of my mother and Fennimore's parents. Every mother wants to see her son or daughter married; grandparents long for the marriage of their children to be fruitful. I knew what was going on in my mother's mind. She liked Fennimore and would welcome him as a son-in-law. I became certain that the Landors would have offered me an equally warm welcome.

And Fennimore? Was it in his mind too? I believe it was. He was not an impulsive man, however; he would wish us both to grow accustomed to each other and the idea of marriage. To him there would be many sides of marriage, and of course he was right.

It seemed to me in those first few days at Trystan Priory that there was a very good chance that one day I would be mistress of it.

Fennimore's mother was eager to talk about the household, and during the second day she asked me to come to her room. She wanted to show me the tapestry on which she was working. She showed me the design which was to depict the glorious victory over the Armada, and she herself had composed it. It would take her years to complete, she told me.

The canvas was set up on a gigantic frame, and on it was sketched the picture she would work. It was attractive. There were the little ships and the great Spanish galleons. There was the King of Spain in his gloomy Escorial and the Duke of Medina-Sidonia with his ships. And on the other hand we had our own Queen at Tilbury and Sir Francis playing bowls on the Hoe. And the battle—the fire ships which caused such havoc and the broken galleons drifting out to sea.

"Why," I said, "it is almost a lifework."

"I shall start it . . . as indeed I have," she said. "It will be for future members of my family to finish it."

It was almost as though she were putting a needle into my hand and telling me to begin.

"It will be wonderful when it is completed."

"I hope to see it finished," she said.

"But of course you must."

"I have hundreds of skeins of silk stored away." She talked of the colors she would use. Reds, scarlets and gold; black for the costume of the King of Spain; scarlet and gold for our Queen. "Oh, my dear Linnet, what a terrible time that was. I hope never to live through such a time. I have never known such a time of wretchedness . . . except. . . ."

She stopped and bit her lip. Then she brightened. "But it is over now. There are still dangers at sea . . . but the Spaniards can do us little harm now. I was always terrified of them . . . terrified that they would come here. And of course, when the men sailed away, I used to shut myself in my sanctuary"—she inclined her head toward a door leading from her room—"and there I used to pray that they would come back safely. But you are a sailor's daughter. You know."

I considered this. It had never occurred to me that my father would not come back. There was something invincible about him, and he always had returned. Though there had been a time when he was gone so long that it had seemed that it was forever.

"If I had lost them," she went on, "that would have been death to me. I should have had no one left . . . no one. After Melanie. . . ."

Her face puckered suddenly and she seemed to come to a decision. She said, "Come with me."

I rose, and she went to the door I had seen. She opened it.

I followed her into a room. It was rather dark as there was only one small window, leaded-paned. In this room I noticed a crucifix and before it a table on which were candlesticks. It was like an altar.

"Sometimes," she said, "I come in here to be alone and pray."

Then I saw a picture on the wall. It was of a young girl

about fifteen, I imagined. She had fair hair which fell about her shoulders and blue eyes. She was remarkably like Fennimore.

"She is beautiful, do you agree?" said Fennimore's mother.

I did agree.

"My daughter. My Melanie."

"I was not aware that you had a daughter."

"I had a daughter. Alas, she died."

"How sad."

She lowered her head as though she could not bear to go on looking at that lovely young face.

"I had the picture brought in here. I could not bear to see it every time I passed it in the gallery. I wanted it where I could see it in private, where I could weep over it if I had to, and look at it and remember."

"Was it long ago?" I asked.

"Three years."

"So recent?"

She nodded.

I was not sure whether she wanted to talk or not, so I tried to convey my sympathy without seeming curious.

"She was murdered."

"Murdered!"

"Please, I cannot talk of it. She was too young for marriage. I should never have allowed it and . . . she died."

"She was your only daughter?"

She nodded.

"You have your son."

Her face cleared a little. "He is the best son a woman could have. Thank God we have Fennimore. But we lost Melanie . . . my little Melanie. I often say to myself, 'I should never have allowed it.' I shall never forget the day she told me she was going to have another child."

"She had had others?"

"No. Attempts. They all failed. It was clear she was not meant for childbearing, and when she told me that yet again . . . a terrible cold fear came over me. It was as though the angel of death had entered. It was here in this room. I can see her now, the fear in her fair young face, and I wanted to . . . to. . . . But never mind. I shouldn't be talking like this to you."

"Please talk if you want to. I will respect your confidence."

"She was different from you. She hadn't your strength. She wasn't meant to bear children. If only I could go back."

She put out a hand, and I took it, holding it firmly.

"I wanted you to know," she said, "because . . . because . . . you . . . you seem like one of us."

It was almost as though she were proposing marriage to me on behalf of her son.

My father arrived that day. The house suddenly seemed more noisy. He was impressed with the Priory and slightly smug because it did not seem quite as grand to him as Lyon Court. Meals had become more elaborate and were taken in the great hall instead of the winter parlor. We dined at the fashionable time of eleven in the morning and supped between seven and eight. There was a great deal of talk at these meals, and my father was often in conference with Fennimore and his parents. I believed that they were getting along very well and that my father was becoming more and more interested in the project.

He had no intention of staying long, though. He was eager to be off. Each morning he rode down to the coast and went on his ship. He was going on around Land's End to the north coast and would be away some weeks before returning home. My mother and I were to travel back the way we had come.

Neither of us had said anything about our adventure on the way. The man had, after all, allowed us to have the better room, my mother pointed out, so we could not complain about his taking it from us. "Your father would make more out of it than was actually there. You know how he loves a fight," she said. "Moreover, we should never be allowed to travel on our own again." So we did not mention it, and it was arranged that we should return as we had come, with Jennet and the two grooms.

There was still news coming in of Spanish disasters, of ships being washed up along the coast, of men who had come to our coasts at dead of night and wormed their way into our villages pretending to be anything but Spaniards. My father could never hear enough of them, and in his opinion no fate was too bad for them.

I could see that the Landors thought him too extreme, but they accepted that a man whose fame was known through the West Country for a valiant seaman and servant of the Queen, must be allowed to express his opinions.

He had a soft spot for all seamen and was faintly critical of the Queen's parsimony toward her sailors. It was the first time I had known him do anything but praise her.

"By God," he said, "these are the men who helped save our country. Are they to go hungry now their task is done!"

"The Chest is better than nothing," said Captain Landor.

"Not good enough for these valiant men," stormed my father. "And why should every seaman have a bit taken from his pay to help those who were wounded in the great fight? Nay, sir. It is the bounden duty of the Queen and this country to care for those who suffered. They gave for England. It is England's turn to give to them."

He was referring to the fund known as the Chest at Chatham, which had been set up to compensate those who had suffered during the fight with the Armada.

"Any seaman who comes to my house," declared my father, "will be cared for. They will find at Lyon Court that sanctuary England fails to give them."

"There must be many of them."

"So much the more reason to care for them," said my father, his face scarlet with righteous indignation. "It has come to my ears that Philip of Spain has set aside fifty thousand scudi for the relief of his wounded. Should the defeated be so well cared for and the victors dependent on their own poor sailors to help them!"

It was true, of course, that the Queen, who loved to adorn her person with extravagant jeweled garments, was often averse to spending money on her subjects, who had given all but their lives to keep her on the throne.

"You may rest assured," said my mother, "that any poor sailors who come to Lyon Court shall be fed."

"We will see to it," affirmed my father, for once in agreement with her.

I could see that the Landors were pleased to turn the conversation to other matters. Whether it was because they realized how unwise it was to criticize the Queen, even faintly, or whether they were so eager to talk of their future plans, I was not sure, but soon they were discussing the possibility of getting more ships afloat and what commodities could be picked up in the various ports of the world.

And so those pleasant days passed, and it was time for us to return home. Before we did so, my parents insisted that we return the Landors' hospitality. They thought it would be an excellent idea if they visited us to celebrate the New Year.

Night at Castle Paling

We spent our first night at the Traveler's Rest. My mother and I had debated whether to do this. It was hardly likely that we should meet the obnoxious Colum there again, and to avoid such a good and tried inn because we feared to, did not appeal to either of us.

The landlord was delighted to see us. The Oak Room was placed at our disposal, and there was no rude interruption that night. We enjoyed the landlord's wholesome table and occupied his comfortable bed in the oak-paneled room. It was true I did awaken in the night and found myself half sleeping, half waking, listening for a thud against the window. Nothing happened. How could it? The man was far away.

We left the next morning. The weather had changed; a wind had risen, dispersing the mist and bringing rain clouds with it. We rode through a fine drizzle, less disturbing than a downpour it was true, but still impeding progress a little. It was dark very early, and we decided that we would not delay putting up for the night, even if it meant making an extra day's journey home.

We were riding through a winding lane—one of the grooms ahead of us and another behind—when we heard the sound of horses' hooves. We had seen no one for the last two hours. "No one would be out on such a day," said my mother, "unless it was absolutely necessary."

The riders were clearly coming up behind us, and we drew to the side of the hedge as they came nearer.

They were alongside; they had surrounded us. There were six men . . . with masks over the faces. Jennet gave a little scream, and there was no doubt in any of our minds that they meant mischief, for they carried cudgels and immediately began demanding our purses.

One of the grooms, attempting to remonstrate, was knocked from his horse while a masked man snatched at my mother's girdle, which was of gold. She dealt him a sharp blow across the knuckles with her riding stock, and he let out a cry of anger. He was temporarily taken aback.

"You are robbers," she cried. "What you want is money. If you treat our persons ill, it will go hard with you, I promise you. I will give you money if you will allow us to make our journey on in peace."

The groom who had been thrown rose shakily to his knees, and at that moment there was a shout from one of the robbers, and again I heard the sound of a horse galloping toward us.

A voice shouted, "What goes?" It was a voice I recognized; I felt an immense relief and excitement. Colum Casvellyn came galloping up.

"By God," he said, "you ladies are in distress. Get you gone, you villains."

Although there were four villains and he was alone, yet I could sense their fear. One of them was very close to me . . . and then in the space of seconds he had seized my horse by its bridle and started off taking me with him.

I tried to stop, but there was nothing I could do. I was being taken along at a breakneck speed, my horse firmly controlled by my captor, while the other three came thudding behind us.

I screamed out my protests, but they went unheeded. The three unencumbered riders passed us, for naturally I impeded the speed of the one who held me. Then I heard the horse coming up behind us. We were being followed, and I knew by whom.

My captor was not going to release me easily. We galloped on and on. Colum Casvellyn shouted to the man to stop. He was close behind, but he did not catch up. He shouted what he would do to the man if he did not release my horse, but still I was firmly held.

It seemed that we galloped for a long time. We went across a plain and along roads. We had lost the three masked men; it was now just a race between the man who had taken me and Colum Casvellyn.

Then my captor made his mistake. We had turned into a road, galloped headlong down it and had come to a wood. Ahead of us the trees started to grow thick, and we must either enter the wood or turn and go back. If we did the latter, we should be face to face with Colum Casvellyn.

We went toward the wood. Our speed was slowing down. I was released so suddenly that I almost fell and only just managed to pull up my horse. Colum Casvellyn was beside me. The other had disappeared.

"That was a chase," he said.

"I suppose I must thank you," I muttered.

"It might be gracious to. I have saved you from that villain. One can guess what his intentions were. I recognize you, of course. You are the lady of the oaken bedchamber."

"You have done me a service, and I thank you," I said.

"It makes up perhaps for my recent discourteous behavior."

"It does. And if you will take me back to my mother and the rest of my party, I shall be most grateful and so will they."

"We can try to find them," he said.

"So you will help me."

"I am at your service."

"Thank you."

He brought his horse close to mine. "You are trembling a little. It was an alarming experience, was it not? The villain! Would to God I could have laid hands on him. I'd have soon had him whimpering for mercy."

"He has gone now and his fellow robbers with him. My mother will be very, very anxious."

"That is something we cannot allow. Do you feel ready to ride on now?"

"It is what I wish. I must rejoin my mother quickly."

"We must try to retrace our way. 'Tis not easy. I did not note the way we came."

"You were riding when you heard the scuffle? Could we go to where you were then?"

"I cannot be completely sure. I heard the shouting and came across country. But we will try. Come, let us start. We must go quickly, for it would not do for me to lose you now, you know. How dark it is. Are you ready?"

I said I was. I felt sick with impatience. I imagined my mother's horror when she saw me being dragged away. I wondered whether she would have recognized Colum Casvellyn. If she had, I did not think that would have given her much comfort.

It was growing darker. There was a dampness in the air. I was shivering, but I was not sure whether it was with cold.

We rode on for a few minutes in silence.

Then I said, "Is this the way?"

"I believe it to be."

"Let us hurry a little."

"As you wish."

On we went. The landscape had changed; there were more hedges, more trees. I knew we had galloped over a plain. Where was that?

I cried, "Are you sure it was this way?"

"I cannot be sure," he answered.

"I think it to be wrong."

He pulled up.

"We are but a mile or so from Castle Paling," he said.

"Your home?"

"My home," he confirmed.

"Then how far from your home were you when you came upon us in the lane?"

"A mile or so."

"Then we could be near the spot."

"Do you think they would be waiting there? My belief is that they would go to an inn and there send out men to look for you."

"Yes, I suppose they might do that. Is there a nearby inn?"

"I know only of two hereabouts."

"Then let us go to them. My mother will be there. You are right when you think that she would go to the nearest inn and get people to look for me."

"We will go then."

The inn was called the Red and White Rose. The signpost creaked in the rising wind, and a man with a lantern came out as we approached. The sign depicted the faces of the Queen's great-grandfather Henry VII of Lancaster and his wife, Elizabeth of York. It was strange that I should notice them at such a time.

Colum Casvellyn had leaped from his horse, and a groom

had rushed forward to take the reins. "Where is the host?" he shouted.

The innkeeper came hurrying out at the sound of that imperious voice.

"Has a party arrived?" said Colum Casvellyn. "A lady with a maidservant and two grooms."

"But no, my lord."

"You are sure?"

"I am, my lord. We have had but one visitor. A merchant on his way to Plymouth."

I felt wretched. I was trying to think clearly. Should I stay here for the night? I wondered. There was nothing much I could do. In the morning I could search for my mother. At least she could be safe, for she had the two grooms and Jennet with her. It was not so much her personal safety that worried me, for the robbers had fled; it was the anxiety she would be suffering at the thought of what might be happening to me.

"There is another place we could try," said Colum Casvellyn.

"Let us then," I said, for I dreaded waiting alone in this inn through the night.

"Host," called Colum imperiously, "if a party such as I have described should come here, pray tell the lady that her daughter is safe and well."

"I will, my lord."

"Now," he said turning to me. "Let us visit the other inn and see if they are there."

We rode away. He did not speak, and nor did I. I felt frantic with anxiety.

We went for a mile or more; then I said, "But how far is this inn?"

"I am not sure, but I believe it to be close by. Ah, wait a moment. I am sure this is the road."

The clouds of the day had completely disappeared now, and the moon had emerged; it was not quite full but just on the wane. I was glad of the light it offered.

"This way," he said. We went up a drive and then I heard his exclamation. "Good God," he said. We were looking at a ruin . . . eerie in moonlight. A sudden horror took possession of me. It was as though I were living in a nightmare. What had happened to me? Here I was in such a place with a man whom I had hated on sight and who had filled me with a sense of fear when I had first seen him. For a moment I told myself this could not be happening in reality. I *was* dreaming. We had gone to the Traveler's Rest, and in the oak-paneled room I was dreaming of the man I had met when I was last there.

How ghostly was that scene! The walls only were standing, for it was nothing but a shell. It seemed menacing, haunted by evil spirits, as the moonlight cast ghostly shadows on the smoke blackened walls.

I looked at the man beside me, and I felt a sudden fear possess me. A faint moaning in the trees sounded like souls in distress. I seemed to hear a warning in the air: "Get away from here. Find your mother. Go back where you will be safe."

Colum Casvellyn was smiling ruefully.

"Who would have thought it? It must have happened recently. It was a flourishing inn when I last passed this way."

"Is there anywhere else where my mother might be?"

"I know of none other."

I said, "I should go back to the Inn of the Roses. I could stay there for the rest of the night."

"A lady alone?"

"I see no help for it. What else could I do?"

"You could come to Castle Paling."

"Your home!"

"It is not so far from here. I would send some of my servants out to scour the roads."

"If I went to the inn, you could still do that."

"There would be delay. I would have to take you to the inn and return home. Then I would have to give my servants their orders. If we went there now, I could have them out on the road in less than an hour."

I hesitated. "I think I would rather go to the inn."

He shrugged his shoulders, and we turned our horses. The strong feeling was with me that I should get away from the man who rode beside me. So strong was it that the thought entered my mind that I should attempt to escape. Let him go on ahead a little, then turn and gallop the other way. But where to and would he not soon overtake me? No, he had helped me so far. I should be grateful to him, and yet I did not trust him, and when I was at the burned-out inn, I had sensed that something was urgently warning me.

I would go back to the inn and there I should wait throughout the night.

We went along at a steady trot side by side. I wondered what the time was. It must have been more than two hours since I had lost my mother. How far had I ridden from that spot? I was beginning to grow frantic.

We came out of a dark road into the open. Before me was a sight which would have been inspiring had it not filled me with apprehension. Dominating the moonlit scene were the stark gray machicolated towers of a castle rising high on the rocky cliffs . . . and beyond the sea.

I stared at the lofty square-shaped structure with its towers on each corner. It was a fortress built for defense, with the protection of the sea on one side and the battlemented towers facing toward the land.

"Welcome to Castle Paling," he said softly.

I turned to him sharply. "I understood you were taking me to the inn."

"Nay," he said. "This is better. I was unsure of the way, and I do not believe your mother would wish you to spend a night at an inn unguarded."

"But . . ." I began.

"Come," he said, "my servants will look after you. We cannot go on riding aimlessly through the night."

"Aimlessly? We are certainly not doing that. We are looking for my mother."

"My dear young lady, what more can you do? You have no idea where your mother went. I have promised you that I will send servants to scour the countryside. Meanwhile, you shall be given refreshment and a place in which to rest while they do so. As soon as she is found, they shall bring her to you here."

"Why should you do so much?"

"It is the only way a gentleman can behave to a lady in distress. Moreover, I am heartily ashamed of my conduct in the inn. Fate has given me an opportunity to remove the bad impression I gave you. Will you deny me the opportunity?"

"You have already made up for it. But I would have preferred to stay at the inn."

"Here I offer you hospitality. You will be safe here. I doubt not in a short time the servants will bring news of your mother. They can escort her here to Paling. And as soon as it is light, you can start for home."

Still I hesitated. I looked at that grim gray fortress. I could hear the faint murmur of the sea. What could I do? It seemed I had no choice. I saw a light moving across what must have been a courtyard. Then I saw another in a window. There were people there. I must go with him. It was the only way. I could not roam, as he said, aimlessly through the night searching for my mother.

He saw that I was relenting. "All will be well," he said gently.

We climbed the incline to the castle.

"I would welcome the pleasure of showing you my home in happier circumstances," he said.

I tried to draw my mind away from thoughts of my mother.

"You are kind," I answered perfunctorily.

"I am glad to be of service. Come, stop fretting. This night will soon be over, and by daylight everything will seem different. Paling has long withstood the force of the elements. It is as strong as it was when the first stone was laid. It needed to be. It had to hold off intruders, and fight the weather. It is of Cornish stone—hard and strong—and has provided a home for my ancestors for generations. The foundations were laid years ago during the reign of the Conqueror."

We were approaching the portcullis. The cool wind fanned my cheeks, and I could smell the fresh, clean smell of sea air. I was aware again of that sense of being warned. It was as strong now as it had been at the burned-out inn. What was I doing? Trusting this man who had behaved so badly at the Traveler's Rest. Oh, when would this nightmare end!

Once more an impulse came to me to turn my horse and gallop away, and I restrained it. What could I do? I had told him that I had wished to go to the inn, and he had brought me here. He was a man who would do what *he* wished. I knew that. He alarmed me, yet excited me in a strange way. I was not sure of my feelings for him. He gave out an aura of immense power, which at this time I needed. I could not help feeling that if he were sincere in his desire to help me in this frightening predicament, he could do it.

I went forward simply because I did not know what could happen to me if I went back.

We had passed under the portcullis.

"Quite a climb," he said. "But you see how strong we are. A lookout on the tower could see people approaching for miles. No one can come near from the other side . . . except by boat, of course, and that would not be easy."

Colum Casvellyn started to shout, and there was an immediate response. Several men came running.

He leaped from his horse, and one of them took it. He

turned to me then and helped me out of the saddle.

He took my arm then and led me across the courtyard.

A door opened. A woman appeared with a lantern. She bobbed a curtsy, and he said, "Gemma, we have a visitor. Let a room be prepared for her and some hot food be brought."

She was off, and he took me through the great hall to the guardroom.

I had a sudden feeling then that he intended to make me his prisoner. On the walls were spears and halberds and at the four corners of the room suits of armor.

"Sit down for a moment," he said. I sat on a chair which seemed to have been made for a giant, so heavy was it.

He leaned toward me and, taking my hands in his, patted them gently. "You are cold," he said. "And so pale. You look different from the spirited young lady of the oaken chamber. It grieves me. How I should have enjoyed receiving you here with your parents in all honor. But let us forget the unfortunate circumstances."

"I find that impossible."

"Indeed you do and most understandably. Here you are, you see, in the castle's guardroom. This is where we kept our prisoners in the past before taking them to the dungeons. Oh, yes, we have dungeons. You see this trapdoor; that is one way to them. There is another. A staircase leading down and a strong iron-studded door which they tell me is impregnable."

I felt the fear grip me again.

"I have brought you here," he said, "before taking you into the castle—for this is but the guardroom. I fear that on our first meeting I made a bad impression on you. It lingers, does it not? Well, I want to say to you if you would rather go from here, I have no wish to detain you. I wish you to think well of me. If you would care to go now, please say so, and I shall not attempt to stop you." He opened the door of the guardhouse and left it open. "It is for you to decide," he added.

I was silent. I could do nothing I knew but stay here, rely on his help and long for the morning.

I said, "I will stay."

He smiled. "A wise decision," he said. "Now I will have you shown to a room which is being made ready for you. Then you shall be refreshed. You may rest in the room provided for you or where you will. Castle Paling is at your service."

I thanked him and reproached myself for my churlishness. It was true he had behaved in a swaggering manner, but he had given up the room to us; then he had called me from my bed when he had tapped at the window. Perhaps that was the most disturbing thing of all. But wasn't it what any high-spirited man might have done? Should I blame him too much? After all, when I had returned to my bed, he had gone away, and he had amply repaid any discourtesy on this night. It was hard to reconcile this man who was so anxious to calm my fears with the arrogant bully who had come to the Traveler's Rest. Had I built up an image of him in my mind which was exaggerated and therefore false? I was apt to do that. My mother often pointed it out to me.

"Now we will leave this grim place," he said, "and I will take you to my sanctum. A small room where I entertain my friends now and then. There food will be brought, and we shall eat. But before that I doubt not that you would wish to wash and perhaps take off your cloak."

He pulled at a bell rope, and I heard a clanging. A serving girl appeared at once.

"Take this lady to the room which is being prepared for her," he said.

She bobbed a curtsy, and I followed her. We went up a staircase and along a gallery. A door was thrown open. Candles flickered in their sconces. There were two women in the room making the bed. They turned and curtsied as I entered.

The room was elaborately furnished. The bed had four posts which were intricately engraved. It was a large bed furnished with heavily embroidered curtains. I wanted to stop them, for I had no intention of sleeping there. I should spend the night listening and waiting for some news.

One of the women brought warm water and a basin in which I washed my hands and face.

Removing my cloak and my bonnet-shaped hat, I shook out my hair. It was my greatest beauty, my mother said. It was a darker shade than my father's, a light brown with golden tints in it, heavy hair, that was difficult to dress and looked its best in disorder.

I was too anxious to be interested in it now, but it was a relief to have it loose.

The woman was waiting to take me to her master, and holding high her candle, she conducted me to a room which was close by the bedroom. Here candles had been lighted and a table laid.

There was hot soup in pewter bowls, and although I did not feel like eating, I realized I was faint with hunger.

He was waiting for me. He bowed and led me to a chair.

"Allow me to help you to this good capon. I am sure you will enjoy it. I can see that you are hungry and thirsty though you feel disinclined to partake of food and drink. Come, there is no good in abstaining. I have already sent men out to scour the countryside, to inquire at inns far and wide. I doubt not that ere long your mother will be here . . . or at least we shall have news of her. That will satisfy you."

It did. I found the capon good, and there was no doubt that my strength was reviving.

"Here is a good wine which will put heart into you. Drink it. It will make you feel better."

He helped himself to the great pie which was on the table and ate hungrily. He drank of the wine.

"Now there is some color in her cheeks," he said. "Come, more wine. Tell me, do you not feel better?"

I said I did.

"Tomorrow you and your mother will be laughing at this adventure."

"I think we shall always shudder with horror to recall it."

"It was a bad moment when that knave galloped off with you. I never doubted that I would catch up with you, though. My great regret is that I was unable to give him his dues. I might well yet."

"You would not recognize him if you met him again."

"Masked as he was mayhap not. I should know his horse though."

He filled my glass. "It is enough," I said.

"Oh, come, your spirits must be revived by the time your mother arrives."

"Do you really think they will find her?"

"How can they fail? There are four of them . . . all going in different directions. They must find her, for she will be either on the road or in one of the inns."

"But there was only one—the Roses. She was not there."

"Perhaps she went there later."

"I should have stayed there."

"Nay, you are better here. . . ."

I was beginning to feel a little light-headed. It was the shock, I supposed, and then the wine. His voice seemed to grow somewhat faint as though it were coming from a long way off.

He was saying, "Let me give you some of this partridge."

The room swayed a little. I thought: God help me, the wine was potent.

He was watching me, smiling at me, cutting the partridge with his knife.

I could not see his face clearly. It was becoming more and more blurred. I heard myself say, "I think . . . I think I should go. . . ."

I stood up. He was there beside me.

I felt the room, everything, slipping away and was only aware of his face near me . . . his eyes were enormous . . . there was nothing but those great black pools of eyes. . . . I felt as though I were trying to swim in dark pools and I was sinking.

I felt myself caught up suddenly. And I knew that he was holding me.

I heard his voice, strange, lilting. "All is well. All is very well."

I started up. Something had happened to me. I did not know where I was. I was shut in a green prison. There was light somewhere shining from outside on the walls. I was different. Something had changed me. I gave a little gasp, for I was naked. There was a light sheet over me and nothing more.

I sat up. I was in a bed. . . . I knew instinctively that it was the four-poster I had seen last night, for in those seconds memory came back. I had come to Castle Paling. My mother and I had been separated. I had sat down to eat and drink, and that was all.

But I knew. Horrible knowledge was tapping on my mind. Did I remember something of it? What had taken place during the night? It could not have been. And yet I knew it. Some hazy memory came back to me. It was the wine. It had dulled my consciousness. It had changed me in some way. I knew this was so. Edwina had told me there were herbs which drug your senses and make you oblivious of what was happening . . . and yet. . . .

I must be dreaming, and yet I was aware of the changes in my body.

It was impossible. Gingerly I knelt on the bed and drew aside the curtains. It was the light of day I saw which had fallen against them and lightened them. I stepped out of the bed. My clothes lay in a heap on the floor. I looked at my body and saw the bruises on it.

I knew then.

He came through a door of what must have been an antechamber to this chamber. He had a robe around his body, beneath which I guessed he was naked. I snatched up my gown and held it against me.

"Such modesty is becoming," he said.

He laughed, and he was the man at the inn then, in all his arrogant triumph. If I had had any doubt before, I could no longer do so.

"I must know what happened," I said.

"Do you not remember?"

"What was in my wine?"

"A little of my special . . . tonic."

"You must be possessed by the devil."

"It is not unlikely."

"You . . . you arranged this."

"It happened."

"My father will kill you."

"I believe him to be a man who is very handy with the sword. I have a similar reputation."

"Do you think you will be allowed to do . . . what you have done and not be punished? You will die for this."

"I was ever gallant. Nothing was done against your will."

"I had no will."

"Then how could it have been done against it?"

"What have you done to me?"

"Made a woman of you, Linnet. What a foolish name. A little bird. There is nothing of the bird about you. You are a very tigress in your passion."

"My passion. . . ."

"Oh, it was there. You were not displeased to be so taken. Believe me. It was a great experience for us both."

"Will you go away? I wish to dress and leave this place at once."

"That's a pity. We were so happy together . . . you and I. And I have news for you. Your mother is at your home. I sent messengers there last night reassuring her that you were safe. . . ."

"Safe!"

"Safe indeed. I said you would be returned to her this day."

I turned away from him. "Oh, God," I murmured, "what shall I do?"

"There are several courses open to you. I will tell you

the most attractive first. I am in need of a wife, and having tested you, I find you well enough."

"You are insulting, and I would rather be dead."

"You are impetuous. You were not so very unhappy last night. You responded very happily."

"I remember nothing, and at least I can be grateful for that!"

"You will remember. Memory will lurk in the dark places of your mind. The little virgin that you were does not want to remember. But you have forgotten you are no longer that little virgin. You were eager enough, I tell you, and who am I to deny a lady whose needs accord with my own?"

"Be silent."

"You must not speak so to your lord and master."

"That you shall never be."

"Why not? We may well be an impatient couple who have forestalled our marriage vows."

"This is a nightmare. It can't be true."

"It is and a simple enough story. You came here. You drank too much wine, and that released your natural impulses. As I have told you, I am not the man—nor would you find many—to refuse what was so charmingly offered. You will never find a lover such as I. Nor one who gallantly offers you marriage after what many would call your wanton behavior. Come, do not be shy. I have seen you naked, remember. And beautiful you are, and will grow more so. What is it to be? How would you like to become the chatelaine of Castle Paling?"

"Go away," I said. "I wish to go. I will not stay a moment longer than I need in this place."

To my surprise he stood up and bowed.

He said, "You must eat before we leave. I will have something prepared for you. Then I shall take you back to your home."

I was alone. I looked at the bed, the curtains drawn back at one side. I shuddered. What a fool I had been. I should never have come here. How clear it all was now. I should have seen it. What a cruel trick of fate to have been delivered into his hands. He had said that I would remember. Did I? Could I recall strange sensations which frightened me and fascinated me . . . as he himself did.

I dressed hastily, anxious to cover up those bruises.

One of the women servants came in with a tankard of ale and a piece of cob loaf and meat. I could not eat, but I did drink a little.

Out in the courtyard my horse was saddled. So was his. He looked fresh and vital.

He helped me into the saddle. He took my hand and looked up into my face, as though he were pleading with me, yet I saw the mockery there.

He said, "We have a long ride ahead of us, mistress."

"I wish to go with all speed."

We did not speak as we rode along and took the road along the coast.

"It is some fifteen miles," he said. "You see we are not such distant neighbors."

"More's the pity," I retorted.

My mother was safe. I believed that, and because I need not fret about her, I could think of the enormity of this thing which had happened to me.

I was not the first who had had such an experience. Many men such as he was did not bother to drug their victims first. At least I had been spared consciousness. Whatever he might say, I could not remember what had happened. There were only those vague, uneasy stirrings of sensation within me . . . only the knowledge that I had changed.

The day was bright and sparkling. The wrong sort of day for my mood. It should have been gray, somber. He broke into song once or twice—they were hunting songs. It was as though he were so pleased with life and himself that he could not suppress his pleasure.

I said nothing except when he spoke to me, and then I replied as curtly as I could.

When we had ridden some miles, he said our horses should be refreshed and so should we be.

We found an inn and stopped there. He rode into the yard in his bombastic manner, which, however, brought him immediate attention. Then, while the horses were being looked after, we went into the inn parlor, where ale and great pies were set before us.

We were alone in the inn parlor, a fact which did not please me. I would rather someone had been there so that I did not have to talk to him.

"Do not be so downcast," he said. "A girl should not mourn the loss of her virginity. It's not all that precious, you know. It is only those who fear they are never going to lose it who have such a high regard for it."

I was silent.

"You are foolish, my girl. I will not call you by that ridiculous name."

"I am no girl of yours."

"But indeed you are my mistress. You know that."

I rose to my feet and lifted my hand to strike him. He caught it.

"Steady," he said. "We do not want to make a noise, do we? What if mine host came in? What should I say? She shared my bed last night and now regrets it."

"You lie."

"It is you who lie. I speak the truth. I'll say more. I have a fancy for you . . . a fair fancy. I'll marry you."

"I would never marry you."

"You might find it right to do so."

"Right to marry you!"

" 'Twas such a night," he said, staring into his ale, "a rare night. What if you should be with child?"

I stared at him. "It is not possible."

"We shall see. 'Twould not surprise me. I'd say you were a lusty wench. You'll breed . . . you and I together. I'd swear that we had started already."

"No," I cried shrilly. "No. Let us go now. I cannot endure any more of your company."

"Then we shall go. I will take you back to your father's house."

"The sooner I am rid of you, the better."

As we went out, he said, "Do not hesitate too long. Who knows, I might find someone else to my taste. I am ready for a wife, and I am not known for my patience."

"I shall commiserate with her when the time comes."

He laughed. "Let us hope it is yourself. Commiserating with oneself is a more frequent habit than with others. My little bird. Pah! Linnet! More like an eaglet I'd say. To me you shall be Girl until you become Wife."

"I am of the opinion that after today you will never have an opportunity to call me anything."

"We shall see," he said.

We rode onward, and I was never more pleased to see the familiar portico with the lions on either side. My mother had heard our approach and came running out of the house. Jennet was with her, and so was my little sister, Damask. I jumped from my horse and threw myself into her arms.

"Dearest child," she murmured. "Oh, my darling Linnet. What a terrible night it has been."

It was so wonderful to see her before me that I forgot everything else but that we were together. She kept looking at me, and I knew what terrible anxieties she had suffered

until she had word that I was safe. I trembled to think what
she would suffer still further when she knew what had
happened to me.

Then I was aware of him. He stood there, his legs wide
apart, watching us with an almost benign expression as
though he had given us to each other. I wanted to run into
the house and hide myself. I saw that he was watching me
sardonically. Was he waiting for me to denounce him as
my seducer that he might tell them that I had offered no
resistance? Did he think they would believe him in prefer-
ence to me?

Those moments in the courtyard seemed to go on for a
long time. It was as though time were waiting for me to
act. I could denounce him. What then? My father was not
here, but when he came back he would kill Colum Casvellyn.
Or he might be killed himself. There was no sense in that.
What was done was done.

I was amazed at myself. Was I reconciled already? I
longed to get away from him and think what I must do. I
must wait, brood on what had happened, ask myself what
I should do about it.

My mother was saying, "It was good of you to send
word that my daughter was safe and again to bring her
home as soon as was possible."

"I only did what any gentleman would do," he said, in-
clining his head.

I was hard pressed not to shout at him and denounce him
for the wicked creature he was, but I saw that it would
only upset my mother more.

"Come into the house and refresh yourself," said my
mother.

She led him into Lyon Court. He complimented her on
the charm of the house. "So modern," he said, "compared
with Castle Paling. They built spaciously in the old days
but without the same view to comfort. Of course, we improve
on the castle from time to time, but it is not the same as
doing it all in the best possible way first."

"Old houses are so fascinating, though," said my mother.

"Oh, yes. So much has happened in them. When I contemplate the villainies of my ancestors, I begin to think the
castle must be populated with evil spirits."

My mother took him into the small room which led from
one of the galleries. Damask looked up admiringly at Colum
Casvellyn. He must have seemed like a giant to her. He
lifted her up and held her high above his head. I was an-

noyed that she showed her adoration so blatantly.

"Damask has taken a fancy to you," said my mother.

"And I to Damask. What an unusual name. You have original names in this family."

My mother looked pleased. She did not see that he was sneering.

"Damask is named after her grandmother. She was born the year Dr. Linacre brought the damask rose to England."

"And Linnet?" he said, smiling blandly at me.

"We thought she would be a boy, and we had decided to call her Penn—a family name. At the last moment we had to change that, and she was so like a little bird. . . ."

I felt sick with shame. What had happened to my mother's good sense? Did she not realize that this man was an enemy? Of course, she did not know how he had treated me. She saw him only as my rescuer. I wanted to shout the truth. I had a feeling that he was waiting for me to do so and in fact was rather hoping that I would, but something warned me. Wait, I cautioned myself. Do not act rashly. Think about this.

I was longing for him to leave that I might go to my room. I wanted to take off my clothes, examine my bruises, wash and put on clean clothes. As if I could make myself clean again . . . ever.

"My dearest Linnet," said my mother, "you are quite exhausted."

"I would like to go to my bedchamber and wash and rest. . . ."

"But of course." She smiled at Colum Casvellyn. "You will understand. But pray do not hurry away. I regret my husband is not at home. We can have a room prepared for you. You will wish to rest awhile after your journey."

"I am used to journeys, and since my mission is completed, must be on my way."

I had risen, and my mother called Jennet.

"You should rest, my dear," she said to me. "It has been an ordeal."

I wanted to shout: You don't know what an ordeal! I could see his eyes on me, mocking, daring me to tell my mother exactly what had happened.

Jennet came in and my mother told her to take hot water to my room, and she herself would bring me a posset which her grandmother had always brewed for exhaustion.

Jennet grasped a reluctant Damask by the hand, and I took a cool leave of Colum Casvellyn.

He bowed. "It gave me great pleasure to be of service, particularly after my manners on the first occasion."

"You did let us have the room," said my mother.

"But, madam, can you forgive me for my churlish manners? I confess I had been drinking too much of the landlord's wine."

"I would forgive anything for what you have done this night."

I wanted to scream, and I could see he was suppressing his mirth. He had said he was possessed by a devil. Indeed it seemed so.

I went to my room. It was easier to think there. Jennet brought my hot water. I took off my clothes. I could not get out of my mind the image of his removing them. I should never wear them again. I washed my body and put on clean garments. Strangely enough I felt better. I went to the window, for I heard voices below. My mother was showing him the gardens.

It was unfortunate that he should have looked up and seen me there.

He lifted his hand to his lips as he had on that other occasion. My mother by good luck had not seen me.

I turned hastily away from the window.

When my mother came in with the posset, I was lying on my bed.

She knelt beside the bed and laid her hands on my forehead.

"Oh, Linnet, I don't think I shall ever forget that moment when I saw that rascal riding away with you. We should never have taken that journey. There should have been more grooms to protect us. Next time I shall see that they are armed. And Linnet, this man, this Colum Casvellyn. . . ." She frowned. "How was he? Did he . . . frighten you in any way?"

Now was the time to tell her, but I could not bring myself to speak of it. Perhaps I could forget it happened, and it would become like a bad dream.

I shook my head and her relief was so obvious that I was glad I had not told her. "He said he would look after me and send his servants to find you," I stammered.

"After all," she said, "he did give up the Oak Room that night, though in the beginning he behaved so badly."

Tell her, I urged myself.

But no, I couldn't. Not yet. I must think about it.

Think about it! I could do nothing else. It was there in

my dreams and when I was awake. Images came into my
mind. I was not sure whether I imagined these things or
whether they had actually taken place.

All I knew was that I could never be the same again, and
as the days passed, I began to realize that I would not speak
to my mother of what had happened. It would be too dis-
tressing to us all.

My father came home, and when the house was filled
with his vital presence, I told myself he must never know.
I was aware what would happen if he did. He would set
out with a cutlass, and nothing would satisfy him but the
head of Colum Casvellyn.

For that man I cared not, but there was a notion of which
I could not rid myself. There was a growing conviction in
my mind that whatever conflict he entered into he would
emerge the victor. He was like my own father, but he was
young and my father was no longer so.

Colum Casvellyn must not be allowed to bring more
tragedy to my family. And the only way I could prevent
this happening was to remain silent.

The hideous happenings of that night must be my secret
. . . and his.

The Hasty Marriage

Christmas came, and there were the usual festivities, although my father had said there would be very special rejoicing in the culmination of this year of victory. It was now over a month since my adventure. It still haunted me. My mother noticed that I had changed and asked me if I was well. I assured her I was, and still I said nothing, which was strange, for previously I had always shared confidences with her. But of this I could not talk.

We decorated the great hall with holly and ivy, and there was much singing and dancing and playing with cards and dice. The servants enjoyed this, for they were only allowed to do it during the Christmas season; therefore, it seemed especially exciting as all forbidden things do. There was a law which forbade craftsmen and servants to gamble, which most of us said was for their own good. Of course a man of substance could do as he wished. My father liked to gamble. He was a gambler by nature, and he was inclined to be very lenient with servants who broke the law in that way.

So Christmas was celebrated with the dice and cards and the mummers and masking, and it was as I remembered it had been all my life.

"Last Christmas," said my mother, "the fear of the Spaniards hung over us like a black pall. This year we are free." I wished I felt free. A greater black pall hung over me, for a national disaster can never really affect us like a personal one.

With the new year the Landors came for the proposed visit. Loving to boast about his possessions, my father had wished to impress them with his wealth. My mother retorted that the Landors were a wealthy family and would not be amazed by that in others, particularly if it were thrust under their noses to be remarked on.

But my father would have it his way. I knew he was very excited about the prospect of new business interests.

New Year, he said, should be celebrated much as Christmas. A Lord of Misrule should be appointed through a certain trinket to be found in one of the cakes or puddings, and that should add to the fun. It was to be a right merry welcoming in of the new year, for he prophesied it would be a year of great prosperity for England.

My mother said to me, "It will be a pleasure to see the Landors again. Do you think so too, Linnet?"

She was looking at me intently, and I could not meet her eye. I said that I should indeed be pleased.

"It seems that they will join with your father. I like the idea. I daresay we shall see a great deal of them in the future."

I could see she was already planning my wedding. Now was the time to tell her. I began, "Mother. . . ." There was a dreamy look in her eyes. I could see she was visualizing the bride and bridegroom and all the preparations that must go into a wedding. And again I could not bring myself to speak of that night at Castle Paling.

On the last day of the old year the Landors arrived. Fennimore took my hands in his and smiled at me. I felt my heart uplifted a little, because he was so different from Colum Casvellyn. How gentle he was, how tender he would be!

My father and mother were in the courtyard welcoming the guests, my father shouting orders and making the servants run hither and thither, my mother taking quiet command.

We took them to their rooms, and they pleased my father by admiring Lyon Court. The smell of roasting and baking filled the house, and it was a very merry party which sat down to supper that evening. Edwina had come over with

Carlos, for Carlos was very interested in the new trading venture and would indeed have a share in it. So would Jacko, and young Penn was determined to learn all he could.

Edwina was beginning to show signs of pregnancy. She had changed; she was more beautiful, I thought, because there was such a lovely serenity on her face. She had always been so anxious when Carlos went away on his voyages. Now, I thought, she will have a child to care for, and she will be happier.

She talked to me about the coming child when we were alone.

"I'm so happy, Linnet," she said. "I've wanted this so much . . . and so has Carlos. We thought it would never happen, and now it has. It is not strange? For so long we have been married and yet some people conceive immediately. I really began to think there was something wrong with me."

I said it was wonderful to see her so delighted and asked what she hoped for, a boy or a girl.

"Carlos wants a boy of course. Men always do."

"My mother says they so admire themselves that they want to see a replica. That is why they want sons."

Edwina laughed. "I simply don't care. I merely want a baby. You'll know how I feel one day, Linnet."

There followed a week of pleasant friendship. The men were often together talking of the merchant vessels they would send throughout the world. My father took the Landors onto those of his ships which were in the Sound, and they planned all kinds of alteration which would render them more suitable for the new project. My mother was very happy. I knew she had decided on Fennimore for me, and she believed that before the visit was over, an announcement would be made.

It was at the New Year that the frightening possibility had come to me. It could have happened. He himself had suggested it. I was not sure, of course, but I soon should be, and what should I do then?

I feigned a headache and shut myself in my room. My mother sent Jennet up with a posset for me. Jennet was a very talkative woman, and her conversation was full of hints about men. It had always been so. My mother used to say, "Jennet was made as she is. I suppose we can't blame her."

Jennet sat on the bed and held out the posset to me.

"There, Mistress Linnet, you drink that. It'll give you a nice sleep, and you'll be right as rain."

"Thank you, Jennet," I said.

She brought her face close to mine and looked at me searchingly. "Mistress Linnet, there's nothing *wrong?*"

"Wrong?" I said. "What do you mean?"

She blushed. She had always had a habit of blushing if her thoughts were indelicate, and although she had been the mistress of many men, she had the air of a virgin. I think that was probably what attracted them.

"Oh . . . nothing, mistress. There was that gentleman at the inn." She giggled. "My dear life, I remember when he came into the inn and would have his way. You could see he was that kind. Reminded me of the Captain, he did." She went on giggling about the man at the inn and watching me covertly. "And then he rescued you. When I watched you being made off with and him after you . . . my dear life!"

I said, "I'm going to try to sleep now, Jennet."

"Yes, mistress." She looked down at me. "And then he took you to his castle. 'Tis like an old tale of knights and ladies that the minstrels do sing of, I do declare."

There was a dreamy look in her eyes which yet held a certain astuteness. I thought: She knows what has happened. It is possible then? And the niggling fear was with me.

Twelfth Night came. This was the culmination of the festivities. The following day the holly and the ivy would be taken down and solemnly burned in the meadow. It was unlucky to leave it up after that.

We had the Twelfth Night cake, and there was a great deal of speculation as to which of us would find the silver penny.

Fennimore was the lucky one. My father as head of the house announced, "I crown you Lord of Misrule till the midnight hour." And the crown which we used every year was placed on his head.

My father, Captain Landor and two of the tallest of the menservants carried him around the hall, and he chalked crosses on the beams wherever he could reach them, chanting, "Protect this house from the curse of devils and evil spirits and of all conjuring and wicked charms."

We played games. My mother had hidden treasure, and we were to hunt for it in pairs. I was pleased when Fennimore, Lord of Misrule, chose me as his companion, and I could not refuse him if I had wished because he was King for the Night.

We went off hand in hand, Fennimore holding our candle high, and I was aware that the eyes of my parents followed us with approval. I was sure that they had decided this would be a fitting time to announce our betrothal. Family ties would cement the business ones. I had to lead the way because naturally he did not know the house as I did.

My mother had devised the clues, and the finding of one led us on to the next. It was a game we had played all our lives, and the treasure hunt was considered the highlight of any of our gatherings. It showed how they trusted Fennimore to allow me to go off with him as they did, for usually young people were paired off by their elders. Of course, Fennimore was the Lord of Misrule and was supposed to have his way, but if someone like Colum Casvellyn had been in his place, they would never have allowed it. Why did I have to think of that man so constantly? What a question to ask myself. How could I ever forget him? What a fateful evil trip that had been for me. It would affect my whole life. How strange that one night could do that.

Fennimore said, "Are you cold?"

"No, no. It was just a passing shiver. Someone walking over my grave, as they say."

And I thought: the grave of my innocence which is now dead but not buried deep enough.

He took my hand.

"Are we going to find the treasure?" he asked.

"That depends on how clever you are."

"You are the clever one."

"I? Whatever gave you such a notion?"

"I suspect it. You are a very unusual girl, Linnet."

"Surely not."

"I think so," he said.

We had crossed the hall and mounted the dais. There was a door there which led into the small dining room and sitting rooms which we used when we were alone, for fashions were changing and in households like ours only on special occasions did people dine in the hall with all the servants seated below the salt.

We looked into these rooms, and we were not very successful with the clues. I think our minds were not on the treasure hunt.

We mounted the staircase and went along the gallery. Fennimore sat down in one of the window seats and drew me beside him. He lifted the candle and looked into my face.

Then he set it down and said, "Linnet, there is something I have to say to you."

My heart began to beat very fast because I knew what he was going to say and I wanted to stop him. I wanted him to wait until I had grown farther away from that night at Castle Paling. I wanted to know whether it would be possible for me to cast it right out of my mind, to forget it so completely that it would seem as though it had never happened. Until I knew, I did not want Fennimore to say what was in his mind.

He went on: "I am so happy that your parents and mine are going to work together. I admire your father so much. He is a bold captain. The Queen has complimented him. He is the kind of man who has saved this country from the Spaniards. That is why it seems so wonderful to me that he should now be ready to fight another campaign . . . a campaign of peace."

"It is not necessary surely to be aggressive to succeed."

"I do agree with you. But what I want to say to you is this: Our families will work together. Linnet, from the moment we first met I felt drawn to you. If your father had not joined with us, it would have made no difference to my feeling."

I must stop him quickly. He must not go on and ask me to marry him . . . yet.

I put out a hand helplessly, and he took it.

He raised it to his lips. Memory stirred within me. I could feel hard lips on my skin. Was I ever going to forget?

How gentle he was, how tender. I needed tenderness. What would I not have given if I could go back two months. . . . If only it had never happened.

He kept my hand in his. "Our families wish it, Linnet. That makes me so happy. It will be so right for us. . . . You will not be far away from your home. Your mother will visit us. So you will not be parted. I know your love for each other."

"Please don't go on, Fennimore," I said.

"Why not, Linnet? Surely you know that I love you. I believe you care for me. . . ."

"I cannot say," I stammered foolishly. "I must have time. It is too soon. . . . I am not ready."

"I should have waited awhile. You are so young and so innocent. . . ."

I was glad that he could not see the deep flush in my cheeks.

He was contrite, eager not to distress me.

"My dearest Linnet, we will say no more. I have been too rash. I should have waited. I did not realize how little you had understood. I should have prepared you. But I have made my feelings known. I will ask you again soon," he went on. "And, Linnet, will you promise me to think about this?"

"I will think about it."

"You see, my dearest, you and I could be so happy together. Our families will work together. We shall be together. You see how it is."

"Yes, I see how it is. Fennimore, you are so good and kind. Give me time."

"You shall have time, my love," he said.

I stood up. "Please, Fennimore," I said, "let us now play this game and try to find the treasure."

He said softly, "Our treasure will be in each other, Linnet."

I shivered again because I was afraid. I longed to be the girl I had been before I had spent a night at Castle Paling. I wanted to be young and innocent and in love with Fennimore. But I was unsure how to act—unsure of everything, of whether I loved Fennimore, of whether I could marry him and, most of all, of what happened that night when Colum Casvellyn had half drugged, half awakened my senses and made a woman of me while I was still a child.

I tried to think of the treasure; I succeeded a little since I was able to solve some of the clues.

We almost won, but Carlos and Edwina, who had chosen to hunt together, were the victors.

My mother was watching me intently.

I knew she was disappointed that she could not announce my betrothal on that night.

The next day we took down the decorations, carried them out to the fields and ceremoniously burned them. Christmas and New Year celebrations were over for twelve months. This time next year, I thought, I shall be so far away from the night at Castle Paling that it will be no longer constantly on my mind.

The whole household was present at the burning. It was a custom that everyone should have a part in it, for to stay away could bring ill luck. It was when the blaze was dying down that we heard shouting in the distance, and one of the servants said, " 'Tis old Maggie Enfield. They be hanging her this day."

I knew Maggie Enfield. She was a poor old woman, almost blind, and her face was disfigured by numerous ugly brown warts. She was known as a witch in the neighborhood and lived in a tiny cottage which was little more than a hut. We used to take food and leave it outside her door. My mother sent this not because she was afraid of what might happen to her if she did not, but because she had real sympathy for the poor old woman.

A few years ago she had been known as a good witch. She grew certain herbs in the patch of land around her cottage and brewed concoctions which had cured many a sickness. She had produced love potions too, and she did what was called the fast. If she fasted for several days and sat silent in her cottage, she brought all her powers to bear on a certain object. She had been known to discover lost articles. If a sheep or a cow strayed away, people went to Mother Enfield and paid for the fast, and almost always she could discover the spot where the animal could be found.

But witches—be they good or evil—lived dangerously, for they could never be sure when people would turn against them. Farmers who suffered a run of ill luck with their stock, parents whose children died unexpected and unexplained deaths, women who were barren—any could be put down to a witch's actions, and when people raged against their own ill fortune, it seemed to soothe them to wreak the anger they felt toward fate against some human victim.

So it had come to this for poor Maggie Enfield. I had heard whispers. Jennet had told me. Somebody's baby had been born dead; someone else had a disease among his cattle. Maggie Enfield had been seen passing the cottage where the baby had died and had been caught looking at the cattle.

And now they decided that she was an evil witch and that she had sold herself to the devil for these special powers, and Maggie Enfield was being dragged from her cottage by those who were determined on vengeance.

They would hang her on one of the trees.

I shivered. I would not go down Gibbet Lane for a long time. I remembered vividly the first time I had ridden down that grim thoroughfare. There were two trees there suitably shaped to form a scaffold. There could scarcely be a more terrifying sight than a body hanging helpless, life-less, swaying on a tree.

And now the celebration of burning the Christmas deco-rations had been spoiled by the thought of old Maggie Enfield in the hands of her executioners.

My father was for going to join the macabre proceeding, but my mother stopped him.

"I will not go," she said quickly, "nor will you, Jake. What will our guests think?"

"They'll think that another of Satan's brew has met her just deserts."

"They are gentlefolk, remember. Such a spectacle will disgust them."

"Justice should disgust no one."

My mother looked impatient, and she turned away from him. She went over to the Landors and told them that we should return to the house without delay or she feared that the meat which was turning before the spit would be burned to a cinder.

My father, amused, as he often was by my mother's defiance, refused to be done out of what he would consider a treat and rode off in the opposite direction.

The subject came up over the meal, and Father was vehement.

"The woman was guilty and had her just reward," he said. "Those marks on her face proved it. Her succubus visits her nightly. The marks were found all over her body."

"Oh, come," said my mother, "they were warts. Many have them."

"Then tell me why she can cure them in others and not in herself."

"I am not skilled in these matters," retorted my mother.

"So it doth seem," replied my father. "Well, Mother Enfield has now joined her master. There she will rot in hell."

"Why should she?" asked my mother. "If she has served her master well, perhaps he will reward her."

"If I had my way, this country would be purged of witches. I'd ferret them out. I'd have the gibbets busy."

My father was a very intolerant man. He had a code, and there was no diverging from it. He had been guilty of rape, I knew. There was Carlos to prove it—the result of a raid on the Spanish coast. What Colum Casvellyn had done to me was exactly the sort of trick he would have played on a woman, and yet he would be outraged because this had happened to his daughter. As my mother had said so often, there was no reasoning with him.

Now he talked fiercely about what he called the cult of Satan. My mother said that witchcraft had stayed with us; it belonged to the days before Christianity came to our land. It was a part of the religion of the ancients. It was anti-Christianity; it was worship of the horned god whom Christians called the devil.

She was knowledgeable about the subject. She said that the Sabbats were in fact a kind of religious ceremony in which the horned god was worshiped, and because there was a need to people the earth, the dances performed at the feet of the horned god were in fact fertility rites.

My father watched her sardonically as she talked—a mixture of pride and derision in his glance. Fennimore said that this was so and the way in which to wipe out witchcraft was not to torture and kill defenseless old women but to lure them from their beliefs in this old pagan religion and make Christians of them.

"Oh, you are a reformer," said my father with a laugh.

"Well, perhaps that is not such a bad thing to be," replied Fennimore.

"It is a very good thing to be," said my mother, smiling at him warmly. There was no doubt that she was very fond of Fennimore.

She managed to turn the subject back to the ever-interesting one of the new project, for it was clear that my father might become too dogmatic and introduce a discordant note.

And so the unfortunate incident of Maggie Enfield's hanging was forgotten, and the rest of the day passed pleasantly.

In the morning the Landors left. Plans had been made; ships were being converted; the new enterprise was about to begin.

I was now certain, and as the fearful truth dawned on me that as a result of that extraordinary night I was going to have a child, I felt as though the bars of a cage were forming around me.

I knew, of course, that I must tell my mother. My father had left on a short voyage, and I chose the time while he was away. I asked her to come to my bedchamber as I had something very important to say to her.

I faced her there and blurted out, "Mother, I am with child."

She stared at me in disbelief, and I saw the color leave her face.

"Linnet. No!"

"I fear it is true."

"Fennimore . . ." she began. "I am surprised. . . ."

"No, not Fennimore, Mother."

I was trying hard to find the right words, and they would not come.

"Not . . . Fennimore!" She was frankly bewildered.

Then the words started to tumble out. "It was that night. He . . . he took me to Castle Paling. It was there. . . ."

"*That* man!" she cried. "But you let me believe . . ."

"I know. I could not bring myself to speak of it then."

"You . . . he. . . . You love him?" she demanded.

I shut my eyes and shook my head. I could hear his mocking laughter. Did I remember it from that night? Had it penetrated my drugged senses?

"He took me to his castle and there . . . I don't know what happened. I was exhausted. He had a room made ready for me. He took me to a room where food was laid out. He said he was sending his servants to find you. I ate and drank . . . and that is all. The next morning I awoke in the four-poster bed . . . I was naked and *different* . . . and he was there. . . ."

"My God," cried my mother. "Your father will kill him."

"So I feared."

Her horror had given way to love. She had taken me in her arms and was rocking me as though I were a baby. "My little Linnet," she said. "Don't fret. We will do something. I could kill him myself."

The burden had dropped away from me as I knew it would when I told her. She would find some answer. She always had. All my problems had been taken to her, and when she knew them, they had ceased to be insuperable.

She sat down on my bed, her arm about me.

"Linnet," she said, "what do you remember of that night?"

"I'm not sure. Sometimes I think I remember something . . . sometimes I believe I have imagined it. I was at the table, and he filled my goblet. He said I was exhausted and needed refreshment."

"The devil!" she cried. "Oh, Linnet, sometimes I hate men." I knew she was thinking of my father. I knew a little of her stormy life, and I believe that she had been ill used. I knew that I had a brother Roberto who was somewhere in Spain, the son of her first marriage; I knew that my father had his bastard sons. And I wished I had confided in her long ago. "And then?" she prompted.

"Then? I drank and the haziness came over me. . . . Everything seemed to slip away. I was aware of him. I think I knew he lifted me up and carried me. Then I woke, and it was morning, and I knew what happened."

She was silent, and her arms tightened about me.

"I have been so frightened," I added.

"You should have told me before, Linnet. But never mind, I know now."

"What can I do?" I asked.

She stroked my hair. "Never fear, we'll find a way. When your father knows, he will go to Castle Paling. It could be the end of one of them."

"Yet he . . ." I began.

"Yes," she said. "Yet he. But men are illogical. What he will think an ordinary occurrence for himself is a violent outrage when performed by others. You are his beloved daughter; it is the daughters of others who may be ill used." She laughed, a sad, bitter little laugh, and she went on stroking my hair. "I cannot bear to think of your keeping this to yourself, Linnet. How was he . . . this . . . man in the morning?"

"He laughed at me. He said that I had not resisted him. He said I had joined him in a merry bed, and it was as much my wishing as his."

"He is indeed a scoundrel. You must hate him."

"I do, and . . ."

"I think I understand," she said. "Nothing can alter what has happened. You are carrying his child. You are sure, Linnet?"

"I think so, Mother."

"We must make sure. But I would not have anyone know of this yet . . . not even my physician. What we have to think of is what we can do. You are unmarried and pregnant, and the man who wishes to marry you is not the father. If only it had been Fennimore, but Fennimore would not have behaved so."

"He is quite different from Fennimore."

"Let us think what must be done. That is of the utmost importance to us now, Linnet. There are herbs, of course. Maggie Enfield could have given them, but she, alas, is hanging on her gibbet, poor soul. There are others, but I fear that sort of thing, Linnet. It is not for you. Fennimore is a good man. He is a tolerant man, and that is rare. I had set my heart on your marrying him."

"I cannot do that now."

"It is not impossible. What if we told him the truth?"

"You mean you would ask him to father another man's child?"

"If he loves you, he would."

"I could not ask him to do that."

"I could explain what had happened. . . ."

I shook my head. "It is impossible, Mother. Colum Casvellyn would know the child is his. On that morning he hinted that I might already be with child."

"The man is indeed a devil."

"He would not let it be forgotten. He lives too near. He might want the child . . . if it were a son."

"That could be so," said my mother. "There seems to me but one thing. You must go to London. I will take you to my mother. She will care for you, and the child can be born there. It can be said that you are a widow whose husband is recently dead. It's so far away none will be able to prove otherwise. My mother will be delighted to care for you and the child. You will be happy there."

"And leave you?"

"The time comes, Linnet, when mothers and daughters must part."

"And you wanted me to marry Fennimore that we might always be quite near."

"Not only that, Linnet. I wanted it because I felt that Fennimore is a good man who would be kind to you. I longed to hear you say that you were betrothed."

"So might we have been but for that night."

"Your father must not know. I fear that man. I feared him when he strode into the inn. I had an uneasy feeling that he was going to bring some evil to us. When he left the inn that morning, I felt such an immense relief that it seemed out of all proportion to what had happened. Now I understand it. If we had only taken a different road."

"You can always say that of life, Mother. It it always a matter of taking the wrong or the right road."

"Now we must be sure to take the right one. I'm glad you have told me, Linnet. Together we will find the solution to this. But there must be little delay. No one here must know that you are pregnant. It is early yet." She calculated swiftly. "It is not yet two months. If we go to my mother, we must do so within the next month."

"What will my father say?"

"We shall have to be very careful with him. He is expecting an announcement of your marriage to Fennimore. He will not understand this sudden desire to go to London and may well oppose it. That could delay us. You know his impatience. Now he has decided to throw in his lot with the Landors he wants you wedded and providing him with grandsons to continue with the business when they come of an age to do so. It is the best way, Linnet. In fact, I think it is the only way. You might of course tell Fennimore. He would be discreet. No one can blame you. And who knows, he might be ready to marry you."

"I couldn't, Mother, not with the child."

"You would grow used to the idea. Perhaps it would be best."

"Please do not tell him."

"We will not act rashly although we must not delay too long. This has been a terrible shock, and I need time to think. Dearest Linnet, I do not want you to go to my mother. To lose you would break my heart, for I should see so little of you and we have been together all your life. Yet it seems to me the best solution, unless of course Fennimore. . . ."

"I am so relieved that you know," I said. "It seems so much easier to bear now."

"We will find a way out, darling," she said. "Together we will find the way."

The way was found for us. A few days after I had told my mother Colum Casvellyn came to visit us.

I was in my bedchamber sewing a button on one of my gowns when Jennet came in very excited.

"He's here," she said. "He's come to call."

"Who?" I asked.

"The one who rescued you and brought you back."

I felt my knees tremble.

"This can't be so."

"Oh, yes, 'tis so, mistress. He rode into the courtyard like as though he were master here, and he leaped down and shouted to one of the grooms who stood gaping at him. Then he saw me, and he said, 'Go tell your mistress, your young mistress, she has a visitor.'"

"You are sure it is this man?"

Jennet blushed in that foolish coy way as though she were a young girl instead of an experienced woman in her forties.

"Oh, yes, mistress, there be no mistaking him."

I said, "Bring him into the winter parlor. I will join him there."

She was off with all speed. I thought: I should find my mother. It would be better if we saw him together. But no, I wanted to see him alone first. I wanted to test my feelings for him.

I could scarcely wait to reach the winter parlor. He was already there, standing with his back to the window, legs apart in that arrogant manner which was characteristic, suggesting that he was the owner of everything in sight.

"Good day to you," he cried, smiling broadly. He strode toward me and, taking both my hands, drew me toward him and kissed me on the mouth.

I flushed hotly and drew back in dismay.

"Coy?" he said. "Reluctant? Oh, no, not after all we have been to each other."

My heart was beating so fast that I could not find my voice. I was filled with uncertainty. I had never felt this overpowering emotion before. It was a hatred, I supposed, but I was not entirely sure.

He looked at me intently. "I came to see how matters stood," he said.

"I do not understand you, sir."

"After such pleasure as we shared there could be results. I was anxious for your health."

"How could you know . . ." I cried.

His eyebrows were raised; his eyes lighted suddenly with pleasure.

" 'Tis so," he cried. " 'Tis so indeed."

He tried to take me by the shoulders, but I stepped back sharply. "By God," he cried, "I knew it. You were meant to bear sons, I'll swear. I sensed it that night at the inn. You and I together. . . ." Then he threw back his head and laughed loudly. It was the laughter of triumph.

I stood back still farther. I wished that I had called my mother to come with me.

"You are sure?" he asked.

"I have told my mother."

His eyebrows were raised again. They were thick, bushy and very arched.

"What says she?"

"You must be gone," I said. "I never want to see you again."

"Not see the father of your child?"

"It must be forgotten. I am going away. We have planned it."

"Going away? Where will you go?"

"I am not prepared to tell you."

"Going away . . . carrying my child!"

I cried out in despair. "Leave me alone, I beg of you. Have you not harmed me enough? Never let me see you again."

"I came here," he said, "to offer you marriage."

"That is noble of you," I said with sarcasm.

"I am a man to honor my obligations."

"This one may pass. You could best make amends by going away and never coming into my life again."

"And the child?"

"Will be taken care of. It shall never know that it was forced on an innocent girl who was drugged to satisfy a cruel man's lust. If you will make amends, go away."

"I am going to look after you and the child. We will marry without delay. Our son will be born a little prematurely for respectability mayhap, but that is not a matter to cause us over much concern."

"How could I marry you?"

"Simply. I could get a priest today. The sooner, the better for the sake of our child."

There was a scratching at the door, and Jennet came in with wine and little cakes. She was dimpling as though it gave her great pleasure to serve such a fine gentleman. I noticed too that old as she was, he was not unaware of her. It was that overwhelming sensuality in her, I supposed, which matched that in him.

I said, "Pray tell my mother that Squire Colum Casvellyn is here, Jennet, and beg her to come with all speed."

He looked at me slyly as though he knew it was a cry for help.

When Jennet had gone, he said reproachfully, "We did not need your mother to decide for us."

"I do not wish to remain here alone with you."

"We were alone remember all through that memorable night."

"How dare you speak in that way? As though . . . I were a party to it."

"But you were a party to it. You made no attempt to run away."

"How could I?"

" 'Twould not have been easy, I'll grant you. But you

were not in truth averse. I awakened something in you. Something you will never forget. That is why you will be wise to accept my offer, give our child a name and give me many more children. I need a wife. I want sons. I know you will be the one to provide them."

My mother came in. She stood on the threshold, and her eyes flashed in rage.

"How dare you come here!" she demanded.

He bowed ironically. "Madam," he said, "I came to ask for your daughter's health and to offer her my heart and hand along with the marriage bond."

"Marriage!" she cried.

" 'Tis only seemly, since as you know we have already bedded and with results."

"If my husband were here . . . ." said my mother.

"Is he not? I wished to meet him."

"It would be an ill day for you if you did."

"Madam, are you being just? I have come to you to right a wrong. I have come to make honorable amends. I offer your daughter marriage."

My mother was speechless. She glanced at me, but I could not meet her eyes. I kept thinking of marrying him, spending my days and nights with him, and I felt a sudden wild curiosity which was almost desire.

He assumed an air of humility which was quite alien to him and gave him an unexpected charm.

"I am a sinner, madam," he said. "I will tell you the truth. I saw your daughter in the inn and, as a young hot-blooded man must do, desired her. I behaved badly." He shrugged. "A sort of revenge if you will, because I knew she was out of my reach. Then I had the good fortune to rescue her from robbers. I tremble to think what her fate would have been had she been left to them. I rescued her; I searched for you; I could not find you; then I took her to my castle. It was there that the temptation overcame me. I deserve your contempt and hatred. But, madam, you do not know what it means to be so deep in desire. There is no conscience, there is no thought for anything beyond the satisfying of that desire. Perhaps your husband could understand. I have heard tales of him, and I think he would. My better nature was subdued. I behaved as I did because I could not stop myself doing otherwise."

My mother said, "You behaved as no gentleman would."

" 'Tis true, alas. And having done so, your daughter has not been out of my mind since that day I brought her home to you. I determined to ask for her hand in marriage, to make amends. I knew that there was only one circumstance in which she would have me. What I hoped is now a fact and I have the temerity to offer myself. She shall be cherished all the days of her life, she shall be my honored wife, the mother of my children, and there shall be no slur on this little one whom she now carries."

My mother was silent. I could see the speculation in her eyes. It was a solution. He was the father of the child; he wished to marry me; I should not be so far from her if I married him. It would have been the best answer but for the fact that I must take this man for my husband.

She turned to me. "I think my daughter will refuse your offer."

"Yes," I said. "I refuse. I never want to see this man again."

"You will see him in your child," he reminded me. "And will you deny him his name?"

"We will make arrangements," said my mother. "We are not without the power to do so."

"I shall want my child," he said.

"Since it was begotten in such a manner, you have no right to it," said my mother.

"A father no right to his child! Come, madam, you are unjust."

"What a pity you did not think of justice when you had my daughter at your mercy."

"Your daughter was, alas, so desirable that my conscience was stilled, and you are to blame for that, madam, for you have brought her up with a spirit and beauty to match your own."

"Enough of this," said my mother. "You have caused us great trouble. You can serve us best by going away from here and never crossing our paths again."

"I have planned it well," he said. "I will ride over with a priest, and he shall marry us quietly. Then I shall let it be known that your daughter and I were so enamored of each other, so eager for the sweets of union that we could not wait for the grand wedding you would certainly want to give us, so we married quietly in November, kept our marriage secret, and now that you know, you insist on a grand wedding if that is what you wish, madam."

I could see that she was thinking of my father. If he were told this story, he would accept it, and although he had hoped with my mother that I would marry Fennimore,

I did not think he would be so delighted with him as a son-in-law as my mother would have been.

She was looking at me. Perhaps he reminded her of my father; she knew what her feelings for him were. Was she asking herself if while outwardly I seemed to hate this man, he aroused unexpected emotions within me? If she was thinking this, she was right.

His size, his blustering manner, the power that exuded from him had a certain magnetism. I could not understand what it was, but when I compared Fennimore with him, Fennimore seemed a little insignificant.

He leaned against the table and regarded the tips of his boots. His expression had grown melancholy. "If she will not accept me, madam, what a plight she will be in! Your daughter condemned as a girl who grants favors before marriage. Oh, I agree, she was forced to it, but such is the way of the world that even so, a maiden's plight is held against her. It is wrong, it is cruel, but nevertheless true. *I* am to blame. I have put her into this condition. I wish to make amends, and I swear with all my heart, madam, that I will do so. We will have our grand wedding as soon as is possible and I shall take my bride with me to Castle Paling. She will already be with child, but why should she not be when she was secretly married to the husband of her choice as far back as November?"

There was silence in the room. I was aware of the thudding of my heart as it shook my body. He was right. It was a way out. Even those who did not believe that we had been secretly married in November would not dare say so. My child would be born with all honor—the heir of Castle Paling. There would be no bitter subterfuge to darken my life. And I should be his wife. The thought, I must admit, filled me with terror, and yet it was a delicious sort of terror. I was beginning to think it was a terror I must experience.

He was the first to speak. "Tomorrow," he said, "I shall come here with the priest."

"We must have time to think of this," said my mother. "Tomorrow is too soon."

"There is little time to waste, madam. Remember, our child grows bigger with every day. I will come tomorrow with the priest. By then you will have seen that this is the answer."

He bowed and went out into the courtyard. I heard him shouting for his horse. My mother and I were silent listening to the sound of his horse's hooves as he rode away.

Then she took my arm. "Come away from here, Linnet," she said. "We must go somewhere where we can talk in peace."

All through that day we talked.

"My dearest child," said my mother, "it is a decision which only you can make. You must not forget that this is for life. Marriage with him would provide an immediate solution, but don't forget you have to consider the future. If such a marriage were distasteful to you, you must not enter into it. Anything . . . yes, anything is better than that. What happened was no fault of yours. Everyone will see that."

"Will people believe it?" I asked. "There will be hints. They will follow me all my life."

"That is not so. You have the example of Romilly. She gave birth to a child, and your own father fathered it. Can you imagine a greater scandal than that? Yet somehow she has continued to live here, and she feels no shame."

"I am not Romilly."

"Nay indeed. The situation is different. He has wronged you and surprisingly has come to make amends."

"He has come because he wants the child."

"He could marry if he wished and have one. Yet he has offered you marriage."

"Yes, it is true," I said.

"But, my dearest, you must think clearly. You must not take a solution merely because it seems easy to you. Tell me what is in your mind."

I raised my bewildered eyes to her face. "I do not know," I said.

"Has he perhaps fascinated you a little?"

"I am unsure."

"I understand it. There is something strong about him. You know something of what happened to me. I did not want to marry your father, yet compared with him, all other men seemed small and insignificant. You see how it is with us. We have always quarreled. Often we have hated each other, and yet there is something between us. Is it love? I don't know. It is a bond, the severing of which would take something vital from our lives. I suppose that is love . . . in a way. As soon as he came into the inn, he reminded me of your father. They are the buccaneers of the world, such men, and this is an age of buccaneers. They are the men of our times and the times are not nice and gentle. We are fighting for our place in the world . . . and we produce men such as these to make and hold our place there. That's how I see it. But such talk does not help us. Tell me how you felt for Fennimore?"

"I liked him. His manners are charming, and he is good to look at. I think he would be a good husband."

"I think so, too. He is kind and gentle and would understand what happened was no fault of yours."

"If there had not been a child. . . . Perhaps I should try to rid myself of it, but I don't want to, Mother. Already I feel that it is mine and in spite of everything. . . ."

"I understand. And I would not allow you to rid yourself of it. Many girls have died through such a thing. Whatever the outcome, you will have the child. Shall we speak to Fennimore? Shall we tell him what has happened?"

I shook my head.

"Then you will go to my mother?"

"I couldn't bear to leave you."

"Then you need not. You could have the child here. You and I would bring it up together."

"My father. . . ."

My mother laughed, and the derisive smile was on her face as though he were there to see it. "He will have to accept what is done."

"There will be trouble. He will never let Colum Casvellyn escape his fury."

"That's true."

"And if aught happened to my father. . . ."

She put her hands on my shoulders and looked at me earnestly. "Linnet," she said, "somewhere in the depth of your mind you want to marry this man."

I lowered my eyes. I could not look at her.

She held me against her and stroked my hair. "You need feel no shame. I understand. So much happened to me. It is not always easy to understand one's emotions. There is a virility about him. You need not be ashamed because you want to respond to it. It is natural. By marrying him, you would be taking a great risk. It would be like going on a journey into the unknown, on a ship of which you knew nothing and an unpredictable captain in charge of the vessel. Well, Linnet, you are a sailor's daughter."

That night I could not sleep. It was after midnight when my mother came into my room. We lay in my bed together, I was clasped in her arms, and she told me of her own youth and what had happened to her, and I knew that there was something of her in me and something of my father too. I knew that a perilous adventure lay before me, but I could no more turn my back on it than either of them could have done.

The next day, true to his word, Colum Casvellyn arrived at Lyon Court. He brought a priest with him. And in the chapel he and I were married.

I was amazed how sober he could be. When the ceremony was over, he embraced me with gentleness, and he docilely agreed to go away until my mother had been able to speak to my father.

She would lie to him, for it was necessary. She wanted no bloodshed. She would tell him that I had quietly married Colum Casvellyn some months before and, fearing his disapproval, as he had wished for an alliance with the Landors, had kept my secret until I was with child and realized that it had to be told.

We stood together watching Colum ride away. Then she turned to me and looked at me steadily.

"So we found our solution, Linnet," she said. "Pray God it was the right one."

The First Wife

Colum and I were riding to Castle Paling.

That morning we had had a second ceremony, this time with the customary festivities.

My father had been far from displeased.

"You sly creature!" he shouted at me. "It's what I'd expect of you. And already carrying my grandson. Take care of him, or it will be the worse for you."

"It might be a girl, Father," I said.

"So you're going to be such a one as your mother are you? Can't get boys. We'll see." His chin wagged with amusement as I remembered so well from my childhood. When he had seemed to be angry and glowered at me and shouted abuse, if I saw that movement of his chin I had known that he was secretly amused. Thus it was now.

We rode a little together, although he wouldn't allow me to gallop. "Remember my grandson," had become a catchphrase. He was pleased. He liked Colum.

"By God," he said, "you've got a man there. And went off and married him in secret, eh?" He slapped his thigh with delight. "To tell you the truth, daughter, I never greatly cared for Fennimore Landor. A good fellow in his way, but no fighting guts. It won't be like that with your man, I'll tell you. There'll be fights in plenty, I doubt not, but remember, you're your father's daughter and fight back. Be like your mother. I'll tell you something—she has the occasional victory."

I could see that he thought that his marriage was the perfect one. A peaceful union, such as I might have expected with Fennimore Landor, was in his eyes faintly despicable.

How different it might have been if he had known the truth.

And so we had married early that morning, partaken of the wedding feast and allowed the guests to continue with it while Colum and I left for the journey to Castle Paling. As it was only some fifteen miles from Lyon Court, I would not be so far from my family, which was a comforting thought, and strangely enough, as I rode along with Colum, although I was conscious of a certain fear, my excitement was intense, and odd as it may seem, I would not have had it otherwise.

He was smiling, well content, and I could not help a little pride because he had been so eager for our wedding. It was nearly three months since that night which had changed my life, but it seemed years ago. I could hardly think of a time when I had not known of Colum's existence.

"Very soon," he said, "we shall come to Castle Paling, your home, my bride. There we shall live happily ever after."

There was a hint of mockery in his voice, but I did not heed it. It was a beautiful day, the kind we get sometimes in the West Country in February, the sort of day when it seems spring is tired of waiting and is making a premature appearance. There were tufts of new leaves on the elder bushes and yellow flowers of the coltsfoot on the banks. In the fields there was a spattering of crimson-tipped daisies, and as we forded a shallow stream, I noticed the purple catkins of the alder trees there, which toned with the butterbur flowers blooming near the water.

I was smiling, and he said, "So you are reconciled to your marriage so hastily enforced by circumstances?"

"I was thinking of the beauty of the countryside."

"It is said," he reminded me, "that when one is in love, the grass is greener and the whole world becomes a more beautiful place."

"I am inclined to think it is the spring," I said.

"I shall soon convince you what a fortunate woman you

are. You will one day bless the night you first came to Castle Paling."

I was silent, and he went on: "I shall have to insist that you answer me when I speak to you."

"I did not think your comment needed an answer."

"It does indeed. You must answer fervently that you will always remember that night as the happiest of your life . . . to that time."

"I did not think I should begin my married life by lying to my husband."

"Nor would you if you said that, for it is true."

"How could I say I remember when I remember nothing?"

"You do remember. There was much of which you were aware."

"Do you mind if we do not speak of it?"

"I am determined to indulge you."

He sang as we rode along, the same hunting song I had heard before.

"It sounds joyous," I said.

"It is the song of the hunter bringing home his prey."

"It is fitting then."

"Oh, entirely so."

Then he laughed in the loud way I was becoming accustomed to, and for some reason, although I feigned indignation, my spirits were lifted.

Castle Paling! My home! It rose before us, grim, forbidding but immensely exciting. I looked up at its gray stone walls which had stood for four hundred years and doubtless would stand five hundred more and even beyond that. There was an invincible durability in those strong walls. They had been built to defend, and they would go on doing so.

Those walls forming a plinth at the base were made to withstand the picks and battering rams of an enemy. There were four towers, two facing the land and two the sea, battlemented and with their lookouts and their apertures for pouring burning pitch down onto the heads of intruders. The window openings on the low levels were few—narrow slits which could be well guarded to prevent intruders.

"Welcome to Castle Paling, wife," he said, and together we rode under the portcullis and into a courtyard.

As if by magic several grooms appeared. Colum leaped from his horse, threw his reins to a groom and lifted me down from my horse.

Side by side we crossed the courtyard, and as we reached

the small door in the great stone wall, he lifted me up in his arms and stepped into the castle.

"The three of us together," he whispered.

Then he set me on my feet.

We mounted a narrow staircase and came to the hall, which was lofty with a gallery surrounding its upper level.

"Your home," he said, with pride. "My family have lived here since the days of the Conqueror—for they came from Normandy with him. We have always been conquerors. It has changed since then, for improvements have been made. My Norman ancestor came here, built a castle and took a Cornish maiden to wife. She gave him many sons and daughters, and they married and bore more so that we became a clan. We have in five hundred years become Cornishmen. Of course the castle was not like this in the first place. Just a fortification—guardroom, dungeons and thick impenetrable walls. We added to it as time passed. I doubt not I shall add to it. Why, I have begun by adding a bride."

Then he lifted me up and kissed me heartily and said, "We are tired after our journey. We will sup quietly, and to bed."

Then we ate and drank together, and it was like that other night in many ways.

It was a different bedchamber, much grander, containing a large four-poster, the tester hung with embroidered silk curtains. Candles burned in the sconces, and I noticed a big court cupboard boldly carved with acanthus and leaf work. There was time to notice nothing else, nor think of it, for my husband was beside me, removing my gown and my petticoats and carrying me to the curtain-shrouded bed.

And after that I knew I would cease to think of that fateful night at Castle Paling because there were others and in time they would all merge into one and I would forget that I had been taken so unwillingly, for as though by magic my unwillingness had gone leaving me eager to embark on the voyage of discovery in which this man, who was already beginning to dominate my life, was showing me the way.

An indication of my feelings toward him was revealed to me in the early morning when I lay awake watching the dawn slowly filter through the silken curtains which shut us in.

He was awake also.

He said, "I arranged it, you know."

"You arranged what?" I asked.

"I was determined to have you when I saw you in the inn. How well guarded you were! By God, your mother is a tigress of a woman. She would have fought to the death for you. I knew I had to plan and could do nothing that night."

"Go on," I said. "Tell me what happened."

"I knew where you were going. Trystan Priory. I know it well. The Landors' place. You were staying for a week. Your maid told one of my servants that you were coming back that way."

"You mean. . . ."

"You begin to understand. They were my men who way-laid you on the road."

"The robbers. . . ."

"Just good servants. I was ready, waiting to rescue you and bring you here . . . where the scene was set. It was not your purse we were after."

"You are wicked," I said.

"It is well that a wife should know her husband."

"You deliberately arranged all that to take place . . . You caused us such anguish . . . myself . . . my mother . . ."

"Sometimes it is necessary to suffer to be happy. All came well in the end. See, you have a lusty husband and a fine home. He has already planted his seed within you. In six months' time our son will be born. And there will be many more, I promise you. For I like what I have, wife. I liked you from the moment I saw you. I know when I want a woman."

"There have doubtless been many."

"Oh, many. But you were the one for my wife."

"Why was that?"

"Well bred, worthy to be mother of my sons. A good family, a good dowry, for your father is a generous man and a rich one. You were suitable in every way. But I wouldn't have had you if I hadn't wanted you. I could find a rich wife without trouble, but I had to have one that pleased me too."

"I should loathe you," I said.

"And you don't. I know that. You couldn't pretend to me, although you tried. Why, even on that first night . . . I could feel your responses. You wanted me, my girl, although you were so helpless and ignorant. You knew it, did you not? Somewhere within your mind was the thought: He arranged it. He is that sort of man. He takes what he wants, and there is no gainsaying him."

I was silent. Had I suspected? I think perhaps I had. But the great discovery was not that he had arranged that this should happen, but that I should know it and be glad that he had.

The weeks which followed my arrival at Castle Paling were ones of discovery of myself and my nature. Strange as it seemed, I was happy—not peacefully, quietly so, but because I was in a state of continual excitement. It could never have been thus with Fennimore Landor, I knew full well.

My relationship with my husband was the dominating factor. I was fascinated by him. He was indeed the lord of the castle, and everyone hastened to do his bidding. His anger could be terrible. I saw him strike servants with his riding whip if they displeased him; they trembled before him. When he was not in the castle, an atmosphere of relief prevailed—it was a sort of respite I supposed from the need to be continually on the alert to please him. His loud voice could be heard echoing through those great chambers. He was indeed the master.

It was a wonderful experience to know that I was so important to him. I laughed to myself when I thought of his planning my seduction. He must have wanted me very fiercely to have gone to such lengths. He had made this obvious to me. He was delighted with me. I was an inexperienced girl, but a passionate one, and he found great pleasure in teaching me. There was no doubt that he was completely absorbed in our relationship, and it did not occur to me to ask myself how long it would last, for I would not remain a pupil forever and very soon I would begin to be less shapely.

He was delighted about the child, and I could see that like my father, he passionately wanted a son. My mother told me that her inability to give my father one had been the cause of a great deal of trouble. She had once said that she believed that if she had given birth to a son, my father would never have turned to Romilly and Penn would not have existed. Who knew?

Colum would talk about "our boy," and I would beg him not to talk constantly of a boy, for it could well be a girl.

"Nay, nay," he would say, feeling the faint protuberance of my body. "This little one is a boy. I know it."

"And if it is a girl, are you going to dislike her?"

"I'll accept her. There's time for boys. I know you will

give me one." He bit my ear rather sharply. "You wouldn't dare do aught else."

And he went on talking of our boy.

He would insist on my taking care. It was very important that I should produce a healthy boy. He wanted nothing to go wrong during my pregnancy. "A man can get lusty boys on serving wenches, but by God, often the fates are against him when he wants a legitimate son. It must not be so with us," he added, as though if it did, it would be my fault.

That was how my father had been with my mother, I dare swear, and she had longed to please her husband, as I did mine.

The castle itself was a strange place to be in. There was so much to know about it. There were so many servants that I could not keep track of them.

The four towers with ramparts and battlements formed the main structure. In two of these towers, the Crows' Tower, which faced the land, and Nonna's Tower, which faced the sea, we lived with our personal servants. I wondered about the other two. From the Seaward Tower—on a level with Nonna and which also looked out to sea—I had seen men and women coming and going. I supposed they were servants, but I had rarely seen them working in that part of the castle where we lived. But the place was so vast that there would naturally be many servants, and it would take a long time to get to know them all.

Sometimes I would go to the ramparts of Nonna's Tower and look through the battlements to the sea. There the great black rocks known as the Devil's Teeth could sometimes be seen, but only when the tide was out. They were a group —cruel, sharp, pointed rocks. Teeth was an apt description, particularly if they were seen at some angles. Then their formation could be likened to a grinning mouth. At high tide they were not visible, lurking as they did just below the surface of the water. They were about half a mile out to sea and almost in a straight line with Castle Paling. Some people called them the Paling Rocks.

The great wall of the castle on the sea side rose up starkly straight, and looking down at the surf below, I thought what a well-chosen spot it was for a fortification. It would have been almost impossible to attack from the sea, and there was only the landward side to be protected.

I found the desire to stand up there and lean on the battlements and gaze down irresistible and dangerous. It seemed to me symbolic of my life here.

Once when I was up there I was seized from behind, and Colum lifted me off the ground and held me high. He laughed in that way of his which I could have called satanic.

"What are you doing up here?" he demanded. "You were leaning over too far. What if you had fallen? You would have killed yourself and our son. By God, I'd never have forgiven you."

"As I should have been past your vengeance, why should I care?"

He put me down and kissed me hard on the mouth.

"I couldn't do without you now, wife," he said.

I put my hand up and touched his hair. "Why do you always call me wife? It sounds unromantic . . . it is as an innkeeper might call his spouse."

"What else are you?"

"Linnet."

"Bah!" he said. "A silly little bird."

"Names change when you are fond of people. You might get to like it."

"Never," he said. "The day I call you Linnet you will know I have ceased to love you."

I shivered, and he noticed.

"Yes," he said, "you should take care to keep me warm. You must always do your wifely duty. You must give me sons and sons."

"Beauty is impaired by too much childbearing."

"That may be. But the sons are a man's compensation."

"But if she no longer arouses his desire?"

"Then he turns elsewhere. A fact of nature," he said curtly.

"I would not wish that to happen."

"Then you must see that it does not."

"And what if a wife is neglected? She might turn elsewhere. What of that?"

"If she were my wife, that would be the time to beware."

"What would you do to her if she were unfaithful?"

He lifted me up suddenly and set me on the parapet. He laughed, and it did indeed sound like the laughter of devils. "I should take my revenge, you may be sure. Maybe I'd give her to the rocks."

He lifted me down and held me against him. "There, I alarm you, and that is not good for our boy. Why should you speak of such things? Have I not given you proof that you are my choice?" He took my chin in his hands and jerked up my face. "And you, are you a wanton then that you talk to your husband in this way? What of Fennimore Landor, eh? Did you not once think of marrying that man?"

"It was mentioned," I said.

"Did he ask you?"

"Yes, he did."

"I am amazed that you did not accept such a model of virtue."

"It was after. . . ."

That amused him. "After I had taught you what it meant to bed with a real man, eh?"

"Remember I was not conscious."

"Enough, though, to realize, eh?"

"I knew that I had been deflowered."

"What a foolish expression! Deflowered! Rather have you been flowered. Have not I given you fertility? Our son will be the flower and the fruit. Deflowered! I did you great honor and much good, as you will admit."

"Yes," I said, "I think I will admit it here, where none can hear but you and the choughs."

Then he kissed me again, and in his hands which caressed my body was that tenderness which was the more precious because it was so rare.

Then he held me against the stone wall, and he talked about the castle, how it was his stronghold and how he had walked the ramparts when he was a boy, how he had dreamed of possessing it and had played wild games in the dungeons and on the winding spiral staircases.

"There are stories of my ancestors which we pass on from generation to generation," he told me. There was in his eyes a yearning, and I knew he was seeing our boy playing in the castle, learning to grow up like his father.

"We have been a wild lot," he said. "What a family you have married into! In the reign of King Stephen my ancestor of that time was a robber baron. He used to waylay travelers and bring them to his castle. He was called the Fiend of Paling. In the Seaward Tower"—he pointed to it—"he used to take his victims there, and he would demand a ransom of their family, and if it were not paid, the victim would be tortured. He would give a grand banquet and bring him out for the amusement of his cronies. At night it is said that the cries of long-dead tortured men and women can be heard in the Seaward Tower." He looked at me sharply, and I could see he was thinking of the child

I carried. "There is nothing to fear," he went on quickly. "It was all long ago. Then Stephen died and Henry the Second was our King. He was for law and order and extorting money for his wars through taxes, so he suppressed the robber barons by means of meting out dire punishments and the Casvellyns had to find a new means of sustenance."

"I have seen men going in and out of the Seaward Tower."

"My servants," he said. "They are fishermen many of them. They catch our fish, and I have a fancy for it. They serve me in many ways. Down there in the lower part of the Seaward Tower are our boats. You may see them venturing out now and then. Have you seen them?"

"No."

"You will know our ways in due time. I will tell you of another ancestor of mine. He had a fair wife, but he was very fond of women. It is a failing—or it may be a virtue—in the men of my family. They adore women. They need women."

"Are you telling me this to put me on my guard?"

"One must always be on one's guard to hold a possession which is precious. You should remember that."

"Should we both remember it?"

"Aye, we will. I was telling you of my ancestor."

"The one who needed women and was unfaithful to his wife. Is that an uncommon story?"

"Not in my family, nor in any for that matter, I'll swear, but where this Casvellyn was different was that being in love with his wife, who was a very fair lady, yet he could fall in love with another who was equally fair. The second lady was a very moral woman, and although she greatly desired this Casvellyn, he knew he could not have her—save by rape—unless he married her. He was not a man for a quick seduction, and that be that. Nay, he liked marriage. He liked the cozy comforts of it. But he wanted more than one wife. So what did he do?" He turned me around, so that we were looking at the turrets of those two towers which faced landward. "There you see our two towers, Ysella's Tower and the Crows' Tower."

"I did not know they all had names."

"Yes, Seaward you know, and Nonna's. They face the sea, and Ysella's and Crows' face the land. Seaward is so called for the obvious reason that it looks to the sea, and Crows' because I imagine crows once nested there. Ysella and Nonna were the names of that long-dead Casvellyn's wives. For ten years Ysella lived in her tower, and Nonna did not know she was there. He kept them apart. He would say farewell to Nonna and ride away. Then he would come back when it was dark and take the secret door to Ysella's Tower and behave as though he had come home after a long journey. He would stay with her for a while and then ride away and return to Nonna."

"I don't believe it. It's not possible. Two wives living in the same castle! Why did they not explore their home?"

"He forbade them to, and wives in those days were obedient. He told Ysella that Nonna's Tower was haunted and Nonna that Ysella's was, and that if either of them ventured near the other, evil would befall the house. He said it was the result of a witch's curse. He would never allow them to leave the castle unless he accompanied them."

"It seems quite incredible."

"It is the legend, and when people used to say, as you do, that it is impossible, my father always replied that with the Casvellyns all things were possible."

"That is blasphemy."

"Maybe blasphemy can be truth."

"And what happened? Did they discover each other?"

"Yes. One day Nonna was here on the ramparts, and she saw a figure on the ramparts of Ysella's Tower. Neither of them should have been where they were. It was part of the forbidden territory. Nonna called her servants, but by the time they came Ysella had disappeared. This gave rise to the legend that there was a ghost at the tower (it was not called Ysella's then, of course, nor was this called Nonna's). Nonna confessed that she had been on the ramparts and asked her husband to explore the tower with her, for she pointed out if they were a party, they need not fear the ghost. He refused, and something in the manner of his refusal made her more curious. It is never good to be too curious, particularly about a husband's secrets. Nonna was determined to find out more about the ghost of Ysella's Tower. One day she took her maid with her and explored. They entered the tower, but they could not get beyond the barred door; they did not know that there was a secret way in close to the rocks. One day she followed her husband when he went away on one of his journeys and, lying in hiding, saw him enter Ysella's Tower by a secret door. She followed him in and came face to face with Ysella. She understood what had happened, and there was nothing for their husband to do but admit his guilt. That day Nonna died. She fell from the top of Ysella's Tower. That was the first time she had entered it. My ancestor then brought Ysella out of her tower and proclaimed her to be his wife. They lived together until the end of their days, but it is said that Nonna haunts Ysella's Tower from that day. There! That is the most colorful of our family legends, do you not think? It is a lesson too for disobedient wives who are too curious."

"Was she overcurious, would you say?"

"If she had not ventured into Ysella's Tower, she would not have died."

"So it was murder."

"Who can say? I am merely telling you what I have heard."

"What a wild family you come from."

"Remember you belong to it now," he retorted. "And take care."

Overhead the choughs were circling. I caught a glimpse of red beaks as they flew near.

"I see," I said, "that this legend is meant to be a warning to wives."

"Why, yes. We Casvellyns have always found it wise to warn our wives." His eyes had grown tender again. "It is chill up here," he went on. "And you are lightly clad. Come. We will go down."

He put his arm through mine as we descended, and although I was still thinking of the story of the two wives, I felt happy and at ease.

My mother visited me at Castle Paling. I was so happy to see her, to show the castle, to take her around and tell her the story of the towers.

"You're happy then, Linnet," she said, as though surprised.

"Life has become so . . . full," I said.

She nodded. "So it was all for the best," she mused. She was very relieved.

She asked me a great deal of questions about my health, and it seemed that what I had to tell satisfied her.

It was the end of April, and what an April that was with the hedges full of wild flowers and the intermittent rain and sunshine. I would listen for the cry of the birds—the ring ouzel, the sand martin and of course the cuckoo. There were many questions to be asked about what was happening at Lyon Court. Edwina's child was due in June, and she was all impatience. Carlos was anxious because they had waited so long. Jacko was courting a girl in Plymouth, and it seemed that ere long there would be another wedding. Little Damask wanted to know why I didn't come home. And my father was eager to know whether there was any sign that the child I was carrying was a boy.

I laughed, recalling them all. They seemed far away from me now, and I was ashamed that I had missed them so little.

My mother mentioned that the Landors had visited Lyon Court again. Business plans were going ahead. Very soon they would be sending out their ships. My father was very busy, and that involved everyone else. There was a great deal of activity, and it was decided that Plymouth should be their headquarters, as was to be expected.

There was something else she had to tell me. Fennimore had ridden over to hear from her the story of my marriage. She said he had seemed quite bewildered. So must he have been, for, according to what we had allowed people to believe, when he had asked me to marry him, I had already been married to Colum.

He had not shown any anger, said my mother, just amazement. "I had to tell him the truth," she went on. "I knew I could trust him. I could not have him believe you to be perfidious. He was very, very sad. He said you should have told him. He would have understood. I begged of him to forget what had happened if he could. I told him that I had spoken to him in the utmost confidence and that what was done was done. He saw the point of it. You were married now. Oh, Linnet, he would have understood. He would have married you. Perhaps we should have told him."

"It is better as it is," I insisted.

"You are happy. You would not have it otherwise."

She smiled at me, understanding perfectly I knew.

She went on: "Soon after, I heard he was to be betrothed to a girl he had known all his life. Her family are neighbors of the Landors. It will be a most suitable union."

"He quickly consoled himself," was my comment.

"We should be glad of that," replied my mother.

I said, "He would face up to the situation calmly, accepting the fact that he and I were not for each other."

I thought how different he was from Colum, and I was glad that everything had turned out as it had. In these short months my emotions had been revolutionized. I could imagine no man my husband but Colum Casvellyn.

My mother, being aware of this, was delighted. I was pleased too to notice that Colum had an admiration for her. She would always be a very attractive woman, not so much because of her features and figure, which were still quite good, but because of that spirit in her, that vitality which I was sure had attracted my father in the first place and still did.

My mother told Colum that she and my father thought it would be an excellent plan if they took me to Lyon Court a little later so that she herself could care for me at the end of my pregnancy.

"You cannot imagine that I will relinquish my wife, even to her parents," cried Colum. "No, madam, my son is to be born in Castle Paling. That is where he shall first see the light of the day in the walls of that castle which will one day be his."

"I want her to have the best care."

"Think you not that I cannot give her that?"

They faced each other squarely, my mother ready to do battle with him as she had so often with my father, and he amused, liking her for it.

They compromised, and it was arranged that in August, that month when my baby was due, my mother should come to Castle Paling. It was the only way, for she was determined to be with me when my child was born and Colum was equally determined that the birth should take place in Castle Paling.

It was mid-May when my mother went home, promising to return at the beginning of August. Colum and I rode some of the way back with her, and when she had left us, Colum told me that I should not be allowed to ride much longer; he was not risking my losing the child. I was happy enough to be so cherished.

The weeks began to pass very quickly. I was preparing for my child, and my mother sent Jennet over to be with me. I might wish to keep Jennet, she said; she was an excellent nurse and had a way with children.

I had always been fond of Jennet. I found her a great comfort, and it was rather pleasant to have a reminder of my old home in Castle Paling.

Jennet was delighted to come, although she missed seeing her son Jacko, but for several years he had been away at sea for long stretches of time and she was used to being without him.

It was not long before she had made friends with one of

the serving men. His name was Tobias, and the manner in which she spoke of him would have led one to believe that she had never known another man.

"He be in Seaward," she told me, so I knew that he was one of those men I had seen going in and out of that tower and about whose occupation I had wondered.

One June day I needed Jennet to do some sewing for me which I wanted quickly, and as I couldn't find her, I went in search of her. I guessed that she was in or near the Seaward Tower, so I made my way there. It was odd, but although I had been in the castle for four months or so, there was a great deal of it I had not seen. I knew the Crows' Tower and Nonna's very well indeed as we lived in them. As Seaward was occupied by the servants, I had not ventured into it, and I often wondered about Ysella's. Once I had wandered across the courtyards and come to the iron-studded door in the thick wall. I had tried it. It was locked. I made up my mind that sometime I would ask Colum to show me every part of the castle.

On this occasion I made my way toward Seaward. I crossed the inner ward, and as I came toward the entrance of the tower I could hear a clamor and the sound of much laughter. I pushed open the iron-studded door which was similar to that barred one which led to Ysella's. Immediately facing me were steps leading down. I went down them cautiously, for I was now beginning to feel less nimble. As I descended, I could feel the strong fresh air on my cheeks and the unmistakable sound and smell of the sea.

I came down into what seemed like a stableyard. I was amazed at the number of horses, and there were some donkeys too. I realized that the voices I had heard had not come from here. On one side of the courtyard was a door, and opening it, I was on a path which wound upward to the coast road. On the shore several small boats were moored to stakes.

The tide was low, and I could see the sharp points of the Devil's Teeth protruding from the water.

I decided Jennet was not there, so I retraced my steps and climbed the stairs. I was now in the small hall-like entrance on the tower side of the iron-studded door. I noticed then another door I had missed, and I realized that it was from behind this that the voices came.

I pushed it open and walked in. There was a large chamber with a big table in the center of it. Seated around it were several men and a few women. Jennet was among

them. These were the people I had seen from the Crows'
Tower—the fishermen of whom Colum had spoken.

I heard Jennet's shrill: "Why, 'tis the mistress."

They shuffled to their feet and looked uncomfortable.

I said, "I came to look for you, Jennet."

"Why, yes, mistress," she said, blushing a little.

"I do not wish to disturb your meal," I said.

One of the men who appeared to be a leader of them
mumbled something.

I said, "Come, Jennet."

She came at once.

I did not know why, but I felt uneasy. These were my
husband's retainers, and I was the chatelaine of the castle.
Why should I feel that there was something strange about
them, that they were not ordinary servants? They were
respectful enough, and yet in a way they seemed a little
shocked to find me here. Why? Wasn't the castle my home?

The man who sat at the head of the table came over to
me and said, "You should be careful, mistress, of the stairs
here. They can be dangerous like. 'Tis easy to trip."

I said, "I went down them. I had no idea there were so
many horses and that there was a path up to the road."

"Aye," he said. "But the master would not wish you to
use the stairs."

"I'll be careful," I said.

I had a feeling that I had met this man before. There
was something familiar about his movements.

I was very conscious of so many eyes upon me. Why
should the fact that I had disturbed my husband's servants
at a meal—in which my own maid was sharing—make me
feel so uneasy?

It's my condition, I told myself. Everything that seemed
a little unsettling could be put down to that.

Jennet and I came out into the courtyard.

I said, "You have soon become friendly with your fellow
servants, Jennet."

She giggled in that girlish way of hers. "Why, yes, Mistress
Linnet, I was always one to make friends quick like."

"And your friend?"

She blushed. "He be a very fine man, mistress. He did
take a fancy to me from the first. All that time ago. . . ."

"All that time ago! You have not been here so long."

She clapped her hands to her lips. A silly habit of hers
when she had said something impetuously; she had always
done it, I remembered from my childhood.

"Well, mistress, he did see me long ago . . . when I were out with you and the mistress."

"I know," I said, "it was when we were returning from Trystan Priory."

She looked so embarrassed that I knew I was right. So she was aware that the plot had been made in this house and that the band of robbers who had beset us on the road were Colum's men.

I felt angry that she should be aware of this; then I shrugged.

"It's all right," I said. "I know what happened. My husband . . . confessed."

Jennet was greatly relieved. "My dear life, what a man he be. There be only one other to rival him, and that be the Captain." Then she appeared to be contrite. I supposed she was thinking of her present lover, who, her optimistic nature would always tell her, was the best she had ever had.

She said, "He do say, mistress, that on the road there he fancied me. He would have run off with me, he says, if orders hadn't been different."

"It is over now, Jennet," I said, "and best forgotten."

Best forgotten! I thought. What a foolish thing to say. How could something be forgotten which had changed one's whole life, which had brought me my husband and the child I now carried.

"Jennet," I said rather primly, "I suppose you will always be the same."

"I suppose so," she said with happy resignation.

I told Colum that I had been to Seaward Tower and met some of his servants who lived there.

"They are good men," he said.

"And women."

"They have their wives and women. That is necessary you understand."

"I understand. My Jennet has joined them."

He burst out laughing. "It does not surprise me."

"She has quickly found a lover there."

"Jennet would find a lover anywhere. Who is the man?"

"I know none of them by name. But I thought I recognized the leader of your robber band."

He laughed again.

"So they know of how I was tricked. I am not sure that I like that."

"They are discreet. They are not like ordinary servants."

"No, they do not seem so. I gather that they do special work for you."

His bushy brows shut up. "What do you mean by that?"

"Such as abducting females on the road."

"Such work they do admirably, you will admit."

"They will be laughing at how I was duped."

"They would not dare. They are good servants and wish me well. They are delighted to have had a hand in bringing me my present happiness."

I was reconciled.

He put his arms about me gently and drew me to him. "You should not wander about the castle without me or someone with you. There are so many dangerous places. . . . Those spiral staircases . . . you could so easily trip and fall. The cobbled courtyards, the unevenness of the stones and all the steep paths. You must not wander off alone. I forbid you to."

"So must the husband of Nonna have talked to her! I am not allowed to ride. What may I do?"

"You may obey your husband. I place no restrictions on that."

"You are . . . despotic."

"I am the ruler of my home."

"The king of your castle."

"Why should I not be? When the child is born, you will have him to occupy you, and then we will ride together out into the country. We will visit your parents. Perhaps we will call on the Landors. I heard that your would-be husband has quickly become reconciled. He is to be married shortly. Of course, she is a wealthy young lady. But he has taken his disappointment well, has he not?"

"I feel little interest in his affairs."

"Why should you when you have a husband and a child of your own?"

"I am content," I said, "deeply content."

July had come, hot and sultry. I often climbed to the ramparts although I knew that Colum would have been displeased if he knew. Sometimes I took Jennet with me. I noticed how often her eyes strayed to the Seaward Tower.

She told me something of life in that tower, of the man who was her lover and who had taken her out in his boat on one occasion. They had fished and brought home their catch, and it had been cooked and eaten at the table in the Seaward Tower.

"There are plenty of boats there and all those horses,"

she said. It was an exciting place, the Seaward Tower. She had helped clean the lanterns there. Never had she seen so many.

I was beginning to feel uncomfortable now. It could only be about six weeks from my confinement. I was so longing for my child to be born that the days seemed as though they would never pass. One day I wandered down through the inner ward and came at length to Ysella's Tower. I looked at the iron-studded door and up at those grim gray walls. Was the story true? It was impossible. How could a man keep someone's identity secret for ten years? Surely she would have been seen? There would be a door on the other side of the tower similar to the one I had discovered in Seaward; there might be a little path there. Had that long-ago Casvellyn been as forceful as his descendant? I was sure he had. He would have forbidden Ysella and Nonna to leave their towers unescorted, and perhaps he had good reason for this in view of what Colum had told me about the robbers on the road. I pictured Ysella up there waiting for the man she believed to be her husband and Nonna waiting for the same man who was hers.

I tried the iron-studded door. It would not move. Had I really expected it to?

I began to feel exhausted and, fearing for the child, retraced my steps back to Crows' Tower.

August came—the long-awaited month. A messenger had arrived from Lyon Court with the news that my mother would be setting out in a few days' time.

One night I awoke startled and found that I was alone. The curtains drawn about the bed made it pitch black. It had been a stifling hot day, and I had been quite exhausted by the weather and my condition.

I could hear something, so I drew aside the curtain. I realized at once that it was the heavy rain. I got out of bed and went to the window. I could hear the rain pelting down on the stones, and a wind was howling. A flash of lightning lit up the sky briefly. I saw the towers against the angry sky; then came the great crack of thunder which sounded as though it were overhead.

I went back to my bed. I could not sleep. I wondered where Colum was on such a night and whether the roads would be sodden when my mother set out from Lyon Court.

I lay still listening for the next clap of thunder, and I suppose because I did now find the days exhausting I was soon asleep.

When I awoke, Colum was beside me. He was in a deep sleep. I rose noiselessly and was dressed before he awakened.

He rose yawning, and I said to him. "What happened last night?"

Did I fancy it or was he suddenly alert? He said, "It was a fierce night."

"What thunder!" I said. "I woke and got out of bed. There was one clap which must have been right overhead."

"I was up," he said. "There was a ship in distress out there."

"How terrible . . . on such a night!"

"I thought there might be something we could do."

"How good of you, Colum."

He smiled at me in that tender way which I always so much appreciated because it seemed unnatural to him.

"When you really know me, you'll see I'm not such a bad fellow after all."

"I am already beginning to ask myself if this is the case."

It was an unhappy day that followed. The ship in distress had come to grief on the Devil's Teeth. All day long the boats were going out to see if there were any survivors.

Colum told me there was none.

How delighted I was to greet my mother. I was watching for her from the turret of the Crows' Tower which gave a good view of the road. I felt a rush of emotion when I saw her sturdily seated on her horse with the grooms and two servants riding with her.

I was waiting at the portcullis to greet her. She swept me up in her arms and then had a good look at me.

"I see you are in good health and spirits," she said. "Nothing to worry about. And by the look of it, it seems as though we shall not have to wait long."

She busied herself with preparations. She admired the cradle in which Colum himself had once lain. Generations of Casvellyns had used it. I wondered whether Nonna and Ysella had had any children and, if so, how they had managed to keep them hidden away. I must ask Colum some time. In any case, it was just a legend.

The weather seemed unbearably hot to me in my condition, and it was a great joy to sit out of doors. There were not the gardens at Castle Paling that we had at Lyon Court, but we could sit in one of the grassy courtyards, my mother spreading a rug for me, and I would lie with my back against the wall and we would talk.

She was very pleased with my marriage. She had become convinced that it was right for me, in spite of its beginnings.

"Colum and Jake," she said, "are of a kind, and that is the kind of man women like us need. It is good when one can look back and say this and that happened for the best."

"It seems so amazing to me that a year ago I did not know Colum," I marveled.

"Time in such matters is not important. I can see you are happy."

"Yet how much you wanted me to marry Fennimore Landor!"

"You would have had a peaceful life with him, but perhaps a dull one."

"When is he to marry?"

"In September."

"How strange that such a man should so quickly make up his mind."

"I gather from his mother that he has known this Mistress Lee for many years. They have been childhood friends. Of course he was fond of you, he wanted to marry you, and it was ideal too in view of the amalgamation. But when you married, he renewed his friendship with Mistress Lee. Their families are pleased about it, and it seems a suitable match.

"They hope to start trading next year," she told me. "These matters take so long to arrange. Your father chafes against delay. You know what an impatient man he is. I am sure it is the thought of getting the better of the Spaniards that makes him so pleased with the venture."

"But the Spaniards are finished."

My mother looked slightly worried. "I am not so sure. Admiral Drake has taken out a fleet of men-o'-war and attacked towns in Spain and Portugal. Why should he do that if they were so defeated? Why should he feel it necessary to give them another blow? I heard before I left that over a thousand gentlemen accompanied him and that only just over three hundred returned. Then our men have seized sixty ships in the Tagus which belonged to the Hanse towns there. It was found that these ships contained stores to fit out a fleet to come against us."

"My father and Colum think that the Spaniard has been beaten forever."

"I cannot believe such a powerful nation could be finished so completely. What I long to see, Linnet, is an end to war and conflict. I heard that a mill has been set up in a place in Kent called Dartford where they are making paper.

Imagine that, Linnet! How much easier it will be for us to write to each other. I call that progress—not one side killing more than the other. And something else. I heard of a new plant the other day. It is called saffron—a kind of crocus. Its stigmas make cakes yellow and gives them a most distinctive flavor."

And so we walked and passed our days most happily, for she had brought with her not only the clothes she had made for my baby and new recipes for my tasting, but that sense of comfort which only she could give me.

She brought back memories of my father and young Damask, who had so wanted to come with her and had made a doll for the baby. My father had insisted that messengers be sent as soon as my baby was born with word that I had a fine healthy boy. Edwina, who now had her own little boy and wanted everyone to know of her contentment, sent affectionate messages. It was like seeing them all.

Even the apprehension which must come to a woman who is about to have her first child was stilled by my mother's presence.

It was not a difficult labor, and to my intense delight I gave birth to a healthy boy.

I had never seen Colum so overjoyed. He snatched the baby from my mother and marched around the bedchamber with him. Then he came and stared down at me. I thought I had never been so proud and happy in my life.

I had reached the summit of joy. I had my beautiful son, whom we named Connell, and he delighted me in all ways. I marveled that this perfect creature was my own son, and I rejoiced in him doubly when I saw Colum's pride.

If he had been out, as soon as he returned to the castle he would go to the child's nursery and satisfy himself that all was well. He would pick up the boy and lift him high in the air. Jennet and I would say that it was no way to treat such a young baby, but Connell did not seem to mind. If he were crying—and he had a lusty pair of lungs, and a strong temper—he would stop when his father lifted him up.

I was delighted. I loved to see the pleasure Colum found in his son.

And I had given him to him. I sometimes marveled that this boy of ours should have been conceived in such a manner. I think Colum did too. But there was nothing that could have made him happier than the possession of this son.

My mother stayed with me for a month after the child's birth, and then she thought she should return to Lyon Court. She had young Damask to look after. The next time she came, she said, she might bring her, although she thought she was a little young to make the journey. My father had set out on the first of his trading voyages and would be home, she believed, by Christmas. We must all spend Christmas together. It was unthinkable that we, living so near, should not. I must persuade Colum to come to Lyon Court, but perhaps because of the baby, they should come to us.

We said good-bye. It was September and a touch of autumn already in the air. The mornings were misty, and the sea was calm but gray. I thought that at Lyon Court they would soon be gathering the apples and pears, and I remembered how we had done it the previous year and stored the fruit in the apple room.

I watched her ride away for as long as I could see her. She did not look around. I fancied there were tears in her eyes. But she had confessed herself well pleased with the way in which everything had turned out. I think she was comparing me with herself, and perhaps on consideration she could say her marriage had been a happy one.

I wished that we were just a little nearer. If Castle Paling had been as near Lyon Court as Trewynd Grange, how happy I would be! The fifteen miles or so which separated us just made frequent visits not so easy to achieve.

The christening of Connell was a great event. There was a big christening cake, and Colum had asked a great many guests from the surrounding country. People whom I had never met before came to the castle, and there was feasting and revelry for two days and nights.

The beauty of the ceremony in the castle's Norman chapel touched me deeply. My son wore the christening robes which had been worn by several generations of Casvellyns, and I wondered whether the husband of Ysella and Nonna had worn them.

Colum had chosen the godparents—friends of long standing, he said. Sir Roderick Raymont was one—a man I did not take to—and another was Lady Alice Warham, a handsome woman who came to the castle with a meek husband several years older than herself.

Lady Alice carried my son into the font, and the ceremony was performed beneath that vaulted roof with its

Norman archway and its massive supporting pillars of stone.

Connell was good and uttered no protest, but I felt a great desire to snatch him from the arms of the woman who held him. I did not know why this fierce jealousy came over me, and I knew I would be glad when all the visitors had departed.

When the ceremony was over and the cake had been cut and the baby had been admired by all, I took him to his nursery and gloated over him and I felt I was the most blessed of women.

The guests lingered for a few days, and it was during their stay that I made a discovery.

The great hall, which was rarely used when there were no visitors, was now the center of our entertainments. All through the day there came from the kitchens the smell of roasting meats and many of the inhabitants of Seaward Tower were pressed into service. "You see," said Colum to me, "there are occasions when we need these servants."

I asked him if he entertained frequently, since we had not done so during the first months of our marriage.

"I did not wish it then," he said. "I wanted to have you all to myself. Moreover I thought it might be bad for the child."

"Will these people think it strange that there were no celebrations of our wedding?"

"It has always been my way to let people think what they will," he answered, "as long, that is, as it does not offend *me*."

Then he talked of the boy and how he was much more advanced than other boys, how he believed that he would grow up into a fine Casvellyn and he could scarce wait to see it.

"As he grows older," I said, "forget not that you will also do so."

"And you, wife," he reminded me.

Then he laughed and held me against him and I was very happy knowing him to be content with our marriage.

I think that was the last time I was entirely contented, for it was that night that I learned something which had not occurred to me before.

It was Lady Alice who began it, and I wondered after whether she did it purposely. I asked myself whether she sensed my complete abandonment to pleasure and, being envious of it, sought to destroy it.

We were at table. The venison was particularly delicious,

I was thinking, done to a turn. The rich golden pastry of the pies was appetizing and the company was merry. Colum, at the top of the table, was flushed and excited, basking in the pride he felt for his son.

I was thinking to myself: May he always be as happy as he is now and may I, when Lady Alice said, "You have made your husband a very proud man."

"It is a wonderful thing to have a child."

"And so shortly married. You are indeed fortunate."

Her eyes were enormous—great dark eyes, not quite as dark as Colum's. I did not recognize the malice in them then.

"Colum, I know, is beside himself with joy. I am not surprised. When you remember the past disappointments...."

"Disappointments?" I said.

"Why, yes, when he hoped and hoped . . . and it never happened. And then the second time he is fortunate immediately. It is not a year, is it, since your marriage and already that beautiful boy. One could almost say it was a happy release . . . although so tragic at the time."

"You are referring to . . ." I began hesitantly.

"The first marriage. So tragic. But it has all turned out for the best, hasn't it?"

I felt a shiver down my spine. His first marriage! He had not mentioned a marriage to me. What had happened? His wife must be dead. Otherwise, how could *I* be his wife? And why was it so tragic?

It seemed as though a chill had crept into the hall. I could see Lady Alice watching me intently. There was a glint of amusement in her eyes. She would realize, of course, that Colum had told me nothing of his previous marriage.

It was in the early hours of the morning before we retired. Together we looked into the nursery next to our own bedchamber, to assure ourselves that Connell was safe.

When we were in bed and the curtains drawn, I said to Colum, "I learned tonight that you had been married before."

"Did you not know it?"

"Why should I? You didn't tell me."

"Did you think a man would get to my age and not take a wife ere that?"

"Why was it never mentioned?"

"The point never arose."

"That seems strange to me."

He drew me toward him. "Enough of others."

But I could not rest. I said, "Colum, I felt so foolish.

That woman mentioning it and I not to know."

"Alice is a sly creature. She was jealous of you."

"Why? She has a husband. Has she no children?"

He laughed loudly. "A husband. That poor stick! Much good he is to her. He is incapable of begetting children."

"I'm sorry then."

"Don't waste pity on Alice. She is not at heart displeased. She has free range to select her bedfellows, and he is complacent enough. As for children, I doubt she wants them. She would find them a nuisance, and they might spoil her figure."

"You know her . . . well?"

"Oh, very well."

"You mean of course. . . ."

"Exactly."

There was a change in his manner. No tenderness now but a certain brusque impatience—the first since the last weeks before Connell's birth. I sensed that he was irritated by my reference to his previous marriage.

"So she and you. . . ."

"Oh, come, wife. What is wrong with you? I've known many women. Did you think Castle Paling was some sort of monastery and I a monk?"

"I certainly did not think that . . . but our guests. . . ."

"You must grow up. You must not be a silly little Linnet twittering in her cage and thinking that comprises the world. Some of us are made in a certain way, and so must it be. I never fancied going lonely to bed."

"So it was jealousy that made her. . . ."

"I don't know. She will doubtless have another lover now. What matters it? I grow tired of this."

"I want to know about your wife, Colum."

"Not now," he said firmly.

But later I returned to the subject. The christening guests were gone, and we were together in the nursery. We had dismissed the nurse so that we were alone with the child, who lay in his cradle while Colum rocked it. The child watched his father all the time. It was an affecting scene to see this big man gently rocking the cradle and I was overcome with a deep emotion. I should have been completely happy, but for one thing. I knew he had had mistresses. That was to be expected, but I could not forget his first wife. I wanted to know something of that marriage, whether he had cared for her, how desolate he had been when she died. Why was he so reluctant to talk of her, or was he? Did he just feel an impatience to go back over something that was over?

"Colum," I said, "I think I ought to know something about your previous marriage."

He stopped rocking the cradle to stare at me, and I went on quickly: "It is disconcerting when people speak of it and I know nothing, and I suppose now we shall be entertaining more. To make a mystery of it. . . ."

"It is no mystery," he said. "I married, she died, and that was the end of it. There was no mystery."

"How . . . long were you married?"

"It must have been some three years."

"That is not very long."

He made an impatient movement with his shoulders, but the hand on the cradle remained gentle.

"What of it?" he said.

"And then she died. How did she die, Colum?"

"In childbed."

"I see, and the child with her?"

He nodded.

I felt sorry for him then. I thought of all the anguish he would have suffered. He had so wanted a boy, and she had died and the child with her.

I was silent, and he said, "Well, is the interrogation over?"

"I'm sorry, Colum, but I felt I should know."

"It is over and done. There is no need to think of it."

"Can something like that . . . a part of one's life . . . be dismissed like that?"

His brows shot up, and he looked angry. "It's over, I tell you. That's an end of it."

I should have stopped, but I couldn't. I had to know.

"You must think of her, Colum, sometimes."

"No," he said firmly.

"But it was such a part of your life."

He released his hold on the cradle and stood up. He came toward me. I thought he was going to strike me. Instead he took me by the shoulders and shook me, but not harshly.

"I am content with what I have now," he said. "I have a wife who pleases me, who can give and take pleasure. It was not so before. Moreover, she has given me this boy. I could regret nothing that has brought me to this. I would have nothing . . . nothing otherwise. Let it be."

I lay against him and felt the tears in my eyes. I knew

he would hate to see them, so I broke away and went to the cradle and knelt down, looking at my son.

Colum came and stood on the other side of the cradle, looking at us both. There was exultation in my heart then. What did it matter that he had married before, that he had been Lady Alice's lover? He was not a man to suppress his desire, and it would always be fierce. Again I thought of my father. These were the two men in my life whom I truly loved. Odd, that they should have been two of a kind. But they suited women like myself and my mother. We needed such men—and it was comforting to realize that they needed women like us.

I knew instinctively that his first wife had been too meek, that he had never cared for her as he had for me. He had told me that, and I could not help feeling gratified.

But there was more to come.

It came from Jennet. She was the sort of woman who could be taken from one place and planted with the greatest ease in another, like some plant that yearns so much to grow that it will flourish in any soil. In the short time she had been at Castle Paling, she had not only acquired a lover but had struck up friendships with other servants and behaved as though she had lived at the Castle all her life.

She was warmhearted, generous in all things, not only her favors, and there was something endearing about her in spite of a certain incompetence. My mother was often impatient with her. I think in her heart she never forgave her for betraying her with my father. After all, it must have been a strain to have one's husband's bastard in the house and his mother too. It was the same with Romilly. My mother was an extraordinary woman. I wondered what I would feel like if Colum brought his mistresses into the house with their offspring. However, to get back to Jennet, she it was who brought this shattering knowledge into my life.

She was now Connell's nurse. After all, I trusted her more than I did anyone else; I knew too of her love for children. She was inclined to spoil the boy, of course, but I suppose we all were.

There she was clucking over him one day and chattering away to him, and she said, "I reckon your father thinks the world of you, my little man. Oh, he does and all. And that's clear to see. And you know it. Yes, you do."

I smiled at them, and I thought of her as a young woman

when Jacko had been born and how she must have loved him.

Then she said, "Boys! They always want boys. The Captain was the same. Show him a boy, and he was that pleased. Nothing too good for his boys. It's the same with this master. It must have been a terrible disappointment to him. . . ."

"What, Jennet?"

"Well, when he couldn't get one with that first wife of his. Well, 'twasn't for want of trying. Time after time he were disappointed."

"You seem to know a great deal about the master's affairs," I said.

" 'Tis common talk in the kitchens, mistress."

"What do they say down there, Jennet?"

"Oh, that she was a poor sick creature and the master wasn't with her as he is with you."

"They're impertinent," I said, but I couldn't quite suppress the glow of triumph.

Jennet did not notice the reproof, and I was glad. I thought: I may find out through Jennet and the servants more than I can from Colum. It was only natural that I should feel a great curiosity about my predecessor, and I could see no harm in doing a little innocent ferreting.

Seeing my interest, Jennet warmed to her subject. There was little she liked so much as gossip.

"Oh, yes," said Jennet, "a poor timid thing, she were. Frightened of her own shadow. The master, they say, do want someone as can stand up to him as you do, mistress. They say you be just the one for him, and he knows it. This poor lady, frightened she were, frightened of the castle and ghosts and things and, most of all, of him."

"Poor child," I said.

"Oh, yes, mistress, and the master he did want a son, and it seemed she could not give him one. She'd be *so*, and then she'd lose it and then *so* again. Only once did she stay her full time . . . and that was the last. Once she went seven months, though. The others . . . they were all quick, as you might say."

"She must have had a very uncomfortable time."

"She did. And the master he were mad like. Shouted he did . . . called her a useless stock. That's what he called her. They'd hear him shouting, and his rage was terrible. Woe betide any who went near him when he was in these rages. They used to be frightened that he'd do away with her. And she was afraid too. She told her maid . . . Mary Anne, it were. She's with one of the Seaward men now and works over there. She told Mary Anne that sometimes she feared he'd do away with her."

I felt I had had enough and wanted to hear no more. Of course, I liked to have confirmation that he was content with our marriage and that he found his second wife more attractive than his first, but I could not bear this talk about his cruelty to her.

"All right, Jennet," I said. "That's enough. Servants exaggerate."

"Not this time, mistress, for Mary Anne did say she was real terrified. And when she was *so* again, she was so frantic she did not know what to do. You see she believed she'd never have the child and she was so sick and ill every time. She thought she would die, and she told Mary Anne that she ought never to try for children. The doctor was against it. She ought never to have married because she knew it would kill her sooner or later. She said she had pleaded with him, and he had said that if she could not give him children, what good was she to him. . . ."

"I don't want to hear any more servants' gossip, Jennet," I said.

"No, mistress, no more you do. But they did wonder why she didn't run away and go home to her family. 'Twas not all that far."

"Oh?" I said.

"I could scarce believe it when I heard," said Jennet, "seeing that we'd been there like and was on terms with the family."

"What do you mean?"

"Well, mistress, the master's first wife was the sister of the young gentleman we all thought you'd take. Her name before her marriage was Melanie Landor."

I felt dizzy suddenly. In my mind I was transported back to Trystan Priory. I was in a small room looking at a picture of a fair young girl.

I could hear a voice saying: She was murdered.

That girl had been Colum's first wife.

Ysella's Tower

It haunted me. I could not get her out of my mind. I could imagine her so clearly in this place, having seen her picture. I could not forget the anguish in her mother's eyes; I could hear the underlying hatred in the voice as she had said, "She was murdered."

And Jennet: "Sometimes she feared he'd do away with her."

Why had he married her in the first place? Had he been in love with her? A fair, innocent young girl. He liked innocence. He had liked it in me. He took some savage delight in destroying that innocence as he had on the first night I had spent in Castle Paling.

I was thinking about him, this man who was the father of my child. What if I had failed as Melanie Landor had? I had delighted him only because I had given him what he wanted.

I could not get her out of my mind. I looked for signs of her about the place. When I walked the ramparts and looked out at the sea, I thought of her standing there and the fear that would have hung over her. It was as though she walked beside me, appearing at odd moments, a shadowy presence to haunt me, to cast a shadow over my happiness.

Poor frail Melanie who had failed to please him and who had died because of it!

No, not because of it. She had died in childbed. Many women did. A husband could not be blamed for that.

I kept hearing her mother's fierce murmur: She was murdered. I must make allowances for a mother's grief. And how strange that she should have been Fennimore's sister. But was it? They were not distant neighbors. Marriages were arranged between people of their position.

What were the Landors thinking now? They would know that I, whom they had chosen to be Fennimore's wife, was now married to the man who had been their daughter's husband.

What had they thought? Why had my mother, who had seen them since my marriage, not mentioned this fact to me? It would have been so natural for her to do so.

I was betraying too much interest in my husband's first wife. Jennet, quick to realize this, garnered knowledge for me.

"It were in the Red Room she died, mistress," she told me. And I had to go to the Red Room.

How dark it was. How full of shadows, and there was the big four-poster bed. I went to the window and looked out to the stark drop to the sea. I could almost feel her then. It was as though a voice whispered: Yes, I thought often of throwing myself down. It would have been quick . . . anything better than my life with him.

Fancy, sheer fancy! What was the matter with me. It was the room with the dark-red bedcurtains—heavy, embroidered in red silk of a darker shade than the background. I pictured her shut in behind those curtains, waiting for him to come to her.

"Her room were the Red Room," Jennet told me. "He would go to her there. She didn't share a room with him like. They did say he were with her only to get a son."

I was ashamed of allowing Jennet to tell me so much, but I had to know; it was a burning curiosity and more. It was not so much that I wished to discover the truth about Colum's relationship with his first wife as to learn more of him.

I pictured his hatred of her. He despised weakness. He liked me best when I fought against him. She was too gentle, too meek, and she was terrified. His only interest in her would be that of procreation.

He would have his mistresses there in the room which I

shared with him now doubtless, and in the dark Red Room she would be visited now and then.

There was terror in this room. It lingered. When she was pregnant, she would be afraid of death, and when she was not, she would be afraid of him.

And how was she equipped to fight against her fate? Poor child, brought up in the gentle Landor home where life went on smoothly and people were kind and polite to each other. I had seen something of life. I knew and had grown to love my father, who was such another as Colum. I was prepared. I was the fortunate one, the loved wife who had not failed him and in less than a year had given him the son on whom he doted.

I wished that I could get her out of my mind. I could not. I could never go near the Red Room without looking in.

"Poor Melanie," I would murmur. "I hope you are at peace now."

Edwina, who was descended from a witch on her mother's side, had certain powers. Once, when Carlos was at sea and involved in a fight with a Spanish galleon, she had had a vision of it and known that he was in danger; sometimes she foresaw events. It was an uncanny gift. I remember Edwina's telling me once that if people experienced violent emotions in a certain spot, they left behind them some disturbance which was apparent to those with special insight.

I now wondered whether Melanie had left something of this behind. I lacked those special powers, but perhaps because I was in her place, I could sense something here.

I half hoped and half feared that she would return in some form. Perhaps that was why I went to the Red Room so often.

I liked to go there at dusk, at that time of day when the daylight is fast fading and it is not quite time to light the candles. Then the room was at its most ghostly.

It was November, the anniversary of that day when Colum had brought me here. He remembered it and had said, "You and I will sup alone together as we did on that day. It is a day I regard as one of the luckiest in my life."

I had dressed myself in a russet velvet gown and wore my hair loose about my shoulders—quite unfashionably but the style most becoming to me—and on that very day I could not resist going along to the Red Room at dusk.

I stood there. There were dark shadows in the room. Soon the light would be gone altogether.

"Melanie," I whispered, "are you there?"

And as I stood there, I felt the hair rise from my scalp, for the door was slowly opening.

I stood watching it. Then it was flung back, and there stood Colum.

"In God's name," he cried, "what are you doing here?"

For a moment I could not speak. He came to me and, taking me by the shoulders, shook me.

"What ails you? What is wrong?"

"I thought you were a ghost."

He caught my hair in his hands and tugged it hard.

"Who has been talking to you?" he demanded.

"I pick up bits of gossip here and there."

"I'll have any whipped who have been pouring poison into your ear."

"You will do no such thing," I said, "or I shall tell you nothing."

"You will tell me what I ask," he said.

"Not here in this room."

"Yes," he said. "Here in this room, with your ghost smirking in the shadows."

There was something grand about him. He was not afraid of anything or anyone. One of the Seaward men had told Jennet that the master feared neither God nor man— and it was true. He would 'be defiant no matter what he faced. So he could not be expected to fear poor Melanie's ghost—if the idea should occur to him that it existed, which I doubted.

"I know that this was the room in which your first wife died."

"Well, she had to die somewhere."

"You never told me that she was a Landor."

"She had to be someone."

"But the Landors. . . . Fennimore Landor's sister! How strange that you should have married his sister."

"Not strange at all. It was a suitable marriage in some ways. The girl was of good family and brought a good dowry with her."

"And you took the dowry and cared nothing for her."

"I had no reason to care for her."

"She was your wife."

He grasped me firmly and, pressing me backwards, kissed me firmly on the mouth.

"There is only one wife for me," he said. "Praise God I have her."

"I wish you had told me that she was a Landor."

"Why? It meant nothing to me that you once had a fancy for that lily-livered boy."

"You malign Fennimore. He was not that. He is brave and dedicated to his work. He has ideals."

"Much good will they do him."

"There speaks the buccaneer."

"This is a buccaneer's world."

"It is changing," I said. "Trade will take the place of war, and those who persist in making war will suffer and those who live peacefully will prosper."

"By God," he said, "you repeat your lessons well. I will have no more of Fennimore Landor in this house. You are well rid of him. I do not wish to hear his name mentioned again."

"Why? Does your conscience fret you?"

"My conscience?"

"Yes, for what you did to the Landors."

"You are mad, wife. What I did to the Landors was to marry their daughter. She died in childbirth as others have done before her."

"But she was sick and ill, and you persisted that she should give you a son."

"God's teeth, girl. Has a man no right to a son?"

"Not if he must kill his wife to get one."

There was a brief silence; the ghostly shadows had crept farther into the room. For a few seconds—and a few only—Colum was shaken. I knew then that he had ignored Melanie's pleas, that he had forced her as in the beginning he had forced me. His will was law in Castle Paling, and if he had to trample over the heart and body of any who stood in his way, he would do so.

In those seconds I seemed to have a vision of the future. It was as though Melanie were warning me. He wants you now. You are important to him, but for how long?

Just that and no more. The moment had passed.

He was laughing. "I can see someone has been talking too much."

"Nay," I said quickly, fearing his wrath for the servants. "I have worked this out for myself. This was the room where she suffered. This was the room where she died. Do you not feel that she is still here?"

"You have gone mad," he said. "She lies in the family vault. She is no more here than your pretty Fennimore is."

"She is dead, Colum, and the dead sometimes return."

"Nonsense," he shouted. "Nonsense."

I saw his eyes look about the room. It would be full of memories for him. His step in the corridor, Melanie shrinking in her curtained bed; the onslaught that she feared—cruel and crude to such a defenseless creature, asking herself what she feared most, his intrusion into her privacy or that pregnancy which kept him away and could bring death closer.

I was full of pity for her.

"You are morbid," he accused.

"I feel drawn toward this room."

"On this night of all nights!"

"Yes, because it is this night."

"You want me to stand in this room and ask forgiveness of her. For what? Because I asked that she should perform her duties as a wife? Because I wanted sons? In God's name for what other reason should I have married a silly, simpering girl who brought me no pleasure."

"You made a mistake in marrying her. We have to abide by mistakes."

"Nay," he said. "If we take a false step, we right ourselves and go in another direction. Enough of this." There was a satanic gleam in his eyes. He pulled me toward the bed.

I said, "No, Colum, please, not here. . . ."

But he would not heed me. He said, "Yes. Yes. I say yes, and by God and all His angels I will have my way."

Later we supped in that room where we had on the first night I came to Castle Paling.

When I was in my chair, he came around to me and in his hands was a solid chain set with diamonds on which hung a locket of rubies and diamonds. He put it about my neck.

"There," he said, "it becomes you well. It is my gift to you, my love. It is my thanks for my son and for giving me that which I have looked for in my wife."

I touched his hands and looked up at him. I had been shocked by what had happened in the Red Room. He had meant to superimpose on my fantastic imaginings a memory of our own. I think he was right in believing that I would not want to go there for some time. I would not want to think of us—which I must—on the bed on which Melanie had died.

How characteristic of him thus to defy the enemy, which in this case was the memory of Melanie.

"You like this trinket?" he asked me.

"It is beautiful."

He kissed me then with that tenderness which always moved me deeply.

"You are glad of that night? Glad a brigand saw you in an inn and decided that you should be his."

"Yes, glad."

I took his hand and kissed it.

"I will tell you something," he said, "there was never a woman who pleased me as you do."

"I hope I shall always do so."

He laughed lightly. "You must make sure that you do."

"I shall grow old," I said, "but so will you."

"Women grow old before men."

"You are ten years older than I am."

"Ten years is nothing . . . for a man. It is only women who must fight off age."

"You are arrogant."

"I admit it."

"Vain."

"True."

"Selfish and sometimes cruel."

"I confess my guilt."

"And you expect me to love such a man?"

"Expect and demand," he answered.

"How could I?"

"I will tell you why. You love me because you know you must. You know my nature. It is all you say it is. But know this too: I am a man who will have my way, and if I say this woman is to love me, then she has no help for it. She must do so."

"You imagine you are a god and all other men are nothing beside you."

"I know it to be so," he said.

"You believe that all you have to do is command a woman to love you and she must needs do so."

"That is true too," he said. "You began by hating me. Now you are as eager for me as I for you. Is that not proof?"

I smiled across the table at him.

"I think it must be," I said.

I was happy that night. It was only in the morning that I thought again of Melanie and wondered whether in the beginning, when they had first married, she had supped with him in that room and whether he had spoken of love to her.

Had it been only when she failed to give him what he wanted that he grew to despise her?

Into my mind had crept an uneasy thought: What if you should cease to please him?

Christmas came. My little Connell was four months old, lusty as ever, doing, as Jennet said, all the things a boy ought to do. Showing temper, showing interest, growing plump and healthy. I wouldn't allow him to be swaddled, and Colum agreed with me. If he had not, I should have prepared to fight against him on this point. I couldn't bear to think of my baby bound up in swaddling clothes for weeks. "I want his legs to grow long so that he will be as tall as his father," I said.

We loved to see him kick, and his legs were straight as a pine tree.

Such celebrations we had that Christmas. My mother and father came to spend the time with us. With them came Damask, Penn and Romilly. I enjoyed decorating the great hall with holly and ivy and giving orders in the kitchens. There were special pies made for my father's pleasure; there were the coins to put in the cakes and puddings, all with their significance, and of course the silver penny for the cake to be discovered by the King for the Day.

The joy in seeing my parents was great. My father insisted immediately on being taken to see his grandson and had brought a carved ship for him which was a replica of one of his own Lions—the *Triumphant Lion*. I laughed at him and told him Connell was too young for such toys, and he retorted that real boys were never too young for ships.

It moved me deeply to see him at Connell's cradle, putting out a great hand before the child's face. Connell reached up, and his hand curled about my father's little finger. I had rarely seen my father so moved. I believe there were actually tears in his eyes.

He stood up abruptly, and he said to me, "So my girl Linnet has a son of her own. Bless you, girl. You've made me a happy man."

Later, when we rode together as we used to when I was at home and the understanding had started between us, he said to me, "I spent years railing against fate that denied me a legitimate son. When you came, I cursed God for giving me a girl. Now I see I was wrong. I learned in time that you were as good as any boy—and so you've proved. Now you've given me my grandson."

I said I was happy too. Then I added, "I have to watch my son will not be spoiled. His father dotes on him even as you do. He must not grow up to think he has but to smile and the whole world will be at his feet."

"Have no fear. That boy will take after his grandfather. I see it. He'll be for the sea. He's got that look in his eyes."

I laughed at my father, but he was serious.

"I'm glad," he said, "you've got a man who *is* a man. Never quite took to Fennimore Landor."

"You are not fair to him. He is a brave good sailor."

"A handsome fellow, I grant you. But you've got a man, and I'm proud of you."

Yes, there was no doubt that my father liked my husband. They rode together and talked a great deal.

My mother too seemed happy, and Damask's infatuation for Colum continued. He was amused by the child, but he took little notice of her, which she did not seem to mind as long as she could sit near and watch him.

It was like the old Christmases I remembered at Lyon Court. I suppose I had made it so. All the servants and their families came into the great hall and were given wine and Christmas cake; they sang carols, and the mummers came and performed.

I did talk to my mother when we were alone.

I mentioned the fact that I had discovered Colum had been married before. "His wife was Melanie Landor," I said. "Fennimore's sister. Did you know?"

"We did discover it after the wedding," said my mother. "What a time that was! First the secret ceremony and then the other. It was all rather hurried, as it had to be."

"When did you realize that Colum's first wife was Melanie Landor?"

"It was after your wedding when you had left for Castle Paling with Colum. The Landors were to visit us. Only Fennimore and his father came. Mistress Landor was taken ill. She admitted to me afterward that she could not face us when she knew that our daughter had married *her* daughter's husband."

"It must have been a shock for her."

"It was. How did you discover? But Colum told you, I suppose."

"No, he did not. I found out through Jennet."

"Trust Jennet!" said my mother half indulgently, half in exasperation.

"Yes, Jennet told me who she was. I was surprised."

"And you mentioned it to Colum?"

Memories came back to me—the darkening room, the red bed with the shadows deepening and the ghost of Melanie lurking.

"I did. He was not very pleased."

"He had not wished you to know?"

"I am not sure of that. He had simply not mentioned it. It was over, she was dead, and he was married to me now. Tell me what Mistress Landor said when she knew I had married Colum."

"Remember that she lost her beloved daughter. She must have been nearly demented when it happened. She did not wish her daughter to have any more children. She was certain that if she did, she would kill herself. Of course she blames Colum. She becomes hysterical over her daughter's death. We must understand that, Linnet."

"She told me that her daughter had been murdered. It was a great shock when I discovered who she was . . . for that reason."

"You must remember she is a mother. That is why she has to blame someone for her daughter's death. Her grief was assuaged by her anger against her daughter's husband. Sometimes when grief like that sweeps over you, anger is an outlet for it."

"I understand. And the Landors have never had any communication with Castle Paling since her death."

"Perhaps in time they will come to see reason. In any case, my dearest, you are happy. You have a beautiful son and a husband who loves you. And it has all happened so quickly. Just over a year ago that we. . . . No matter. I rejoice. May God bless you, my darling, and may you always be as happy as you are now."

She wanted to see the castle. I told her about Ysella and Nonna. "Ysella's Tower is locked up. It is used as a kind of storage place. Seaward is where certain of the servants live."

"A whole tower to themselves?" said my mother.

"There is so much space in a castle, Mother."

"I remember the Abbey where I spent my childhood. It is very beautiful here and so interesting. I like to think of my little girl as the chatelaine of a great castle."

When I was showing her the rooms in the castle, we came to the Red Room.

It was the first time I had been in it since that night when Colum had found me there. I noticed that there was a layer of dust on the planked hutch and the bedposts.

My mother noticed it too and raised her eyebrows. As she grew older, she had become a meticulous housewife.

"The servants don't like to come in here alone," I said.

"The haunted room, is it? Now I see it has that air. What legend is there attached to this place?"

I said, "It was the room in which Colum's first wife died."

"Ah," said my mother, "if I were you, I would take down those red hangings and the bedcurtains and put in another color. Change it."

"I hadn't thought of that."

"The only legends that should be preserved are happy ones," said my mother.

"I will consider it," I said. And I thought at the time: She is right in a way, but changing the curtains and putting in new furniture would not alter the fact that within these four walls Melanie had lived, suffered and died.

After the New Year my parents went back to Lyon Court. I missed them very much, but I was happy watching my child grow bigger every day. He flourished, and our delight in him was greater than ever. But oddly enough I could not cast out that morbid fascination which the Red Room had for me, and I still went there. I did think of changing the curtains. I even went so far as taking my little seamstress along to discuss the matter with her.

I noticed how reluctant she was, and I could see that she was afraid of the task.

At last she admitted that she thought it might bring bad luck.

"Nonsense," I said. "Why should it?"

"It might be, madam, that this is how she wished it to stay."

Then I knew that I should really do as my mother said. I must change the room entirely so that when people entered it, they would not think of poor dead Melanie.

But I didn't. I found I had no heart for the task. I assured myself that to do so was to give way to superstition. But that was not quite true.

Somewhere deep down in my mind was the thought that Melanie had left something of herself behind and that one day I might need her help.

I will admit it was a thought which flashed in and out of my head and was dismissed immediately, but it came back. It was there in the Red Room, and on dark nights I thought I could hear it in the murmur of the wind on the sea.

What if he should tire of you as he tired of Melánie? Tire of me? The mother of his son . . . and the other children we should have. For we should have them. He was sure of that, and so was I.

There was a great deal I had to discover about my husband. I knew so little of him. That was doubtless why I was so fascinated by him.

I would keep the Red Room as it was, and I would attempt to learn more of my husband. I must know where he went when he was not at the castle. I must share his life.

I would find out. Oddly enough—and how right this premonition was to prove—the notion filled me with a certain apprehension.

Spring had come, and I was once more expecting a child. I was delighted but not more so than Colum.

"Did I not tell you that you would havè a quiverful? Give me another boy. When we have half a dozen of them, we'll think about a girl or two."

I retorted, "I do not propose to spend my life in a continual state of pregnancy."

"Do you not?" he retorted. "I thought that was a wifely duty."

"To provide a few children, yes, but she needs a little respite."

"Not my wife," he said, and he lifted me in his arms and looked at me with love.

I was happy. Gloomy thoughts had gone. I visualized a future—Colum and I grown older, more sedate, and our children playing about us.

As soon as I knew I was to have another child, my desire to discover receded. I was happy. I wanted to go on in my contentment. There were times when he went away for several days at a stretch. I used to wonder where. He was not very communicative about his affairs, and one thing I had discovered was that he hated to be questioned. When I had asked, he had answered me vaguely, but I had seen the danger signals in his eyes. I had seen his sudden anger flare up against some servant, and I had always been afraid of arousing it. At one time I wondered whether he visited a mistress. I did not think this was so because when he went away, he took a retinue of servants with him.

Again I learned a little through Jennet. She was supposed to sleep in the servants' quarters in the Crows' Tower, but I knew she slipped out to Seaward to join her lover there. One night I discovered that she was not going to Seaward Tower.

Colum had told me that he would be leaving early the next morning. He was going on some business and would be gone before I was up.

I remembered then that Jennet had not gone to the Seaward Tower on another occasion when Colum had been going away. I decided to question as discreetly as I could, because I was growing more and more interested in Colum's journeys.

When I awoke the next morning, I sent for Jennet. I said, "I gathered you spent the night on your lonely pallet, Jennet."

She blushed in that manner which had sometimes irritated my mother but which I could not help finding rather endearing.

"Orders," she said. "I was not to go to Seaward last night."

"There should be such orders every night, Jennet," I said.

"Yes, mistress," she answered. " 'Tis always so," she volunteered, "the night before he do go on his journey. He be busy preparing like late into the night and sets off with the dawn."

"Does he tell you where he is going?"

"No, Tobias never will say, mistress. Shuts up tight when I ask. He's a mild man, but he gets angry if I as much as mention it. 'Keep thy mouth shut, woman,' he says, 'or that'll be the end twixt you and me.' Yet he be a mild man in all other matters."

It certainly was strange. I wondered why there had to be this secrecy. Colum was not a man to make an effort to keep anything quiet. His implication was that if people did not like what he did, he cared not a jot of it. Yet he was quiet about this business of his.

When he returned from those journeys, he was invariably in good spirits and glad to be back with me. It was June, and the warm sunshine filled the castle. It was three months since my child had been conceived, and I had recovered from the first uncomfortable stages of pregnancy and had not yet reached the cumbersome one. I felt well and energetic and Colum and I rode out together. We should be away for the night, he told me, as he had some business to transact.

I was delighted because I thought at last he was taking me into his confidence. I was actually going with him on a business venture; I was making the most of my riding too, because I knew that very soon I should be forbidden to ride.

This is the loveliest of all months, or perhaps it seemed so to me because I was so happy. The sky was cobalt blue with only the faintest hint of wispy white cloud. The choughs and the sea gulls swooped and rose above the water, and as we rode away from the sea into the lanes, I was enchanted by the countryside. The white chervil on the banks reminded me of lace, and the grass was spattered with blue forget-me-nots and red ragged robin.

The sun was warm, and I was happy. I felt well and strong. My son was in good hands. The care of children was one thing Jennet could really be trusted with.

Colum sang as we rode along—it was the old hunting song which was such a favorite with him.

I did not recognize the road until we were almost at the inn. And there it was before us—the Traveler's Rest—and there was the host who had been in such a quandary on that other night. Now he was beaming with delight, hands crossed on his chest.

Colum leaped from his horse and lifted me down. Grooms ran to take our horses.

"The Oak Room, host," cried Colum.

"At your service, my master," replied the host.

And we were mounting the stairs and there was the room I remembered so well—the big four-poster bed in which I had slept with my mother, the lattice window from which I had looked down and seen Colum standing before me.

The host was saying, "There is venison, my master, cooked as you like it. And natlin and taddage pies as will tempt your palate. And if my lord so wishes, metheglin to wash it down."

"Lay it on," cried Colum. "For we have ridden far and are hungry."

The host bowed and shuffled out and left us standing there looking at each other.

Colum came to me and laid his hands on my shoulders. "I always promised myself that you and I should sleep in that bed."

"You are a man who cannot endure to be balked."

"What man worth his salt is not?"

I laughed. "You planned this," I said, "because of what happened here when I came with my mother."

He shrugged his shoulders. "I had business to transact so I thought, why should I not do it at the Traveler's Rest? I will take my wife with me, and we will share the Oak Room, for it will bring home to her the fact that she has a husband who will have his way sooner or later."

"I can never understand why a man who is acknowledged as the king of his castle should have to go to such lengths continually to stress the fact that he is."

"Because he is not sure that one person fully realizes it, and to tell you the truth, it is that person he is most anxious should."

I laid my head against his chest and put my arms about him.

"I am content with life as I have found it, Colum. You are a strong man. I should be the last to deny it, but whatever I was made to accept I should always have my own views . . . you appreciate that."

"I would not want a foolish simpering creature . . . like. . . ."

I was glad he stopped, but I knew of course that he was referring to Melanie.

To change the subject I said, "You say you have come here to do business. Do tell me, Colum, I am most eager to know."

I saw a shadow pass over his face. He went to the window and looked out; then he turned his head and said to me, "What do you know of my business?"

"Nothing much at the moment, but I should like to learn."

"There is nothing to learn," he said. "I have some merchandise I wish to show to a merchant. We are meeting at this inn."

"So it was because it is business, not because of that night."

"A little of each, shall we say?"

"What merchandise have you to dispose of, Colum? Where does it come from?"

He did not answer that question.

He said, "Ere long two of my men will arrive with pack horses. They will bring the goods."

"What merchandise is this?" I persisted.

"It varies."

He drew me to the bed and removed my cloak.

"Colum, there is much I wish to know. When I come to think of it, there is so little I do know. You are my husband. There is nothing I want so much as to share my life with you, and if I do so, I must know. . . ."

"Know what?" he said, loosening my hair from the net which held it. "What should you, a good and obedient wife, wish to know but that you please me?"

"I want to please you, yes. In every way I want to please you. But I want to help you too."

He kissed me with more gentleness than I was accustomed to. "You please me, and you please me most when you wait for me to tell you what I will."

"You mean this business of yours is a secret?"

"Who talks of secrets? What a woman you are for creating drama from ordinary events. You store up ghosts in the Red Room."

"You were secretive about that."

"Secretive! I! Because I forgot something in the past which it can do no one good to remember. You should be grateful that my first marriage was a failure. It makes me more than ever contented with my second."

"I know you are content, Colum, but I want to help you. I want to understand . . . everything."

He laughed and pressed me back on the bed. He kissed my throat. Then he said, "Nay, the host's table is awaiting our attention. We will eat, and then mayhap I will attend to my business, and when that is finished, you and I will be together here in this Oak Room as I yearned to be when I first saw you here."

He rose and pulled me to my feet.

"But, Colum," I began.

"You have a hungry husband, madam," he told me. "He must needs eat before he can answer more questions."

We went to the dining room. Memories came back. I pictured his sitting there eating with gusto, catching my skirt as I passed. How I had hated him then. It was incredible that in so short a time that hatred could have turned to this passionate love.

He ate heartily, doing full justice to the muggety pie made of sheep's entrails and taken with cream—a Cornish custom which we of Devon had never indulged in, although we were as famous for our clotted cream as the Cornish were. He drank the metheglin but rather sparingly, I thought, and while we were eating, two men put their heads into the dining room.

He acknowledged them, but he did not introduce me. They did not remain in the dining room but went away, I believed to wait until Colum was ready. They looked like merchants in their best clothes. One wore a russet jacket with camlet sleeves, and there were pewter buttons on it. The other was in brown with gray kersey hose, and they both wore steeple-crowned hats.

"They are friends of yours, Colum?" I asked.

"They are the men whom I have come to see."

"On business," I said.

"Aye, business."

"I had thought you a man of means, not a merchant."

"Merchants are men of means, wife. I have rich lands, a castle and many servants. To keep up such an establishment and maintain a wife is costly in these days. So now and then, when the mood is on me, I am a merchant."

"What is your merchandise?"

"Whatever comes my way."

"So it is no particular commodity?"

"Enough of questions. Your curiosity will make a scold of you yet."

"It is only because I would serve my husband that I wish to learn his habits."

"He will keep you acquainted of the best way to serve him. Now I must leave you for a while, so I will take you to the Oak Room and then you will go to bed. You may be sure that the moment I have completed my business I will be with you."

He took me to the Oak Room and left me there. I sat on the bed and thought of him down there transacting his business. What business? The men had arrived with the packhorses. I wondered what they had brought. It was strange for the squire who owned a castle and was the lord of his neighborhood to barter over merchandise. I wondered again what it was and why he should be so reluctant to discuss this with me. There could be two reasons. The first was that wives were not supposed to share in their husband's business affairs. They were not supposed to understand them. I knew that Colum while delighting in my spirited nature was also determined to subdue it. He seemed to ignore the fact that if he ever did, he would lose interest in me. Perhaps deep down in his heart he wanted to. Perhaps he wanted to keep me as the mother of his children and go off in search of erotic adventures with other women. I was sure that was what he did before we had married. In a way he chafed against this passion between us. Once he had said with a sort of exasperated anger, "None will satisfy me now save you." He was a strange man. He hated above all things to be shackled. It might well be that he wished to keep his business apart from me because he did not want to share everything. He wanted to exclude me because he feared I was becoming too important to him. The other reason was, of course, that it was something of which he was ashamed. Ashamed! He would never be ashamed. Something that must be kept secret perhaps.

So I pondered, and I longed to creep down the stairs and into the room which the host would have set aside for them and listen at the door.

I sat at the window for a long time thinking, and I was still there when I heard a bustle below. Looking down, I saw the two men who had looked in at the dining room. A groom was leading two packhorses. They were not ours. Then came Colum with the two men. I drew back but not so far that I could not see them.

They talked together. Then the men mounted their horses and rode away.

I knew that Colum was coming up now, so I left the window and sat on the bed.

In a few minutes he was in the room.

"What!" he cried. "Still up! What do you here? 'Tis time we were abed."

I could not sleep well that night. I had bad dreams. I was not sure of what, for in them events were jumbled, but Colum was there and so were the merchants and the packhorses, and Melanie too . . . for my dream had shifted to the Red Room. Melanie was warning me, "Don't be too curious. If you are, you could uncover something you would rather not know."

In the morning we rode back to Castle Paling. It was a beautiful morning. There is nothing like sunlight for washing away the fears which come by night. They are exposed as nothing but vague shadows conjured up out of the darkness. I reveled in the green of the conifers and the call of the cuckoo, though he was beginning to stammer now. All was well. In six months' time my child would be born, and now I was going to my home where my son would be waiting for me.

It was August. I could no longer ride, and the days seemed long and tedious. One night there was a violent storm, and I awoke to find that Colum was hastily dressing.

I sat up in bed, and he told me to lie down and keep the curtains drawn. He was going out because he thought there might be a ship out there in distress.

I said should I not be up in case there were something I could do? He said, no, he would forbid it. I had to think of the child I carried.

Nevertheless, I rose and went to look in at the room adjoining ours where Connell slept. He was a year old now. I thought the thunder and lightning might frighten him. Nothing of the sort. He shouted with delight as the flash lit up the room, and he clearly thought the violent thunder was part of a game which had been devised for his benefit.

I laughed with him, glad that he was not frightened, and because I did not wish him to see that I had expected him to be afraid, I left him.

I went back to my bed and drew the curtains around me, and I thought of that other night when there had been a storm and Colum had gone out to see what could be done.

He had told me that on dark nights he caused a lantern to be put in the turret rooms of the towers facing the sea as a warning to sailors that they were close to the Devil's Teeth.

He said, "It has been the custom of our house to give this service. When sailors see the lights, if they know they are on the Cornish coast, they will realize that they are near the Devil's Teeth and keep away," so in Nonna's and the Seaward Towers these lanterns shone on all dark nights.

So I lay in bed and prayed that if any ship were being buffeted by the violent winds, it would come safely through.

The storm died down, and I slept. It was light when I awoke, and Colum had awakened me by coming into the room.

His clothes were sodden with the rain, and there was a hot color in his cheeks.

"Was a ship in distress?"

He nodded. "She's broken on the rocks."

"She couldn't have seen the lights in the tower."

"She was blown onto the rocks. We did what we could."

"You are soaked." I rose and started to dress.

"There is nothing you can do," he said. "It is over. You'll see her when it's thoroughly light. It's a sorry sight."

I did see her—poor sad vessel that had once been so proud. I could not stop myself looking at her, and I thought of my father who had gone off on an expedition to the East Indies. Fennimore had gone with another ship, and Carlos was captaining another. This could happen to any of them. It was terrible to contemplate the hazards of the sea.

As I stood by the window, Colum came beside me and put an arm about me.

"Do not go out today," he said.

"Why not?"

"Why must you always question?" he demanded with a touch of irritation. "Why cannot you obey me like a good wife?"

"But why should I not go out?"

"The ground is slippery. I'd never forgive you if aught happened to the child."

That afternoon Colum went away for a day or two. I watched him go, and then because the sun was shining and the sea was calm—only a slightly muddy color to suggest last night's trouble—I felt the urge to go out was irresistible.

I would walk with care, but I must go out into the sunshine. I would not take the cliff path which could be treacherous, but I would just walk in the precincts of the castle.

Thus I came to the cobbled courtyard before Ysella's Tower. I looked up, remembering the story and asking myself how it was possible for a man to keep two women in the same dwelling and one not know the other was there. "Preposterous!" I said aloud. But if they were meek women who obeyed without question the husband they shared, it might have been managed. No, I could not believe it. Although with the forceful Casvellyns perhaps anything was possible. Colum would like me to be as docile as Ysella and Nonna must have been.

Then I noticed the sand among the cobbles. There was a good deal of it. I wondered idly how it could have got there. Could it have been blown up in the storm? Impossible. It would have to come right over the top of the tower to get there. The only answer was that people who had been on the beach had been walking there. Strangely enough I had been here the day before and not noticed it.

It was there on the stone step also, close to the iron-studded door, so whoever had brought it in had stood on that stone step.

As I stood there, I saw a glittering object and stooping

to pick it up I saw that it was an amulet. It glittered like gold.

I examined it. It was oval in shape, about an inch wide and two inches long. It was beautifully engraved, and what was depicted fascinated me. It was the figure of a beautiful youth about whose head was a halo, and at his feet lay a horned goat; one of the youth's feet was resting on the goat as though he had vanquished it. There was a name engraved on it in very small letters so that I could scarcely read it: I took it to my room and examined it, and at last I made out the name to be VALDEZ. So it was Spanish. Someone must have dropped it. Someone who had been on the shore and brought the sand up on his boots.

I put the amulet in the drawer.

Colum returned two days later. I saw him riding toward the castle with the men and the packhorses. They were unladen.

I went to the kitchen and ordered that the joints should be set on the spits immediately and that one of his favorite pies should be made without delay—squab perhaps as there was plenty of bacon and mutton and Colum had the Cornishman's love of pastry.

We dined alone in the little room where we had our first meal together. Colum always wanted us to be there alone on occasions like this. It showed an unsuspected sentimentality.

I put on the diamond chain with the ruby locket, and it was a very happy evening. It was when I was putting the chain and locket away that I opened the locket and, looking at the space for a miniature inside it, decided that I should like to have a picture of my son there, after the custom.

I smiled thinking of suggesting this to Colum and that he might be a little disappointed because I did not choose to have his picture. But would he ever allow himself to be painted? Then of course I might have other children, and I should want pictures of them all. While I was thus idly thinking, I was stroking the edge of the locket and to my amazement the layer in which was space for a picture sprang up and I was looking into a woman's face. She was beautiful with clouds of dark hair, an olive skin and languorous dark eyes. So cleverly had it been painted that in spite of the fact that it was so small, all this was apparent.

How strange that an unknown woman's face should be depicted in a locket which was given to me by my husband.

It could only mean that the locket had belonged to some-one else before me.

Colum came into the room while I sat there holding it in my hand.

"Look at this, Colum," I said, and gave it to him.

He took it and looked down at the woman's face.

I could see that he was taken aback.

"This is very strange," he said.

"Clearly it once belonged to someone else. Where did you get it?"

I saw that for the moment he was nonplussed. Then he recovered himself.

"It could not have been the one I wished made for you. The goldsmith has lied to me. People dispose of their valuables and articles of gold, silver and precious stones are sold as new, for how could one be sure whether such articles had been freshly wrought or not?"

"So the goldsmith sold you the locket as new."

"And," said Colum, "it was not. I must take the fellow to task. How do you feel about it now? Can you wear some-thing that was not made especially for you?"

I said, "I don't want to part with the locket. Perhaps someday I might meet this mysterious lady. It is exquisitely done. The painter must have been a man of talent."

"Give it to me," said Colum. "The miniature shall be removed. You can put in something of your own family. I shall have your initials engraved on it. That goldsmith must do this, since he has sold me a secondhand article for a new one."

"Later on," I said. "I'll keep it as it is. Perhaps I could have pictures of my babies in it. That reminds me." I opened a drawer and took out the amulet. "I found this, Colum," I told him.

He frowned and almost snatched it from me.

"Where?"

"In the courtyard."

He examined it in silence, and I wondered whether he was as interested in the article or just trying to control his annoyance.

"Which courtyard?" he snapped.

"The one before Ysella."

"I told you not to go there."

"It was perfectly safe, and I must walk somewhere since I can't ride. What is it? I thought it looked like an amulet."

"It *is* an amulet. I'd say this belonged to a Catharist. I have seen them before."

"What sort of people are they?"

"It is a sect that has been in existence for many years and has its roots in pre-Christian times. These people, though, profess to believe in two gods, the good one and the evil one."

"As Christians do."

"It is so. But the general belief is that these people serve the devil. They profess they do not, and this is the kind of amulet they carry with them to prove it. But they meet at midnight in what are called covens, and they worship the horned goat. This shows the good triumphant. I have seen this kind of thing before."

"I wonder whose it is. Do you think we have one of the Catharists in the castle?"

"I will discover," he said, holding out his hand for it.

"It is beautifully engraved," I pointed out. "See, there is a name on it. Valdez. That's Spanish, is it not?"

"By God, so it is. Who could have come by it?"

"I like it," I said. "It conveys the idea of virtue prevailing over evil."

"I must find who owns it."

He put it into his pocket.

"Let me know when you do find the owner," I said. "I should like to know who would have such a thing."

I sensed he was faintly disturbed.

Later that afternoon I went down to the shore. It was warm, and there was a faint mist in the air. I could see the sorry sight of a vessel caught on the rocks, toppling drunkenly as the waves washed over her. I thought of the people who had confidently set out from some place on their way to a destination which they had never reached and wondered how many had perished in the storm.

Parts of the vessel still floated on the water, useless pieces of wood—the remains of what had once been a stalwart ship—and again I thought of my father sailing on the treacherous waters which could be so calm and smiling and in a brief hour so cruel. All people who went to sea did so at their own risk, of course. They all knew that they needed good fortune as well as skill to come safely to land. All his life my father had been a sailor, and he had come safely through. Men such as he was thought themselves invincible. Even the sea could not tame them.

A piece of wood was being brought in by the tide; in it

came and was carried back, in and back, each time a little nearer. I watched it, feeling a great desire to hold it in my hands.

Nearer and farther, tossed hither and thither on the waves. Now a big one brought it right to my feet.

I picked it up and saw that it had letters on it. They were, "San Pedro."

So the ship out there was a Spaniard. A thought flashed into my head then—the amulet which I had found in the courtyard was also Spanish.

There seemed some strange significance in this, but I was not sure what.

My time was fast approaching, and my mother had come with Damask to stay with us. She also brought Edwina and her little boy with her, for it was almost Christmas. My father was on the high seas; so were Carlos and Jacko, who was now married to a girl from Plymouth.

They had not returned from the East Indies, and my mother told me that much would depend on the success of that first enterprise. I was always happy to have her with me. Edwina I could see was anxious; my mother seemed to have a placid belief in my father's survival through all conflicts.

She did tell me during her stay that Fennimore's wife had that September given birth to a son, who was named after his father.

My mother and Edwina decorated the castle hall. I was too cumbersome, my confinement being hourly expected.

And on Christmas Day of that year 1590 my child was born.

This time I had a daughter. I think Colum was a little disappointed, for he would have preferred another son, but it was only a fleeting displeasure. I was twenty years old and already the mother of two healthy children.

My mother was delighted with the child.

"Daughters can be such a comfort," she told me and kissed me.

Damask loved the baby and in fact, when my mother went back to Lyon Court, wanted to stay with us. However, that was not possible, and they left after the New Year.

For some time I was absorbed in my children. Connell was a lively child. I used to tell myself that this was just how Colum must have been at his age. He was going to be tall and strong, I was sure, and fond of his own way. Colum doted on him and was impatient for him to grow up, and sometimes it seemed that the boy was too, for to us in the castle he appeared to be far in advance of his years.

Mothers, I know, are supposed to love their children equally, but I loved my little daughter with a single-mindedness which I believed I could never feel toward any other child I might have. Perhaps it was because her father showed less interest in her than he did in the boy. Perhaps she seemed more vulnerable than Connell ever had.

He had appeared to be born with that self-confidence which he had inherited from his father. We called her Tamsyn, the feminine form of Thomas, the name of Colum's father, and I added Catherine to that for my mother.

Through the rest of the winter, the spring and the summer I felt cut off from the outside world, so completely absorbed was I in my nursery.

Jennet adored the baby, and she and I became more friendly than we had ever been, and I was glad my mother had sent her to me.

In the August of that year my mother came to stay with us. She was eager to see the children. Tamsyn was now nearly eight months old and showing a decided character of her own. She was going to be a spirited girl. She had lost that air of helplessness which she had had as a little baby and was beginning to show a lively interest in everything around her.

My mother's news was a little disturbing. My father with Fennimore and his father, Carlos and Jacko had all returned safely from the expedition to the East Indies. They had brought back rich goods and had started to trade with that part of the world. Alas, the journey had been a hazardous one, and not all the ships which had set out had returned. They had mustered a fleet of fifteen vessels. Some had foundered and gone down with all hands; two had been captured by pirates; three had been engaged in an action against foreign ships, the identity of which was unknown, but clearly they had been some sort of traders. Out of the fifteen only eight had come into harbor, but they had been richly laden with spices, ivory and gold. Therefore, the venture could be said to have been profitable.

"I thank God that our men returned safely," said my

mother, "but I pray for those poor souls who have not been so fortunate."

I nodded, and the memory of the *San Pedro* smashed on the rocks came back to me.

"I sometimes wish," I said, "that my father and the rest were not seafaring folk. How much better if they pursued a profession ashore."

"You are fortunate," replied my mother, "in that Colum is occupied with his lands. I am glad for you, Linnet, that he does not take these long and hazardous journeyings."

I nodded, and I thought of Colum, whi left mysteriously now and then and did not tell me where he had been.

My mother stayed until the end of September. I missed her very much after she had gone, and a certain restlessness came over me. It was in this mood that the certainty that a great deal went on in Castle Paling of which I was ignorant persisted.

It was October. The evenings were fast drawing in, and there was more than a touch of autumn in the air. Soon, I thought, the gales will be with us, and my thoughts again went to the *San Pedro* which I had never quite been able to get out of my mind.

I found myself in the courtyard facing Ysella Tower where I had discovered the amulet, and as I approached the iron-studded door, I was aware of something different about it.

Then I realized what it was. The door moved. It was swinging ajar on its hinges.

The impulse was irresistible. I pushed it open and went in.

The first thing that struck me was the smell. It was strange, yet familiar. The place was close, of course—little air came in. Then I realized what it was. It was the odor of sea water, seaweed and a sort of musty dampness.

The door opened onto the hall, which was very similar to that of the other towers. It was dark not only because little light came in, but because this hall was full of articles. There were great boxes and piled objects of all kinds strewn about the floor. My foot touched something which made me cry out. I thought it was a man lying there trussed up. It was a bale of cloth. I bent over it. The sea smell was strong. It was slightly damp.

I made my way across the hall, stepping carefully around the objects which littered the floor. There were goods of all descriptions. What on earth could it mean? I could not understand it. How long had these things been here, and whence had they come?

I went up the stairs. Along the gallery everywhere was permeated by this damp sea smell.

I pushed open a door and went in. I saw a wooden case. I went over to it and looked inside. Some trinkets lay in it. They looked like gold and silver. I lifted one. It was a long gold chain. The workmanship reminded me of the chain Colum had given me with the ruby-studded locket.

As I stood there, I heard a noise. I felt the hair on my head rise a little. I remembered suddenly that I was in Ysella's tower, the haunted tower, the tower where Ysella had lived all those years ago in secret.

Almost immediately I overcome my fear. Someone was in the hall below. The door had been opened. Someone must have come in to get something.

I started along the gallery and reached the staircase. There was no one in the hall. Hastily I descended the stairs. A sudden feeling of panic had come over me. It was because the hall seemed darker than it had when I had entered. I saw why. The great iron-studded door, which had been open and which I had left open, was closed.

I hurried to it. I could not open it. Then I realized that it was locked.

I pulled at the enormous handle, but of course it would not move. The answer was simple. Someone had come in here, had either been in here when I entered and not seen me, or gone out for a while, leaving the door unlocked, and then returned and locked the door.

Whatever had happened, the fact remained. I was locked in Ysella's Tower.

I banged on the door with my fists. Whoever had locked the door could not be far away. But I realized quickly that this could do little but bruise my hands. I shouted, but my voice could not penetrate those thick walls.

I was faced with the alarming fact that I was locked in Ysella's Tower.

What could I do? Was there possibly some other outlet? I must not panic. I must explore. There might well be another door. I knew the layout of the tower because it was similar to others. I wished I could escape that horrible musty odor which seemed to grow stronger every minute. I found my way into what in Ysella's day must have been the kitchens. There were the great oven, the fireplace and the roasting spits. There were a few caldrons. They were filled with objects. There were some coins in one. I looked at them; they were not English coins. In another pot there was some more jewelry.

I thought then: When Colum wishes to give a gift to his wife, he comes down here and selects it.

There was a door in a small passage close to the kitchens. I tried it; it was securely locked. There was no way out there.

I made my way back to the hall. The horrible realization came to me that it would soon be dark, but I consoled myself that I should be missed and they would come in search of me, but would they think of looking in Ysella's Tower?

I came into the hall, tried the door again, banged my fists against the stubborn wood and called at the top of my voice. Then I made my way up the stairs again. Perhaps I could find my way to the ramparts. If I could and made some sign up there, it might be possible that someone would see it.

The spiral staircases were like those in the other towers— the stairs narrow at one end and wide at the other, demanding care in mounting and descending, and there was a rope banister to help one up or down. They wound around and around so that I had the sudden fear that as I turned a bend, I might come face to face with some terrifying sight.

The tower was haunted, it was said, haunted by Nonna's ghost, because Nonna had discovered Ysella here, and soon afterward she had died.

She should not have been so curious, Colum had said lightly. And if I had not been so curious, *I* would not now be in this predicament.

I looked into several of the rooms with their long, narrow windows cut out of the thick walls. It was chilly, and the sea odor had permeated even up here.

The door onto the ramparts was not locked, I was delighted to see. I pushed it open and was in the fresh air. For a few seconds I could think of nothing but taking in great gulps of it. I looked through the battlements. There was Seaward Tower looming up before me. I leaned over and looked down. I shivered. Far below was the courtyard where I had found the amulet. I knew now that the amulet, had it not been dropped in the courtyard, would doubtless now be in the wooden box or one of the caldrons with the other trinkets.

I looked up at the sky. Clouds were being bustled across

it by a tetchy wind. I called out, "I'm here. In Ysella's Tower. Somebody come and get me out."

My voice was lost in the wind. There was in any case no one down there.

I took off my petticoat and waved it between the battlements. I was hoping someone would see it. There was no response.

I called again. Who could possibly hear? Gulls were circling overhead. They were coming inland, which was said to mean that the wind was rising and there could be a storm at sea. They made their melancholy cries as they circled overhead.

What am I going to do? I thought. They'll miss me. But will they think of looking in Ysella's Tower?

I shouted again. I waved my petticoat. I was beginning to get a little frightened because it was growing dark rapidly and I had an uneasy feeling that no one was coming back into Ysella's Tower and that no one could see me from the ramparts.

There was a chill in the air. I missed my petticoat. I thought: I can't stay up here until someone finds where I am. On the other hand, the thought of going back into the tower repelled me.

It was quickly growing dark. How stupid I had been to come so far inside. I should have stood at the door and looked about me, and then, when someone came along—as someone must have—I could have insisted that whoever it was accompanied me on my tour.

I had been foolish, and what could I do now?

I walked farther along the ramparts. Here the battlements were fairly low. I leaned over. It made me feel dizzy. Nonna had died after she had found Ysella. She should not have been so curious. It was as though the evil-looking faces carved out of stone up there on the battlements were laughing at me.

Suddenly I heard a shrill, piercing scream, and looking down, I saw one of the women servants running through the archway which led from Ysella's courtyard to another.

I shouted, but I was too late, for she had disappeared, and again my voice was carried away by the wind.

She must have seen me up here on the ramparts. She would think I was the ghost. But she would tell someone, and perhaps they would come. I waited expectantly.

But no one came. It was almost dark now. I could not spend the night up here. It was better to go into the castle.

On impulse I threw my petticoat over the ramparts. They would search for me and that would let them know that I had come here. They would open the door then and come and find me, for the garment would surely give them a clue to my whereabouts.

I watched it flutter to the ground. It was uncanny. It looked as though it were a woman falling down. What had Nonna felt when she discovered her husband had been unfaithful to her? Life was no longer good for her, and she had decided to take her life.

It was the fading light, it was the tension which I must necessarily feel in this situation which had made me fanciful, but it did seem as though that was a human being falling. There was a screech as it fell, but it was the gulls startled perhaps by what would seem to them a gigantic bird floating down. Several of them rose overhead, calling protestingly.

I stood there shivering.

Someone will find the petticoat soon and come for me, I promised myself.

I found my way down the spiral staircase, not so easy to manage in the gloom. I reached the gallery and went down to the hall.

It looked different now. There was very little light coming through the windows, which were few and so narrow. The tower was built for defense, and the lower windows were meant to supply the minimum light and air, for in a fortress the lower part was the most vulnerable.

I picked my way between bales of cloth that had been sodden and were drying out, garments, spices, goods which had been carried from one place to another—gold, silver, ivory; the kind of commodities in which my father and the Landors were dealing.

So much slipped into place. Colum going out on the nights of storm. His clothes soaked with rain and sea water. The Ysella Tower to be locked and intrusion into the courtyard discouraged. Jennet dismissed from the Seaward Tower on the nights when Colum and some of his men were going on a journey. The men who inhabited Seaward Tower who were not quite the same as the other servants. "They are fishermen, they catch our fish, and I am very fond of fish," he had said. They were men of the sea, those who inhabited the Seaward Tower. There were boats there; there were horses and donkeys, packhorses.

I felt sick. I did not know whether it was the smell of these sea-saturated goods or the knowledge which had come to me or the thought of Colum's anger if he ever knew that I had intruded into his tower. And he would know. Even now he would be looking for me. He would search for me, and they would find my petticoat in the courtyard. That would surely lead them to Ysella's Tower.

It was clear now. These goods which filled the tower had come from shipwrecked ships. On the night of a storm, when ships were unable to withstand the fury of the elements, when they broke up on our coast, Colum and his servants were there. They salvaged the goods and stored them in Ysella's Tower, and then Colum made bargains with men such as those he met in the Traveler's Rest.

And it was secret.

Was it against the law then to take goods from the sea? Was this why it must be done in secret? He had been angry when he had discovered my curiosity about the tower. He had told me the story in the hope that I would be afraid to go near it because it was said to be haunted.

When I found the amulet, he knew that it had fallen from some merchandise which had been brought into the tower. The locket he gave to me he knew to have been part of these goods. When he gave me a present of jewelry, and he had given me one or two, he came down here and selected it. Something which looked like new . . . or would have done if I had not discovered the secret spring and the name in it.

What was this business of his? It seemed that there was something callous about a man who could come by his wealth through the distress of others.

I shivered. Deep down in my heart I knew that there was something frightening about Colum. I knew that had I married Fennimore Landor, I should have lived a peaceful, happy life, my only anxiety would have been when he took his sea voyages, and that would have been for his safety, not for my own.

What a strange thought that was. But my mind felt so lucid now. It was as though a misty mirror had been wiped and I could now see clearly what was reflected.

Colum would be angry. What form would his anger take? If he raged against me, if he struck me—he never had, but there were times when I had thought he was about to—I think I should be more at ease than if he silently accepted what I had done.

He would give me some explanation, of course. But I did not need an explanation. I knew the answer. This was his profession. He owned much land, it was true, and he was said to be rich. But was he so because he sold jewels and the like which he took from sinking ships?

No wonder he was a little contemptuous of my father's plan and that of the Landors. Here was an easier way of bringing in merchandise than sailing the seas for it; here it was brought to his own shores.

It was growing darker. There was very little light coming into the hall. I could make out the shapes of the various objects, and I thought of people who had sailed with them. I could see it so clearly, the wind and the storm lashing their useless masts, the creaking of their vessels, the dying cries of the drowning and the cargo breaking free to be flung hither and thither on the frothing waters of the sea until it was picked up by the scavengers.

The scavengers! That was how I thought of them. I knew this much. I hated my husband's profession. And he must be ashamed of it, or why should he attempt to keep it a secret from me?

I looked about the hall. If I could but find some light, I thought, I would feel better. I hated the gloom of the place. It was eerie, ghostly.

I sat down by a bale of cloth and tried to shut out its musty odor.

"Oh, come, someone," I prayed. "Rescue me. Am I to spend the night here?"

They would miss me, of course. They would come to search for me. Perhaps already Jennet was telling Colum that I had not come to the nursery to put my children to bed, for that was a task I insisted on doing myself.

It was dark now. I sat very still listening. A strange scuttle on the stairs. It would be mice perhaps. Or rats. I shivered. Rats who had secreted themselves in some of the bales. They always left the sinking ship.

One imagines noises. That sounded like a step on the stairs. Could it be the ghost of Nonna? She had given way to her curiosity and died soon after. Died because of it. Nonna had been murdered. She was the unwanted wife.

The wind was rising. How clearly I could hear the sound of the sea. It was washing now about the foundations of the castle; it was completely covering the Devil's Teeth. Somewhere out to sea a ship might be in distress. And Colum would be watching so that he and his men might go out and profit from it.

I hated this. Yet my father had been a pirate. He had

thought it right to rob the Spanish galleons that crossed his path. How many times had he sailed home with the hold of his ship crammed with treasure—filched from the Spaniards.

How dark it was. How the wind buffeted the great walls of the castle. And then the lull and the silence which was more frightening than the noise of the wind. The sudden noise from above. What was it—some rat or mouse . . . or the footfall of one who was dead and could not rest?

I am fanciful, I know it. I do imagine things. I kept staring into the gloom, expecting at any moment to see the ghostly figure on the stairs. Nonna walking slowly, coming toward me, a terrible coldness enveloping me as I am close to the dead and Nonna whispering, "I warn you. I have come back to warn you."

It was imagination. There was nothing . . . only the dark hall with the shapes I could see as my eyes had grown accustomed to the gloom.

What time is it? I wondered. How long had I been here? Long enough for them to miss me.

I am going to spend the night in Ysella's Tower, I thought. I remembered how many times I had wished to look inside. Well, now I had, and here I was, a prisoner.

I was trembling. I was certain I was not alone in the tower. The thought sent a shiver down my spine. What had Nonna felt when she knew that her husband had a mistress whom he kept in this tower? I could picture her bewildered grief. And then she had died. Had she died of her own will, or was she helped to her death?

I wondered how long I had been in the tower. It must be two hours. It had been about three o'clock when I came. Now it must be five. They would have missed me by now. I was sure of it.

If only I had a light. If only I could find a candle. I would set it in one of the windows. What of the serving girl who had seen me on the ramparts? Had she not gone back to her fellow servants and told them what she had seen? They would laugh at her. How many times had one of the servants sworn she had seen the ghost of Ysella's Tower?

Perhaps I should go up to the ramparts. Someone might come into the courtyard. If I shouted, someone might hear me in time.

I stood up. The fearsome eeriness wrapped itself about me. I almost fell over a bale which I had not noticed. Its sea-damp odor swept up as I touched it.

My footsteps echoed hollowly on the stone flags as I groped my way to the gallery and found the spiral staircase. I could feel the rope and I grasped it.

I really felt terror going up that staircase. I was overcome by an awful presentiment that something malignant was waiting for me at the turn. Still I went on. I had to get out of this place, and I had more chance from the ramparts. If I shouted, there was a faint chance that someone might hear me, for they would surely begin to look for me when they found me missing.

I must surely be nearly at the top of the staircase. I seemed to have come a long way. I touched the wall—it was cold and clammy. I turned. The staircase was less curved than it had been. Gingerly I felt my way, taking care not to lift one foot from the stone before I was sure the other was firm.

I could feel the cold air from the ramparts, and then suddenly my heart leaped in terror, for a flash of light illuminated the scene and came to rest on the hideous face of a gargoyle carved in the stone. He leered at me in the sudden light, and I gave a scream as I fell backward.

I could not have fallen far, though, because the turn of the staircase stopped that. I lay inert on the stone staircase, and I felt consciousness slipping away from me.

Noise everywhere—voices. I was lifted in a pair of strong arms.

"Colum," I said.

He said, "It's all right. You're safe."

I knew I was in Ysella's Tower because of the smell. It was everywhere. It was light now because there were several men, and they all carried lanterns.

Colum brought me down the staircase to the hall. It looked different now with so many lanterns to light it up.

He said, "I'll carry my wife. She cannot walk, I think. She has hurt her ankle."

Two of the men went ahead, their lanterns lighting our way. I was aware then of the darting pain in my ankle.

I was taken up to our room, and Jennet was sent up to me. She took off my clothes and wrapped me in a warm gown. Then she drew the curtains about my bed. Some of the women came up—those who were specially skilled with herbs and such like. One of them examined my foot and put a paste of herbs on it and wrapped it up tightly.

I must not stand on it, I was told.

So I lay there, thinking of Ysella's Tower, and I went on living those moments as I had mounted the stairs. Then I was given a posset to make me sleep, and I did.

I did not see Colum the next morning. I remained in my bed, for it was painful to walk, and it was dusk when Colum came into our bedchamber. I still lay on my bed.

He drew the curtains back and looked at me lying there.

"Now I wish to know what you were doing in Ysella's Tower," he said.

"I found the door open and looked in."

He leaned over me. His eyes were narrowed. He looked cruel. "You have been told not to go there."

"The door was open. I saw no harm in looking in."

"Yes," he said, "that has been taken care of."

"What?" I asked.

"He who left open the door has been punished."

"Punished. How?"

"You ask too many questions."

"It was my fault for going in."

"It was indeed," he said. "You know you had no right."

"I saw no harm," I retorted. "I wanted to know what was in there."

"If I had wanted you to know, would I not have told you?"

"If it had been something of little importance, you would have told me. As you did not, I knew it was significant."

"I expect you to obey me. Has it ever occurred to you what could happen if you angered me?"

"You could kill me, I suppose, as your ancestor killed his wife Nonna."

There was a silence in the room. He did not move; he stood like a stone statue, his arms folded.

Then he said slowly, "Do not provoke me. You have yet to learn that I can be an angry man."

"I know it well. I have seen something of your rages."

"You have seen nothing yet."

I had a feeling then that I did not know him. He was a stranger to me, though he was the father of my children. I felt that he had worn a mask and that it was slowly slipping from his face.

I was not afraid of him, oddly enough. I knew that his rage could be terrible; I had lost sight of the man who had stormed into the inn, who had taken me to his castle. I had forgotten that man in the gratified husband who was so delighted with his son. But he was still there.

I thought: He is capable of killing me if I angered him or if he wanted to be rid of me.

It was almost as though the ghost of Nonna had lingered with me, warning me to take care.

Yet I felt strangely reckless. I was going to confront him with my discovery. I was not going to pretend.

He stood there in that pose as though he kept his arms folded to stop their seizing me, and whether they would have caressed me or his fingers would have gripped my throat and he strangle the life out of me, I could not be sure.

What I realized in that moment was that I knew little of this man.

He said, "You should not have been in the courtyard. You should not have entered the tower. You could have stayed there for days and we not discover you. But for the fact that one of the servants was hysterical because she had seen a ghost on the ramparts and we found your petticoat there, we might not have found you. When I knew you were missing, I sent men out looking for you. You caused me great alarm."

"I am sorry to have done that."

"So should you be. Never behave in this way again or you will be sorry."

"You sound . . . murderous. I believe you would kill me."

"It is right that you should fear me."

"I did not say I feared you. I said I thought you capable of killing me. You are hating me now because I have discovered the nature of your business."

"What have you discovered?"

"That in the tower there are goods salvaged from the sea."

"And why not?"

"You could tell me why you wish to keep them so secret."

"Is it not better for me to take them than to let the sea have them?"

"They are cargoes of wrecked vessels. Do they belong to you?"

"Salvage belongs to those who bring it in."

"Surely sometimes there are survivors. What then?"

"If there were, then the goods would doubtless be theirs, but if there are none, we take the salvage from the sea."

"But why did you not wish me to know?"

"I do not intend to answer your questions. It is you who shall answer mine. Have you spoken of this to anyone?"

"How could I? I have seen no one except Jennet."

He leaned forward suddenly and gripped my wrist.

"You will speak of it to no one. Do you hear me?"

"I hear you perfectly well."

"What happens in my castle is my affair. Remember that. No one else's."

I said, "I never want to wear the ruby locket again."

He said, "You will wear it."

"It belonged to someone . . . someone drowned in a ship. Did you take it from her corpse?"

"Be silent, you foolish woman. Be glad that you have a husband who cherishes you enough to bestow gifts on you."

"I don't want those which have been snatched from the dead."

He turned away and went to my trinket box. When he came back, the chain with the ruby locket was in his hand.

"Put it on," he said.

"I prefer not to."

"You will put it on," he told me.

I refused to take it.

With a savage gesture he fastened it about my neck. I felt it cold against my skin.

I shut my eyes and lay there. I felt helpless to resist him, although my whole body cried out for me to do so.

He threw himself down beside me.

He caressed my neck and played idly with the chain.

He said, "You please me now as you ever did. I have never been so long delighted with a woman. You are fortunate, wife. We have our children, and they please me. I want more sons, though. We'll have them. And there is something else we'll have. You will do as I say and be happy to. You will say I have no will but his. And whatever he does, still for me it will be right. Say it."

"Nay," I said. "You may put a chain I do not want about my neck; you may do to me what you did on the night you drugged my wine. But you cannot change my feelings. If I do not like what you do, even if I do not say so, I still dislike it, and nothing will change that."

He laughed aloud.

"You've got spirit. I grant you that. That's good, for I want to see spirit in my sons. What should it be like if they inherited the mealymouthed fear of a silly woman? Nay, you please me." He had my ear between his teeth suddenly, and he bit it savagely. "But know this," he went on, "I will do as I will, and you will not spy on me. You

will talk of nothing you see here. Is that understood? You
will close your eyes if you are squeamish. You will accept
what you see here, and you will never whisper a word of
it to anyone. Do you understand?"

"I understand what you say."

"And you understand that you will be expected to obey."

"And if I did not?"

"Then you would let forth the full force of my wrath,
and that can be terrible. Remember it."

Fear came over me then. I felt as though I had been
deceiving myself, and when he made love to me, I knew
there was no tenderness; there was only the will to force
me to his.

The coldness of the dead woman's trinket seemed to cut
into my flesh. I kept seeing the dark, beautiful eyes in the
miniature. I wondered: Did he see them in reality? Did
he take the necklace from her while she still lived?

I began to wish that I had never ventured into Ysella's
Tower. I had been more at ease in my ignorance. Yet something told me that if there was evil, it was better to be
aware of it. Evil! Was I applying that word to my life with
my husband?

I knew that life had changed. I was now aware and alert,
waiting for something . . . I was not sure what.

The Woman from the Sea

I tried not to think too much about what was happening during those nights when Colum and his servants were out on their scavenging expeditions. They almost always took place during nights of storm, and I would lie frozen in my bed waiting for Colum to come in. I could picture it all so clearly: the ship in distress; the goods floating on the water; the men scrambling aboard the sinking vessel. And what of the survivors? Why were they always so docile?

In those days I was guilty of closing my eyes. I realize now that there was so much I did not want to know. I was not exactly in love with Colum, but he was important to me. There was an immense physical satisfaction in our relationship for him, and for me as well, and that was something which we both wished to preserve. I was fascinated by him, nonetheless so because he was something of a figure of mystery. He was a strong man, and I believe that for some women—such as myself and my mother—power is the essence of physical attraction. When I was with Colum, I could not help being aware of his strength and his power to subdue everything and everyone around him. I found a thrill in standing out against that power and in his knowledge that I did. I enjoyed his efforts to subdue me which were triumphant for him because he could tell himself he had imposed his will on me, but I knew that whatever he did to me or insisted I do, I would always preserve a part of my freedom to think as I wished.

Secretly he was aware of this. It balked him and irked him, while it fascinated him.

So the months passed. My mother visited us now and then, but I told her nothing of what I had discovered in Ysella's Tower.

She would talk a great deal about how the business my father and the Landors were building up was progressing. There were disasters, but it was growing, and they must not expect to succeed completely at the beginning. Such an endeavor needed years of planning and work.

Once she said, "I wish the Landors were not so averse to meeting you and Colum. They would like to see you, of course, but would not see your husband."

"Do they still blame Colum for the death of their daughter?"

"I have tried to explain that it was a natural happening, but they won't have it."

"What of Fennimore?"

"He lives at Trystan Priory with his wife when he is not at sea. I believe the little boy is very well."

"Surely their grandson will make up to his parents for the loss of their daughter."

"He does, I am sure, but it is natural that they go on brooding for her." My mother changed the subject. "So many people believed that we had beaten the Spaniards off the sea with the defeat of the Armada. It was not so. They still have great strongholds in America, and Sir Walter Raleigh and the Earl of Cumberland backed by the City of London are amassing a fleet of men of war to attack the settlements in America."

"This will mean more war."

"We will always be at war with the Spanish, your father says. They are scattered all over the world. They have possessions everywhere."

"We defeated the Great Armada though, Mother."

"Yes, praise be. I would to God they could take their ships out for trading only."

"Dear Mother, how wonderful if everyone felt the same! People don't, though."

She shivered. "When I think of the men of our family— your father, Carlos, Jacko and Penn—every one of them a seaman. You should be thankful, Linnet, that your husband does not go off on those long voyages when you cannot know what is happening to him and whether he will come back."

I was silent, thinking of stormy nights when Colum was about his business. I wished that I could have confided in my mother, but I resisted the temptation to do so.

She went back to Lyon Court in September and it was on the last night of October, the thirty-first and what we called Halloween, that the woman from the sea came into my life.

That was a night which was to influence my whole life. There was always a certain amount of excitement at Halloween. In Cornwall the weather was usually mild and damp at that time of the year. The spiders' webs seemed to be festooned over every bush, and little globes of moisture clung to them like glittering jewels. In the lanes there were carpets of leaves, all shades of brown from gold to russet, and the trees lifted their denuded branches to the sky to form a delicate lacy design, making them as beautiful as when they were in leaf.

Jennet chattered a great deal about the excitement in the servants' hall. Halloween was the night when witches rode on their broomsticks to attend the Sabbat only they knew where, and woe betide any who walked out at midnight and strayed into their coven.

It had happened, said Jennet, to one of the Seaward Tower women years ago. She had never been seen again in the form by which they knew her, but there was a black cat who haunted the place, looking for someone who would sell her soul to the devil in exchange for certain favors.

"So, mistress, don't 'ee go out on Halloween."

"I'm not likely to," I replied.

" 'Twill be a thorough stormy night, I do believe," prophesied Jennet with a shiver, "but witches take no heed of weather."

When it was dark, a fire was lighted on a hillock outside the castle precincts; I wrapped my cloak around me and took the children to see it, but I would not let them go near it, for the wind was rising fast and the sparks could prove dangerous. Connell, now three years old, was an adventurous boy, and I took Jennet with me to help me look after them lest they should be too bold.

The servants danced around the fire, and when it died

down, they picked up the ashes which they would treasure.

"They'll bring luck," said Jennet. "Protection against the evil eye. I'll get you some, Master Connell, and you too, Mistress Tamsyn."

The children watched round-eyed, and Connell asked questions about witches. I wouldn't let Jennet answer them for fear she instill some terror in them. I told them there were good witches who cured people who were sick.

"I want to see a wicked witch," declared Connell.

It was difficult to get them to sleep that night. The wind was rising and making ominous whistling noises throughout the castle.

I felt uneasy because a storm was brewing. It was one of those nights when Colum was out, and I knew that that meant there was a ship in distress.

This had happened before. I lay in bed experiencing a dreadful unrest. It was near midnight, and I knew that I could not sleep. I thought of the people on the sinking ship and of Colum and his men rowing out to pick up the salvage.

Why were there never any survivors?

I felt that I was propelled by an irresistible impulse. I could not lie there waiting, letting my imagination conjure up a scene. I must know what was happening. I got out of bed and put on a cloak with a hood and heavy boots. I went out of the castle.

The wind caught at me, buffeting me. Walking close to the castle walls, I came out to the path. It was difficult to stand up, and I almost crawled down to the shore. In the lee of the castle there was a little shelter. I saw dark figures running hither and thither. I stood as close to the water's edge as I dared go. The waves rose like giant monsters and came thundering onto the sand. I heard Colum's voice shouting, "We can't go out yet. Wait a while."

There was a ship out there, I knew. Caught, held fast on the Devil's Teeth. The wind caught my hood and threw it back; my hair flapped about my head. The wind and rain lashed at my skirts. It blinded me.

As I cowered there, a figure loomed up before me.

"Good God," cried Colum, "what are you doing here?"

"There's a ship out there," I cried. "Can't we do something?"

"Do what?" shouted Colum. "In a sea like this. What in God's name! Go back. Go back at once."

He took me by the shoulders. I could not see him very

clearly, but from what I could I thought he looked satanic. "Don't dare come out again. Go back. By God, do as I tell you."

"I want to help. . . ."

"Go back. That's the way to help." He pushed me from him, and I stumbled toward the castle.

I knew there was nothing I could do by remaining there. If I could have done something to help those people on the ship I could not see but knew to be there, I would have defied him. But there was nothing.

I made my way to the shelter of the castle and leaned against the wall. The sharp stone cut into my hand. I was shivering with the cold, for my clothes were saturated with rain and sea water from those gigantic waves.

And as I stood there, I saw the men with their donkeys; they were coming toward us, and each man was carrying a lantern. They did not see me standing there. They walked around the path to the Seaward Tower.

I went into the castle. I took off my wet clothes and rubbed myself dry. I felt sick with horror. Something told me that I did not know everything of what happened on nights like this.

I wrapped a cloak about me and went to the window. I could see nothing but the darkness. I could hear nothing but the groaning and shrieking of the wind and the sound of the waves pounding against the rocks in their fury.

I knew that down there the little boats would be going back and forth. They would be bringing what they could find from the vessel. They would carry it stealthily into Ysella's Tower, and in a few days Colum would go away and find a buyer for what he had to sell. Then a little later Jennet would be told she was not to go to the Seaward Tower to her lover because he had other work to do than entertain his mistress.

And out there in this fierce, malignant sea, men would be dying, and there would be no one to save them. It was not men's lives they were interested in—it was the ship's cargo—and if they saved lives what complications that might bring. What if the saved ones demanded to keep what was salvaged from their ships? So it was to the interest of Colum and his men that all perished.

It was this that I could not forget.

Soon after dawn I dressed myself and again went down to the shore. It was there that I found her. She was lying in the shallow water; her long dark hair floating about her.

Her face was pallid, and I thought she was dead.

I waded out and caught her arm. When the wave had subsided, I dragged her nearer to the shore. The next wave came and nearly carried me out with her, for the sea had not yet calmed down, and the waves were still strong. But I managed to drag her free of them.

She was lying on the sand, and I knelt beside her.

She is dead, I thought. Poor woman.

I took her wrist and felt a pulse fluttering. Then to my horrified amazement I realized that she was heavily pregnant.

My father had taught me something of how to revive the drowning. I turned the woman's body so that she was lying face downward, her head turned to one side. I knelt and placed my hands on her back, and keeping my arms rigid, I pressed with the weight of my body. Thus I drove the water out of her lungs and, I believed, saved her life.

I waited beside her. I rubbed her hands and wrapped her in my cloak. I watched her lest she should need further attention and in due course was rewarded, for I could see that she was breathing more naturally.

What I wanted now was to get her into the castle. I wanted to put her to bed and make sure that she had the care she so urgently needed.

I left her lying on the shore and went back to the castle. I called several of the servants. I told them what I had discovered, and we took a mule down to the shore, and dazed and shocked as the woman was, we managed to get her onto the animal and bring her to the castle courtyard. There I ordered several of the men to carry her to a bed.

They took her into the Red Room, wrapped in my cloak as she was, and laid her on the four-poster bed. I had not wished her to go to that room, but they had put her there before I could prevent them, and it seemed unwise to move her again.

She lay very still, and I said to Jennet, "We must not disturb her yet, but bring clean clothes from my bedchamber. Her condition is dangerous, for she is pregnant."

"My dear life," cried Jennet. "The poor soul will surely lose her baby."

"We shall try to see that she does not," I replied.

I sent one of the men to bring the physician. He lived five miles away, but he would come at once if there was a call from the castle. Then I ordered that hot soup should be brought, and between us Jennet and I undressed the woman.

I was surprised that she was younger than I had thought. I guessed her to be my age or perhaps a year or so older. Her skin was smooth; her limbs most beautifully formed, and in spite of her pregnancy, it was possible to see that she was an exceptionally beautiful woman. She was only half-conscious, but she seemed grateful for what we were doing. Her hands were long and slender; they had never worked, that much was clear. There was a patrician air about her face, an unearthly beauty, but perhaps that was because she was almost more dead than alive. Her hair was magnificent—thick, silky and black with that almost bluish tinge which is so rarely seen in England and, when it is, usually means foreign blood. Her lashes were as black as her hair, and their blackness was accentuated by the pallor of her skin.

"She were on that ship," whispered Jennet.

"She must have been," I answered. "There is no other reason why she should be lying in the sea on such a night."

Jennet's eyes were dazed with memory. "The sea can be terrible," she said.

"We will nurse her to health," I insisted.

It was amazing how quickly she recovered. I was able to feed her with the hot soup, and when she was lying in clean clothes in the warm bed, the faintest color came into her face. It was as though a light had been placed behind the alabaster. Her skin glowed. I thought: I don't think I ever saw such a beautiful woman.

I had to face Colum. I knew he would be angry. What would he have done if he had found the woman? Left her to the mercy of the sea, I knew, which would have soon finished her.

I went into our bedchamber and came face to face with him.

"So you have brought a woman in?" he said.

"She was half drowned. I am nursing her. She is to have a child."

"Why did you bring her into the castle?"

"She would have quickly died had I left her there."

He gripped my wrist. "What concern is that of yours?"

"If I see someone dying, I would do everything I could to help that man or woman."

"So you bring her into my castle."

"It is my home."

"Forget not that you live here through my clemency."

"And forget not," I said, "that the dowry my father gave

me has been very useful in maintaining the castle."

He narrowed his eyes. I knew that he was passionately interested in wealth. It must be for this reason that he had become a scavenger; he had married me not only because he had desired me but because I brought a good dowry with me—as good as any girl of the neighborhood would bring him . . . doubtless as good as that which came with Melanie Landor. My mother had prevailed on my father to endow me well. It was important, I being in the condition I was, that I should marry the man who had put me in it.

"You are becoming a shrew," he said.

"And I am beginning to learn something of you."

"Learn this then," he said. "It is I who will decide who shall be a guest in my home."

"What do you propose to do, turn this woman out? She is sick, or will be if she is not cared for. What would become of her?"

"Is that my affair?"

"Perhaps it should be as you will help yourself to the merchandise which was being carried by the ship in which she traveled."

"What should I do? Let the sea swallow them?"

"Perhaps they should be salvaged and returned to their owners."

That brought out a peal of harsh laughter. "I can see my clever wife should indeed be managing my affairs." The laughter died out suddenly; his mouth was grim. "On the contrary, I can see I shall have to teach her to manage her own. And that is that she interferes not with what she sees and that if she attempts to, she will soon be wishing that she had never done so."

"What will you do then? Strip me naked to the waist and tie me to the whipping post as though I were a servant who had misbehaved? Will you wield the whip, or is that too menial a task for your noble hands?"

He took a step toward me and lifted his hand. He had done it before, and as before, the blow did not come.

"Take care," he said. "You would find that if I were truly angry with you, my wrath would be terrible."

"I will not be your puppet. I would rather be dead."

He laughed. There was just a hint of tenderness in his face. He seized me and held me tightly against him. "You are my wife," he said. "You gave me the best son in the world. I am not displeased with you. But know this. I will not be crossed. My will is law. You have my favor. No woman ever pleased me for so long as you do. Let us keep it so."

"And what of this woman from the sea? Will you turn her away?"

He was thoughtful for a moment. I could see he was thinking deeply. He was angry because there had been a survivor from the ship and that I had brought her into the castle and may well have preserved her life. He would have preferred her to die, so that there were no witnesses. He could send her away, but what if she lived to tell the tale?

"Not yet," he said. "Let her stay awhile."

"She is with child."

He was silent for a few seconds; then he said, "When is the child due?"

"It is difficult to say. I should think the birth may be some two months away."

He remained thoughtful, and then he said, "She may stay at least until the child is born. Have you spoken to her?"

"She is in no condition to speak. She looks . . . foreign."

"A Spaniard," he said, his lips curling.

"It was a Spanish ship?"

He did not answer that.

"Keep her for a while," he said. "There is no need to decide yet."

"I am sure she is of noble birth."

"Then we will make her work in the kitchens to forget that."

I thought: At least he will not turn her out until her child is born. Poor woman, where would she go then? There were dismal tales of Spanish sailors who had been wrecked on our coasts at the time of the Armada, but they were men. The idea of a woman turned out in an alien land to beg her bread with a small child to care for made me sick with horror.

He said, "You say she has a foreign look. Where is she?"

"In the Red Room."

"My first wife's room. The one you think is haunted. Well, perhaps the ghost will drive our visitor away. I'll look at her. Come with me."

Together we went into the Red Room. He threw open the door and walked to the bed.

She lay there, looking as though she had been carved out of alabaster. Her hair now dry lay about her shoulders. The perfect symmetry of her features was more than ever apparent. Her heavy lashes lay against her skin. I wished that she would open her eyes. I was sure that if she did, the effect would be dazzling.

Colum stood staring at her.

"By God," he said, "what a beautiful woman."

In a few days she was able to get up. It was astonishing how a woman in her condition could have come through such an ordeal. I sent for the midwife who had attended me at the birth of my children and asked her to examine our patient. The verdict was that she was in a good condition and that her ordeal appeared to have had no ill consequences for the child.

She spoke a little halting English. She was Spanish, as I had thought, a fact which would not help her, for the hatred of that race persisted in our country although we had beaten the Armada.

She could tell us little. When I asked questions, she shook her head. She could not remember what had happened. She knew that she had been in a ship. She did not know why. She could remember nothing but that she had found herself in Castle Paling.

I asked her what her name was, but she could not remember that either.

During the first week in November when the sea was as calm as a lake, I made one of the men row me out to the Devil's Teeth. It was perfectly safe, for those men knew every inch of that stretch of sea; they knew exactly where the treacherous rocks lay hidden beneath the water.

I saw the ship caught there on the rocks, a pitiful sight. She was broken in half; the sharp rocks must have been driven right through her, and I read on her side the words "Santa Maria."

I wondered why that woman had been on the ship. She must have been traveling with her husband; perhaps he was the captain of the vessel. How strange it was that she could remember nothing. She would in time. Such a shock as she had experienced could rob a woman of her memory. Perhaps, poor soul, it was as well that she could not remember; perhaps it would stop her grieving too much until she recovered a little.

Her child was due toward the end of December, the midwife told me. I think that perhaps the fact that she was pregnant was the reason for her serenity. I imagined that the great importance to her was the welfare of her child, and I determined to make her as comfortable as I could, for I felt a great responsibility toward her. There was one picture which kept coming into my mind and which I could not dismiss. It was that of the men returning to the Seaward Tower with their donkeys and lanterns. Where had they been? I had an idea, but I would not face it. I could not bear to because I thought that if I did, I could not stay here.

The woman had to have a name, and because the name of the ship was *Santa Maria*, I called her Maria. I asked if she would mind if I called her by that name.

"Maria," she said slowly and shook her head. I did not know whether she meant we could call her by that name, but we did. And very soon she was known throughout the household as Maria.

By December it was clear that the birth of her child was imminent. With Father again at sea, my mother came to spend the Christmas with us, and Edwina and Romilly accompanied her.

I had insisted that the midwife stay at the castle, for I still feared that Maria's adventure when she was so advanced in pregnancy might have had some effect which was not apparent. I was fanatically anxious that nothing should go wrong. It was not that I had any great affection for Maria. She was not an easy person to know. Her aloofness might have been due to her ignorance of our language, but it was certainly there. She accepted our concern and help as though it were her right, and she never seemed overgrateful for it. I felt, however, that her child must be born and live. The uneasy thoughts which had come into my mind on the night when the *Santa Maria* had sunk persisted, and I could not dismiss them.

When my mother was introduced to Maria, she was clearly surprised. I had mentioned her in a letter but only briefly, and I had discovered that everyone who met Maria was astonished by her. It was something more than mere beauty, but I could not yet quite understand what.

"What a beautiful woman," said my mother when we were alone. "So she is the lady of the shipwreck. One thing is certain. She is of high birth, patrician to the fingertips. Where will she go when the child is born?"

"I don't know. She cannot remember whence she came. Perhaps after the child is born, her memory may return."

"Then she will wish to go to her family, I doubt not."

"If she is Spanish, that could be difficult."

"There is no doubt that she is Spanish," said my mother. "I could speak with her a little in her native tongue if I remember it. My first husband was a Spaniard, as you know, and during my life with him I learned a little."

"She would be glad if you did," I replied warmly. "It must be difficult for her with no one to talk to."

"I will see what I can discover," replied my mother.

Later she talked to Maria, but although Maria was clearly glad to converse with someone who could speak her native tongue a little, she could not or would not tell her anything about herself. She vaguely remembered the storm and the ship's trying to come into port. Why she was on the ship was still as much a mystery to her as it had been on her arrival here.

My mother shared the opinion that after the child was born, her memory might return.

In the afternoon of Christmas Eve, Maria's pains started. Jennet brought me the news of this, and I immediately summoned the midwife. The child was born without her, though. She went into the room and found a beautifully formed little girl.

She was astonished.

"All is well?" I asked urgently.

"I was never in attendance on such an easy birth."

Maria lay calm and beautiful on the red curtains drawn back from her bed, and I thought: On that bed poor Melanie must have suffered her many miscarriages, and finally, she died there trying to give Colum the son he wanted. Now a child has been born there—a strong healthy child.

It was a strange Christmas Day. We had the usual rejoicing, but it was not the same. I could not forget—nor could my mother and Edwina—that a child had been born under our roof.

There was feasting and singing and the games we played at Christmastime, but my thoughts were in the Red Room where Maria lay in the bed with her child beside her. I had had brought in the cot which I had used for my children when they were babies. Now that lovely little girl lay in it.

It was the day after Christmas that Edwina passed me on the stairs.

She looked strained, I thought. I said, "Edwina, is anything wrong? You look . . . worried."

"Oh, it's nothing, Linnet. My fancy, nothing more."

"But there *is* something, Edwina."

"It's just that I feel that something has changed here . . . that there is something. . . ."

I was suddenly nervous, although before I had been inclined to shrug aside Edwina's fancies.

She gripped my arm suddenly, "Take care, Linnet," she said. "There is something evil in this house."

"What on earth do you mean?" I demanded.

"Oh, nothing. I shouldn't have said that. Forget it. It was just a thought that came into my mind."

"Ah," I said, "I know what it is. It's the cry of the gulls. They do sound as though they are warning us."

But she lived by the sea. She was accustomed to the cry of gulls. She was used to the weird sound the sea sometimes made when it thundered into the caves or over the rocks.

No, she had sensed something evil. Oh, yes, there was evil in this house. I had long suspected it . . . long before the coming of Maria and that night when I had seen the men returning to Seaward Tower with their donkeys.

But I hid my fear from Edwina. So we laughed together and pretended to forget, but what she had said lingered in my mind.

Maria was up almost immediately. She surprised me not only by her quick recovery but by her lack of interest in her child.

Jennet snatched up the baby and cared for her, taking her to her mother only when she was to be fed, and Jennet saw that this happened as regularly as it should.

"Unnatural," grumbled Jennet. "Foreigners, that's what."

The child was well formed and clearly healthy. I felt sorry for her, and I took her to my nursery and showed her to my children. Connell was not very interested, but my little Tamsyn, who was just two years old, was enchanted by her. She followed Jennet about when she held the baby and liked to look at her. She was far more interested in the baby than any plaything.

I talked to Maria. "What plans have you?" I asked.

She looked vague and either did not or pretended not to understand.

"You must recover from your confinement first," I said. "We can decide when you are completely recovered."

She did not seem in the least anxious about her future.

"The child must be named," I said. "What would you choose for her?"

"Name?" she said and shrugged.

I waited for her to decide, but she did not, and I asked if she would like to give the baby one of our Cornish names.

She smiled gravely. When she smiled, one could not help gazing at her in amazement. It was like a beautiful statue coming to life, and indeed with the passing of each day she became more beautiful.

But as she said nothing about the baby's name, I asked if I might choose one for her. She nodded, and so I began to cast about for something suitable. Thus I hit on the name Senara, the patron saint of Zennor. This seemed very suitable as Senara is one of the saints about whom nothing is known.

And so the child became Senara.

The household had altered subtly. Colum had changed. He hated Maria, I believed, and some of that hatred was directed at me, implying that I should never have saved her and brought her into the house.

All through the month of January, when it was cold exceptionally for us, for there was snow, she scarcely moved from the Red Room. She ordered that a great fire should burn there throughout the day and most of the night, and I did not countermand this order. When I felt inclined to, I remembered her lying there in the water so near to death and the men coming in with their donkeys, and I could do nothing.

My mother stayed until mid-February because the weather was too bad for traveling, and while she was there, I did not notice the change so much. It was after she had gone that it seemed more apparent.

I gathered from Jennet's conversation that the servants were aware of it.

"They don't like going to the Red Room," she told me. "They'm in and out quick as can be. They say they'll look up like and see her eyes on them. 'Tis like she be fixing a spell on them."

"A spell, Jennet!" I said sharply. "What nonsense!"

"Well, she did come on Halloween, mistress."

That alarmed me faintly. They were going to fasten the name "witch" on Maria.

I knew that she would be able to look after herself, but it was dangerous. Witches were taken and hanged or even burned to death on the flimsiest suspicion. I did not want the shadow of witchcraft to touch our household.

"It just happened that she was on the wrecked ship," I said sharply.

"That's what 'twould seem, mistress."

"That's what it *was*, Jennet."

"Well, they be saying that if she be a witch, she'd make her coming seem natural. She could stir up a storm at sea if need be."

"Nonsense," I said. "If they accused her of being a witch, what of Senara?"

Jennet then did look alarmed.

"They would soon be accusing the daughter of a witch," I went on.

"She be but a babe."

"Would they care for that? If they took one, they'd take the other too."

Jennet's face was as resolute as it could only be when there was a child to be protected.

" 'Tis all a parcel of nonsense," she said hotly. "There were a wreck, and she were from that broken ship. And just because it happen to be Halloween."

I could see that I had said the right thing.

I was sure Jennet would have had some effect on the others, but she could not eradicate suspicion altogether. Maria had come at the time of Halloween, and to a community that was beginning to be more and more obsessed by witchcraft that was significant.

March was unusually mild, and the spring feeling came early that year. There appeared to be a bigger crop of daisies and dandelions making the meadows a mass of white and gold. I had inherited a love of flowers from my grandmother Damask, and I always took special delight in their coming. At this time of year I would ride out and search for the wild daffodils and wood anemones and the purplish blue flowers of the ground ivy which I called gill-go-by-the-ground, a name I must have heard from my mother, who got it from hers. This year was different. When I rode out, I would be thinking about Maria and wondering what was going to happen to her and Senara, for they could not stay indefinitely at Castle Paling.

In time, I suppose, Maria would tell us. She had been in the house five months. Of course, if there had not been the child, she could not have remained so long.

I wondered why Colum ignored her presence. She was living as our guest, and I had to admit that at times she behaved almost like the mistress of the house. Colum was not of a temper to tolerate such an invasion into his house-hold, yet he had raised no objection after the first outburst. I could not get Edwina's warning out of my mind, for Edwina's prognostications had so many times proved to have some substance.

Returning from one of my rides on a lovely day in March, I left my horse in the stables, and as I was coming into the courtyard through the narrow arch, I heard voices.

I paused, for I recognized those of Colum and Maria, and it so surprised me that without realizing I stopped short. From where I stood they could not see me, nor I them, but Colum's voice with its deep timbre was one which carried easily on the air.

They were quarreling, and I sensed the suppressed fury in him.

"Get out," he said. "I will not have you under my roof. Get out and take your brat with you."

I heard her laugh. It was a deep laugh, full of malice and hatred.

She spoke haltingly, but there was no doubt of the gist of her remarks. "This you owe me. As long as I wish. You destroy our ship. . . . You . . . *you*. Murderer. You take our goods . . . you take our lives . . . I live . . . my child lives . . . and because this is so, you owe us all we take."

"I owe you nothing."

"Think, lord of the castle. I go from here. I tell. . . ."

"You tell . . . tell what?"

"How you become rich. . . ."

I drew back into the shadows. I felt sick with fear.

"Some things I remember," she said. "The ship . . . the lights. . . . The big rocks are there . . . in the sea. There were lights to warn us. . . . But the lights were not where the rocks were. . . . I know what you do. You lure the ship to the rocks, and you plunder us."

"Who will believe this nonsense?" he cried.

She laughed again.

I could not stand there. At any moment Colum could come striding from the courtyard and find me there, listening.

I turned and fled. I went up to my bedchamber. I could not say that I had had a shock. For some time the thought had been in my mind . . . ever since I had seen the men on the donkeys . . . and perhaps before.

So this was what he did. He sent his men out on the donkeys with their lanterns, and they would stand some miles away with their lanterns to indicate that that spot was Castle Paling and the Devil's Teeth were just before it, and thinking to avoid the treacherous rocks, the ships would come straight onto them.

It was diabolical.

And this he did that he might salvage the cargoes and sell them. How many ships had suffered in this way? I could remember five storms and the nightly activities of the men. They might not have succeeded in every instance, but that he could do this horrified me and changed my feelings toward him.

I did not know what to do. He was my husband, the father of my beloved children, and his profession—if such it could be called—horrified me.

It was a mistake to have come to the bedchamber, for within a short time the door was open, and there he stood flushed with rage after his encounter with Maria.

I faced him. I could not keep silent.

I said, "I have just come up. I was in the courtyard. I overheard what Maria was saying to you."

He looked at me in astonishment, his eyes narrowed suddenly. "Well?" he said.

"I know it's true. Oh, Colum, it's horrible."

"You too," he said. "Have done. I am in a mood to do you a mischief . . . both of you."

"She was right. You lured the ship in which she was sailing onto the rocks, for the sake of its cargo. By chance she managed to survive. I. . . ."

"And you, by God, brought her here. Had I known what you were doing. . . ."

"Yes, you would have thrown her back into the sea, for that is the kind of man you are. You care nothing for human life. You dispense with it if it is in your way. It sickens me to think of it."

"Then, madam, you had best prepare yourself for this state of sickness. If I have married a lily-livered woman, God help her, for I will have her obey me and keep her mouth shut when I command it."

"I have suspected this."

He came toward me suddenly and caught my arm. "You have mentioned this to any?"

"To whom should I mention it?"

"To your mother perhaps."

"How could I? She would be disgusted. She would insist that I return to my home with her."

He released his grip on my arm. "This is your home,"

he said, "and by God, you shall stay in it as long as I wish to keep you. As for your mother's disgust, I do not believe your father is so nice in his ways. I wonder how many Spaniards he has killed."

"We were always at war with Spain."

"Was it for war that they met their deaths or because they had gold and treasure? Answer me that."

I could not. I knew what he said was true. And I knew that my mother, who was honorable and good, remained with my father and loved him in her way, in spite of his bloodstained hands.

I wanted to go away, to be by myself, to think. To ask myself what I wanted to do, for I could not be sure. I wanted to be with Colum. I had to admit it, he satisfied my senses. When we were together, I could forget everything. The strength of him, the power he wielded over everything and everyone in the castle. At such times I felt I wanted to be subdued, I welcomed his rough lovemaking, it satisfied a part of my nature; but when he was not there, when I thought about him, I felt repulsed and wanted very much to go back to Lyon Court. I wanted to talk to someone, to understand myself. I could not talk to my mother because what I had to tell I believed would cause her great concern. She would not want me to go on living with a man who lured people to their deaths for the sake of profit. Yet she had lived with my father.

It was a cruel world. Once my mother had said, "Was it so vicious in the past? Will it be so in the future? I find it hard to reconcile myself to the fury of the times. Perhaps I was born into the wrong world."

I remembered that now and asked myself: Was I?

Colum was watching me, his black eyes alight with a passion that I had seen in the early days of our acquaintance.

He shouted, "Answer me. Answer me."

"What other men did has no bearing on this," I said.

"Has it not? You have a fine opinion of your father. I shall insist that you have as fine a one of your husband."

"You cannot force people to have opinions."

"We shall see," he said. Then he came close to me and took me by the shoulders. "Now you know the nature of my business," he said, "what do you propose to do about it?" I was silent, and he went on, "I will tell you. You will accept it. You will help me in all I do, as a good wife should."

"I would never help to . . . murder."

He shook me violently. "Have done," he said. "A ship founders. I have as much right to its cargo as any."

"A ship that has been *helped* to founder?"

"Should I be blamed because a captain does not know how to navigate?"

"If you lead him astray with false information, yes, you are to blame. You have caused the death of countless people . . . so that you could grow rich on their possessions."

"Have done, you fool. Why did you have to save that woman from the sea?"

"Because I am not like you . . . a murderer."

"You have brought her into this house with her brat. What good will that do us?"

"At least it has saved two lives to set against all those you have taken."

"You have the tongue of a shrew."

"As you have long discovered."

"And you are too virtuous, are you, to stay under this roof?"

"I . . . think I would like to go to stay with my mother."

"And leave your husband . . . and your children?"

"I could take the children with me."

He laughed. "Never," he said. "Do you think I would allow them to leave this roof? Or you either. They shall be brought up as I wish."

"You would make a murderer of my son."

"I would make a man of mine."

"I will take my daughter and go."

"You will leave your daughter and stay."

"I have to think about what I have discovered."

"There is one lesson you must learn, and I had hoped you had learned it by now. I am the master here and of you and my children. You disobeyed me when you brought that woman here."

"You had given no order that she should not be brought . . . *master*," I added with sarcasm.

"Because I had not seen her. She will bring no good to you. Rest assured of that."

"I was not thinking of the good that might come my way. She was in distress, and as any normal human being would, I saved her."

"You are a fool, wife, and I doubt not will live to regret your folly."

"Why am I foolish?"

"Because she is as she is. . . ."

"I understand not."

"You must not think you are the fount of wisdom."

"I must be alone. I want to think."

"To plan your departure. You will stay here. I will not let you go. Take off your riding habit."

"I am not yet ready to."

"I am." He snatched my riding hat from my head and threw it onto the floor. He caught my hair in his hands and pulled it in the rough manner with which I was familiar. I could sense the rising passion in him, and although I thought of this later, there was something different in it. He wanted to teach me a lesson.

Now, I had talked of going away, and he would show me that I wanted him as he wanted me. I could not do without him just as he was pleased with me, in this respect.

It was as before—but there was this difference. Perhaps I should have known. But like so many significant things of life, it only occurred to me later.

Maria stayed with us. Her status in the household had changed, and she behaved like a guest. She joined us at meals, and her daughter was cared for in our nursery with our own children.

I was not sure how this had come about. Colum and I rarely ate alone, but when we did, it was in the room which I called the winter parlor—after the one at Lyon Court—the small, intimate kind of room which people were beginning to use instead of the great halls where all the household sat together.

There were occasions when we dined in the hall. If there were visitors—which there were quite frequently—and on special occasions, then it was natural that Maria should be there. What was strange was that when we dined in the winter parlor she should join us. I could not understand why Colum accepted this.

I guessed that in a way either his conscience worried him—although that was difficult to believe—or that she was threatening him in some way. It was hard to imagine his allowing anyone to threaten him, but she had accused him of being a murderer. He had been responsible for the death of her husband—for I had to believe she was traveling with her husband—and perhaps even he would feel he should make some amends.

Colum kept me with him a great deal after that encounter. He seemed determined to make me accept him for what he was. He told me, soon after that scene, that if I attempted to leave him, he would come to Lyon Court and get me, no matter if he had to kill my father in the attempt.

He said, "Don't provoke me, wife. Never provoke me. You would find my anger terrible. I would stop at nothing to gain satisfaction. Is that something you have learned yet?"

"I begin to," I said.

"Then be a good wife. Deny me nothing and you will be cared for. I want more children. But all this time after Connell and our daughter you have been barren. Why?"

"That question must be answered by a higher power."

"Not so. You have slipped away from me. You have become critical of me. I will not have that. Take care, wife."

"Take care of what?"

"That you continue to please me."

What did he mean? I wondered about slipping away. Had I during that first year or so of marriage loved him not only with this physical passion of which I was so acutely aware, or had my feelings for him gone deeper than that? Had I built up a false image? Had I seen him as the man I wanted him to be? I could do that no longer.

And he allowed Maria to join us. Those meals *à trois* were not easy. Colum and I talked in rather forced fashion; she appeared to watch us thoughtfully and contributed very little to the conversation.

I had a feeling that this state of affairs could not continue. We could not go on day after day sitting thus at table together. Something was going to happen. Then suddenly I was aware.

I caught his gaze fixed on her, and he looked just as he had looked at me on the memorable night when I had first seen him at the Traveler's Rest.

I felt a wild twinge of alarm.

I was deeply aware of them. They were playing a kind of game together. She was haughty and scornful of him, and he was maddened by her attitude. It was something of a repetition of what had happened between him and me.

There was an occasion when she stayed in her room and sent one of the maids down to say she was indisposed, for all the world as though she were the mistress of the house. We ate alone on that night. Colum was moody, speaking scarcely a word.

She had taken one of the horses from the stables and made it her own. I had supplied her with riding clothes; I had set the seamstress to make garments for her. That was in the beginning when I was sorry for her and wanted to make up for the wrong which had been done to her by my husband.

She never hesitated to take these things. She herself designed her clothes and was with the seamstress while she was working. When they were completed, they were beautiful in an exotic way. She walked gracefully and held herself so proudly that she looked like a queen. Her beauty seemed to intensify with the passing of the months. She loved the sun and on hot days rode off and sometimes did not come back all day.

Colum continued to watch her broodingly, and he had ceased to mention her to me.

When we entertained, she joined the company. She would seat herself at the table on the dais and even though Colum and I were in the center, she would have given the impression to a stranger that she was the mistress of the house, not I.

There was often something jaunty about her manner; it was as though she were secretly amused. One of the neighboring squires had fallen in love with her and implored her to marry him. She would not give him a definite answer, and consequently he made pretense after pretense to visit us.

"Young Madden is here again," Colum would say. "Poor lovesick fool! Does he think she will have him?"

Once I said, "Colum, how long will she stay here?"

He turned to me angrily. "I thought it was your pleasure that she stayed. Was it not you who were so eager to make up for my cruelty?"

"Yes, but she doesn't belong here, does she?"

"Who shall say who belongs where? Once you did not belong; now you do."

"Surely that is different. I am your wife."

"Remember it," he said rather sourly.

That was a strange long summer. The heat was intense. The sea was as calm as a lake and from the turret window looked like a sheet of silk shot with blue and gray light; its murmur was gentle as it washed the walls of the castle. I would often look out at the sharp teeth of the Devil protruding above the water and the dark smudge of battered vessels there. I wondered what Maria thought when she looked out and saw the remains of the *Santa Maria*. Did she think of her husband who was lost to her forever? One could never tell; she glided about the castle with that remote look in her eyes, and no one could know what she was thinking.

Colum was different. He talked often about another child. What was wrong with me? Why did I not conceive? He had changed toward me. There was a certain lack of spontaneity in his passion. I thought I knew why.

I wished that my mother would visit us. In the month of June I wrote and asked her to come. I told her how I missed her and how long it seemed since we had been together.

There must have been a plea in my letter, for she wrote immediately and said she was making plans to leave. I felt relieved then. I had decided that I must confide in her. I knew that was the last thing Colum wanted, but I did not care. I felt I must talk to someone. But she did not come. Damask had a fever, and she neither dared leave her nor bring her.

"When she is well, we will come, my dear Linnet," she wrote. She told me what was happening at home. My father had returned from his second voyage, and this time he had been equally successful as far as trading was concerned and had achieved this without the loss of ships. The Landors had visited them.

"Fennimore's little boy is the pride of his life," she wrote. "He is called Fenn and must be a month or so older than your own little Tamsyn."

Her letter brought back so clearly to me the great hall in Lyon Court and my father at the head of the table talking of his adventures and my mother, watching him and now and then bickering with him.

There was a great comfort in thinking of my mother and father. I had once imagined that Colum and I were rather like them. Their marriage had survived the years, and it was clear that they could not live happily without each other. But now we could never be like that, I told myself.

I watched Maria walking to the stables. She swayed as she walked, so graceful was she. When she sat a horse, she looked like one of the goddesses from Greek mythology. I thought that so much beauty concentrated in one person was disconcerting.

I wondered where she went on her long rides. That was a mystery. Mystery must always surround Maria.

July came, and the heat had turned sultry.

"There'll be thunder," said the weather-wise, but they were wrong. The heat persisted. St. Swithin's Day came, and we watched for the rain. It did not come.

I remembered my mother's quoting to me:

> St. Swithin's Day, if thou dost rain,
> For forty days it will remain.
> St. Swithin's Day, if thou be fair,
> For forty days 'twill rain nae mair.

But what did I care whether it rained or the sun shone? The weather could not alter the strangeness in the castle.

Then came August—hot nights when the bedcurtains were drawn back to let in a little air. There was a swarm of wasps. Connell was stung, and I treated the sting with a remedy Edwina had given me. How I wished I could see Edwina. I remembered then how she had said that there was something evil in the house.

Evil. Yes, it was evil. There was no mistaking it. In my heart I thought: It was brought here by the woman from the sea.

I awoke in the night. It was too hot for sleep. Colum was not there. How many times had I awakened and found him gone? I went to the window and looked out to sea. It was calm and still. A shaft of moonlight made a path on the still waters. I could see the tips of the Devil's Teeth clearly. There was no ship in sight.

Some impulse made me take my robe and wrap it around me. I opened the door and stepped out into the narrow corridor.

It was dark, for there were no windows to let in the moonlight. I went back into the room and lighted a candle.

I knew where I was going, and if I found what I felt I might find, what should I do? I would go to my mother. I would steal out of the house in secret and take the children with me. Or I might write to her and tell her that she must come, for I needed her even as young Damask had when she was ill. She could come to me, and she must.

The candlelight threw shadows on the thick stone walls. I stood outside the Red Room, my fingers on the latch. Yet I could not bring myself to open the door. In my mind's eye I could picture them. It would be as it had been with us, for she had bewitched him.

Why did I use that word? Bewitched. It was wrong.

There was no question of witchcraft. She was a beautiful and voluptuous woman; he was a sensual man. He desired her as he had once desired me, and did I not know that he would allow nothing to stand in the way of his desires?

The room of ghosts and shadows, I thought. She suffered here, poor Melanie. And if he visited Maria here, what did the poor sad shade of Melanie think? Could it be true that unhappy people walked as the servants said? Did they hope to regain some happiness by so doing? Did they seek revenge on those who had made them suffer?

How like him it would be to join Maria in that room, on that bed where Melanie had died . . . just as he had made me share it with him. I remembered then his passion had been not only desire for me but a need to show Melanie's ghost if it existed that he cared not a jot for it. It seemed that in Colum's passion there must always be double motives.

Quietly I opened the door. The curtains were drawn back from the bed, and a shaft of moonlight shone straight onto the bed.

It was empty.

I felt ashamed as I tiptoed back to my bedchamber. I lay on the bed. Colum did not join me. It seemed strange that they were both absent on that moonlight night.

September had come, and the heat was still with us. I had to see my mother. I told Colum that either she must come to me or I would go to her.

He did not answer me; his thoughts appeared to be on other matters.

There had been no disasters at sea during the summer months. Colum rode off on long journeys by himself and often stayed away for several days. He never told me where he had been. Maria was at the castle—quiet, brooding almost; there was a secret smile in her eyes.

Colum came back after one of his long journeys. It was September—nearly a year since that night when I had gone out and rescued Maria from the sea, yet she seemed content to stay at the castle and made no attempt to get away. James Madden would have offered her a way of escape through marriage with him, but although she allowed him to go on hoping, she would give him no definite answer. She did not try to speak to anyone as far as I knew. Her English, it was true, was limited but it seemed strange that she should appear to accept her fate so placidly.

Senara was taking notice now. Her eyes would light up

when I entered the nursery. I wondered what happened when Maria did. But of course she rarely did. She had borne her daughter and passed her over to us, as though it were our duty to care for her.

Soon the autumn would be with us. A whole year would have passed, and at the end of October it would be Halloween again.

When I rode inland, I saw the birds congregating, ready to leave for a warmer climate. The butcher-bird, the nightjar, the chiffchaff and the common sandpiper were leaving us. Our ever-faithful gulls would remain to wheel over our coasts and utter their mournful cries.

I said to Colum, "I have written to my mother. It seems so long since I saw her. I am insisting that she come."

He looked at me steadily, his dark eyes cold.

"You have not heard," he said. "I did not wish to disturb you. The sweat is raging in Plymouth."

"The sweat!" I cried. "Then she must come to us at once."

"Nay, that she will not. Dost think I will allow my children to run the risk of catching it?"

"She may be ill."

"You would have heard had she been."

"I must go to her."

"You shall stay here."

"But if she is in danger."

"I doubt she is ill. But she is near the sickness, and it spreads like wildfire. You must stay apart."

"I want to see her so much," I said.

"You talk like a peevish child. You have your home to think of. Know this. She shall not come here, nor shall you go to her. I'll not have danger brought to the castle."

I was worried about my mother, but letters came. The sweat was taking toll of many people in the neighborhood, she wrote. She did not go into the town. She had feared that Damask was sickening, but it turned out to be only a return of the fever she had had earlier.

She wrote that she thought it unwise of her to come to see me or me to go to her.

"I shall write often, my dearest child," she said. "And until this terrible thing passes, we must be content with our letters."

She sent me a pair of stockings such as I had never seen before. The art of weaving had been introduced by a gentleman of Cambridge. He was the Rev. Mr. Lee, and my mother wanted to know if I had ever seen such stockings.

"See how they mold themselves to the leg as stockings never did before," she wrote. "I have heard from your grandmother in London that they are always worn by the quality, and she says that soon there will be no other kind. I have more news from London. A Mr. Jansen who has been making spectacles has invented an instrument which makes things far off seem close. It is called a telescope. What will happen next? I wonder. What times we live in! I would instead they could find some means of preventing this terrible sickness breaking out every few years—and a cure for it when it comes."

To read her letters offered me some comfort; but I wanted so much to talk to her. I wanted to tell her of the strange atmosphere which was slowly creeping into the castle.

That it had something to do with Maria, I was certain, and Colum was involved in it.

Are they lovers? I wondered. If they were, that would explain so much.

It was Halloween again. Now the weather had changed. There was rain—a light drizzle which was little more than a mist.

Jennet's eyes were dark with her thoughts. I wondered what she knew.

" 'Tis a year," she said, "since she came here. T'as been a long year . . . a long, strange year."

So Jennet had felt it too.

"And little Senara is ten months old."

"A proper little miss," said Jennet, her eyes softening and the mysterious look going out of them. "It does me good to see young Tamsie with her. Proper little mother. And Senara, she knows her too. Screams for her. I swear she said 'Tamsie' the other day. Mark my words, that'll be the first word that one says."

I was glad that my daughter was kind to the baby. It showed a pleasant trait in her character that there was no jealousy, for I knew that Jennet spoiled Senara. How far away that nursery world seemed from what was going on in the rest of the castle!

Halloween was with us. A dark and gloomy day—quite windless, the mist hanging over the castle, shrouding the turrets and penetrating into the rooms. The coastline merged into a bank of mist. It would be hard for any ships that were near our coasts in this. They would not need the lights from Colum's donkeys to deceive them. They would not be able to see anything through the mist.

It was a silent world—chill and dark. I thought of the raging storm of last year. I wondered whether Marie was remembering too.

There was no bonfire that night.

I asked Jennet why.

"Weather bain't fit," she told me.

But I didn't think it was only the weather. Many of the servants believed there was a witch among us, and it might have been that they feared to offend her.

So the night of Halloween passed quietly.

But in the morning we discovered that Maria was missing. The bed in the Red Room had not been slept in. All that day we thought she would come back. But she did not. And as the days began to pass, we began to realize that she had disappeared.

She had left us Senara as a memento of that night a year ago, but she herself had gone as suddenly as she had come.

Christmas Night
in the Castle

What a strange time that was. Christmas came and passed. My mother did not visit us because of the threat of the sweat. Silence had settled on the house; the servants whispered together. None of them would go to the Red Room.

Every day I waited for something to happen. Sometimes I would go to that room and quietly open the door, expecting to find her returned. The room was empty, silent, yet I sensed a presence there. Was it Melanie, or did some mysterious aura of Maria remain?

The servants were convinced that she was a witch. She had come and gone on Halloween. I could imagine that that was some wry joke of Maria's, for I had often had the feeling that she was laughing at us in a contemptuous kind of way.

I thought during the first days that she would be back. In the first hours I had thought she might have eloped with James Madden. That was soon dispelled when he arrived at the castle. The news had reached him that she had gone, and he had to discover for himself. I had rarely seen a man so stricken. At least it proved that she had not gone to him.

A month later he had killed himself. He was found hanging in his bedchamber.

When we heard the news at the castle, the servants were horrified. They were certain then that she had been a witch.

I myself wondered if this were true. Once I spoke to Colum about it. He did not seem disturbed by her departure. In fact, at times I thought he seemed relieved that she had gone. He had been attracted by her without doubt, and when I think of that incomparable and rather strange beauty, I was not surprised. I knew it must have been irresistible. I warmed toward Colum. It was amazing how easily I could. I believed that he had been attracted against his will and that now temptation had been removed he was glad.

With each day I felt myself growing away from the horror the first revelation of his way of life had brought to me. Could one grow accustomed to such things? My mother had. Was I the same?

As that year progressed, we settled into a way of life which did not change much. There were one or two wrecks, but I tried not to think about them. While the torrent raged, I would lie in my bed, the curtains drawn and try to shut out of my mind the thought of what was happening outside the castle. There were one or two facts which forced themselves on my attention. I knew that Colum had agents in various foreign shipping ports—and English ones too—who informed him when cargo ships were leaving. He would know what route they would take and if they were likely to come near to our coast. Then he would watch for them. His men would be out on the coast, and if the weather favored him, he would attempt to bring the ship onto the Devil's Teeth.

I would lie there trembling sometimes, saying to myself: "You are a devil, Colum. You are cruel and wicked, and I should take my children away from you. What can happen to them with such a father?

My daughter was safe. She was essentially mine. Colum was proud of her healthy looks, but he showed little interest in her. The boy was all his. Connell, now five years old, was beginning to look like his father. Colum would take him out on his pony; I had seen the boy riding on his shoulders. Connell could give that unadulterated adoration which Colum wanted. I think that Colum loved Connell more than anything on earth. He was determined to "make a man of him," and that meant bringing him up in his own image. He was succeeding admirably. The boy came to me only when he was sick, which was rarely. Then he would be like any other small child needing his mother. Colum had little patience with sickness, although if Connell was ailing, he would be frantic with anxiety.

How different was my little Tamsyn. She was a bright child. Although a year and four months younger than Connell, I could see already that she was going to be more intelligent. She had a quick, probing mind and asked continual questions. She was by no means pretty; she had a rather snub nose, and she had missed her father's darkness—which Connell had inherited—and was mid-brown, with large hazel eyes. Her mouth was too large and her brow too high, but to me she was perfect.

There was in Tamsyn a protective quality. It may have been that she sensed something of the relationship between myself and her father and instinctively knew that it was not all that could be desired. I always fancied that when Colum was in the nursery, she was standing guard to protect me. To look at that small, stalwart figure, ready to do battle on my behalf, moved me deeply. She had the same protective attitude toward Senara, which showed an uncommon trait in her character. She was going to be of the kind that fights for the rights of others.

Then there was that other occupant of our nurseries: Senara. She had been ten months old at the time of her mother's departure and had very quickly forgotten her. Maria had never played an important part in her life in any case. It was Jennet and myself who gave her that affection and security which children look for.

It very early became clear that she was going to be a beauty. It seemed impossible that it could be otherwise with such a mother. Her hair was of the same black and silky texture as that of Maria, her eyes were long and dark, her skin of the magnolia petal kind, her nose was straight and perfectly formed, and she had a lovely mouth. I wondered whether she would be as beautiful as her mother—it was too soon to say, but there was a sweet innocence about her which I felt sure Maria could never have had even in her cradle.

When Maria had left and there was all the talk about her being a witch, I feared that some harm might come to Senara. She was, after all, the witch's child. Some of the servants would not go near her, and I talked seriously to Jennet about this.

"Jennet," I said, "you must always let me know what the servants are saying. What do they think about Maria's going away?"

"On Halloween which was when she came," said Jennet. "It goes to show. There can't be no gainsaying that."

"They are saying she's a witch no doubt."

"She be a witch, mistress. How did her come, and where be her to now?"

"We know how she came. She was shipwrecked. Where she has gone is a mystery. People often go away discreetly."

"To a lover like as not," said Jennet, touching her lips with her tongue. "She were the kind who would bewitch a man. Why. . . ."

I stopped her. I knew she was going to say she had bewitched the master. Jennet's tongue always ran away with her.

"It is Senara who worries me, Jennet."

"Senara!" Jennet's maternal feelings began to bristle. "What be wrong with Senara?"

"Nothing wrong with her health. You have been like a mother to her."

"It do make you feel young again, mistress, to have a little one in your arms."

"Make sure no harm comes to her."

"What should, mistress, a baby . . . little more?"

"They will say she is the witch's child."

"They wouldn't harm a baby."

"Make sure they don't, Jennet. Watch over her."

"My dear life, mistress, no one's going to harm that pretty creature while I'm there."

"What of those nights when you're at Seaward with your lover?"

Jennet blushed like a schoolgirl. "Well, there be those," she admitted. "But there's the girl, Amy. I talk to her. 'If any harm should come to my babies,' I said to her, 'I'll break every bone in your body.' And there's young Tamsie. She's there. She'll look after Senara. They lie close together, and Tamsie holds her hand all through the night. If she cries, Tamsie soothes her. A regular mother she be. Nay, no harm will come to Senara."

So the time began to pass and although the servants refused to go into the Red Room and crossed themselves when they passed it, I was sure that there was less talk of witchcraft in the kitchens than there had been.

It was not until August of that year that my mother came. It was wonderful to see her. I told her in detail of Maria's departure, and she was pleased that she had gone. "A woman like that is unsettling in a household," she said.

She loved the children, and Tamsyn was her favorite. There was something very appealing about my grave little girl.

My mother had all the latest news from London, where she told me in hushed tones twenty-eight thousand people had died of the plague.

"These terrible epidemics." She sighed. "Is there no end to them? How I wish some means could be found of stopping them!" She went on: "You must come to Lyon Court and bring the children with you. Your father complains that he sees you rarely."

"He should come here with you."

"He is always engaged on a voyage or preparing for one."

"Is he getting along amicably with the Landors?"

"As well as can be expected. You know your father. He is not the easiest man to work with me. He wants all his own way."

"And Fennimore . . .?"

My mother looked at me sharply. She sensed that something had changed at the castle, and I knew she was wondering if I were regretting my marriage. I was not sure whether I could truthfully say that I did. I could confess to myself that now and then I thought of Fennimore Landor, with the gentle, kindly face and the idealism of his expression. He wanted to make a better world. He was that sort of man. Colum cared nothing for the world, only his own profit. Now I was beginning to think, as I had long ago, of how different my life might have been if I had not gone on that journey and met Colum. I should, I was sure, have married Fennimore. We should have had children. I should have spent my time between Trystan Priory and Lyon Court, and I was sure I should have been happy—in a quiet, secure and peaceful way.

Did I regret? How can I say? At times, yes. But then my children would not have been Connell and Tamsyn, and when you have children whom you love, how can you wish that you had others, which you undoubtedly would have had with a different father.

"Fennimore," said my mother, "is as enthusiastic as he ever was. He believes wholeheartedly in his ventures. And so does your father now. They have built a new ship. They have named her the *Landor Lion*. She is due to go out to the East Indies early next year."

"And his son . . . ?"

"He is at Trystan Priory with his mother."

"You see them now and then?" I asked.

"Oh, yes, indeed." I wanted to ask what Fennimore's wife was like and if he was happy with her and did he ever think of me. Which was vanity, of course. It would be better for us both if we never thought of each other.

"And . . . his son? Are they any other children?"

"There is a girl besides young Fenn."

"What is she called?"

My mother hesitated a moment, and then she said, "Melanie."

"I see. After Fennimore's sister. They are happy, I suppose?"

"Yes. It is a quiet household. Of course, Fennimore is away at sea a great deal, as your father, Carlos and Jacko are too. Romilly misses Penn a great deal, for he sails now with your father. You are lucky to have a husband who does not go to sea."

I was silent, thinking of Colum battling with the waves in his small boat, luring men to their deaths for the sake of their cargo.

I was on the point of telling my mother, but as was to happen so many times, I did not.

Time was passing, and Maria was hardly ever mentioned now. I often wondered whether Colum thought of her. There were my mother's visits, but Colum raised objections when I wished to go and stay with her. I had the feeling that he believed I should never come back. There would always be an excuse when my mother wanted me to go. He had heard that there were robbers on the road and could not himself spare the time to take me. How could I travel with three young children? There was always some excuse. I must wait until he could travel with me.

"Vagabonds and robbers are being driven out of the big cities," he told me. "And where will they come? Into the country? There are so many of them in the cities that the mayor of London and the Star Chamber are determined to rid the capital of them. They beg constantly and make a nuisance of themselves, and because they persist, they are hanged on the gallows in London as a warning for all to see. And what will they do? Come to the country. They will beg by the roadside, and if you do not give they will take—and like as not murder you for good measure. Do you think I am going to allow my children to make a journey in such conditions!"

There was truth in this, for my mother wrote that she had heard from London that those who persisted in begging were hanged by order of the magistrates.

So we did not go to Lyon Court, though my mother made the journey to us. When she came, she brought a bodyguard of servants and any robbers would have had short shrift against them. I suggested to Colum that I travel likewise protected, but he would not hear of it.

That Christmas, however, he agreed that we should go to Lyon Court, and we traveled there with the three children, Jennet and two other women and about four grooms.

My father was home and delighted to see us, particularly the children. He was greatly attracted to Connell and loved to see my son, legs apart, imitating his grandfather and father. I sighed to myself because I knew that he was going to be such another as they. They sensed this too but it delighted them.

My father took him on his ships and was eager to make a sailor of him. I encouraged this. I would rather he followed my father's trade than that of his own father. Tamsyn was my mother's favorite and I was so pleased that my little daughter was determined that Senara should not be left out. Not that my mother would have attempted to do that, but wherever Tamsyn was, there was Senara.

The child was three years old, rather precocious and undeniably beautiful—quite the beauty of the family. My father studied her closely and nodded at her. I could see he thought that she was one of Colum's bastards.

He listened attentively to the story of Maria's being washed up on the shore and brought to the castle to bear her child. I could see the twinkle in his eyes as he surveyed Colum. It meant he understood. This was Colum's way of introducing his child into the castle.

He would not have thought so if he had seen that poor half-drowned woman I had found on the shore. His connoisseur's eye was quick to note Senara's appearance.

"She'll be a little beauty, that one," he commented and choked with laughter. He liked to think of other men's misdemeanors. I supposed that made his own seem in the natural course of events.

I remember the fierce arguments that Christmas. My

father raged against the Spaniards as he used to in the days of my childhood. He choked with rage when he talked about the descent they had made on Penzance that July.

"By God, the dons have raided our coast. Have they forgotten we have driven them off the seas?"

"Have we?" said my mother. "If that is so, how did they get to Penzance?"

"Our own coast!" spluttered my father. "What say you, son-in-law? Do you think we should take out ships and harry them?"

"I do indeed," said Colum.

"Trade," spat out my father. " 'Tis fair enough when we have done for the dons. But while they show such impudence and raid our coasts, there's only one thing to do. Raid theirs."

"You disconcert them more by taking their trade," said my mother.

"Disconcert them," stormed my father. "I'd murder the lot of them. I'd wipe them off the seas."

He was all for diverting his ships from their trading ventures and putting them in action against Spain.

"We haven't finished with the Spaniards yet," he growled. "By God's teeth, will they never learn their lesson?"

Colum and my father talked of the Spaniards with loathing. My father was pleased with Colum, except that he could not understand why Colum did not go to sea.

"I would," said Penn, "that I could discover a gold mine, like Sir Walter Raleigh."

"He has not discovered it yet," my mother reminded him.

"He will," cried Penn. "I know he will."

"He has to," put in my mother, "if he is to regain the Queen's favor which he lost through seducing one of the maids of honor."

"Poor Raleigh!" said my father. "I doubt not she asked to be seduced. No woman is taken against her will to my mind."

"You men imagine you are quite irresistible, I am sure," said my mother, "but you have unwilling victims now and then."

My father's eyes were on my mother, suppressing his amusement. I looked up. Colum was watching me.

I thought: I wish I could stay here with my mother, and my children with me always. Here I feel safe.

Edwina and her son were, of course, with us. Carlos was at sea and at such times she more or less lived at Lyon

Court. My mother knew how anxious she could be and with that strange gift of hers my mother was always afraid that she would see some disaster.

Edwina talked with me during that visit when we were alone.

She said, "I feel happier about you now."

"Were you unhappy before?"

"I had an uneasy feeling that there was something evil at the castle. You remember I told you."

"Yes, I remember. It had something to do with Maria. She disappeared, you know, as suddenly as she came."

"It was a strange feeling . . . vague, insubstantial. That's how it is often. Now I feel . . . much happier."

"So I'm safe," I said rather lightly.

She answered: "It is as though the evil which threatened has receded. I can't explain more than that."

It was clearly the influence of Maria. I often wondered what became of her. She went away taking nothing with her. It was all very strange.

Edwina embraced me. "Take care, Linnet," she said.

And I wondered whether she was still a little uneasy about me.

That year slipped away almost unnoticed. I was glad that Maria seemed to have been forgotten; I felt that was better for Senara's sake. The Red Room was still the haunted room, but Maria's name was only occasionally mentioned.

Senara was growing up to be a normal little girl, and the only difference between her and others was her exceptional beauty. The devotion between her and Tamsyn had not diminished but was even more marked. Senara, who had a tendency to naughtiness, could be called in order immediately by Tamsyn.

I spent a great deal of time in the nursery. I was teaching the children, so this was necessary. I daresay I was prejudiced, but my daughter's quick mind was a delight to me. Her affectionate nature charmed me, perhaps most of all that protective streak which was so marked in her relationship toward me and toward Senara.

I tried to shut out my doubts and fears about Colum. I had my children, and my mother was not so very far away. I knew that she had suffered a great deal because such a long distance separated her from her mother, so I told myself I had much to be thankful for.

If I had never discovered the nature of Colum's business, I could have been very happy during those years. There were to be two more of them before I realized that they were but a lull, a waiting period, and that the storm which had begun to gather about me had merely receded and could return and break over my head.

During those years the country remained at peace, although there were skirmishes with Spain, the perennial enemy. The defeat of the Armada had saved us from invasion, but it had not completely eliminated the threat.

It was a sad day for the country—and particularly for the West Country—when we heard that Sir Francis Drake was dead. He and Sir John Hawkins had set out with a fleet of men-of-war to attack the Spanish settlements in the West Indies. Both of them had died. If they had but stayed at home, both of these men would have lived. It seemed a pity that Sir Francis, who had done so much good, should have gone away to die. He had brought water to the town through the River Meavy and had built six mills for the grinding of corn. He went into Parliament—representing Plymouth naturally—and he had organized the building of walls and fortifications there.

My mother was sadly angry. "So much good he did in peace, why did he have to go on this expedition? What did it matter that the Spaniards had a treasure store in these places? Let them keep it. Better so than that a great man should lose his life in attempting to take it."

But that was the way of such men. "He died as he would wish to die," growled my father.

Then there was the apprehension when we heard that the Spaniards had taken Calais. Did this mean that our enemies were rising again? The Queen entered into an alliance with the French, but they were not liked much more than the Spaniards.

There was great rejoicing when Admiral Howard plundered Cádiz. My father talked of it for a whole year. "The Spaniards' losses amounted to twenty million ducats," he gloated.

We would hear such news, and then there would be silences of months. What happened in the capital affected us little.

I was now visiting my mother often. The more I made the journey, the less arduous it seemed. The children were getting a little older, and that made it even easier.

My relationship with Colum was changing. I was no longer so necessary to him. There were occasions when the passion flared up between us, but at others he seemed almost indifferent to me. He was away a great deal more than he had been. I had learned that it was unwise to ask where he had gone. Nor did I wish to know. I shut myself away. I could see no way out of my situation. I must accept Colum and what he did or refuse to and leave him. To leave him meant leaving my children. That I could not do. So I did what seemed to me the only thing I could do. I shut my eyes to what I did not want to see, and I stayed.

My visits to my mother were my salvation. Sometimes my father was there; sometimes he was not. The Landors, I knew, were frequent visitors, but they were never there when I was. It was not only due to my earlier relationship with Fennimore but the fact that I had married Melanie's husband. My mother, with her extreme tact, arranged that our visits never coincided.

I heard that the company was doing well. It now owned a fleet of ships. There was an amalgamation of several trading companies that could well be incorporated under a charter.

"Of course," my mother said to me on one occasion, "it is Fennimore Landor who is at the heart of the business. Your father is enthusiastic at times, and then his enthusiasm wanes. His heart is really in buccaneering, but I tell him that more good will come to our country this way than all the fighting."

I knew she was right, and I knew also that my father would never agree with her. And how I wished that Colum would join them instead of plying his horrible trade!

There was one matter which surprised us both. Since the birth of Tamsyn I had not conceived. Sometimes I thought that this was something to do with my state of mind. I was willing myself not to have another child. I might say that I did not want a murderer of men and women to be its father. Deep within me I could not reconcile myself; I think too that I believed that some opportunity would arise, and then I would escape.

If I could be free of him, if I could take my children away, if I could go back to my old home, could I start afresh and be happy?

I did not know. I sensed somehow that this was a waiting period. My children were no longer babies. They were growing up fast. Later on, I promised myself, I shall make a decision.

Then the strange thing happened.

I had been to Lyon Court for several weeks and returned home.

It was a hot, still day. The children were pleased to be back home, as they always were, although they enjoyed Lyon Court. Looking at the castle towers as I rode up, I felt the thrill I always did when I had been away for some time. The first that came into view were Ysella's and the Seaward Towers, and I could never look at Ysella's without thinking of that day when I had been shut in there. I could still smell the musty, damp smell of stale sea water. I thought too of the ridiculous legend of the two wives who lived so close to each other and never knew of the other's existence. It would always be with a kind of apprehensive fascination that I returned home.

Connell was eager to see if Jerry, the groom, had looked after his dogs and falcons during his absence. Tamsyn, Senara and I went to my bedchamber, and then Jennet and the little girls went off to their own room together.

I looked about that bedchamber of many memories. There was something different about the place on this day. Was that so, or was I imagining it? When I came back after an absence, the antiquity of the place forced itself upon me. Lyon Court was modern in comparison, and modern houses seemed less touched by the past.

The little chambers, the short spiral staircases, the unexpected nooks, all these things had the effect of taking one out of this world into another era. I almost felt on that afternoon that I was impelled toward the Red Room.

I went along and stood for a few moments outside the door. Edwina would have said some uncanny force had sent me there.

As I opened the door, I felt a shiver run down my spine, and the hair really did rise from my scalp. It was not a bright room—perhaps it would never have acquired its reputation if it had been—for very little light came in from the long slit of a window, but my eyes, accustomed to the gloom, saw clearly and I am sure did not deceive me. I knew as soon as I opened the door that someone was in the room. Then, as I stood there, the shape took form, emerged, as it were, from the hangings on either side of the window.

I caught my breath. I felt my knees tremble.

Then she came toward me—gliding slowly. The musk scent enveloped me. She brushed past me and went into the corridor.

For a few seconds I could not move. I was too shocked.
I just stood still, that unmistakable scent assailing my nostrils.

Then I said, "Maria! What are you doing here?"

There seemed to be a terrible silence, and then my limbs
suddenly regained their bones.

I ran from the room. There was no sign of her.

"I have seen a ghost," I said aloud.

Where was Maria? No one knew. I could not keep my
vision to myself.

I told Colum. "I saw her, Colum. I saw her as clearly as
I am seeing you now."

"How could you have done so? Where is she?"

"I swear I saw her. She came toward me and walked
past me. I smelled her scent."

"Then why did you not take hold of her? Wouldn't that
have been the reasonable thing to have done?"

"I was so taken by surprise. I just stood there."

"And let her pass you!"

"You don't understand how shocked I was."

He took me by the shoulders and shook me, in an exasperated way.

"You're as fanciful as the servants. If she had been here,
how could she have got away without someone's seeing
her? Be reasonable, wife."

I was certain . . . and then not so certain.

Where did she go? I had been as though rooted to the
floor, it was true. I had given her a few seconds to escape,
but as Colum said, where could she have gone to?

I told no one but Colum what I had seen.

Jennet volunteered the information, though, that the
servants were more convinced than ever that the room
was haunted.

"Have any of them *seen* anything, Jennet?" I asked.

"They've *heard*," replied Jennet. "There was young Jim
who had to pass the room after dark one night, and he
said he heard something in there . . . something that would
make your hair stand on end."

Edwina would have seen significance in the vision. Did
it mean that danger had come back? Was I once more
threatened as I had been before?

I became convinced that I had seen a ghost.

I could not keep away from the Red Room. I used to
fancy I could smell the musky scent there. It was in the

pillows. I would turn sharply, expecting at any moment to see her standing behind me.

I felt the uneasiness returning.

My mother wrote exuberantly. There was great rejoicing at Lyon Court and Trystan Priory. The trading company had come so far that it was to be incorporated by charter under the title of the Governors and Company of Merchants of London Trading to East Indies.

"Our branch here is being swallowed up by the bigger ones, and Fennimore is delighted. Your father less so. He says he doesn't want interference from outside. But you see what it means, Linnet. It means Fennimore's venture is more successful than he ever dreamed it possibly could be.

"This will be a great company. It is planned to form agencies all over the world. Factories will be built. I cannot tell you how excited Fennimore is. For him it is the realization of a dream."

I told Colum. A cynical smile played about his lips.

"A great deal of effort to achieve what? The sailors will do all the work, and the profit will go elsewhere. Mark my words."

"They seem to think that the company will help make England great. It is what they wanted."

"Who is they? Your Fennimore! Are you thinking you should have married him?"

I was thinking it. What was the use of pretending otherwise. I had known little of Fennimore really—except that he was personable and an idealist. I thought too of men like Fennimore planning a great company which would bring good to England. I should have liked to plan with him.

Suppose I had never gone to the Traveler's Rest; suppose I had never met Colum. I pictured us all at Lyon Court. The great table would be weighed down with food, and there would be rejoicing because the object which had been so near to Fennimore's heart was showing great promise.

I felt then that fate had gone against me. I should have married Fennimore Landor. I should have been beside him in his triumph now. I could never share Colum's, for his successes meant disaster for others. I longed to share in Fennimore's enterprise, and how I hated those of my husband.

It was a mistake, I told myself desolately. A tragic mistake.

The gales came early that year. October had scarcely begun when they started roughing up the seas and throwing showers of sand against the castle walls. I was apprehensive. There were the times when there was nightly activity at Paling. Visitors to the castle brought news of ships that would be sailing near our coasts. I had gradually come to understand how well this diabolical business was organized.

I would lie in my bed alone and fearful, wondering what was happening outside. At such times I would promise myself, when the children are older, I will go away. I will set out as though on a visit to my mother and never come back. I could not take Connell. He would never leave the castle. He was his father's boy. But Tamsyn, who was now ten years old, and Senara would come with me. I would tell my mother why I could not return.

I knew this was only dreaming—a kind of sop to my conscience because I felt sullied by those murders. Sometimes I could not rid myself of the conviction that I was in a way involved, simply because I accepted what had happened and remained a wife to Colum even though I knew what he was doing.

During a long spell of fine weather, when there were no wrecks on our coast, my conscience would be lulled, and I would say to myself: A wife's place is beside her husband. She promised to remain with him, for better or worse. I had made my vows.

There came the night in mid-October. The wind had been rising all day. I was sickened by the now-familiar signs of activities. The lanterns in the two towers would be doused, I knew, and the donkeys would be out with their lights high on the cliff some miles away. News had come that a ship with a rich cargo was passing our way.

I lay in bed.

Was there not something I could do, should do? But what? How could I stop disaster? I could only pray that the captain of that ship would steer clear of the Devil's Teeth.

I scarcely slept at all. Soon after dawn I was up. I went down to the shore. Colum and his men were busy going out in their little boats bringing in the salvage. I saw one of the men down there, and I stopped him.

I said, "What sort of ship this time?"

"One of the finest, mistress." His eyes were cruel; his tongue came out and licked his lips. I could sense his excitement. He was doubtless calculating what his share in the profits would be. "One of them East India men we hear about—one of the *Lions.*"

The *Lions!* They were my father's ships. Did he not know that? I had begun to tremble. I said, "Did you see her name?"

" 'Twere the *Landor Lion,* mistress."

It was as though the waves rested in midair; there was a deep silence and then the sound of a madly beating drum which was my own heart.

The man looked at me oddly; then embarrassment was obvious on his face. He had forgotten for the moment who I was. I had come from Lyon Court: my father was Jake Pennlyon, the owner of the Lion Line.

He touched his forelock hastily and made off, terrified, of course, that he had given information which should be kept secret.

I just stood there looking out to sea. So high were the waves that I could see little. Somewhere out there was one of my father's ships lured to destruction by my wicked husband.

There could be no more complacency. This was the end of it.

Then the terrifying thought struck me: Who was on that ship?

I did not know what to do. What could I do? Could I take a boat out to the wreck? Impossible in such a sea. One of them must take me. I must know. I could not bear the suspense. What if my own father had been navigating that ship? It could not be. He knew this coast so well. But if he were deceived by the lights? I could not believe it, not of Jake Pennlyon, who had sailed the Spanish Main and come through unscathed after years of adventure.

What could I do? I must know.

I went into the castle and climbed the stairs to the ramparts from which point I should be able to get a long-distance view. The sun was coming up, and I could see the Devil's Teeth; I could see what must be the ship . . . the floating mass on the water . . . rich cargo, and bodies like as not. What if there were survivors? What did they do to survivors?

What had I been doing in this place all these years? Why had I allowed myself to become involved even for my children's sake?

I felt as helpless against the tide of my emotions as I was against the sea.

Later that day a body was washed up on our coast. I was the one who found it. I had been walking along the shore sadly, my thought in a turmoil, asking myself again and again what I could do.

He was lying there on the shore. I sank to my knees and looked at him. It was Fennimore. Dead.

It was years since I had seen those noble features. There was nothing I could do. The sea had taken him. Oh, Fennimore, who had had his dreams, Fennimore, the idealist who had lived long enough to start his noble enterprise, to see it expand, that scheme which was going to make his country great as wars never could.

The face of a dreamer, the man who would love an idea more than anything else, Fennimore, who might have been my husband.

I knelt and lifted his head into my lap. . . . I smoothed the wet hair made a darker shade of blond by the sea water. How fine his features were. And those glassy eyes had once shone with enthusiasm for a scheme and with love for me. He was a man who would accept fate unflinchingly. But his love was gentle; I married, and he took another wife. I wondered if he loved her. He would in a calm and gentle way, of course. He must have wanted sons, and he had one, named Fennimore as he was.

I thought how strange life was. If he had not come into my life, I should never have set out to visit his family and so come into Colum's orbit. His life was bound up with mine, in a way.

I could not leave him. I stayed there with him.

It was Colum who found me. I saw his face darken as he looked at me there with the dead man's head in my lap.

He cried, "In God's name. . . ."

"Yes," I said, " 'tis another of your victims."

"You interfering woman. Keep to your nurseries, will you?"

"No, I will not. You have destroyed one of my father's ships."

"If her captain had known how to steer her. . . ."

"Stop it," I shouted. "This was her captain. She was the *Landor Lion*—the ship my father and the Landors built. They brought back rich cargoes from the East Indies. You wanted those cargoes. One night's evil work would give you that which they had taken months of planning and labor to get together. I hate you and everything you stand for."

"A nice thing," he said, "to find a wife mourning her lover."

"He was never my lover."

"Nay, he had not the spirit for it. He wanted you, but being the lily-livered dandy he was, he was willing to pass you over and take another. Do you think you would have had the night sport with him you have had with me?"

I laid Fennimore's head gently down and rose.

I said, "He must be given a decent burial. On that I insist."

"Who are you, madam, to insist?"

"Not your slave, but your unfortunate wife."

"He shall be thrown back into the sea."

"Do not dare do such a thing. If you do, I will let it be known how you have made your fortune."

"You talk to me of daring. Know this, I will have my way, and you shall obey me."

"Why should I?"

"Because if you did not, you would regret it all the days of your life."

"I do not care for the rest of my life. Do what you will to me. Kill me if you will. Mine will not be the first death to be laid at your door."

"Go into the castle," he said.

"I shall not leave Fennimore Landor until he is taken reverently from here. I wish his body to be placed in the chapel and a coffin made for it. Then he will be buried beside his sister, that poor lady who was once your wife."

He looked at me and I saw the grudging light of admiration in his eyes.

"I marvel," he said, "that I should be so soft with you."

"I shall wait here," I said, "until he is taken into the chapel. I wish to stay with him for a while. I wish to arrange for his burial."

"And if I say no?"

"Then I shall leave the castle. I shall go to my father's house. I shall tell him what happened to the *Landor Lion* and its captain."

"Inform against the husband you have sworn to obey! Break your vows to me!"

"I shall have no hesitation in doing so."

He caught me by the arm. "Do you think I'd let you?"

"I would make the attempt."

"By God," he said, "I believe you would. You defy me; you give me no more children, and yet I have a softness

for you. You shall have your way in this, wife. He shall
be taken to the chapel, and he shall be buried beside his
sister. There shall be no name on his gravestone, and do
not let me hear the name of his ship pass your lips again.
It must be thought that he perished far from here. You
see how I indulge you."

I did not answer him. I dropped to my knees and looked
into Fennimore's dead face.

Colum went away, and shortly afterward four of the men
came to the shore.

They carried Fennimore's body to the chapel.

The next day he was buried beside his sister in the burial
grounds of the Casvellyns close to Ysella's Tower.

It was the end of an era. I could never forget it. I was
haunted by the memory of Fennimore's dead face. I wondered what would happen when my mother visited us. I
could no longer keep secrets from her. I was rather glad
we did *not* meet, for I was sure she would realize the change
in me.

The storm had taken place at the beginning of October.
Colum had strangely enough tried to woo me back to some
semblance of affection. I could not respond. The sight of
Fennimore dead on the shore had killed something in me
forever.

It was Halloween again, the night when witches rode on
their broomsticks to their covens where they worshiped the
devil in the form of the Horned Goat.

The day was misty and so typical of November in our
part of the world—warmish and everything one touched
was damp.

Because it was Halloween, the servants were talking. I
wondered if any of them remembered Maria. It was seven
years to the day since she had gone, and Senara was nearly
eight years old. It was a long time to remember.

But Jennet must have talked to the children of witches,
for when I went to the nursery, Senara was asking questions,
and Tamsyn was answering them, and she could only be
repeating what she had heard through Jennet.

"They go to covens," Tamsyn was saying.

"What are covens?" asked Senara.

"That's where they meet. They fly there on broomsticks
and there is their master, the devil. Sometimes he's a big
black cat, and sometimes he's a goat. He's ever so big . . .
bigger than anybody has ever been, and they dance."

"I want to go," said Senara.

Connell said, "If you go you're a witch. Then we'll catch you and tie you to your familiar and throw you in the sea."

"What familiar?"

"It's a cat perhaps."

"Could it be a dog?"

"Yes, a dog," cried Connell, "anything. Sometimes it's a mouse or a rat or a beetle . . . or a horse. It's anything."

"It could be Nonna," said Senara. Nonna was her own special puppy whom she had named after the tower. Her eyes were round. "Perhaps Nonna's my familiar."

"You can't have one," said Tamsyn protectively. "If you did, they'd say you were a witch."

"And we'd take you out and hang you on a gibbet," cried Connell with relish—his father's son.

"He wouldn't," said Tamsyn protectively. "I wouldn't let him."

"I'd hang him instead," said Senara.

"I'd like to see you try."

Connell had Senara by the hair. She kicked him. It was time for me to intervene. In fact, I did not know why I had allowed the conversation to go on so long.

"That's enough," I said. "You are all talking nonsense." Then I made them take out their books, and we read from Sir Thomas More's *Utopia*, which was far removed from the distasteful subject of witchcraft.

That night Maria came back.

Colum and I were supping together in the winter parlor. It was a rather silent meal as our meals had become. He made no effort to converse. Sometimes he would eat and leave me at the table.

I think that even he accepted the fact that after the death of Fennimore there was an unsurmountable barrier between us. I could sense a tension mounting; I wondered whether he cared. He did not always share the bedchamber; he had been away from home for several nights, presumably arranging for the disposal of the cargo salvaged from the *Landor Lion*, but on those occasions when he came to me, I sensed it was to let me know that he would still claim his rights. It was like staking a claim, an assurance of a right-of-way, I thought cynically. I hated those encounters, yet I still found excitement in them, and there was a sense of disappointment when he was not with me.

This was the state of affairs on that night.

She must have walked straight into the castle, for she came and stood in the room.

For the moment I thought I was seeing the ghost again. Then she spoke.

"I have come back," she said.

Colum stared at her—as I did.

"Come back," cried Colum. "Good God. Maria!"

"Yes," she said. "I come back. I live here again."

"But . . ." began Colum.

I stood up. I could feel myself trembling. "Where have you been?" I demanded. "Why have you come back?"

"It is nothing to you where I been," she said, in her halting English. "It matters not. I am back."

"You think you can just walk in . . ." said Colum.

"I think yes. You took my ship. . . . You kill my friends. You owe me home. I stay. Do not try to turn me away. If you do . . . you will be sorry. You owe me this. I take."

I said, "This cannot be."

"Yes," she answered, "it can." She was looking straight at Colum.

She was even more beautiful than I remembered. She wore a velvet cloak with a hood, which fell back to show her shining dark hair, which was piled high on her head. Her dark eyes were long, and smiling serenely. There was something unearthly about her. I am dreaming, I thought. This cannot really be Maria.

"I go to my room, my Red Room," she said.

"You cannot stay here," I began.

She ignored me and turned to Colum. "My belongings will come soon," she said. "I stay here for a while."

Then she left us.

I stared at Colum. "What does this mean? She has gone to the Red Room. This can't be true. Where has she come from?"

"She will stay here," he said.

"It is the price you must pay for murdering her people," I said. "Is that it?"

"Say what you will," he answered. "She shall stay."

Then he left me there.

And so Maria came back to Castle Paling.

The household was agog with rumor. The witch had returned. She could not have timed her arrival at a better time to suit their theory. First she had come on Halloween, a year later precisely to the day she had gone, and now she had returned seven years later on Halloween.

And she lived in the Red Room, that room where the servants had heard strange noises and where I myself had seen—or thought I saw—her ghost.

The servants watched Maria furtively. If she gave an order, they flew to obey her. They were terrified of the evil eye.

She went out riding alone. Once I met her; she did not acknowledge me but galloped off in another direction, her hair streaming behind her. Each day she rode.

It would soon be Christmas, and I longed to see my mother. I was very depressed when I heard from her.

"My dearest Linnet," she wrote. "The Landors are spending Christmas with us. As you know, they have suffered a terrible tragedy. Fennimore is almost certainly lost, and the *Landor Lion*, which was due to arrive home more than a month ago and had been sighted within ten miles of the coast, has not returned. We feared it might have been lost in that fearful storm we had at the end of October. Your father and Captain Landor have much to talk of. The loss of the ship alone is a great blow to them. But that Fennimore should have gone with it is more than his poor mother can endure. She is distraught, and I am going to have them here, with poor Fennimore's wife and children. I shall try to make them forget a little. It means, my dearest child, that we shall have to forgo our Christmas together, for you could not come without Colum and he could not come for reasons that you know. The loss of Fennimore has brought bitter memories of Melanie's death. As soon as they have gone, I shall come to see you. Or perhaps you will come here."

The days seemed long. It was late before the sun rose, and it set so early. "The darkest days are before Christmas," my mother used to say.

Into the house had crept something evil. I was sure if Edwina were here now, she would warn me again.

I could feel it. It came from the Red Room, and it menaced me.

Perhaps it was true that she was a witch. Perhaps she had not really been on the ship. Perhaps she had lain in the sea waiting for me to find her. I began to be beset by fancies.

What a beautiful woman she was! Perhaps it was evil beauty, but it was none the less seductive for that. She seemed to possess many personalities, and she would shed them as a snake sheds its skin. That was how I thought of her—as a beautiful sinuous serpent.

Everything about her was so mysterious. Where had she been during her absence? Where had she acquired the garments she possessed in such rich abundance? I began to suspect that the figure I had seen in the Red Room was in fact Maria herself and not a ghost. The servants heard noises in that room. I knew that Colum was not indifferent to her. Could it be possible that he had brought her to the castle, that he had been in touch with her all this time, perhaps keeping her in a home somewhere? It was a situation which would appeal to him. How could I be sure, but it seemed a plausible explanation. She was a Spaniard of noble birth, I was well aware, but it would not have been easy for her to return to Spain, and if she had, she would never have come back to England. I was sure that she derived a great satisfaction in creating this mysterious aura about herself, and for this reason she preserved this secrecy.

The children were fascinated by her too.

"Does Senara's mother live with us now?" asked Tamsyn.

"She will perhaps for a while," I replied.

"Most mothers live all the time with their children, don't they? But Senara's mother is different from all other mothers."

Senara said, "You are my real mother. She is my dream mother. I like to look at her. But I like best to know you're there."

"I'll always be here if you want me, Senara," I told her.

Connell said, "Maria is the most beautiful mother in the world."

Tamsyn watched me closely, her face growing red. "That's not true," she said, and blushed deeper because she was lying. "My mother is."

Dear Tamsyn, the protector!

How strange that during those days a thirty-year-old woman should turn to a ten-year-old child for protection. Protection! What an odd word to use.

In the matter-of-fact manner of children they accepted Maria's visitation as natural enough. That the servants talked of it in their hearing I did not doubt, but there she was, and they accepted her.

Maria was interested in her daughter now, for Senara was like her; one could see the relationship immediately—the same long eyes, the black hair, the perfectly shaped features. But Senara lacked the mystery; she was an ordinary little girl.

Maria was indeed shedding her skin. She was bringing out a different personality from that we had seen during that long-ago year she had spent in our household. She was becoming like a normal woman. She visited the schoolroom and listened to the children at their lessons. She petted Senara and gave her presents. She instructed the seamstress to make dresses for herself and Senara.

Senara was naturally a little vain. Such a lovely child could not help being aware of her beauty. She was naïvely proud of it, and my dear Tamsyn, who could be called almost plain in comparison, was proud of it too.

I was pleased to see that the coming of Maria had made no difference in their relationship. They shared a bedchamber and were never really content if they were separated for long.

Maria tried to charm my daughter. Sometimes I had a feeling that she was trying to break the great affection between us. She could not do that in the smallest way, and I fancied that Tamsyn had grown even more protective toward me. It was almost as though she were aware of some menace in the house. It may have been, though, that I, being aware of this, had become nervous and showed it.

What was most disturbing was the effect she was having on Colum. I could feel the tension rising. I, who knew him so well, realized that he wanted her as fiercely as he had once wanted me. I could see the smoldering light in his eyes when he surveyed her. She would join us at our intimate suppers. The three of us would be there at the table, the candlelight flickering on our faces—I knew that mine must have been alert and watchful. I knew too that neither of them paid much attention to me.

I cannot endure this, I thought. I must get away. I must go home to my mother. I should have confided in her long ago. She would have advised me what I must do.

Maria's beauty was unearthly. Satanic in its way, and I could understand that Colum found it irresistible.

Sometimes I thought they were lovers. Then I was not so sure. Those nights when he was not with me, where was he? In the Red Room?

I would lie in my bed unable to sleep. When I did doze fitfully, I would be beset by dreams—wild, fantastic dreams of visions. Maria was always in my dreams. And sometimes Colum. I saw them together writhing in an embrace. I would awaken clammy with sweat and fear and believe that there was someone in my room.

Tamsyn said, "You are not well, Mother. Shall I make a brew of the herbs Aunt Edwina gave us? I know how to."

"What would you give me, Tamsyn?" I asked.

"The pimpernel brings laughter, so I would give you that. But it is not the time of year for pimpernel. Poppy brings sleep. But there are no poppies either. But I have an ashen branch, and if that is put beneath your pillow, it will drive away evil spirits."

"My dearest child, I am happy just to be with you."

"I *am* your dearest child," she said. "More dear to you than any of the others. I know it. It makes me happy. I will look after you always."

"Bless you, my darling," I said.

She was silent for a while. Then she said, "If I were older, you would tell me what ails you."

"Nothing ails me in truth."

"I think something does. But I will look after you."

"Then I shall soon be well," I said, and I held her against me.

Maria came riding into the courtyard. I saw her from my window. She leaped from her horse, and a groom hurried to take it away and feed and water it. She came into the castle and, I suspected, went to the Red Room. I sat at my window, wondering about her. Ten minutes later Colum came in.

I said to myself: He has gone to the Red Room.

I knew that he had.

What did he say to her there? There would be no need for words. They were lovers. I sensed it. It was two weeks since he had come to me. I felt a sick resentment against her for being more beautiful than I, more desirable to him.

I hated him; I feared him. There had always been something of these emotions in me.

I wished I could have talked of this to my mother. I felt she would have understood. I wished I could talk to her of these sudden bouts of fear which possessed me. There was no one to whom I could talk. I seemed to hear my daughter's voice: "If I were old enough, you could tell me."

Oh, Tamsyn, I thought, if only I could!

They were making love in the Red Room. Afterward they would talk. Would they talk of me? How did they talk of me? But why should they? Of what importance was I to them—only of course that if they wished for marriage, I stood in their way.

He was tired of me. I knew that. He would no longer be indulgent as he once had. I would irritate him. Was this how Melanie had felt? He despised her. Did he bring his mistress of the moment into the castle? Was she of so little account to him that he did not care?

It could never be thus with me. Once he had wanted me so urgently that he had gone to great lengths to get me.

He would not come to me now. Perhaps never again. I had not given him the children he wanted. Only two and one a girl.

He wanted sons, many sons, lusty boys, whom he could train in his hideous profession.

I went to bed. I lay there, the curtains drawn back. I could not bear to have them closed because if I did, I would have frightening fancies about what was happening in the room.

As I lay there, I heard footsteps in the corridor . . . slow, creeping footsteps. My blood seemed suddenly cold. They had paused outside my door.

I could hear the sound of the latch being lifted.

"Who's there?" I called out in alarm.

There was no answer.

"Who is it?" I said.

I lay there waiting. Terror upon me. Who could it be? Whom did I fear? Maria? Colum?

For some seconds I lay there. Then I rose and went to the door. I opened it.

There was no one near.

The children were decorating the hall with holly and ivy.

I went out with them to bring in the yule log; they shrieked with happiness, and I could feel myself being temporarily caught up in it. The damp, soft air made my skin glow, and I felt better than I had for some time.

Even the castle seemed less grim. The Christmas spirit had entered the house. And when it was over, I promised myself I would go to my mother. I had made up my mind that I would tell her everything. I thought she might advise me not to return to the castle, and that is what I wanted.

I had always been careful with my journal—if such it could be called—because I dared not let Colum see it. The thought of his reading it had from the start embarrassed me; now I supposed it would be more than that. So when I had finished writing, I always put it carefully where only I would know where to find it.

Since Maria had come back into the house, I felt it was even more necessary than ever to keep my writings out of the way.

Because I kept it hidden, I had always felt that I could write freely, which is the only way in which one can write a document such as this.

As we grew nearer to Christmas, both Maria and Colum changed so much that I could, if I had not written down my feelings and what actually happened, have forgotten half of it and perhaps convinced myself that I had exaggerated. So I often looked back and read what I had written at the time it happened. It was amazing how it helped me to realize the truth of my situation. I somehow thought that it was because of this that I had felt this fear.

Now Colum was full of bonhomie and Christmas spirit. Maria had become human. She became less secretive. It seemed that the Christmas spirit of goodwill to all men had crept into the house.

"We shall not have your family here this Christmas," said Colum, "nor go to them. We shall have to make up for that. We'll have the mummers in to do a play. How's that?"

The children were delighted. Tamsyn and Senara made a Christmas crib, and while they were making it, Tamsyn decided that they should do a Nativity play themselves and the grown-ups should be their audience.

Tamsyn was cleverer at her books than the others, and she wrote the play, which they would present in mime, for Connell declared that he would not learn words. Two or three of the local squires were being invited, and as they had children, these would be brought in to play their parts.

Senara was to be the Virgin at first, but somehow she didn't look the part, but she did make an enchanting shepherd boy who saw the star in the East, and to her surprise Tamsyn was the Virgin. I was pleased because in spite of her somewhat retroussé nose and her wide mouth, there was a purity about her, and I set about devising her costume. This was where Maria showed herself in a new light. She found materials for the costumes and appeared to enjoy helping them to dress up. Even Colum watched with amusement, and Connell, who might so easily have imagined such mummery only fit for girls, was delighted to be one of the three kings.

There was a great deal of speculation as to who would

find the silver penny and be King for the Night. Connell boasted of what he would do if he were.

There was to be dancing music and singing: the children would sing madrigals in which we would all join; then they would show their skill with their lutes and recorders.

From the kitchens there came the smell of baking. There was to be feasting as never before.

I was almost lulled to a sense of security, but not quite, for as soon as I retired for the night and was alone in my room, I would begin to wonder what was in store for me, and I would remember glances which I had—or imagined I had—intercepted between Colum and Maria. The excitement of Christmas could not dispel the suspicions that they were lovers. I think perhaps at the heart of my fears was the fact that Colum should seek to hide this from me. I was sure he had hidden nothing from Melanie. Why should he attempt to delude me if he no longer cared for my feelings? Was it because he realized this passion for Maria was a fleeting thing? Did he fear that she would disappear again as she had once before?

There was one night about a week before Christmas when these fears seemed stronger than ever. I tossed and turned in my bed, and it must have been soon after midnight when I could stay there no longer. I got out of bed, wrapped a gown about me and sat at the window.

What thoughts came back to me then as I looked down on the sea, calm as a lake, with a shaft of moonlight making a path on the waters! I could see the Devil's Teeth just protruding, for it was going to be a high tide. The gentle swish of the waves soothed me, and I began to nod.

Then suddenly I was awake. I felt a tingling down my spine, that previously experienced raising of my hair on my scalp. I gave a little cry, for there had been a sound in the room, and in my half-sleeping state I believed that the door had opened and someone had looked at the bed and then at me. I was sure I heard a click as the door closed.

As before, I ran to the door. There was no one there. It was a bad dream. But I was trembling. I could not go back to bed. I was afraid that if I did so, frightened as I was, I should sleep. Something warned me. I *must* not sleep. Twice I had thought someone had meant to enter my room. The first time I had called out, and whoever it was had not entered. The second time that person had entered and seen me at the window. If I had been sound asleep . . . what then?

I was haggard in the morning. I had scarcely slept all night.

Tamsyn looked at me with anxious eyes. "Are you well, Mother? You look not well."

I said, "I did not sleep well. I had a bad dream, I think." She nodded gravely.

That evening Jennet came up with a posset.

"The master said you were to have it, mistress."

"Why?" I demanded.

"He said he thought you were doing too much for the Christmas preparations and had got tired. He said he was worried about your health, and if you did not improve, he was going to call the physician."

I thought of that other beverage which had been prepared for me, the one which had made me lose my senses on that very first night in the castle.

I said to Jennet in sudden alarm, "Did he make the posset?"

"Oh, no, mistress. He but bid me make it."

"Then you know what's in it."

"Surely I do, mistress. 'Tis the posset I make always when the children have their ailments. I have the herbs by me, dried they be and all in their sweet-smelling jars, as I did learn from your mother, as learned from hers. This be a good one if you are feeling out of sorts. There be goose grass to sweeten the blood and a sprig of woodruff for the liver, for 'tis very often the liver as will affect you poorly."

"Give it to me, Jennet," I said. "I will drink it, and tomorrow you will see me brimming over with health."

So I drank the posset, and indeed it did soothe me to such an extent that when I lay on my pillow, I was almost immediately fast asleep.

I awoke startled. Someone was in my room, standing at my bedside. I felt as though a thousand ants were crawling over my skin. I could not see very clearly. The moonlight must have been obscured by dark clouds. Hands were reaching out. I was caught and held.

"No," I screamed.

Then a soothing voice said, "It is all right, Mother."

"Tamsyn."

She was laughing as she clambered into my bed.

I held her tightly against me. "Dearest Tamsyn."

"I frightened you," she said.

"I must have been dreaming."

"I should have awakened you gently. How you shiver!"

"It was waking suddenly. Why did you come, Tamsyn?"

"I was worried about you. I couldn't sleep. You looked so tired yesterday. Not like yourself at all. Then I thought I will go and be with her. She may need me. And without thinking very much, I came."

"Oh, Tamsyn, it makes me so happy to have you with me."

"Do you feel comforted then because I am here?"

"Greatly so."

"I shall stay with you."

"Yes, do. I feel so happy to have you with me."

She clung to me.

"You feel better with me here?"

"I feel so happy, Tamsyn. So much better already."

After a while she said, "I thought to find my father here with you."

"Nay, he is not always here."

She was thoughtful. Then she said, "He is away so much. I'll swear he does not want to disturb you."

"That may be so, Tamsyn."

"You are getting sleepy."

"Yes, I am."

"I shall stay with you, because I feel you like it better when I am here."

"I feel so happy to have you, Tamsyn . . . so safe."

"Let us sleep then, Mother. You need to sleep. Then you will be gay and happy as you used to be."

So we slept together, and in the morning I felt better.

Tamsyn said, "I shall stay with you, Mother, until you are quite well again. I think you need me. Who knows, you might want something in the night."

It seemed absurd, but I felt a great relief sweeping over me, for it was true that with my little daughter there I felt safe.

Christmas Day came, and in the morning the carol singers arrived. There was a great bowl of mulled wine from which everyone drank, and we all joined in the singing. We gave each other gifts, and we kissed and declared no presents could have pleased us more than those we had received.

In the afternoon the children did their miracle play. I was deeply moved to watch Tamsyn in her role. It was declared a great success, and the children enjoyed it very much as did we all.

I sat with our guests and watched Colum and Maria.

Perhaps it was not obvious to others, but it was to me. There was something about the manner in which they avoided looking at each other and then suddenly they would be unable to prevent it. There was scorching passion there. I sensed it. The children played their recorders and lutes, and the feasting began. The table was laden with food of all descriptions; there was beef, mutton, sucking pig and boar's head, pies of various kinds—muggety, natlin, squab, leek and herby. There was dash-an'-darras, a kind of stirrup cup, and metheglin and all kinds of wines—cowslip, gilly-flower, blackberry and elder.

All seemed to eat heartily, and afterward there was dancing, singing and the choosing of King for the Night. Strangely enough this fell to Colum. There were loud cries of protest as he produced the silver penny. He was lord of the castle in any case. Connell was bitterly disappointed. Then the games began, and when we went in search of the treasure, Colum chose me as his partner.

I was suddenly happy and told myself that I had been mistaken in him. Perhaps he really still cared for me. He could have chosen Maria, who had gone off with one of the visiting squires; and all knew that for the grown-ups this game was an opportunity for getting together and being alone.

Colum said, "It has gone well, eh?"

"The children are enjoying it, which is the main thing."

"Nay," he said banteringly, "we have as much right to enjoy Christmas as the children. Come," he went on, and we climbed the stairs to the ramparts.

We were up there alone in the cool night air.

It was a beautiful night—the calm sea, the slightly protruding Devil's Teeth, and to our left the Seaward Tower with the light burning from the lantern.

Colum leaned over and looked down.

"How far away it seems," he said.

"A long drop," I answered.

Then he came close to me and caught me around the waist, and I had a panic-stricken moment when I thought he was going to throw me over. I felt my body go rigid with terror.

"Yes," he said slowly, "it's a long, long way down."

I drew away from him and looked at him in the night light. His eyes were brilliant. I thought: He is going to tell me something. He is going to tell me that he loves Maria.

For a few seconds the thought flashed into my head that he was inviting me to throw myself down there onto the rocks.

I said in a voice the steadiness of which surprised me, "I think we should join our guests. Someone will have found the treasure by now."

"*We* must not find it," said Colum. "That would be wrong. They would say it was contrived. It is bad enough that I should have found the silver penny and become King for the Night. King for the Night . . . anything I want tonight is mine. Whatever I ask, eh?"

"Are you not always king in your castle?"

"Can it be that you recognize this at last?"

I laughed coldly, and we went down to join our guests.

Connell and his partner, the young daughter of one of the squires, had found the treasure—which were two little gold amulets in a box. The box was brought to Colum, who then presented it to them with the customary remark that the contents of the box would protect them from cursed devils, sprites, bugs, conjuring and charms.

Connell was delighted. It was a consolation for not finding the silver penny.

There were bound to be casualties, and one was Senara. She was sick, and Tamsyn said she would take her to her bed.

Several of the visitors were staying for a few days, and in due course they were lighted to their rooms.

I went to mine, and I could not resist writing my account of what had happened that day. I liked to do it while it was fresh in my memory. As I wrote, I heard footsteps outside my door, and I hastily put the papers away.

It was Tamsyn.

She had come every night to look after me.

"Senara is very sick," she said. "She wants me to be with her. She says she is better when I am there."

"Go to her, my dear," I said.

"Well, you are better today, Mother."

"Yes, my love. Do not fret about me."

"Jennet is giving Senara a dose of herb twopence. She says that will cure anything."

"She will be better in the morning."

She clung to me for a moment. "You are sure, Mother, that you are all right without me?"

"Of course, my darling. Good night. Go and look after Senara."

I kissed her fondly and she went out.

I went on writing. I would finish right up to that moment when I had kissed her good night. Then I should put the papers away and go to bed.

Part Two

TAMSYN

The Unknown
Sailor's Grave

Christmas is never a happy time for me. I can never forget that it was at Christmas that my mother died, and although it happened six years ago, I remember it as vividly now as I did the first Christmas after.

I was ten years old at the time. It had been quite a merry Christmas Day. We had done a miracle play, the mummers had been to the castle, and we had danced, sung and played our musical instruments.

I often thought that if I had been with her on that night, it wouldn't have happened. For several nights before I had slept in her bed, and then Senara had been ill and I had stayed with her.

I would often think of those nights when my mother had been so pleased to have me with her. I was very young then, and children don't always see things clearly. I had imagined that she clung to me and that it seemed so important that I should be there.

And the next morning she was dead.

Jennet found her. I often go over it all. How I had heard Jennet scream and come running to me, and I couldn't get a coherent sentence out of her. I went to my mother's room, and there she was lying in her bed. She looked unlike herself—so still and cold when I touched her cheek.

The strange thing was that there was nothing to indicate how she had died.

My father's physician came and said that her heart had failed her. He could find no other reason why she should have died.

She had been ailing for some weeks, my father said, and he had been very anxious about her. We all confirmed that.

I felt sick with anger against myself. I had the notion that had I been with her, this would never have happened. I had sensed in those days before her death that she was afraid. Then I wondered whether I had imagined it. At ten years one is not very wise.

There was a great deal of whispering in the castle among the servants, but whenever I appeared, they stopped and said something quite banal so that I was well aware that they had changed the subject.

My grandmother arrived from Lyon Court. She was stunned. She looked so bewildered, just as I felt, and she took me in her arms, and we cried together. "Not Linnet," she kept saying. "She was too young. How could it have been?"

No one knew. People's hearts sometimes failed them, said the physician. Their time had come. God had seen fit to take them, and so they went.

My grandfather was away at sea; so were my uncles Carlos, Jacko and Penn. Edwina came, though. She seemed so strained and frightened. She broke down and said that she ought to have done something, that she had seen it coming. She wouldn't explain, and we didn't quite know what she meant, and she was too distressed and hysterical to say more. But I felt drawn toward her because she blamed herself in much the same way as I did, for I continued to feel that had I been with her, it wouldn't have happened.

There was a service in the old Norman chapel, and she was buried in our burial grounds close by Ysella's Tower. She was put next to the grave of the unknown man who had been washed ashore when there was a wreck at sea earlier that year. On the other side of the unknown man's grave was my father's first wife.

More than anyone—even Senara—I had loved my mother. This was the great tragedy of my life. I told my grandmother that I would never get over it.

She stroked my hair and said, "The pain will grow less

for you, Tamsyn, even as it will for me, but it is hard for either of us to believe that yet."

She said she would take me back to Lyon Court with her. It would be easier for me there, she said. I longed to go with her. I kept thinking of my mother and the last time I had seen her. I should never forget it. She was in her bedroom, and when I came, she was standing up and looked as though she had hidden something. But perhaps I imagined that.

Senara said I should not reproach myself. She had been so sick, and naturally I stayed with her.

"Besides," said Senara, "what could you have done?" She was only eight years old then, and I couldn't explain to her this uncanny feeling I had. It was because my mother and I were so much in harmony. I felt she knew something that she hadn't told me. If she had, I might have under-stood. I remember how angry I was with myself for being so young.

When my grandmother suggested I go back with her, I said that I couldn't leave Senara, so she immediately said that Senara must come too. I told Senara, and she was pleased; she wanted to get away from the castle. My father raised no objection to our going. I had never known my father so quiet before.

I felt a little comforted to be at Lyon Court. I had always enjoyed my visits there. Lyon Court was a young house compared with the castle. It seemed open, frank, candid . . . which doesn't seem the right word with which to describe a house, but I use it in comparison with the castle—which was sly, in a way, full of secrets, having stood so long, I suppose. There had been a castle there in Norman days, and of course it had been improved on over the Plantagenet years. My grandmother said that Lyon Court was ostentatious and that the Pennlyons wanted everyone to know that they had made a fortune. It was the sort of house which was proud of itself if you can think of houses having personalities, which I do, and it was a happy one.

The gardens were famous in the neighborhood for their beauty, and my grandmother liked that to be kept up. At this time of year there was not much blooming naturally, but there was that air of promise, of spring and summer glory.

We could see across Plymouth Hoe and out to the Sound with the ships coming and going. Senara loved it, and as she had not suffered as much as I had over my mother's death—although she had loved her too—she began to be excited about being at Lyon Court. Sometimes she would laugh aloud and then look at me in dismay. I would tell her she was not to worry if she forgot now and then because that would please my mother if she were aware of what was happening here. She would not wish us to mourn more than we could help.

My Aunt Damask who was fifteen—young for an aunt— was told by her mother to look after us and she did; but she was unhappy, for she had loved my mother dearly, as all seemed to who had known her.

Looking back at the visit, I think of sadness. We could not escape our sorrow by leaving the castle. This was my mother's old home. At the great table in the lofty hall she had sat; she had climbed the staircases, walked along the gallery, ate here, slept here, laughed here. The memory of her was as strong here as it was at the castle.

But it was not unrelieved gloom because of the Landors. They had been staying with my grandmother for Christmas, and when she had heard of my mother's death and had come at once to the castle, they had left Lyon Court and gone to visit other members of the trading company and were calling back for another brief stay on their way to their home at Trystan Priory. I had heard the name Landor now and then, and I knew that this family was connected with my grandfather's business, which was often spoken of with a kind of awe. I had gathered that my father was a little skeptical of it, for I had seen his lips curl when it was mentioned.

Senara and I were in the gardens with Damask, who was playing a song she had learned. I knew her mother had told her that she must try to take my mind off my mother's death, and this was what she was attempting to do. There was a clatter of horses' hooves and the sound of voices, all of which I connected with arrivals. Damask stopped playing and said, "Someone has come. I wonder who."

Senara jumped up and was ready to see who it was. She was volatile and impulsive. I continually had to curb her.

I said, "We ought to wait until we are sent for, shouldn't we, Damask?"

Damask agreed with me. "People often come," she said. "Do you have many visitors at Castle Paling?"

I thought of the visitors—the squires of the neighborhood who came when invited for Christmas and such festivities; we had always known when to expect them. There were others though who came unexpectedly. They weren't ordinary visitors. They came to talk business with my father, and I remember that my mother always seemed uneasy when they were in the house.

"We have a few," I said.

"We have lots," said Senara, who liked everything of hers to be bigger and better than anyone else's. She had a habit of deceiving herself into thinking that it was. I checked her when I could.

"When your grandfather is here, the house is often full," said Damask.

I was glad he was not there. I knew his grief would be loud and vociferous. He would be angry because my mother had died and seek to blame someone. He always looked around for a culprit when anything went wrong. He would demand why doctors had not been called and blame my father. I knew he would. I did not want my father to be blamed.

"We shall soon know who it is," I said.

And so we did.

I believe now that meeting Fenn Landor at that time helped me far more than anything else could. He too was ten years old—a few months older than I was. A good-looking boy with deep-blue eyes; he was very serious. Perhaps because we were of an age, he singled me out for a special companion—Senara was too young, Damask too old—and through him I began to be interested in life again as, in my ten-year-old ignorance, I had thought I never could be.

He liked us to be alone so that he could talk. He chafed against his youth and longed to be a man. We would go off together and lie on the cliffs looking over the sea, or sometimes we would ride together. My grandmother, watching us closely, allowed this. I realized that she thought that Fenn could do more for me than perhaps anyone. He was not part of my old life as the rest of them were. He was someone entirely new, and when I was with him, I could cease to think of my tragedy for half an hour at a time.

He told me about his father, who, according to him had been the finest man in the world. "He wasn't rough and swaggering as so many men are," he told me. "He was good and noble. He hated killing people. He never killed a man in his life. He wanted to bring good into people's lives."

"When did he die?"

"People say he is lost, but I don't believe it. He'll come back one day. He was due to come home. We watched for him every day. Every morning, when I wake up, I say to myself, 'This will be the day.' And it goes on and on. . . ."

I could see a look of blank despair in his face, and I longed to comfort him. I knew that although he said he believed his father was alive, he feared that he was not.

"His ship was the *Landor Lion*. It was a joint venture—the Pennlyons and the Landors, you see. My family and your grandfather's."

"Ships are often delayed for months."

"Yes, but you see this one was sighted off the coast in October and there was a great storm."

"I remember the great storm."

"So you see. . . ."

"Go on hoping," I said. "Unexpected things happen to ships. It might not have been his ship that was sighted. You can't be sure."

"No," he said firmly. "You can't be sure."

Then he told me about the new East India company which had been founded, and he talked glowingly of the progress it had made and how his father had been instrumental in making it great.

"It was his idea really, you see. It started long ago before I was born. It was after the defeat of the Armada. My father believed that peaceful trading was the answer to our problems." I noticed with a touch of sorrow that he talked of his father in the past tense, and I knew that in his heart he could not help thinking he was dead.

"How old will you have to be before you join your father?" I said deliberately to restore his belief.

He smiled suddenly dazzlingly; he had a beautiful face when he was happy.

"Sixteen perhaps. Six whole years."

I was able to tell him about my mother's death and that was the reason I was at Lyon Court with my grandmother. I found I could talk to him of that sad event more calmly than with anyone else. It was because he too had lost a deeply loved one. The bond instantly formed between us. I knew he had loved and admired his father more than anyone just as I had loved and admired my mother.

Thus we could comfort each other.

I made him tell me about ships and the company. His father had talked a great deal to him. I could imagine the sort of father he had been—a father of whom his children need never be afraid and for whom they had the utmost love and affection and, above all, respect. An ideal father. To have had such a father was a great blessing, but alas, to lose him must be the greatest tragedy.

Once he said to me, "Why is it that we have never met before? We often come here. You must do too, for this is the home of your grandparents."

I admitted it was odd, for we had come frequently.

"We must just have missed each other."

There was no doubt that Fenn and I did a great deal for each other, and my grandmother was pleased about this.

There was one strange incident which happened during that visit and which I could never forget.

Senara, Damask and I shared a room at Lyon Court. It was a big room, and there were three beds in it. One night I lay sleepless, for I had not slept well since my mother's death. I dreamed a good deal about her, and I would wake up suddenly and imagine she was calling to me to come to her, for she was afraid of something. This dream was a recurring one. In it I was always fighting to get to her and was unable to reach her. I would call out in my despair, and then I was awake.

This is what happened on that particular night. I woke up wretched and sat up in bed, being unable for the moment to realize where I was. Then out of the gloom the familiar objects took shape—the planked hutch, the table with the carved panels and the two other pallets on which lay Damask and Senara.

I could hear the sound of someone's crying. I got out of bed, wrapped a robe about me and opened the door. I went into the corridor. The crying was coming from the room next to ours.

I knocked lightly on the door, and as there was no answer, I opened it gently. In the window seat sitting very still, the tears falling unheeded down her cheeks, was Fenn's grandmother.

She started up as I entered. I said quickly, "I'm sorry. I heard your crying. Is there anything I can do?"

"It is Tamsyn," she said. "Did I awaken you?"

"I was not sleeping very well."

"You too are grieving," she said. "My poor child, you have lost your mother. I have lost my daughter and my son."

"Perhaps he did not drown."

"Yes, he did. He comes to me in dreams. His eyes are

empty sockets, and the fishes swim around him; the sea has him; he lies deep on the sea bed, and I shall never see my beloved son again."

There was something alarming about the wildness in her eyes, and I could see that her grief was an illness and that she was deeply stricken by it.

"Both my son . . . and my daughter," she said.

"Your daughter too?"

"My daughter was murdered," she said.

"Murdered!" I whispered.

She caught her breath in a gasp of horror, and then she said, "You are little Tamsyn Casvellyn. I must not talk to you of my daughter."

"You may talk to me of anything if it comforts you to do so."

"My dear child," she said. "My poor dear child."

I cried a little because, as Fenn helped me forget my grief, she brought it back in all its vividness. I was right back in that dreadful morning when I had gone into my mother's bedroom and seen her lying there. I could hear Jennet babbling of what she had found, and all my misery swept over me afresh.

She rocked me to and fro. "Life has been cruel to us both, my child, cruel . . . cruel. . . ."

"When did your daughter die?"

"Before you were born. . . . It had to be before you were born." I did not understand that, but I had already discovered that she was incoherent.

"She was murdered by her husband. He is a murderer. One day fate will catch up with him. You see. It will be so. I am sure of it. And now my beautiful boy is taken from me by the sea. He was so young to die. Why did it have to happen to him? Within a few miles of the coast he was. . . ."

"Perhaps he will come back."

"Never," she said. "I shall never see his face again."

"At least," I said, "you have hope."

And I thought: I have no hope. I have seen my mother laid in her grave. Vividly into my mind there flashed the picture of the family burial ground—the grave of my father's first wife and that of the unknown sailor and my mother's.

She started to talk then, of her son, Fennimore, and his ambitions. "No mother ever had a better son. He was noble; he was good. He was a great man. And my daughter . . . my little girl. She was frail. She should never have married.

But it seemed natural and there was that . . . that"—her voice sank to a whisper—"that monster!"

I tried to soothe her. I said she must go back to bed. But she would not be soothed; she started to lament loudly, and I could not calm her.

I did not know what to do because she was becoming hysterical, and I thought she must be ill. She clung to me, but I managed to disengage myself, and I went along to my grandmother's room.

I wakened her and told her what had happened.

"Poor woman," she said, "she is in a sorry state. This terrible disappearance of her son has brought back the tragic loss of her daughter. She gives way to her grief, and I fear it will unhinge her mind."

We went back to her. She was sitting there, her hands covering her face while she rocked back and forth in her misery.

My grandmother said to me, "You should go to bed, my child."

I did not take any notice. I felt there was something I could do.

"Come, Janet," said my grandmother, "you should go to bed. I will bring you something to make you sleep." She took Janet Landor's arm, and I took the other. We led her to her bed.

"Lie still," soothed my grandmother. "Try to sleep. Don't brood. It can do no good. We can best help ourselves and others by stifling our grief."

I was proud of her because I knew how she suffered from my mother's death, and I wanted to be like her.

"That child's mother," whispered Janet, "was she murdered too?"

My grandmother had taken me by the arm.

"She is rambling," she whispered to me. "Now, Tamsyn, go back to your bed. Try not to disturb the others. I will look after this lady. Good night, my child."

I went away wondering about poor Janet Landor, and there was one phrase which kept ringing in my head: "That poor child's mother . . . was she murdered too?"

She must have been referring to my mother, and what did she mean?

My grandmother had said she was rambling, and she was certainly hysterical. She could not have been referring to my mother!

I did not see Janet Landor for several days, and when I

did, she was quiet again, and although I forgot that nightly disturbance, the memory of it was to return to me with some force later.

Senara and I stayed with my grandmother until the spring. It was May when we went back to the castle.

A surprise awaited us. Our father had married again. Senara's mother was to be my stepmother.

After coming back from Lyon Court, Castle Paling seemed an alien place, even though it had always been my home. Everything seemed to have changed since we had been away. My mother's influence had been eliminated entirely, and in its place was something new—intangible, it was hard to say what.

Some of the furnishings had been changed—the bed-chamber which my mother and father had shared was entirely different. There were rich velvet hangings about the bed and at the windows. There was a foreign look about it. I looked into the Red Room. That had been left exactly as it always had been. I remembered all the stories I had heard about its being haunted. My mother's sitting room, which she had used so much, was also left untouched. There was her carved wooden chair and the table on which stood the rather large sandalwood writing desk of which she had always been fond.

Senara was secretly proud that her mother instead of being a mysterious guest in the castle was now the undis-puted mistress of it. She had previously, I think, felt some-thing of an outsider, and that was why I constantly tried to remind her that I thought of her as my sister.

The servants had changed. They whispered a lot; they were constantly crossing themselves as though for protection against the evil eye. I knew that they were afraid of my stepmother, Maria; sometimes I thought even my father was a little.

I could not suppress a certain resentment. In the first place, I hated to see someone in my mother's place; in the second, I thought it had happened too quickly. Three months after she had died my father had married my stepmother, and the fact that she had been living in the castle was somehow even more shocking.

My father had never taken much notice of me. Connell was his favorite. He had little regard for girls—at least not for his own daughter. He kept out of my way after my return almost as though my presence embarrassed him. He knew how very devoted my mother and I had been to each other.

At first Senara gave herself airs, but that was very soon at an end. The friendship between us was too firm for anything to harm it. The fact that her mother had taken my mother's place might have caused a rift in some cases, not with us.

My father engaged a tutor to give us lessons because my mother had done so in the past, and he was already installed at the castle—a Master Eller. He seemed aged, but I doubt he was much more than forty-five. He was strict and serious, and even Connell had to pay attention although he hated lessons and at twelve years old thought he should have been beyond them.

Jennet had scarcely changed except that she had aged a little. I think my mother's death had shocked her deeply. She was only a year younger than my grandmother, and I knew she had regarded my mother as her own daughter. She used to go about muttering to herself, and she harbored a dislike for my stepmother which she was afraid to show.

So many people were afraid of my stepmother. It was because she had come on Halloween, and that was the time for witches. That she was different from other people was clear. She never appeared to be angry, but if she were displeased, there would be a glitter in her eyes which was as frightening as my father's loud displays of temper. Everyone and everything were different. The castle seemed full of shadows. Servants were afraid when the darkness fell. Jennet, who had been so talkative and pleased with life, was no longer so. On her face was a perpetual expression of bewilderment. Once she broke down and wept. "I knew your mother when she was a baby," she told me. "I held her in my arms when she was but a day old. Your grandmother was good to me but sharp. She lifted her hand against me more than once, but Miss Linnet. . . ." She broke down, and we cried together.

Then Jennet crossed herself suddenly and said in a hollow voice, "God help us all. That good lady's place . . . my little Mistress Linnet's place . . . be took by. . . ." Then she looked over her shoulder and after a long pause she murmured, "By . . . by another."

Like everyone else, Jennet was afraid of my stepmother. I wondered about my father. His eyes followed her wherever she was. I heard one of the servants say, "He be spellbound."

Now and then I found her dark eyes fixed on me. I don't think she understood me. She was expecting me to be resentful toward her for taking my mother's place; stepmothers were not generally liked by the children of their predecessors. But I knew that hating her could not bring my mother back. She was Senara's mother, and Senara thought her wonderful. My misery did not take the form of wanting to blame someone. When she understood this, she ignored me, and I was glad of that. Although she had never shown affection for Senara, she was anxious for her future. She made sure that Master Eller made an educated lady of her, and she engaged a young man to teach us dancing and singing. His name was Richard Gravel, and we called him Dickon. He played the lute and the virginals in such a manner as to raise the spirits or bring tears and make the heart melt, and he could dance so beautifully that when he performed, it was impossible to take one's eyes from him. Senara was enraptured by him and was eager to excel at both music and dancing. We learned country dances, morris dancing, but chiefly those which would be performed at balls and banquets. It occurred to me that my stepmother wished to make a great lady of her daughter, and because I was her companion, I shared in the tuition too. It vaguely entered my mind that she did not believe Senara would be in the country all her life. This training was to make a court lady of her.

But we were far from the court. Deep in my mind was the knowledge that if my stepmother desired it, so would it be. I had heard one of the servants mention that she had the powers. I had never heard the expression before, but I understood immediately what she meant.

It is surprising how very quickly young people can adjust themselves to situations. Before the year was out, my home no longer seemed an alien place; the extraordinary had become commonplace. It was not that I forgot my mother; I should never do that. I used to go to the burial ground and put flowers on her grave, and because it seemed unfair to leave out those other two, I put flowers on them

There were of course several long-dead Casvellyns in the burial grounds, but these three graves were together, and I was sorry for my father's first wife, Melanie, and the unknown sailor. To set my mother's apart, I planted a rosemary bush on hers, because rosemary is for remembrance. When I planted that tree, the notion came to me that my mother was not completely lost to me; she was close to me at all times and particularly so when I needed her help. Whatever the delights of heaven, she would never leave me entirely alone. I sensed her presence watching over me, guarding me from evil. It was a comforting thought, and once it had come to me, it stayed with me and I began to be happy again.

Life settled down to a new pattern. Lessons with Master Eller and singing and dancing with Dickon took up a great deal of our time. We rode with the grooms; we visited Lyon Court, although my grandmother never came to us, and she was never pressed to do so. I believed that she did not want to be in a household where my mother had lived, nor did she wish to see my father's third wife. But I was encouraged to go to her whenever I wished, and when I went, Senara accompanied me. It was inconceivable to either of us that we should be parted. We quarreled occasionally, but we both knew that those differences would be quickly settled. We were very different in temperament. I was quiet, rather serious, not easily roused to anger and enjoyed looking after people. Senara was impatient with me sometimes, although she liked me to look after her. She was full of life: she hated lessons. Master Eller despaired of her, but she played the virginals and the lute with passion and flair; she could sing prettily, and she danced so gracefully that it was a great joy to watch her. I was serious and loved books, and she would be jealous of my reading. Is that more interesting than talking to me! she would demand. I would truthfully answer that it was, whereupon she would endeavor to tear the book from my hands. Then I would try to interest her in what I read, but her attention soon strayed. In spite of these differences, we were very happy in each other's company.

And so the time passed.

When I was thirteen years old, the Queen died. I was staying with my grandparents at the time. It was March of the year 1603. I remember feeling depressed, not so much because the Queen was dead but because the realization was brought home to me that my grandparents were old and if the Queen, who had seemed immortal, should die, so could they. My great-grandmother Damask, who was named after the rose, had died at a great age just after my mother had. It was a double blow for my poor grandmother, for although she saw little of her own mother, she being in London, there were the same kind of ties between them as there had been between my mother and hers.

Death was in the air. " 'Tis something as don't come singly," said Jennet prophetically.

My grandfather, the once lusty sea captain, no longer went to sea. He must have been over seventy years old, for my grandmother was sixty-three. He used to sit on the Hoe for hours looking out to sea, I supposed dreaming of the days of adventure. He walked with a stick because one of his legs was stiffening and gave him a certain amount of pain. He still roared about the house, and my grandmother still berated him, but I felt they behaved as they did not because they felt any animosity toward each other but because they wanted to go on as they always had. Uncles Carlos and Jacko were at Lyon Court often when they were not at sea, and they would sit with their father and talk of their latest exploits. They were devoted to him. Edwina was often at Lyon Court too, and her sons with her. Damask was going to marry one of the captains in the trading company. It was with a certain sadness that I realized how everything was changing—a little here, a little there, until the entire picture was different.

On the day the Queen died we sat at the table in the great hall because there were guests in the house. There were the parents of the young man Damask was to marry, and he was there too, and there were several others who worked for the company.

The talk was naturally all of the Queen: what a great reign it had been and that her death was sure to mean changes. She had been ailing for some time, and we should have been prepared, but we had all thought she would continue to reign over us forever. All my life people had talked of the Queen as they might have talked of the earth. It was impossible to imagine England without her.

My grandfather adored her. To him she was the symbol of England. She had once sent for him to go to London, and he had sailed up the Thames and had gone to Greenwich, where she most graciously received him. It was before the defeat of the Armada, and she had been fully aware of how useful men such as Jake Pennlyon could be to her. She had complimented him on his exploits and he hinted that she looked to him to go on robbing Spaniards of their treasure and bringing it home and making sure that a goodly proportion of it made its way into the nation's purse, while at the same time she let the Spaniards believe that she was admonishing her pirate seaman. That had appealed to my grandfather. He had constantly declared he would serve her with his life.

Now she was dead. That proud spirit was no more. We had always listened avidly to the stories about her: how she was so vain that with her painted cheeks and wigs she had believed the courtiers who had told her she was the most beautiful woman on earth (had she really, or had she appeared to in order to attempt to convince them that she was?); how she had loved the Earl of Essex, yet had agreed to his execution; how right to the very end she had expected men to fall in love with her and thought them traitors if they did not: how furious she had always been when they married or took mistresses, although she had no intention of giving up one small bit of her sovereignty by marriage; how she had three hundred dresses in her wardrobe, how choleric she was, how calm and shrewd, how cruel, how kind she could be. Whatever she was, she was a great Queen.

"We shall never see her like again," mourned my grandfather.

She had gone to Richmond when she had become so ill, for she believed the quiet and the air would help her recover; for a while she had seemed better there, but then she had fallen into a state of stupor. She had had a notion that if she went to bed she would never rise again, so she commanded her servants to bring cushions, and she lay on them on the floor.

Captain Stacy, the father of Damask's betrothed, had recently come from London, and he had special information. He had heard from some present at the time that she had named her successor. She had said to Cecil, her Secretary of State: "My seat has been the seat of Kings and I shall have no rascal to succeed me."

"By rascal," said Captain Stacy, "Her Majesty meant none who was not a King, for she went on: 'Who should succeed me but a King.'"

"She was referring to King James of Scotland, the son of her old enemy the Queen of Scots," said my grandmother. "I doubt not that is a most excellent choice, for he is indeed the true heir."

"And a good Protestant," said my grandfather, "in spite of his Papist mother."

So died our great Queen. She was seventy years of age and had reigned for forty-five years.

We had a new monarch. King James I, who had been the James VI of Scotland.

"I wish my mother had lived to see this day," said my grandmother. "This union between England and Scotland is bound to bring peace. Peace was what she wanted all her life, and although she came to find it in her own household, all through her life there was conflict throughout the country—religious conflict."

"Do you think that is over now, Grandmother?" I asked.

She looked at me, and a sad look came into her eyes. She shook her head slowly.

There was a great deal of talk about our new King and Queen. At the beginning of a new reign everyone was full of hope. They believed that the old evils would disappear and be replaced by blessings. The news we heard regarding our new King was mixed. He was said to be very clever and wise and was known as the British Solomon; it was believed that the harsh laws against Catholics would be modified. After all, had not his mother been one of the greatest Catholics of them all? We had to learn what manner of King we had, but when he came to England with his Queen, there was a great revival of the scare of witches.

Although it had happened some thirteen years before when the King's Queen, Anne of Denmark, had come to England from her native land, the story was recalled.

She had been married by proxy to King James of Scotland (as he was then), and a great fleet had been prepared to take her to her husband. In September of the year 1589 she set out with the Earl Marshal and eleven ships to accompany her. As they neared the coast of Scotland, such a storm arose that they could make no progress against it and were very soon in danger of drowning. There was nothing to be done but to allow themselves to be blown onto the coast of Norway. Oddly enough, although they waited there until the storms had abated, when they set out again, no sooner had they sighted the coast of Scotland than the storms arose once more and drove them back.

Peter Munch, the Danish admiral, had no doubt that the repetition of this disaster was due to witchcraft. He took Queen Anne back to Denmark, and there began to cast about in his mind for anyone who might bear him a grudge. There were several people suspected. As these were men and witchcraft was usually attributed to women, he arrested the wives of these men, put them to such torture that they broke down and confessed and were then burned alive.

The party then set out once again for Scotland, and again no sooner had the coast of the Queen's new country been sighted than the storms blew up again and they were driven back to Norway. By this time winter had set in, and the admiral dared not undertake the journey yet a fourth time.

Another incident occurred. Jane Kennedy, who had served Mary Queen of Scots with great devotion, married Sir Andrew Melville, another loyal supporter of the late Queen, and these two were greatly favored by James. He immediately appointed Jane chief lady of the Queen's bedchamber in readiness for her arrival. The new Lady Melville made her way immediately to the palace, but in doing so she had to cross Leith Ferry. No sooner had she begun this brief journey than a storm arose, and the boat in which she sailed was crushed by another, and she drowned.

This was considered to be too much of a coincidence to be natural, and witchcraft was again blamed. There was a hunt in Scotland this time, which resulted in the torture and burning of old women. The King in due course had gone to fetch his bride and did succeed in bringing her to Scotland, but that period had become known as the Time of the Witches, and now that James had become King of England and traveled south with his bride, it was remembered that they had been the victims of witchcraft, and the interest in and persecution of witches were revived.

Although I was young at the time, I was struck forcibly and with a kind of horror at the manner in which ugly rumor can arise, seek its victims and destroy them. In that year when our Queen died and we had a new King on the throne I saw my first witch. It was horrible, a poor old woman hanging grotesquely on a tree in a country lane. Senara and I were riding with Damask, her betrothed and his father when we came into a lane.

I stood and stared. At first I did not know what it was. Then I felt a horrible revulsion sweeping over me. I could not believe that poor revolting creature had ever really harmed anyone.

None of us spoke about it; we turned our horses and rode as quickly as we could away from that horrible sight.

Senara had a nightmare that night. She crept into my pallet. We still shared a room with Damask. She was fast asleep.

"What is it?" I said.

"I dreamed of that witch, Tamsyn."

"It was horrible."

"Not just of her."

"What then?"

"I dreamed it was my mother."

"It was only a dream."

"I have heard the servants whispering about my mother."

"Servants always whisper about the families they serve."

"There *is* something strange about my mother."

"She is the most beautiful woman I ever saw."

"I've heard them say beauty like that comes from the devil. I used to be proud of her but after this afternoon...."

"People will always be envious of those who have what they have not."

"It was so clear. We were riding ... just as we were this day and I felt myself forced to go and look at her ... and when I got close, it was my mother."

"It could never be."

"But it could, Tamsyn."

"Nay, nay, she is much too clever ever to be caught...." I was amazed by what I had said and added quickly, "Even if she were a witch. But how could your mother be that?"

Senara said, "She's your stepmother, Tamsyn."

"And my father's wife, so you see...."

"It's just servants' talk. It is because she is so much more beautiful than anyone else."

We were silent for a while. Then Senara said, "Tamsyn, even if she were ... it wouldn't make any difference to us, would it? We'd still be as now."

"Nothing would ever make any difference to us," I promised her.

That seemed to satisfy her. But she was shaken and would not go back to her own pallet.

When I was fifteen, there was a great scare throughout the country concerning Catholics. The new King had been on the throne for two years, and to us far from the court the new reign had brought little change in our daily life. There was perhaps one difference. At Halloween a special atmosphere seemed to pervade the castle. Everyone would seem to be very much aware of my stepmother then. She knew this, and I imagined she was secretly amused by it.

But I was not really thinking of what was happening in our castle but outside. More witches seemed to be discovered; there were constant rumors of old women being taken and put to the tests and having been examined, their bodies revealing certain marks which proved they had intercourse with the devil and because of this acquired special powers of evil. Sometimes, when riding, we would come upon a group of shouting people. I always turned and went off as quickly as I could because I knew that somewhere in their midst would be a poor old woman, and I could not rid myself of the thought that she had only to be old, ugly, squint or have a humped back to be accused. The new King had a special abhorrence of witches, and this sharpened everyone's interest in them.

When I watched my stepmother—and it was a pleasure always to watch her because she moved with a grace I never saw in any other person—I used to think how different she was from the old women who were suspected, tortured and killed.

But witchcraft was a subject which always made me uneasy, which might have been due to the effect I knew it had on Senara. She could be really frightened by it. I would see the shadow pass across her face and then she would get out her lute and play a gay song and ask Dickon if we could practice some new dance. I knew her better than anyone else did and that her nature was—as it had always been—to thrust aside unpleasant things and behave as though they had never happened.

I thought afterward how like the coming of a storm it was because there is so often a first faint rumble of thunder in the distance and you scarcely notice it. Perhaps you say, "Oh, there is thunder about."

So at this time when I was fifteen years old, there was witchcraft "about."

The Catholics seemed a greater menace, and when a plot to blow up the Houses of Parliament was discovered, the whole country was agog.

I was allowed to sup in the great hall when there were guests coming, and because I was given this privilege, so was Senara. We used to enjoy these occasions. We would listen avidly to the conversation and afterward watch the dancers. Dickon was brought in to give displays which were always highly applauded, and several times Senara had danced with him for the company. She loved those occasions, for she yearned for admiration; she had to be continually assured that she was beautiful, attractive and desirable. I, who was given to looking for a reason for everything, had convinced myself that she had become like this during the years when her mother had not been at the castle. But now, of course, her mother was the chatelaine, and it was I who was often set aside for her. I didn't mind this, I saw that it was natural for a mother to love her own daughter more than a stepdaughter, and I often wondered whether I was a constant reminder of my mother.

I remember at this time how the conspiracy which was called the Gunpowder Plot was discussed.

When my father talked, his voice boomed down the table, and most people stopped their private conversations to listen. My stepmother sat beside him, and on either side of them were the important guests. The servants no longer sat below the salt—that was an outmoded custom.

My father said, "Guy Fawkes talked when racked. He has betrayed the whole party of them, and they will lose their heads for this."

Senara listened, eyes wide. It seemed that a Robert Catesby with his accomplices, Sir Everard Digby and Francis Tresham, were the leaders. They were joined by a relative of the great Percys of Northumberland and a soldier of fortune, Guy Fawkes. Tresham, whose brother-in-law was Lord Monteagle, wrote to Monteagle and warned him against going to the Houses of Parliament on a certain day. The letter was shown by Monteagle to Lord Cecil, who had the vaults searched and there were found two hogsheads and barrels of gunpowder. This was at two in the morning. The man Guy Fawkes was discovered when he arrived to ignite the gunpowder. He was seized, and only after severe tortures did he betray his accomplices. However, the Houses of Parliament were saved, and throughout the country the people marveled at the miraculous chance which had led to the discovery.

Everywhere throughout the country people discussed the Gunpowder Plot. It was something which must never be forgotten.

And so at our table the Catholic menace was discussed.

"We'll never have Papists here," cried Squire Horgan, one of our neighbors, his face flushed with wine and fury. "Depend upon it."

My stepmother smiled in her mysterious way, and I wondered whither she had come when the sea had thrown her up that night long ago before Senara was born. There was an aloofness about her as though she were despising these people at her board. She was it was said from Spain. She certainly had Spanish looks. My grandmother said there was no doubt of her origins, and she would know because before she had married my grandfather, she had been married to a Spaniard on the island of Tenerife. Spaniards were Catholics, very staunch ones. But I suppose witches had entirely different religion.

I pulled myself up sharply. I must not think of her as a witch. She never practiced religion, I believe. She was never in the chapel, though Connell, Senara and I went regularly. I rarely saw my father there either.

The Gunpowder Plot was to have its effect on our family. Very soon after that night, when I had sat at table and listened to the talk about it, a messenger came to us from Lyon Court with very sad news. My grandfather had died. My grandmother wished Connell and me to go over to her for the burial.

My father raised no objection, and when Senara heard that we were going, she wanted to go too. I was always flattered and touched by her devotion to me. It really seemed as though she were unhappy without me, and as her mother seemed indifferent to what she did, she was allowed to come.

How sad Lyon Court was without my grandfather! I knew it would never be the same again. He had been such a big man—I mean in more than size. Lyon Court was always different when he was there. He was constantly shouting about the place, often abusing either the servants or my grandmother or any member of the family. It all seemed so quiet and silent.

My grandmother looked old suddenly. She seemed to have shrunk. After all, she was sixty-five years of age.

Three deaths of people she loved most dearly—her mother, my mother and now my grandfather—had left her frail, bewildered, as though she were wondering what she was doing on the earth without them.

I had an uneasy feeling that it would not be long before she followed them.

Connell was very upset because he had been my grandfather's favorite. The old man had loved boys, but of course his love of women had been one of the pillars of his nature. Perhaps I should say he had needed women. Young boys, members of his family, had pleased him as girls never could. His mistresses had been numerous, yet it was my grandmother whom he had loved. She had been so suited to him— so fiery, such a fighter, far more so than my mother had been or I could ever be.

She used to say that I took after *her* mother.

She took me into the chapel at Lyon Court where his coffin had been set up. Candles burned at either end of it.

She said, "I cannot believe that he has gone, Tamsyn. It seems so empty without him. There doesn't seem to be much meaning in anything anymore."

Then she told me how he had died. "If there had been no Gunpowder Plot, I am sure he would be with us today. His rages could be terrible. He never tried to control them. I was always warning him. I used to say, 'One day you'll drop down dead when you let your passions get the better of you.' And that was what happened after all.

"He heard of the plot. 'Papists!' he said. 'That's who it is. The Spaniards are behind this. We defeated them in fair battle, and they'll come back by foul means. God damn them all.'

"Then he fell down, and that was the end. The Spaniards killed him in the end, you see, Tamsyn."

She found great comfort in talking to me about him. She told me how they had met, how she had hated him, how he had pursued her and of the adventures she had had before she finally married him.

"Somewhere in my heart, Tamsyn, I always knew that he was the one for me. Always, when I was far away from him, I remembered that he was there in my life. And now he is there no more."

I tried to comfort her. I told her I felt that my mother was not really gone. "I seem to feel her there close to me," I said. "When I am unhappy or frightened, I call to her. Then I'm not afraid anymore."

"May God bless you, little granddaughter," she said.

Fenn Landor came to be with us on the day of the burial. He had grown up and was different from the boy I had met before. He would soon be sixteen—and so should I. We were no longer children.

My grandfather was buried in the Pennlyon burial grounds. They were not as large as ours at Paling, for the Pennlyons had been in the house only for a few generations.

Connell, Senara, Fenn and I used to go riding, and Fenn and I always seemed to find ourselves together. He liked that because he wanted to talk to me about the trading company of which he was now a member. He was going to take his father's place, he said. He still talked a great deal about his father.

"One of these days," he said, "I shall find out what happened to him."

I remembered his grandmother who thought he was at the bottom of the sea. We would talk together about our parents, both being in the same position, and we were very happy together.

Senara grumbled. "You and Fenn Landor are always going off together."

"Why should we not?"

"I think he's a bore."

"You may think what you please. That does not affect my opinion."

She stamped her foot. "If I were a witch," she said, "I'd put a spell on him."

"Don't dare say such things, Senara," I retorted angrily.

She looked a little frightened.

"I would, though," she went on. Then she was soft and clinging. I never knew anyone to change moods more quickly than Senara. "Don't like him better than you like me, will you, Tamsyn?"

"As if I could."

But she set me wondering.

I did like Fenn. I liked him very much indeed, and I hated saying good-bye to him when it was time to return to Castle Paling.

"We shall meet again soon," he said. "I will call at the castle, and you must come and visit us."

When we went home, Fenn rode with us. It was on the way to his home of Trystan Priory, he said.

My grandmother was a little dubious when she heard that he proposed accompanying us; then she lifted her shoulders. "Why not?" she said. "He will protect you from the dangers of the road."

Later, when we were alone, just before I left, she said, "The two families have never met since the death of your father's first wife. It used to be rather awkward when your mother was alive. We saw so much of the Landors, being involved in business together, and Fenn's grandmother could not be induced to see anyone connected with your father."

"Whyever not?"

"Your father's first wife was her daughter."

"Her daughter. The one she said was. . . ."

She stopped me before I could finish. "She was hysterical with grief. She refused to see things as they really were. She wanted to blame someone for her daughter's death, so she blamed the daughter's husband. What happened was that your father's first wife died in childbed."

"And she blamed my father for that!"

"She was of the opinion that her daughter was too frail to bear children and should never have been allowed to try to do so."

"That seems unreasonable of her."

"People are not always reasonable in their grief."

"And for that reason she would not meet my father!"

"That's true, Tamsyn."

"She made a strange remark about my mother. Do you remember when I went into her room on that night and found her crying?"

"I remember it well. It was just after the disappearance of young Fenn's father. Poor soul! I think the loss of her children unhinged her mind."

"But what she said about my mother. . . ."

"I cannot bear to think of it, Tamsyn. My daughter . . . she was so young. And to die in her bed."

"Her heart failed, they said."

"And she had been unwell and had not told me. The greatest regret of my life is that I was not there to nurse her."

"She did not appear to need nursing. I was with her on the nights preceding that one. But on her last night I was not there."

My grandmother covered my hand with hers.

"My dearest, we must try not to grieve. So Fenn is going to ride back with you. He will stay a night or two at the castle, I daresay, for I am sure your father will not object. You like Fenn, do you not?"

"Oh, I do. He is so interesting and so . . . good."

She smiled. "At one time I thought his father might have married your mother. The son is so like the father that sometimes I could believe it is Fennimore who is here and the girl who likes him so much my own Linnet."

"Did you want her to marry that Fennimore?" I asked.

She turned her head away and did not answer. Then she said suddenly, "She wanted your father. In the end it was her choice."

I did not quite know what she meant by that, but I believed the subject was painful to her, and I did not want to make her more unhappy than she already was.

I forgot a little of the sorrow I had left behind me at Lyon Court when I was riding along with Fenn. He talked a great deal about the trading company and how they would miss my grandfather. "But it is some years since he went to sea. He was a great sailor. I don't think he ever quite got over the loss of the *Landor Lion*. It seemed so strange to disappear like that . . . after it had been sighted quite near the Sound."

I was afraid he was going to talk about his father, and although I was very interested, I knew it was a depressing subject and I wanted to get away from depression. I kept thinking about my mother, who might have married his father and, if she had, how different everything would have been.

It had put an idea into my head which might have been there before. What I mean was that I recognized it was a possibility, and it was one which gave me a great deal of pleasure.

What if I should marry Fenn?

I was sure my mother, if she could do so, would approve of this. She had been very fond of Fenn's father. He must have been very like Fenn; then why had she married my father?

During that ride home I thought now and then of my father. I seemed to see him for the first time. I did not love him in truth, although I had always thought I had, simply because it was the dutiful thing to love one's father. I was happier when he was away; I kept out of his range as much as possible. He had very little interest in me, I was sure. Connell had always been his favorite. I wondered then why my mother had loved him more than Fenn's father. He had probably decided that she should. He was the sort of man who made people's decisions for them. He was hard and cruel, I knew. I had seen men after they had been whipped because they disobeyed him. There was a whipping post in the courtyard before Seaward Tower. The servants were terrified of him.

I wondered what Fenn would think of him, Fenn who was kind. That was what I liked about him. He was so *kind* and gentle too. If he had boys and girls, he would never allow the girls to see that he preferred the boys, even if he did. Yet in a way I suppose I was glad my father was not as interested in me as he was in Connell. Connell had had many a beating because he had failed to please my father. I was never beaten because I neither pleased nor displeased.

I was suddenly looking at my home with a new clarity because I was wondering what Fenn would think of it.

My father was at home when we arrived, and he and

my stepmother came down to greet our guest. I saw the curl of my father's lip as he studied Fenn, which meant that he did not think very highly of him.

My stepmother smiled a welcome. Even Fenn was startled by her. I tried to look at her afresh. I could not understand quite what that magnetic charm was. She was very beautiful, it was true, but it was not only beauty. There was a sheen about her; it was in everything she did, in her smile and her gestures.

"Welcome to Castle Paling," she said. "It is good of you to go out of your way to look after my daughters on the road."

Fenn stammered that it had been his pleasure and was no means out of his way.

"It's rarely that we see a Landor within these walls," said my father. "The last one was my first wife. She would be your aunt, would she not?"

"That's so," Fenn replied.

He seemed to shrink before my father, and I felt that old protective instinct, which had amused my mother, rising within me.

I wondered whether my father was going to make sport with him, to trick him into betraying his enthusiasm for the trading company and then show his contempt for it.

My father shouted to one of the servants to prepare a room for our guest and to send another with wine that he might welcome him on his first visit to the castle.

The wine was brought. We drank it, and we talked of the death of Captain Pennlyon and the sadness it had caused at Lyon Court.

"A great sailor, my father-in-law," said my father. "One of the old buccaneers. I'd like to have as many golden crowns as Spaniards he has put to the sword."

"It was a cruel world in those days," said Fenn.

"And has it changed? Why, young sir, whether men go in trade or war, 'tis all the same. Booty is what they are after, and blood and booty go together."

"We aim to trade through peace."

My father was laughing to himself. "Aye, 'tis a noble sentiment."

I was glad when the servants came down to tell us that the room was ready.

"I have ordered that it shall be one of our best rooms," said my father. "Some of the serving women will tell you it's haunted, but that will not affect you, I know."

Fenn laughed. "I'll swear you have ghosts and to spare in a castle such as this."

"Ghosts!" said my father. "On the stairways, in the corridors. I'll tell you you would be hard pressed to find a room that couldn't boast of one. This is a castle of legends, sir. A haunted castle. Dark deeds have been done here, and some say they leave their mark."

"I promise you, sir, I fear them not."

"I knew you would have a bold spirit. Your profession demands it. Though they tell me that sailors are the most superstitious men on the earth. You tell me, is that true?"

"When they go to sea, it is. There are so many evil things that can befall a ship. But those sailors who fear that which is not natural at sea are bold on land."

"We are on land, but the sea laps at our walls, and it would sometimes seem that we are on neither one nor the other. Come, you will wish to go to your room. 'Tis but an hour or so to supper."

He signed to the serving girl to show him where he would sleep.

I knew he was being taken to the Red Room.

Supper was a merry meal. My father was in good spirits. My stepmother decided to charm him. She did a little, I noticed with some dismay. She sang a song—in Spanish, I suppose it was. I could not understand the words, but it throbbed with tenderness. My father watched her as she sang as though he were bewitched. In fact, I think every man present was. I wondered, as I had on many other occasions, what she was thinking.

That night I could not sleep. I kept thinking about Fenn and my grandmother's hints that I might marry him. I knew that I wanted to. I realized that I loved Fenn, and I was the sort of person who would not change. It seemed to me like a pattern. My mother and her Fennimore, both marrying other people to make the way clear for their children.

I was seeing everything with that new clarity which had come to me through the ride from Lyon Court. My home was indeed an unusual one. My father accused by his mother-in-law of causing the death of his first wife; his second wife dying mysteriously in her bed; and his third wife a witch.

And the castle—it was a haunted castle, haunted by specters of the past. There were secret happenings at night. One awoke and was aware of things going on; one had grown accustomed to them and accepted them without asking what they meant. The servants were often uneasy; they were frightened of my father, and those in the Seaward Tower were different from those who attended to our needs in the castle. I had grown up with these things and had accepted them . . . until now.

Strangest of all was my stepmother—that foreign woman who spoke so little, who could enchant all men at will— be they young or old; there were rumors about her. I knew my own mother had saved her from the sea on Halloween, which, said my practical grandmother, was why the rumor had started.

Perhaps that was so, but it was brought home afresh to me that my mother had been dead but three months when he had married her.

"Tamsyn, are you awake?"

It was Senara. We had continued to share a room. We could have had one each, for there were plenty in the castle, but Senara was against it. She liked the room, she said, and she might want to talk in the night. It was like many other rooms in the castle, big and lofty, but it did have one unique feature. One of my ancestors had put in what was called a ruelle. He had lived in France and liked the idea. It was a sort of alcove which was curtained off by a heavy red curtain. Senara had always been fond of hiding behind it and springing out on me in the hope of frightening me.

Now I said, "Yes, I'm awake."

"You're thinking about *him*." She said it accusingly.

"Whom do you mean?" I asked, knowing full well.

"Fenn Landor."

"Well, he is our guest."

"You think he is a *special* guest, don't you?"

"The guest of the moment should always be a special guest."

"Don't elude me, Tamsyn. You know what I mean. You like him too much."

"I just like him."

"Too much," she insisted.

I was silent.

She got off her pallet and knelt by mine.

"Tamsyn," she said very seriously, "no one is going to take you away from me. No one."

"No one shall," I said. "You and I will always be as sisters."

"I would *hate* anyone you liked more than you liked me."

I thought: She is very young. She'll grow up.

"Go back to bed, Senara. You'll catch cold."

"Remember it," she said.

The next day, when I was showing Fenn around the castle, we came to the burial ground near the old Norman chapel. I showed him my mother's grave in that spot with the other two so that they were a little apart.

"Why," he said, "that is my aunt's grave." He went to it and knelt beside it. "My aunt and your mother. Who is the other?"

I said, "It was a sailor. He was drowned and washed up on our coast. We buried him here."

"I wonder who he is," said Fenn.

"I wish I knew. I daresay he has those to mourn for him."

Fenn was sad, and I knew that he was thinking of his father.

"There must be many sailors," he said, "who are lying in graves unknown to their families."

"Few are washed up on the shore."

"No," he said, "the ocean bed is the graveyard of many, I'll swear."

"Do you still think so much of your father?"

"It is six years since we lost him, but he is as vivid in my mind as he ever was. You would understand if you had known him. He was a kind, good man in a world that is far from good and kind. That was what made him so outstanding. My mother says he was born before his time. He belonged to a different age, when men had become wiser and kinder because of it."

"That's a wonderful thing for a wife to say about her husband."

"He was a wonderful husband." He clenched his fists suddenly. "I know I shall find out one day what happened to him."

"Isn't it obvious? His ship must have been lost at sea."

"I suppose you are right, but I have a feeling that someday I shall hear."

"How wonderful if he came back to her. My grandfather was away for years—captured and made a slave and my grandmother never gave up hope. And he did come back. Poor grandmother, she feels his loss sadly."

He was very thoughtful, and I longed to share his thoughts.

Then he said suddenly, "Tamsyn, would you do something if I asked you?"

"I am sure I shall. What is it?"

"You have planted rosemary on your mother's grave."

"She loved it, and so did I, and it's for remembrance."

"Will you plant a bush on this grave?"

"Of course."

"An unknown sailor. Who knows where *his* family is? Plant the rosemary, and it will be as though you plant it for my father. Will you do that for me, Tamsyn?"

"You may trust me to."

He stood up and took my hands in his. Then he kissed me lightly on the forehead.

I was blissfully happy because that kiss while we stood close to my mother's and the unknown sailor's grave was a symbol. It was like plighting my troth. I knew that I loved Fenn. I was not sure whether he loved me, but I thought he did.

Fenn left the next day but not before I had planted my rosemary bush. I saw how pleased he was.

"I know you are the sort of girl who would keep her promises," he told me.

Before he left, he said that he wanted me to come stay with his parents. He would arrange that they should soon invite me.

I waved farewell to him and then went right up to the ramparts so that I should see the last of him.

Senara came and stood beside me.

"You're madly in love with him," she accused me.

"I like him," I admitted.

"You show it. You shouldn't do that. You should be aloof; it is for him to fall madly in love with *you*. Now I suppose he will ask for your hand in marriage, and then you will go away to that place of his, and I shan't see you anymore."

"What nonsense!"

"It's not nonsense. I shall be left here, and I don't like it."

"When I marry—if I do—you shall come and stay with me."

"What's the use of that? We've always been together. We've shared a room. You've been my sister ever since I could remember."

She was pouting and sullen. Then her eyes were suddenly mischievous. "What if I made an image of him and stuck pins in it? Then he'd die because I'd pierce his heart. No one would know how he died . . . except me."

"Senara, I hate to hear you talk like that. It's all such nonsense."

"People do die . . . cows die, sheep die . . . as well as people. No one knows what killed them. There is no sign at all. . . . They just die. It's the evil eye. What if I put it on your precious lover?"

"You couldn't, and you wouldn't . . . even if he were my lover, which he is not. He is merely a good friend. And, Senara, I beg of you do not say such things. It is dangerous to talk so. People hear it and take it seriously. You mustn't say it."

She dodged back from me and put out her tongue, a favorite gesture of hers which was meant to irritate.

"You are no longer a child, Senara," I said. "You must be sensible."

She stood still, her arms folded, mocking me.

"I *am* sensible. They are always saying my mother is a witch. Well, I'm a witch too. Nobody knows where we came from, do they? How do I know, how do you know, who my father is?"

"Senara you are talking dangerously. Your mother had the misfortune to be wrecked at sea. My mother saved her life. You were about to be born. It is all easy to understand."

"Is it, Tamsyn? Is that what you really think?"

"Yes, it is," I said firmly.

"You always believe what you want to. Everything is good and nice according to you. Other people don't always think so. And one thing, don't imagine you are the only one who has a lover."

"What do you mean?"

"Ah, wouldn't you like to know?"

I very soon did know. It suddenly occurred to me that Senara had inherited that indefinable quality from her mother. In the days which followed she seemed to grow more beautiful; she was passing out of her childhood, and she was of a type to mature early. Her body had become rounded, her long eyes languorous and full of mystery— so like her mother's. When she danced with Dickon, she was so lovely that it was impossible to take one's eyes from her.

Dickon adored her. When he danced with her, there was

such happiness in his movements that it was a joy to watch them. He would sit and play the lute to her and sing songs of his own composing. They seemed all to be about the charms of a dark-eyed maiden, who tantalized him and tormented him while she enchanted him.

Enchantment! Bewitchment! These were words which occurred again and again in his song. She beguiled his senses; she had this elusive quality which he could not define.

One day in the music room Maria discovered her daughter in the arms of Dickon, the music teacher. Senara told me about it afterward. She was hysterical, half defiant, half fearful.

"Dickon always wants to make love to me," she had said. "He has a passionate nature, and so have I. *You* wouldn't understand, Tamsyn. You are so calm and dull about these things. I love Dickon. He is beautiful, do you not think so? And the feeling he puts into his songs . . . and when we dance together, I seem to melt in his arms. I am ready to grant any request he might make of me. That's how Dickon affects me, Tamsyn."

"It sounds like a very dangerous state of affairs," I had replied with trepidation.

"Dangerous. Of course, it's dangerous. That's why it's exciting. When I am going for my lessons, I make Merry curl my hair and I choose my ribbons very carefully to match my gown. Merry laughs. She knows."

Merry was the maid who had been given us now that we were growing up. She worked for us personally, looked after our clothes, did our hair and was in fact a lady's maid whom we shared. She was youngish—a little older than I was in fact—and she was in love with Jan Leward, one of the men servants who lived in the Seaward Tower. They were going to marry one day, she had confided in us, and she was very pleased with life because of this. Senara tricked her into giving confidences about the progress of her love affair with Jan.

"Oh, Senara, take care," I had begged.

"That is something I prefer to leave to others," she had retorted. "Care! It's dull, and I hate dull things. No, I shall never take care. I shall be bold and reckless. That is how I intend to live my life. I think Dickon is handsome. More so than your Fenn Landor, and I tell you this, Tamsyn, you are not going to be the only one with a lover."

"What other people have has nothing to do with loving."

"So wise," she had mocked me. Then came this indiscretion. She told me about it. "The door of the music room opened, and my mother stood there. We were seated at the table. My lute lay on it, and Dickon had his arms about me. He was kissing me, and suddenly we knew that we were not alone. You know how silently my mother comes into a room. She stood there and looked at us. She said nothing. It would have been better if she had. Dickon started to tremble. You know how they can all be so afraid of her. Then she walked to the table. We both stood up. Dickon's face was scarlet. He has such beautiful fair skin. Mine doesn't change color like that. But I was as frightened as he was. She picked up my lute and gave it to me. 'Play,' she said. 'Play a love song, a sad one, for love songs are often sad.' I took the lute and she said, 'Play "My Love Has Gone and Forever More I Mourn."' I did, and she sat there listening. Then she looked at Dickon and said, 'How well have you taught my daughter?' He stammered that he had done his best and that I was an apt pupil. She sat there for a while. Then she got up and went out. We don't know what will happen, but Dickon is afraid."

We soon discovered what had happened.

Dickon did not appear in the music room again. He had been sent away.

Senara was violently angry and quietly sad in turns. She used to cry at night and talked constantly about Dickon. I had thought her feeling for him superficial, but this did not seem to be so, for as time went on, she continued to remember him and speak of him with bitter and sorrowing regret.

Senara changed after that incident. She seemed always to be trying to score over me. I think there was a streak of envy in her nature and particularly where I was concerned. I used to remind myself that in the early years of her life she had been the waif about whom so little was known. Her very name betrayed that. The admiration she had had from Dickon had softened her considerably, and when it was snatched from her, she had really suffered.

At first she had confided more in Merry than in me. She insisted that I had my Fenn Landor, and she spoke of him as though we were betrothed. I must confess I did not stop her as I should have. I was, I suppose, so enamored of the idea of being betrothed to Fenn that I couldn't resist deluding myself into thinking that it was so.

Then my stepmother—no doubt influenced by the Dickon

affair—said that now we were all growing up there should be more entertaining at the castle. She would invite the best of the neighboring families. Some of them had eligible young men who might be interested in us, and there was Connell also to be considered.

My father evidently agreed. He seemed always to agree with my stepmother. At least I never saw any conflict between them. When I compared them with my late grandfather and grandmother, I thought how different their relationship was and that there was something more normal in the bickering of my grandparents than in the quietness I observed between my parents—my father being the man he was. I sensed that when they were alone, they were far from quiet, and sometimes the thought came into my mind that my stepmother was indeed a witch and even my father was in thrall to her.

"The young man who brought you from your grandmother's," she said, "was very charming. I believe he has a sister. Perhaps we should invite them both to stay here."

I was delighted. I said I thought they would be pleased to come.

"We shall see," said my stepmother.

The seamstress was working hard making new gowns for us. When we entered into a new reign, fashions always seemed to change. In the country as we were we were always a year or so behind, but even so we were now getting what was called the short Dutch waist and the full fardingale. We had cartoose collars and tight sleeves under long sleeves hanging from the elbow. We had dresses with divided skirts to show barred petticoats usually much finer than the gown itself. Ruffs had disappeared—for which I was thankful—and in their place we had stand-up collars. The sewing room was littered with cloth of all kinds, taffeta and damask, some silk and velvet and a mixture of silk and some other thicker material called rash and mochado which was mock velvet.

The sewing room was a symbol of the fact that there were three marriageable young people in the castle and weddings were to be expected. It was strange how gay that made everyone feel.

Merry was no ordinary maid, for we were both fond of her, and she was very pretty too and full of life. She talked a great deal—particularly to Senara—of Jan, her lover, and how one day they were going to get married. There was great excitement when she was wearing a ring. It looked like gold—a thick band.

"It be my token ring from Jan," Merry told us solemnly.

Alas, her triumph was short-lived, for it seemed Jan had stolen the ring. He had taken it from my father's possessions, and when it was discovered, there was a great upheaval in the castle.

Merry quickly lost her token ring and wept for it, but even more bitterly did she weep when Jan received his punishment. We three shut ourselves away so that we could hear nothing of it, but quite a number of the servants gathered in the Seaward courtyard. Jan was tied to the whipping post and given ten lashes.

" 'Twill be the shame of his life," sobbed Merry. "He be such a proud man. He only took to give to me."

Senara's eyes flashed with anger. "A curse on those who are beating Jan," she cried. "May their arms rot and. . . ."

I silenced her. "Whoever lifts the whip against him does so on orders," I said. "And, Senara, please do not say such things."

"I mean them," she cried.

I knew who had given the order for punishment. It was my father.

We comforted Merry as best we could. Senara prepared an ointment, for she was interested in such things, and we sent it over for Jan's back.

"It will let him know that we are thinking of him," said Senara, "as well as help cure him."

The atmosphere of the castle had changed. An air of melancholy had descended on us.

There was a letter from my grandmother.

She was glad to hear that Fenn and his sister were coming to stay with us. "I'm afraid this could never have happened while his grandmother was alive," she wrote. "Now, poor soul, she is at rest, and perhaps the feud between the two families will be over. I could understand, of course, her bitter sorrow when her daughter died, and some people must lay the blame for their sorrow on other shoulders. It's a great mistake. You will see Fenn again, and I am sure you will enjoy his company. I believe his sister, Melanie, is a charming girl.

"My dearest Tamsyn, how I should love to join you, but I fear the journey would be too much for me. Perhaps later you would come to me. I have not been very well.

Edwina is often here. I shall look forward to your being here soon, my dear child. Let me know about Fenn's visit."

It was high summer when they came—Fenn, his sister, Melanie, his mother and their servants. They were to stay for a week, and my stepmother had made great preparations for them. She had evidently taken a fancy to the family; I was worldly enough to know what it was because they were rich. They had large estates about Trystan Priory, and although in the beginning they had lost money in the trading venture, that had now proved very successful.

When they arrived, a warm welcome was given them. My stepmother was gracious and charming, and my father too received them with a show of pleasure. Fenn looked pleased to be back, and I was thrilled to see that when his eyes alighted on me, they showed clearly his pleasure. There was something open and candid about him; he was the sort of man who would never be able to hide his feelings even if he wanted to. His sister, Melanie, was rather like him in appearance, she was quiet and gentle in manners, and their mother was a very gracious lady. I couldn't help thinking that Trystan Priory must be a very pleasant, comfortable household.

Fenn was put into the Red Room once more, and Melanie and her mother shared a room close by.

Supper that night was taken in one of the smaller rooms— so that we could talk together, said my stepmother, before other guests arrived. So there were my father, my stepmother, Fenn, his sister and mother, and Connell, Senara and myself. Conversation was of the estates and of the trading company of which Fenn spoke with such enthusiasm and how pleasant it was for families like ours to get to know each other.

I could scarcely sleep that night; nor could Senara. We lay awake on our pallets talking about the evening.

"What *mild* people they are," commented Senara. "They look as if nothing could arouse them. I have a good mind to set fire to their bedchamber. I daresay that girl Melanie would sit up in bed and say, 'How peculiar. I believe the room is on fire,' and then calmly walk out as though nothing had happened. Shall I set fire to it just to see if I'm right?"

"What a horrible idea! You do think of the strangest things."

"One day I shall do them."

"Please, Senara, you know I hate you to talk like that."

"Why should I care what you hate? I hate to see you

looking at that Fenn as though he's Sir Lancelot or one of those knights who were irresistible to the ladies. You don't care about that."

"You have a very jealous nature."

"Anyone who feels anything is jealous. It is only people like you and your silly Landors who don't. They're calm because they don't feel anything. I think you're all made of *straw*."

I laughed at her, which infuriated her.

"Don't think you are the only one who knows about love." Her voice broke, and there was a sob in it. "I wonder what is happening to Dickon now."

"I daresay he found another post teaching music and dancing to a susceptible young girl. They now gaze at each other over the table, and he sings songs to her as he plays his lute."

"Don't talk so," cried Senara.

"I'm sorry. Do you still care about him?"

"Of course I don't, but I don't want him laughed at."

"I'm not laughing at him. I'm sorry for him. I hope he found a good post quickly."

She changed the subject. "That Melanie will soon be living here. They've chosen her for Connell."

"What!"

"It's true. Merry heard them talking about it, and she told me. It's more or less arranged. They only have to like each other. Connell will, I daresay. His father wants him to, so he has to, and as long as he can frolic with the serving wenches, he's ready to marry whoever is chosen for him."

"Where do you get such ideas?"

"*I* keep my eyes open. Servants talk to me more than they do to you. They'd be afraid to tell you. You're so proper."

"Connell and Melanie," I said.

"Don't sound so surprised. Is it not obvious? It's time Connell married . . . you know, get sons to carry on the line. Connell will be rich—he'll inherit all this—and she will have a good dowry, you can be sure. Just imagine, in a little while, I'll warrant we have dear prim little Melanie installed as our sister."

"Well, I think Connell will be lucky."

"You would! And Connell, what of him? He won't get much fun with her, I'll swear. Well, the serving girls are always willing when it is the master of the house, which he will be in time."

"You talk too freely, Senara."

"What should I do? Cloak my thoughts as you do . . . or try to. Don't think I don't know you, Tamsyn Casvellyn. I see clearly what is in your mind. You betray it, and if you did not, I have means. . . ."

I laughed aloud. "Oh, I see, this is the witch's daughter speaking."

"Never underestimate a witch, Tamsyn."

"How many more times do I have to tell you not to speak of yourself as a witch? It's dangerous and growing more so."

"This is only in the four walls of our bedchamber. I trust you, Tamsyn, not to betray me. You would never betray anyone. Least of all your sister, Senara. We are as sisters, Tamsyn. Do you remember when I made you cut your wrist and I cut mine, and we mingled our blood and swore that we would come to the aid of the other when that one was in danger?"

I laughed. "How you loved those dramatic gestures when you were a child."

"I love them still. It's part of my nature."

"Hush!"

"What! Do you think the witchfinders are lurking in the court cupboard? Do you think they are going to spring out and search my body for the marks? There are no marks on my body, Tamsyn, not yet."

"Go to sleep," I said.

"I can't sleep. I'm thinking of the future. Of Melanie coming here and your going away. An exchange, that's what they want—you will go to Trystan Priory as the bride of the holy Fenn and Melanie comes here to take your place. I won't have it. I won't have her in place of you. You are my blood sister, and where you go I shall go."

"I could take you with me."

"See, you have already made up your mind to go. Do not think that I shall allow you to go to your lover. I must have a lover, or I must be with you. Perhaps I will take your lover, and I will be the one to go to Trystan Priory as the bride, and you will come there and stay with *me*. That would be a complete turnabout."

"I never heard such nonsense. I am going to sleep now if you won't."

"Tamsyn," she wailed.

But I did not answer her. I lay still pretending to sleep, but of course I could not. I kept thinking about Connell's marrying Melanie. I did not think she would be very happy. Then I thought of my marrying Fenn and going to Trystan Priory, which would be my home forever after.

The next morning Fenn asked me if I would take a ride with him. I was very happy to agree to this, and I wondered whether during the ride he would ask me to marry him.

Before we went to the stables, he said he would like to visit the burial grounds, and we did. The rosemary bush was flourishing.

"I watch over it," I said. "See this creeper. It is going from my mother's to the grave of the unknown sailor."

"In time," he said, "it will cover them both."

He stood and took my hands in his.

"Thank you for caring for this grave, Tamsyn. I daresay you will think I am fanciful. You see, I don't know where my father lies, and in a way this is a sort of substitute."

"I understand absolutely. I should feel the same. Rest assured that I will always care for the grave."

He looked at me very solemnly and I thought: This is the moment. But then I heard someone calling my name. "Tamsyn. Tamsyn, where are you?"

It was Senara.

She was at the edge of the burial ground, dressed in her riding habit. It was of mulberry-colored velvet, and she had a riding hat, rather like a man's, with a band about it and feather at the back. She seemed to grow more beautiful every day; she was beginning to look very like her mother, but the mysterious look of her mother in her was a vitality which made her more human than her mother could ever be.

She studied us rather mockingly. "Why," she said, "you are about to ride too. Why should we not all go together?"

Other guests arrived at the castle. When we rode out, it was in a large company. My father hunted the deer some miles inland and made up a party. Fenn was in this, and they were away two whole days, for the forest was so far that it took them some hours to get there and they were staying the night at a hunting lodge which belonged to a friend of my father's, who was entertaining the party there.

That meant that Melanie and her mother were left for us to look after. Melanie was very interested in the domestic side of the castle. She met some of the servants. Merry said afterward that she was a very gracious lady and she hoped Master Connell would not be another such as his father.

I was very drawn to Melanie—perhaps because she was Fenn's sister. Senara dismissed her as spiritless, but then Senara judged everyone by herself.

When the men returned, they brought some fine deer with them, and these were to be roasted for the grand banquet which would be given on the night before the Landors returned.

In the afternoon of that day Connell and Melanie went riding together. I went with Senara because she was determined to come. I knew that she was not going to leave me alone with Fenn. I could not help smiling because I was sure that if Fennimore intended to ask me to marry him, he would not be deterred by Senara. I was amazed too by the force of Senara's affection for me, if it was affection. Or was it perhaps the determination that I should not have what she could not?

There was a great deal of chatter in our bedchamber as we prepared for the banquet. Senara's gown was of red silk and her petticoat of embroidered damask, and the silk divided in the skirt to give an ample view of this magnificent petticoat; her bodice was tightly laced with gold thread: on her head she wore a jeweled ornament which her mother had given her. When she was dressed, she studied me. "You look quite beautiful in your blue velvet," she told me, her head on one side. "Now, Merry, who is the more beautiful, do you think?"

Merry looked embarrassed and said, "Do not ask such questions."

"You discomfort poor Merry," I said. "You know you are, so why do you wish to make her say it?"

"It is always good to speak the truth," said Senara demurely.

What a night that was. The smell of roasting venison filled the castle; the great table in the hall was laden with food of all descriptions; there was beef and mutton, besides the venison, and all manner of pies and pastries of which the people of our part of the country were especially fond. Squab and lammy and taddage all served with clotted cream, which made them overrich for my liking; I preferred those savored with herbs and some of the flowers like marigolds and primroses when they were in season. Before the banquet began, dash-an'-darras, the stirrup cup, was lavishly taken, which meant that the company was in high spirits before it reached the table.

There mead and metheglin were freely served with sloe gin and wines made from cowslips and gillyflowers. When the company had eaten its fill and the musicians were about to play, my father stood up and said he had news to impart which gave him great pleasure.

"My friends," he said, "you are this day celebrating the betrothal of my son, Connell, and Melanie, whose mother and brother are here with us. Alas, that her father could not be here also, but I promise her she will find in me one who is willing and eager to take his place."

There was a filling of goblets, and glasses and toasts were drunk, and Connell and Melanie rose and stood beside my father, holding hands in the traditional way.

I caught Fenn's eye, and I could see that he was pleased. Indeed, everyone seemed to think the betrothal highly suitable.

Then my father called to the musicians to play and he rose from the table, and taking Melanie by the hand, he opened the dance with her. Connell took Melanie's mother as his partner, and Fenn took me. Others of the company fell in behind us, and we danced around the hall. Some of our guests remained at the table drinking and watching us as we danced.

I said to Fenn, "This betrothal pleases you."

"I like well," he replied, with a pressure on my hand, "that our families should be united. If your brother makes my sister happy, I shall be well content."

"I trust he will," I answered fervently.

"There had been a restraint between our families because of my aunt's marriage to your father. It was wrong of my grandmother to blame him for her death. She was somewhat unbalanced and became very strange before she died. But that is over now. Now there will be friendship between us."

I was happy dancing with Fenn. I felt certain that our families were going to be united by more than by that marriage tie.

Then the happiness of the evening disintegrated. Above the sound of the music came the sound of piercing screams. The dancers stopped; so did the musicians. My father cried angrily, "What means this?" But the screaming went on.

The door at one end of the hall opened into the kitchens, and it was from this direction that the screaming came.

Senara and I were close behind my father as he flung open the door.

Two of the serving girls were being held up by others, and they were the ones who were making the noise.

"Silence," cried my father.

So great was their fear of him that he could silence them whatever the state of their minds.

I saw that Merry was there. She curtsied and said, "Master, these two girls have seen something terrible."

All the guests were crowding around the door, and my father said, "You'll be whipped for this. What think you you are doing disturbing my guests in this way?"

My stepmother had taken charge. She said, "The girls are beside themselves with fear. You had better tell me what has happened."

" 'Twas what they did see, mistress," said Merry.

"Let them speak for themselves," said my stepmother. "Jane. Bet. What was it?"

The two who had been screaming stared at my stepmother with round, frightened eyes. But they had recovered their senses. There were as frightened of her as they were of my father—though for different reasons, and I had at times wondered which they feared most, the whipping which he would order or the vague terror which she could inspire.

"We did see a light, mistress."

"A light! What light?"

" 'Twas in the burial ground. . . . 'Twas moving hither and thither like . . . a ghostly light. 'Twere not natural."

"Is that all? You saw a light and you make this noise?"

"Bet she said to me she'd wager I wouldn't go with her . . . and I said I would and then we wished we hadn't, but we went and . . . oh, mistress, I dursen't speak of it."

My father said, "A pack of silly girls. Their foolishness will be beaten out of them. What did they see?"

The girls looked at each other; they seemed to be trying to find their voices and could not and were going off into hysterics again.

I said, "We'll search the burial ground and see who's there. It must be someone playing tricks."

"Let's go now," cried Senara, her eyes alight with excitement. "Let's go and see what it was that frightened those silly girls."

Our guests were quite clearly amused by what was happening. Senara was chatting gaily to Squire Horden's son, who was very taken with her.

"It must have been someone's ghost," she said. "We've lots of ghosts. Melanie, do you like ghosts? You'll get to know them when you come to live here."

Melanie smiled serenely and said that she would have to wait until she had made their acquaintance before she could tell Senara whether she liked them.

It was a beautiful moonlit night. "We should have had the musicians out here," said Senara. "We could have danced in one of the courtyards."

"The cobbles would have been hard on our feet," I answered.

Senara came and walked on the other side of Fenn as we came into the burial ground.

"Why did the ghost need the flickering light?" someone asked. "He could see well enough in the moonlight."

Fenn and I with Senara had walked over to the spot we knew so well. Senara gave a cry and said, "Look."

There was a stone on the grave of the unknown sailor. On it had been printed in large black letters:

Murdered October, 1600

Everyone crowded around to look.

I saw my father clench his hands; he cried, "Good God. Look at that."

My stepmother came forward and stared at it. "Murdered," she repeated. "What does it mean?"

"Some joker. By God, a poor joke. He'll be flayed for this," cried my father.

He pulled it from the earth and in an excess of anger threw it from him. It landed with a thud among some brambles.

He turned to the company and said, "This is the grave of a sailor who was washed up on our shores. My wife was anxious that he should be given decent burial. Some foolish joker put that stone there, hoping to frighten the maids. Come, we will go back to the hall. Those stupid girls will wish they had not disturbed us, I promise you."

In the hall he commanded the musicians to play, but some of the gaiety had vanished. I noticed that Fenn was particularly affected.

We sat together on a window seat, neither being in the mood for dancing. I had imagined our sitting thus while he asked me to marry him, but after what we had seen in the burial ground, I realized that Fennimore could think of nothing else. He had so identified that unknown sailor with his father that he was shocked to see that inscription on his grave, and he could not get it out of his mind.

The next day we talked of it.

"You see, Tamsyn," he said, "it was in October, 1600, that my father disappeared."

"That was the year the sailor was buried. It was the year my mother died. It was on Christmas Day."

"I couldn't sleep last night," said Fenn. "Every time I closed my eyes I could see that stone with those words on it. Who put it there, Tamsyn? Who could have done such a thing?"

"Perhaps we shall discover," I said.

He was shaken. So was I. I could see that the discovery of that strange stone had made it impossible for him to think of anything else.

He did not mention our betrothal.

And he rode back to Trystan Priory still not having spoken of it.

Yet the wedding was to be in a few weeks' time and we should all travel to Trystan Priory to celebrate it.

At Halloween

There was great excitement in the preparations for the wedding. Connell was pleased to be the center of attraction. I was certain that he was not in love with Melanie. Senara said, "How could he be? He's in love with himself. People can only be in love with one person at a time, and one thing I am certain of, Connell will always be faithful . . . to himself."

Whatever his emotions, he liked the thought of getting married.

We did not discover who had put the stone on the unknown sailor's grave. Strangely enough, my father had not pursued the inquiry as fully as I expected him to. The two hysterical serving girls who had interrupted the company's entertainment were questioned, but all they would say was that they had seen lights in the burial ground, had been wagered they wouldn't go and look and then had gone out and seen the stone.

My father shrugged his shoulders and said it was someone's idea of a joke and if he discovered who the culprit was, *he—or she—*would discover it was something quite different.

Perhaps it was the excitement of the wedding which

made people forget, but now the burial ground was included as yet another part of the castle in which ghosts lurked.

Senara, Merry, the seamstress and I were once more busy with our gowns. I was very excited at the prospect of seeing Fenn again. Senara knew. She taunted me when we were in our bedroom at night.

"I know what you're thinking, Tamsyn," she said. "You're thinking he's going to ask you this time. Perhaps he will. It will be so neat, won't it? Melanie comes here, and you go to Trystan. What an excellent arrangement, *they* will think. I shan't. I don't want that silly dull creature here."

"I thought you considered me rather dull."

"In a different way. A foil to my liveliness. She's different. I don't want her. Just think when we come back, she will be with us."

"I believe she will be a very pleasant addition to the household."

"I shall ignore her."

"Poor girl, how upset she will be!"

"Don't mock. What really concerns me is that the laggardly Fenn might at last find the spirit to ask *you*. You'll accept him. I know that full well. I never knew any girl throw herself at a young man as you have thrown yourself at him."

"That's not true."

"You can't see yourself. All adoration and submissiveness! Asking him all the time to marry you."

"I'm going to sleep."

"You're not," she said.

"If we are to be fresh tomorrow, we must sleep. It's a long way to Trystan."

"There's a change in your voice when you mention the house even. Confess, you are longing to be mistress of it."

"I refuse to discuss such nonsense."

"Nonsense it is. Listen to me, Tamsyn Casvellyn. You are not going to marry him. I'll marry him myself rather. That would be fun, wouldn't it? Suppose I married him instead of you? *I* will go to Trystan Priory. I will be the mistress there, and poor sad Tamsyn will stay behind in the Castle Paling until she is old and crabbed and filled with bitter envy because her blood sister Senara married the hero of her dreams and lives happily ever after at Trystan Priory with her ten children and her handsome husband whom she had turned into the most attractive man on earth."

"Good night, Senara."

"I will not be dismissed."

"Will you not? Then go rambling on, for I intend to sleep."

She went on talking, and I pretended not to listen, and after a while she was quiet.

The next morning early the packhorses were loaded with our baggage which contained our wedding finery, and in a big party, at the head of which rode my father and my stepmother, we set out for Trystan Priory.

What sad news awaited me there! Fenn had been called to Plymouth, where he must join his ship. He had wanted to remain to see his sister married, but that was not possible. He had to take his ship on a venture from which he hoped to return in six months' time.

Senara looked at me mischievously.

"I arranged it," she whispered.

I turned away impatiently.

"When our Queen came from Denmark," she went on, "the witches of Scotland and Norway raised storms so that she was almost lost at sea. If they could do that, why should not someone be sent to sea?"

"You talk such nonsense," I said shortly.

"You call it that because you don't understand."

I was uneasy about her, but she had always loved to tease people. She teased Merry about Jan Leward and Jennet about her lovers, but this attitude toward me and Fenn was beginning to upset me.

The wedding was celebrated two days after our arrival. Melanie made a beautiful bride with her blond hair falling about her shoulders and her gown of fine silk and her kirtle decorated with threads of gold; two of her boy cousins led her to the church; they looked very charming with bride laces and rosemary tied to their sleeves. Connell was already there, led in by two young men who must be unmarried to perform this duty, and each of these had bride lace on branches of broom tied to their arms. Carried before Melanie was the bride cup, on which was more rosemary gilded and tied with ribbons of many colors. The priory musicians followed them into the chapel, and all the young girls, including myself and Senara, followed. Senara and I, being closely related to the bridegroom, carried big bride cakes.

It was impressive as such ceremonies always were, and Melanie looked radiantly happy and Connell well pleased. It would have been a wonderful day for me if only Fenn had been there.

Senara whispered to me as the pair was repeating their vows, "Whose turn next? Yours? Don't be too sure of that, Tamsyn Casvellyn. It might be mine."

I ignored her.

The ceremony over, the feasting began; it went on during the day, and then we put the couple to bed with a certain amount of ribaldry. My father cried that he hoped they would give him grandsons and "without delay," he added.

Connell looked a little sheepish, and I was amazed by Melanie's tranquillity.

Senara said afterward that she had come to the marriage bed in absolute ignorance.

Within three days we were riding back to Castle Paling, my father, stepmother, my brother and his new bride at the head of the party.

Having Melanie in the house made very little difference. She was so quiet no one noticed her very much. A nonentity was Senara's verdict. Connell took very little notice of her. He scarcely saw her during the day but shared her bed every night.

"Once she is pregnant," commented Senara, "he will find his pleasure elsewhere."

"You are coarse," I told her.

"My dear Tamsyn, I am not as innocent as you."

"I trust you *are* innocent."

Senara shrieked with laughter. "You would like to know, would you not?"

"I do know."

"You know nothing. You are blind to what is going on. You are another Melanie. You don't gossip enough. That's your trouble. Servants are the best informants. They rarely fail. Then of course I have my special powers."

"I don't want to hear about them," I said, "because I know they do not exist."

"One of these days the truth will be brought home to you." She looked mysterious. "Now I am going to brew a spell. Your Fenn is on the sea somewhere. What if I brew up a storm, as the witches of Scotland did? What then, eh?"

I felt sick with fear suddenly, and Senara went off into peals of laughter.

"You see, you do believe. It's all very well to pretend you don't when the result doesn't matter."

"Please, Senara, stop this talk of spells and such like. Servants overhear. I tell you it is dangerous." I took her

by the shoulders suddenly. She had really frightened me
when she had talked of Fenn. "If there should be a scare
throughout the neighborhood, if there should be such a
noise about witches, and witchfinders came down here, do
you not see that you would be suspected . . . you and . . . ?"

She finished for me: "My mother." She smiled then, and
her mood changed suddenly. It was soft and loving. "You
do care for me, don't you, Tamsyn?"

"You are as my sister."

"No matter what I do."

"It would appear so," I said.

Then she threw her arms about me in the impulsive,
lovable manner which I knew so well.

"I taunt you because we belong together. I could never
endure to lose you, Tamsyn."

"Nor shall you," I promised.

After that she was gentle for a while, and when she was
in that mood, no one could be more charming or loving
than Senara. If only she would always be so.

We had been back from the wedding for a week or so.
The sun had shone almost unceasingly for four weeks without a drop of rain, which was unusual for Cornwall. I
decided that I would water the plants on the graves, for
the earth was so dry it was cracking in places.

Since that night when the stone had been found few
people went near the burial grounds. They were certain
that the stone had been placed there by some ghostly hand.
Sailors who were drowned at sea often could not rest. It
was said that at night one could hear cries coming from
the Devil's Teeth where many a ship had foundered. The
fishermen coming in at dusk always avoided that stretch
of water, not only because it was dangerous—they did not
fear this because they knew those rocks so well—but because they believed it to be haunted.

I took my watering can and, entering the graveyard, went
to that spot where the three graves were. I saw it immediately. I stared and knelt by my mother's grave. The stone
which my father had hurled into the bushes on that night
had been discovered. It had now been planted on my
mother's grave.

I stared at it; the words, which had been changed, danced
before my eyes. "Murdered 1600."

I pulled at the stone. It came away easily in my hands. I
touched the black letters. I knelt by that grave, and I thought

back to the day when I had gone into my mother's room and seen her lying there quiet and still.

Pictures flashed in and out of my mind. Had she been afraid before she died? I had slept with her because my presence had given her comfort. I remembered the occasion I went to her and stood by her bed. She had awakened in fright. Why? Had she been expecting someone else? Did she know someone was planning to murder her?

Murder her! I looked back at the stone. Who had put it there? Why? And after all this time. It was seven years since my mother had been buried here. Why only now should someone put that stone on the unknown sailor's grave and then on hers?

When I considered that, I was comforted. It was some practical joker with a distorted idea of humor. How could a sailor who was drowned at sea and washed up on our coast have been murdered!

I remember my father's anger when he had seen it that night. Naturally he was angry because his guests had been disturbed. He had flung the stone into the bushes. Who then had found it and put it on my mother's grave?

I stared down at it. What could I do with it? Mechanically I laid it on the ground and watered the graves.

I would not leave the stone there. I picked it up and carried it into the house. I put away my watering can and took the stone up to my room.

I hid it at the back of the court cupboard, first wrapping it up in an old petticoat.

For the rest of that day I kept thinking about it and trying to remember the last months of my mother's life. How could she have been murdered? Who would have murdered her? And if so, how? There was no sign on her body that she had suffered violence.

The next day I would take the stone with me when I rode out and I would go alone. I would take it far away. I would bury it in a wood and try to think no more of the matter.

What was the use of deluding myself? I knew that I should go on thinking of it.

I sat at my window and looked out to sea. There were the Devil's Teeth crudely protruding from the water. Someone had once said, when the tide is neither high nor low, it looks as though the devil were smiling. It would be a wicked smile, a satisfied smile, the smile of one who knows that men will be lured to disaster.

I did not throw the stone away because when I came to take it next day, it was missing.

I opened the door of the court cupboard and felt for the petticoat. There it was, rolled as I had left it. But it was light, and the stone was not there.

I could not believe it. I had wrapped it so that it was hidden. No one could have known it was there. I knelt with the petticoat in my hand, and a terrible apprehension crept over me. Could it really be that some other force—not human—had placed that stone first on the sailor's grave and then on my mother's? Was it really true that the ghosts of the castle were manifesting their existence in this way?

Hands caught at my throat, and I screamed out in terror. My head was jerked back, and I was looking up into Senara's laughing face.

"What are you doing caressing that old petticoat? And I frightened you, did I not? Did you think it was an enemy? Have you such a bad conscience?"

"You . . . you did startle me."

"I wondered what you were doing on your knees. I watched for minutes . . . well, a few seconds . . . I couldn't make out why you kept looking at that old petticoat."

She snatched it from me and unfurled it.

"Look, it's torn. What possible good is it? That ribbon on it is rather pretty, though. . . ."

I rose, and she studied me anxiously.

"You're not ill, are you? You look scared."

"I'm all right. It was just. . . ."

"I know. Cold shiver. Someone walking over your grave, as they say."

I pulled myself sharply together.

"Yes, something like that," I said.

I was obsessed by memories of my mother. I had loved her dearly, and she had rarely been far from my thoughts, but now the memories were with me all the time. I wished that I had taken more notice at the time. I had only been ten years old then, and there was so much I had not understood. If only I had been older. If only my mother had been able to talk to me.

I remembered something Senara had said about our servants knowing so much about us, and that led me to think of Jennet, who was still in our household. She was getting old now; she was nearly as old as my grandmother, and there had been talk of her going back to grandmother when my mother died, but she had wanted to stay.

She and my grandmother had been through many adventures together, and because my grandfather had given Jennet a child, there was always a touch of asperity in my grandmother's attitude toward her. They were fond of each other in a way, but I think Jennet preferred to be with me.

When my mother had died, she had said, "There's young Tamsyn. I know Mistress Linnet would have wanted me to keep an eye on her."

And in a way she had kept her eyes on me. In the last year she had become resigned to age as she had through her life become resigned to everything that had befallen her. The prospect of a baby in the house—we were all expecting every day to hear that Melanie was pregnant—revived old Jennet a little. If that baby came, she would want to be in the nursery.

She said to me once, "Men! I've known scores of them and very good company too and from that company comes the best of all things—little babies, dear little babies."

Now I wanted to talk to her about my mother. Jennet was easy to talk to; reminiscences flowed from her.

"Mistress Linnet," she said, "she were a wild one at one time. Stood up to her father she did. But she never had quite the fight in her that her mother had. Cat they called her, and Wild Cat I'd heard the master say more than once—that was the Captain—a regular one he was. I reckon there wasn't another like him. You see, your mother wasn't wanted by him. He was mad for a boy, and it seemed your grandmother couldn't give him one. He let her see it, and Mistress Linnet, she let him see that she knew it, and then sudden like they understood each other, and then my dear life, there was something between them. He was proud of her. My girl Linnet's as good as a son, he said. Then she met your father. And when she came here, I came with her."

"She was happy here, wasn't she, Jennet?"

"Happy . . . what's being happy? Most people are happy one minute and sad the next."

"You're not, Jennet. You've been as happy as anyone I ever knew."

"I had a knack of it. Good things happened to me. I've had a good life, I have."

I smiled at her fondly. I was not surprised that my mother had been fond of her.

"You were my mother's personal maid, weren't you?"

"Oh, yes, I was. I was sent over here to be that. Your grandmother trusted me for all she could be sharp with me. She knew that I was the best one to look after her daughter."

"Why did she think my mother needed looking after?"

"Oh, you know how it is . . . a young girl bride. She wants some of the old familiar faces around her."

"How was she . . . toward the end, I mean?"

Jennet looked back into the past and frowned.

"She got a bit quiet like . . . as though there was something. . . ."

"Yes, Jennet, go on. As though there were something?"

"Something she wasn't sure of."

"Did she ever say anything?"

"Not to me. I reckon there was one person she would have told, and that was your grandmother."

"Why not . . . my father. . . ."

"Well, what if it should have concerned him?"

"What do you mean by that?"

"I don't know. Just that if she was worried about him, she wouldn't have him to talk to, would she?"

"Do you know why she should worry about him?"

"Wives do worry about husbands, you know. There's reasons. Why, your grandmother. . . ."

But I was not going to be sidetracked.

"How did she seem during those last weeks, Jennet? *I* felt there was something."

"She was always writing. . . . I caught her at it more than once."

"*Caught* her at it!"

"Well, that's how it seemed. She be there at her table writing away, and if I came in, she would cover up what she was writing, and I never saw where it went in the end."

"She must have been writing letters."

"I don't think so. She never sent so many letters away. But when I came back to her room, it would all be put out of sight. I never saw any sign of it then, which was odd. I often wondered where she kept it."

"I wonder what she was writing."

"It was some sort of diary, I always thought. People do that. They like to write things down."

"That's interesting," I said. "I wonder where she put her diary."

"'Tis my belief she hid it away."

I thought to myself if she did that, she must have felt there was something she must hide.

I didn't want to discuss her anymore. I started Jennet talking about the old days at Lyon Court and Captain Jake, my grandfather. That was a subject for which she would turn away from any other.

I was excited, though. If my mother had written a diary and if she had recorded everything that happened to her as it did, surely there would be some clue in it to what she had been feeling during those last weeks of her life.

I was determined to find my mother's journal or diary, whatever it was. I could not forget that moment when I had seen the stone on her grave. Why had it been put there? Because someone knew that her death had not been natural?

Perhaps I thought the mischief-maker had meant to put it on her grave in the first place and had in mistake put it on the unknown sailor's. I went down to the shore, where I could be quiet, to think of what had happened. I found the rhythm of the waves soothing. I looked up at the straight gray walls of the castle, and I said to myself: Someone in there knows what happened to my mother.

My father. He had married within three months of her death. It was very soon, too soon, said some. But my father was a law unto himself, and he did not consider convention.

Did my father wish to be rid of my mother that he might marry my stepmother? Did my stepmother wish her dead that she might marry my father? Had my mother discovered a secret which someone in the castle wished to hide?

If she had kept her journal faithfully—and what was the point of keeping it if not faithfully?—she would have written it there. She must have done so, for she was so anxious to keep it hidden where no one could see it. What had happened on that last night of her life? Had she written in her journal and then gone to that bed from which she had never risen?

I must find the journal. I would have no rest until I did.

Where would it be most likely to be? In the bedroom she had shared with my father and which he now shared with my stepmother?

No, I did not think so, for she would surely not wish my father to see it. There was her sitting room in which she had spent a great deal of time. No one used it now. I would begin my search there.

It was a small room and not very light—no room in the castle was, for the long, narrow slits of windows had originally been built more for defense than to let in air and sunlight.

As I entered the room, I felt deeply moved. I remembered so well her sitting there. She liked to sit in the window seat with me beside her or at her feet while she talked to me.

There was the chair on which she sat, and there was the table. On it was a book and her sandalwood box, a kind of desk. I went to it and opened it. That part on which one wrote lifted up to disclose a cavity in it. There was nothing there but some sheets of blank paper.

It was the obvious place in which to put one's journal, though she would hardly keep it there if she wished to hide it.

Where then? I looked around the room, at the chair with the paneled back decorated with inlay and carving; it was one which my grandmother had had made for my mother and of a modern design. Not so the old settle. That had been in the castle for as long as I could remember. My mother said it was there when she came, and it had probably been built in the middle of the previous century, long before the defeat of the Armada. It was really a chest with the back and arms put on it, the top of the chest making the seat and the extensions the back and the arms. I went to it and lifted the seat. I pulled out some old garments. There was a hat with a feather which I remembered seeing my mother wear. I was excited. This was her room, and it had not been changed since her death. I was certain that somewhere here I would find her journal.

In chests such as this there were often secret compartments. What more likely than that she should have hidden her papers in this very chest?

I took out the clothes to examine it better. On either side the wood appeared to be thicker and I felt that this could quite easily conceal a cavity. I tapped gently on the wood. It seemed hollow. I was certain that somewhere there was a secret spring.

And as I knelt before the chest, I heard a noise. What was it? Only a footstep in the corridor. Only someone passing the door. Keeping my kneeling position, I stared at the door. My heart started to beat wildly as the latch of the door moved and the door was silently and slowly opening.

My stepmother was standing on the threshold of the room.

She was always mysterious; I knew the servants feared her, and at that moment so did I. She remained silent for what seemed a long time but could only have been a few seconds. What was it that was so frightening about this moment? I realized suddenly that her face did not move or change very much. When she smiled, her mouth turned up a little at the corners—that was all. I suddenly felt that I was in the presence of evil. This is what the servants felt. But who could say whether it was because of the reputation she had or whether there really was something satanic within her.

Her lips moved slightly in her immobile face.

"Are you clearing out your mother's clothes?"

She had walked in; the door shut behind her. I felt a great desire to dash past her out of this room. I was deeply conscious that I was here with her . . . alone.

"Why . . . yes," I said. "All these years these things have been here."

"Did you find anything that you were looking for . . . particularly?"

"There are only her clothes."

I stood up.

"Nothing else there?" she said.

"Nothing," I answered.

She picked up a shoe, cork-soled, high-heeled and round-toed.

"Hideous!" she said. "Fashions are better now, are they not? Look at this ruff. The lace is beautiful. But an ugly fashion, do you not think? It is well that it is no longer the mode. It had one virtue, though. It made the ladies hold their heads high."

I picked up the things and put them back into the chest.

"Do you propose to leave them there?" she asked.

"I do not know what else to do with them."

"I thought perhaps you had some purpose in gathering them together. The servants perhaps would like them. But even they are conscious of the fashion."

I picked up the things and put them in the chest. Then I shut down the lid and it was turned into a settle.

"It is not an unpleasant room," she said. "We should use it. Or did you feel that since it was your mother's . . ."

"Yes, I do feel I should like it to remain just as it is."

"It shall be," she said, and went out.

I wondered if she had been aware of the tension I was feeling.

I went to my bedchamber. I was glad Senara was not there. After a while I felt better. Then I asked myself what had come over me to make me feel so disturbed because my stepmother had discovered me looking into the chest.

Jennet had been gossiping. Poor Jennet, she could never resist it. I heard through Senara.

"Your mother was always writing," she said. "She wrote in a book she had every day. Did you know?"

"Jennet mentioned it the other day. So she told you too?"

"Not exactly. Merry said she was talking about it in the kitchens. It all sounded rather mysterious."

"Why should the fact that she was keeping a diary be mysterious? Many people do, I believe."

"Well, she hid this away apparently."

"Who said so?"

"Well, where is it? Have you got it? I believe you have."

"I haven't."

Senara looked at me intently. "If you had it, would you read it?"

"Why do you ask that question?"

"For the reason people usually ask questions. I should like an answer."

I hesitated, and she went on. "People put their secret thoughts into diaries. If she had wanted you to read it, she would have shown you, wouldn't she?"

I was still silent. I was thinking of Jennet's spreading the news that my mother had written down what happened to her every day and had been so anxious that someone should not see what she had written that she had been very careful to put her writings in some secret place.

I thought of the diary I had once kept when I was a child. It read something like this: "Rained today." "There were visitors at the castle for my father." "Hotter today." And so on, except at Christmastime when there would be a description of the festivities. Nothing to be hidden away there.

Then I thought of my mother's stealthily writing and finding some spot where she could secret her journal for fear it should be read by someone in the castle.

Senara went on: "There was something wrong with her, wasn't there . . . just before she died."

"What do you mean . . . wrong?"

"You used to go and sleep with her every night. Why?"

"I just had a feeling that I wanted to."

"What a baby! Who wanted to be with her mother!"

"Perhaps I did."

"It wasn't that. *You* were playing the mother. You always

seem to like it when there's someone who wants to be looked after. You're always finding animals to nurse. Do you remember that gull you brought home with the broken leg? The others were pecking him to death and you found him there, making horrid squawking noises. I remember how you brought him home and nursed him, but it didn't do any good, did it? He died in the courtyard. 'Miss Tamsyn at it again,' they said. And look how you're always clucking over the peacocks at Lyon Court. So you went to look after your mother. Why? You would have been there the night she died if I hadn't been sick. Oh, Tamsyn, do you blame me for that?"

"Don't be silly. Of course I don't."

"I did drink too much mulled wine. It was horrid. I shall never forget the feeling. I'll never do it again. But I wonder why your mother hid away her diary. Wouldn't it be fun if we found it?"

Then I guessed that Senara had mentioned the diary to her mother and that Maria had known for what I was looking when she had seen me at the chest.

We were approaching Halloween, always remembered at the castle with a certain awe because it was on Halloween fifteen years ago that my stepmother had come to us. Jennet remembered it well, and while Jennet had a tongue in her head, it would not be allowed to be forgotten.

There is something about the autumn which has always fascinated me. Spring was the season my mother had loved because of all the wild flowers she found in the hedgerows. She knew the names of most of them and tried to teach me, but I was not a very apt pupil and tried to learn to please her more than for any special interest. For me the special time of year was autumn when a little inland the trees sported their bronzed and golden leaves and there were carpets of them in fields and lanes and the spiders' webs were draped over the hedges. I liked the mists of the mornings and evenings and even the chill in the air. I used to think before my mother died: soon it will be Christmas, the time of holly and ivy and yule logs, and families being together and forgetting their differences. It was a time to look forward to. Autumn was the looking-forward time, and so often anticipation is better than realization.

Jennet told me that in the days before that Halloween when my mother brought the woman who was to replace her into the house, the servants used to make a large bonfire which was said to keep off witches, and when it was burned out, they would scramble for the ashes which they would preserve to keep off the evil eye.

The castle was filled with the autumnal shadows; when I awoke in the morning and looked out to sea, there would often be nothing but a wall of gray mist. I pitied sailors in such weather, and I thought often of Fenn and wondered when he would be home. I used to make sure that the lanterns in the Seaward and Nonna's Towers were always alight.

The day came bringing with it an air of excitement. My stepmother seemed to glide rather than walk about the castle. There was a secret smile on her face as though she knew everyone was expecting something to happen and she was at the heart of it.

The drama came at supper. Senara was missing. When she failed to appear at the supper table, I began to be alarmed. She was often late, but never for meals where my father would be. Unpunctuality infuriated him, and anyone who could not be at the table was sent away without food and often cuffed for it.

My father noticed her absence but did not comment. If she failed to put in an appearance, she would go without her supper. My stepmother showed no anxiety, but then she never did show very much.

After the meal she was still missing, and I began to be frightened.

I went up to our bedchamber.

"Have you seen Mistress Senara?" I asked Merry.

She shook her head. "She went off early in the afternoon."

"Went off," I said. "Where?"

"She were on her horse, Mistress Tamsyn. Jan saw her riding away from the castle as though she were possessed."

I wished they would not use such expressions and on Halloween of all times. It was easy to see how their minds worked. For them my stepmother was still the witch to be placated and feared, and Senara was her daughter.

"When was this?" I demanded.

"Early this afternoon."

"Did she say where she was going?"

"No, mistress. She just put on her riding clothes and her best hat with the blue feather and went off."

"Which of the grooms were with her?"

"Well, mistress, I did see none of they."

I thought: She has gone off alone!

Although we knew most of the neighboring squires, their families and retainers, robbers lurked on the roads, and we were forbidden to ride without at least two grooms.

Yet she had gone off alone and on Halloween.

I went up to the ramparts of Nonna's Tower and looked out. If it had been daylight or a clear moonlit night, I might have been able to see something. On such a night as this I could see very little but the four towers of the castle.

I went down, very anxious. She had gone riding alone that afternoon. Anything could have happened to her.

I went to find my father and stepmother. I must tell them that Senara had not merely missed her supper but that she was not in her bedchamber either and something must be done about it.

As I came down to the hall, I heard arrivals in the courtyard. With great relief I hurried out. One of the grooms was holding a lantern, and I saw an unfamiliar man on a horse.

My father was greeting him, and my stepmother was with them.

"Come into the castle," said my father. "You must be weary."

I said, "Father, Senara is not in the castle."

"I know, I know," he said. "This good gentleman has ridden here to tell us she is safe. Tell the servants to bring mulled wine and refreshment, for he needs to revive himself."

Relief filled me as I ran off to do his bidding.

The gentleman was Carl Deemster, and he had recently bought, from Squire Northfield, a mansion some five miles inland. He had come from Lincolnshire with his family two years before. He was rather somberly but neatly dressed, and his accent was unfamiliar to me. He explained that Senara had lost her way and called at his house. The mist had arisen, and it was growing dark, and his wife had invited him to stay the night while he rode to the castle to tell us that Senara was safe.

My father was very hospitable. He said that the mist was thick and it would not be an easy journey back. The kind Carl Deemster must spend the night at the castle, and supper must be brought for him immediately and a room prepared.

This was agreed upon. Our guest ate very sparingly and drank nothing, but he and my father seemed to find a great interest in each other.

Carl Deemster talked about the sea and clearly knew something of ships.

When I went up to my bedchamber, the mist had penetrated into the room. It seemed stark and empty without Senara! Merry came in to put my things away.

"So she be safe," she said. "I thank God for it."

"Of course Senara is safe," I cried. "What did you think?"

"Its being Halloween I did wonder. And her going off. Jennet said it reminded her. . . ."

"Jennet," I said, "is always being reminded."

"She said it was such a day when the mistress went away."

"You mean. . . ."

Merry crossed herself. "I mean the mistress . . . she who is mistress now. She came on Halloween, and she went on Halloween. You were but a baby at the time as it was years ago. And we thought that Mistress Senara being her daughter and none knowing where she came from. . . ."

I was always uneasy when the servants talked of Senara's background. I could never hear the word "witchcraft" when I did not fear for her. She was in a way to blame. There would always be mystery attached to her mother, but Senara nourished it. Even on this occasion she had to get lost on Halloween. It was almost as though she wanted to be accused of witchcraft. Did she not realize how dangerous this could be?

My uneasiness stayed with me. I was longing to get through the night and be united with her. I wanted to hear how it was she had managed to get lost on Halloween.

I was up early in the morning, and so was our guest. He had broken his fast with a goblet of home-brewed ale and meat and bread and told me that he wished to leave early. He was sure that his wife would realize that he had spent the night with us on account of the mist, but he would like to return to Leyden Hall as soon as possible, for she might be anxious if he were late.

I asked if I might ride with him. We could take two of our grooms and bring Senara back with us.

He said his wife would be delighted, and so it was arranged.

It was a beautiful morning when we left. The mist had lifted, and the air was balmy. We rode inland through lanes and across meadows and finally we came to Leyden Hall, a charming old house, built I should say at the beginning of Queen Elizabeth's reign—about the same period as Lyon

Court and very like it in style, with its vaulted roof and wings on either side.

But how different was Leyden Hall from Lyon Court, with its ornamental gardens where peacocks strutted symbolically. My grandfather and his father had loved ostentation. It always seemed to me that everything at my grandfather's home was meant to impress. I was immediately struck by the simplicity of Leyden Hall. I had been to this house when it belonged to Squire Northfield. What a different place it had become. There were no pictures on the walls: everything that was decorative had been taken away. I met the mistress of the house, Priscilla Deemster; her gown was of a simple calico material which came from Calicut in India—clean and neat without lace or ribbons. She greeted me with a show of friendship plainly expressed. I felt that I was in the kind of household I had never seen before.

The Deemsters had two sons who were both married and lived with their wives at Leyden Hall. They were all dressed in the same simple manner. Among them Senara looked like one of the peacocks of Lyon Court in her blue riding habit. I had rarely seen her as lovely or as excited as she was then. Her beauty was as breathtaking as that of her mother.

"We were so anxious about you," I told her.

"It was the mist," she said and there was a lilt in her voice. "It has been a wonderful experience for me. I have been so comforted in this house."

Her voice had taken on a tone unusual with it and which somehow belied the sparkle in her eyes.

"I am so sorry to have caused you anxiety," she said. "Master Deemster, out of the goodness of his heart, so kindly offered to let you know."

"It was indeed kind," I said.

As it was nearly noon, I was invited to dine with the family, and I gratefully accepted this. I was very interested in this household, and I particularly wanted to know why Senara was so pleased with her adventure.

The table was set on trestles in the great hall which I remembered as being so grand in the time of the North-fields. The food on it was simple. It mainly comprised vegetables, which were grown in the gardens—and there was salted pig. Here the whole of the household congregated—every man and woman in the household—and then I understood Senara's elation, for seated at the table was Richard Gravel, Dickon, her onetime music master.

Senara looked at me mischievously.

"You remember Dickon."

He smiled at me. He had changed as much as this house had. He had been rather dandified, delighting as he did in his music and dancing. Now he was dressed in a plain jerkin, short trunks of a brown material, and his long hose were of the same shade. His hair, which had been wonderfully curling, was now cut short and flattened about his head as though he were ashamed of its beauty. He had been fun-loving and bold; now his eyes were downcast, and there was an air of modesty about him which I could not entirely believe in.

We sat down, and grace was said. It seemed a long time before our host finished his exhortations to us to be grateful.

The pork was not very appetizing, and I secretly was not all that grateful for it. We ate very well at home and always in the most tasteful manner, and there was invariably a variety of dishes to choose from.

Dickon told me during that meal what he must already have told Senara.

When he had been turned out of our house, "and rightly so," he said in his newfound humility, "for I ill repaid my master, I knew not where to go. For two days I trudged the countryside and had but a crust all that time. I was wondering where I should find another bite to eat, and feeling faint and hungry, I settled into a hedge and there awaited some evil fate to overtake me. As I lay there, unkempt and famished, a man came along the road. He too was without means of sustenance, hungry and footsore. He told me that he was going to call at Leyden Hall, for the gentleman and lady who now lived there would never turn any away. I said I would perforce go with him, and so I came."

Senara was watching him with an intentness she rarely displayed.

"When I felt the goodness, the serenity of this household, which was unlike anything I ever knew before, I asked if I might stay here in any capacity whatsoever," went on Dickon.

"You do not teach dancing and singing?"

"Nay, nay. That is over. It is all part of my sinful past life. Such frivolities find no favor in the sight of heaven. I shall never sing and dance again."

"That's a pity! You did them so well."

"Vanities," he said. "Here I tend the gardens. The vegetables you are eating have been grown by me. I work with my hands for the good of the house."

"You see," said Senara, "Dickon has become a good man."

It came to me to say that although attempting to seduce his master's daughter might not find favor in the sight of heaven, I did not believe there was anything wrong in singing and dancing. Did not the angels sing? But I made no comment. We had received excellent hospitality at the hands of this family, and our host had had the courtesy to ride over to us and inform us that Senara was safe with them. I did not wish, therefore, to say anything which might be hurtful to them.

I could see that they believed firmly in their doctrines and such people could easily be hurt and possibly angered by those who disagreed with them.

When we had eaten, Senara and I prepared to ride back. It was still only one o'clock, for they did not sit over their meals as we were inclined to do. I gathered that eating here was not to be regarded as a pleasure but a necessity. Our horses, fresh for the ride back, were brought to us, and with many thanks we left them.

Senara and I rode together—two grooms ahead of us and two behind.

"Now," I said. "I should like an explanation of how that came about."

Senara opened her eyes very wide and smiled sideways. "I have told you. I was lost in the mist. I came to Leyden Hall and explained my predicament. I was made welcome and as I was not allowed to find my way home alone I stayed there. You know the rest."

"It seems to me a strange coincidence that you should be lost near the house in which Dickon is a servant."

"Life," said Senara demurely, "is full of strange coincidences."

When we reached the castle, the servants looked at Senara with awe. I saw one of them cross herself when she thought we were not looking, which filled me with a vague apprehension. As usual Senara did everything to encourage it.

"Why," she cried to one gaping serving girl, "did you think I'd flown off on my broomstick?" Then she went close to her and narrowed her eyes so that the girl grew pale. "Perhaps next Halloween I might."

When we were alone in our bedchamber, I admonished her, but she laughed at me. She was excited as I had rarely seen her.

"Imagine Dickon a Puritan!"

"Is he sincere, do you think?"

"Dickon is always sincere. He believes wholeheartedly in everything he does . . . at the moment. That is what I like in him. He made me feel that I could be a Puritan too."

"You, Senara! You are a pagan, which is the very opposite."

"I could change," she said, "perhaps. He talked to me about it. It is inspiring . . . in a way."

"Inspiring to you! I never knew anyone who loved finery as you do. One day you want to be a witch. The next a Puritan!"

"Dickon talked to me about the sect. They are very noble. The Deemsters are fond of him. They love converts. You see, when he went there, he was such a beautiful young man, with his feet firmly planted on the road to hell. They have saved his soul. You know how attractive anything that you have saved is."

She had learned something about the Puritans. The Deemsters came from Lincolnshire. Master Deemster's mother had been Dutch, and they had ties with Holland. "They believe that life should be simplicity," she said, "and abhor all Papist idols."

"As we do."

"For the Puritans their religion is the most important event in their lives. They care for nothing but their simple goodness. They do not believe in the riches of this life. They believe we should live humbly, simply and that all vanity is an offense to God. They would die for their beliefs."

"I pray God they do not have to. The King is against them and has sworn to harm them."

"They know that well."

"He believes that they are as the Scottish Presbytery, of which he has had some experience, and he has said that that agrees as well with a monarchy as God with the devil."

Senara laughed as though this pleased her. I think she was enamored of the Puritans because by pursuing their brand of religion, they courted danger.

"Moreover," I went on warningly, "the King has said at the Hampton Court Conference that he will harry the Puritans out of the land or else do worse. They must either conform or take the consequences."

"Oh, yes, they know this, and they care not for his threats. They are planning action. One thing they will never do is give up their religion."

I could see that she was excited by her adventure and that this was in some measure due to the fact that the Puritans were in danger.

I was very disturbed indeed when I discovered that she had known Dickon was at Leyden Hall. One of the servants had found out that he was there and told her. She had staged her little adventure for Halloween—what a fearless, reckless girl she was!

From then on she talked of him a good deal and often called at Leyden Hall. She began to learn a great deal about the Puritans and their beliefs and aims, which was strange considering she was Senara.

The Turret Lights

It was Christmas Day, my eighteenth birthday and Senara's sixteenth. My stepmother had invited people to the castle. She seemed eager to find husbands for us both and particularly for me perhaps because I was two years older.

During the last weeks Senara liked to go off alone. I believed she was riding to Leyden Hall.

She had taken the feather out of her riding hat and wore it plain. She would put on a demure expression which ill matched her brilliant long eyes with the mischief in them. Of course, I had never been absolutely sure of Senara.

She talked to me about the Puritans, and often she would become quite earnest.

"They want to make it all as simple as possible, Tamsyn," she said. "And religion should be simple, shouldn't it? Do you think God wants all that ceremony? Of course He doesn't. One should worship Him in the simplest possible way. The church is always ready to persecute those who don't conform."

"You are really interested, Senara," I said. "You've changed since you arranged to get lost near Leyden Hall."

"I arranged it, as you know," she said. "I couldn't believe Dickon had become a Puritan. I had to go and see."

"Surely he is not making one of you?"

"Can you imagine me . . . a Puritan!"

"That is something beyond my powers of imagination."

"No, I should never be a Puritan at heart, but I admire them in a way. Think of Dickon."

"It seems to me you think of him a good deal."

"He is so beautiful . . . even now in his plain clothes and his curls pressed out he is still more handsome than any other man . . . even your Fenn . . . who has gone away without declaring his feelings . . . even he looks quite ugly compared with Dickon."

"You are bewitched by him."

"You forget I am the one who does the bewitching."

"So it is he who is bewitched by you."

"I think that in spite of his new Puritan ideas, he is a little. For I am a very bewitching person, Tamsyn."

"In your own opinion certainly."

"It is so interesting," she said, "and so *dangerous*."

"Keep away from religion that is dangerous."

"What a thing to say! Surely that is quite cynical. How can people help what they believe, and if you believe, shouldn't you defend that belief with your life if need be?"

"Our country and my family have been torn by religious beliefs. One of my ancestors lost his head in the reign of Henry the Eighth; another was burned at the stake in the reign of Mary. We don't want any more religious conflict in the family."

"You're a coward, Tamsyn."

"That may be, but that is how I want it."

"They are talking of going away."

"Who, Dickon and the Deemsters?"

"Yes, to Holland. They can worship there as they wish. Perhaps one day they will go far away and make a land of their own. They talk about it a good deal."

I laughed.

"What amuses you?"

"That you, Senara, of all people, should be caught up with Puritans. Of course it is not the Puritans, I know. Can it really be Dickon?"

"How could it be? I would never be allowed to marry a man who was our music master and now grows vegetables and works for a family like the Deemsters."

"I cannot see you in the humble role of wife to a man in such a lowly position."

"Nay, nor could I. For I came from such nobility that is

far beyond anything I have had here."

"Oh, how do you know this?"

"My mother has told me. In Spain she moved in very noble circles——royal in fact. So you are right when you say I could not marry Dickon."

"Don't look sad. It's the first day of Christmas. We shall make merry this night. You will dance and sing for the company, and no one will be merrier than you."

"It will be a very different Christmas at Leyden Hall," she said.

"I can picture it. They will make of it a purely religious occasion. There will be no feasting, dancing and making merry, as we do, no King for the Night, no blessing on the hall, no mummers, no carol singers. This is more to your taste, Senara."

"It is!" she cried, and that night she was beautiful in a blue velvet gown, her dark hair caught back in a gold band.

I was not the only one who thought her the loveliest of all present. There were several young men who did and would doubtless in due course ask for her hand, which was what her mother wanted.

There was Thomas Grenoble for one, who came from London and was connected with the court. He was young, rich and good-looking. I knew he was one my stepmother had chosen for Senara. He could do the latest dances, which she quickly mastered, and I wondered whether as she danced with Thomas Grenoble, she thought of Dickon. If she did, she gave no sign of it.

Melanie had been brought up by her mother to be a good housewife, and I don't think our household matters ever went so smoothly as they did that Christmas. Melanie was quite unobtrusive and gentle; Connell was inclined to ignore her and flirt with some of the young women guests, but Melanie remained unruffled. She reminded me very much of Fenn, and how I wished that he were with us!

I mentioned him to her and asked if she had heard from her mother when he was expected back.

"It was not to be a long voyage," she answered. "My mother thinks he will be back by the spring."

That gave me new hope.

I was still looking for my mother's diary, and when it seemed that I had looked in every possible place, I began to think that it never existed. Jennet was known to exaggerate, to romanticize, particularly now that she was getting older. Had she seen my mother writing once or twice and imagined she had been writing something which she wanted to hide? That seemed very likely.

And my mother's death? People did die suddenly when they were not very old. One heard of them now and then, and no one was skilled enough in medicine to know the cause. If one was in court circles and known to have enemies, people thought of poison. I wondered how many men and women had been believed to be poisoned when they had died of natural causes.

Then on some days my feelings would change, and I would be certain that my mother had not died naturally. I could not forget the stone I had found on her grave. And who could have removed it from the cupboard in which I had placed it?

That was what had started my speculations. It was certainly mysterious. My mood fluctuated. At times I would think it was nonsense; then at others the certainty that my mother had not died naturally would be with me. Then I would start to look again for the journal, for if there was a secret, would it not be in that? But if she had not known she was about to die, how could it have been! But had she known? Why should she have been afraid during those last days of her life?

It would be in the book, and if that book existed, it must be in the castle.

I could think of nowhere in her sitting room where it could be. I had searched that, and the settle had yielded nothing. In the bedroom which she had shared with my father and was now that of him and my stepmother? That had been refurbished after my mother's death. Surely if the book had come to light, it would have been mentioned—or destroyed perhaps.

There were turret rooms in the towers of both Nonna's and Crows' where perhaps something could be hidden. In one of my exploratory moods I decided to look.

In those rooms there were some very old pieces of furniture, among them several stools and a table and a pallet or two. The stools were interesting because they were made like boxes and articles could be stored under where one sat.

When I was in the turrets with their long, narrow windows, I was always fascinated to look out to sea, and my eyes invariably came to rest on the jagged rocks of the Devil's Teeth. A gruesome sight! I was not surprised that they were said to be haunted.

These rooms were used fairly frequently, for high in the walls of those facing the sea were windows in which lanterns hung. They were reached by stepladders which were kept in each room so that they could be easily reached. The lanterns had been hanging there for many years and had been placed there by one of my ancestors. He was known as Good Casvellyn in contrast, I had heard, with so many of the family who were far from good. The Devil's Teeth had always been responsible for a good share of the wrecks along our coast, and Good Casvellyn had had the idea that if he carefully placed lighted lanterns in the top of his towers of Nonna's and Seaward, it was possible that they could be seen some way out to sea and the sailors who saw them would know they were close to the treacherous Devil's Teeth. Therefore, they would steer clear of them.

I liked to think that the kindly action started by Good Casvellyn had saved the lives of sailors. Of course, it often happened that in spite of the lights, there were disasters on the rocks.

I was always anxious when I heard the wind rising and the spring tides were up and there was a storm at sea. How many ships had foundered on that grinning mouth? I imagined that many a sailor who was unsure of his whereabouts and saw the lights in Nonna's and the Seaward Towers blessed Good Casvellyn for his lights.

It was the duty of one of the men from Seaward Tower to make sure that each night they were shining out to sea.

I had searched everywhere in the tower rooms at Nonna's. I examined the stools with the greatest care because I suspected that in one of them there must be a secret compartment.

It was soon after Christmas that I started to search again, and the more I thought of the matter, the more certain I became that one of the stools up there could be a hiding place for those papers. I examined them all. There was indeed a secret compartment in one of them, which made my heart beat fast, but there was nothing in it when I finally succeeded in opening it.

I sat on the floor feeling exasperated. There is nothing so maddening as to search for something when you are not even sure of its existence.

Then suddenly, as I sat there, I felt a cold shiver run down my spine. I sensed, rather than heard, that someone was close watching. I stood up. There was no one in the room.

"Who's there?" I said in a sharp, aggressive voice which betrayed my fear.

There was no answer. I hurried to the door and threw it open. I was looking straight at the spiral staircase which wound a few steps from the top so that if someone were just a dozen steps down, one would not see that person. But I did hear a light footstep, and I knew that someone had been watching me.

Why had he or she not answered when I called? Why was it necessary to watch me unobserved?

There came to me then the thought that someone knew what I was looking for and that that someone was very anxious to know if I had found it.

The light was beginning to fade. I looked around the room. Soon the man who was in charge of the lantern would arrive to light it. I did not want him to find me here. Nor did I wish to stay here. That step on the stairs had unnerved me. For if someone was eager to know whether I had found the papers, why should this be so?

Was someone afraid that I would find them? Was someone else looking for them even more fervently than I? If so, there could be but one reason for this. That person might be afraid of what was in them.

Who would be? The one who had killed my mother.

Thomas Grenoble called often. Senara would play the lute to him and sing languorous songs of love.

She had another suitor too. He was a young man with hair and eyes as dark as her own. He was a visitor at Squire Marden's house. Some years older than Senara, he was intense and passionate, I should imagine. He was not English, though his name was not really foreign. He was Lord Cartonel. He spoke with a rather careful accent, and some of his expressions were un-English.

He told us that he had been in several embassies for the late Queen and that he had lived abroad for many years, which was why there appeared to be something a little foreign about him.

There was no doubt that my stepmother admired him, and I guessed that she had chosen either him or Thomas Grenoble as Senara's husband.

Senara was delighted to have these two admirers.

"It is always good," she said, "to have a choice."

"And what of Dickon?" I asked.

"Dickon! You can't seriously think that I am considering him."

"If he were of noble birth. . . ."

Her face flushed with sudden anger. "But he is not!" she said sharply and changed the subject.

It was late February when Melanie came to me one day, "My brother is home. I have a letter here from my mother. She says he will be staying for a while before his next voyage."

"I wonder if he will call here."

"I think he will want to," she answered, smiling her gentle smile.

I used to wake up every morning after that saying to myself, "Perhaps he'll come today." Whenever I heard arrivals, I would dash to my window and look down, longing to see him.

February was out. He had been home three weeks, and he had not come to the castle.

Why did he not come? Melanie looked puzzled. Surely if he did not want to see me, he would wish to see his sister?

Senara was faintly mischievous as she always had been about Fenn.

"I hear the good Fenn Landor has been home some weeks. Yet he does not call here."

I was too wounded to retort sharply, so I shrugged.

"He has forgotten all about us," she went on. "They say sailors are fickle."

A few days later we heard that Thomas Grenoble had returned to London.

"Without asking for my hand!" said Senara demurely. "What do you make of that, Tamsyn?"

"I thought he was deeply enamored of you. It seems strange."

"He was. But I was not going to have him."

"He has not asked, remember."

"He was on the point of it. He is a very rich man, Tamsyn. He will have a high-sounding title one day. He is just the man my mother wanted for me."

"Yet he did not offer."

"Because I did not want him to."

"You told him so?"

"That would not have stopped him, but I had to stop him somehow because if he had, I am sure the temptation would have been too much for them to resist. So I worked a spell."

"Oh, Senara, do not talk so. I have asked you so many times not to."

"Nevertheless I stopped him. It was a very natural sort of spell. A man in his position at court could not have a witch for a wife."

"Sometimes I think you are mad, Senara."

"Nay, never that. I am so pleased that my spell worked that I want to tell you about it. Have you ever thought, Tamsyn, how we can make our servants work for us? They can do so much with a little prompting. I have made good use of servants . . . always. You are not attending. You are wondering whether Fenn will come soon. I will tell you something. He won't come. He doesn't want you any more than Thomas Grenoble wants me. Let me tell you about Thomas Grenoble. I made the servants talk . . . my servants to his servants. It was so easy. I made them tell him of my strangeness, my spells, the manner in which I was born. I wanted him to think that the servants were afraid of me, that I never went to church because I feared to. That strange things happened, that I could whip up a storm at sea, that I could make a man see me as the most beautiful creature he had ever seen . . . and he believed them. So that is why he went so suddenly to London. He is putting as great a distance between us as he can."

"You did not do this, Senara."

"I did. I did. I knew they would force me to marry him if he made an offer. And he was on the point of it. He was besottedly in love with me. But his fear of being involved with witchcraft was greater than his love. People are becoming more and more afraid of it, Tamsyn. It's a growing cult. And the more people fear it, the more they discover it. I am free of Thomas Grenoble."

I did not entirely believe her. I thought she was piqued because he had gone away.

I accused her of this, and she laughed at me.

"His love could not have been very strong," I said, "if he could so quickly forget it."

"You should comfort me, Tamsyn. Have we both not lost a lover?"

As I walked away, I heard her shrill laughter. And I thought: She is right. I have been foolish to hope for Fenn. I misunderstood his friendship. But if he is a friend, why does he stay away?

A little later I saw Senara riding away from the castle.

I thought: She is going to Leyden Hall. She is going to see Dickon.

I remembered then how she had adored him when she was younger and how they had danced and sung together.

Could it really be that she loved Dickon? Was it really true that she had rid herself of Thomas Grenoble in this way?

One could never be sure with Senara. If she loved Dickon, she was heading for sorrow, for she would never be allowed to marry him.

And for myself, I knew I could never love anyone but Fenn Landor.

Senara and I, I thought, we shall have to comfort each other.

March came in like a lion, as they say. The winds were violent, and the salt spray dashed itself against the castle walls. The waves were so high that it was dangerous to walk on the sea side of the castle. One could easily have been caught and washed away.

One evening, when a storm was rising, I had an uneasy conviction that the lantern was not alight. There were occasions when it went out, but in such weather special attention was supposed to be given to it.

I climbed to the tower carrying a taper with me, and sure enough, that reassuring glow was not there and the turret rooms were in darkness.

I thought of going to the Seaward Tower to tell them that someone had forgotten to light the lanterns in Nonna's. Then I thought it was quite a simple matter to light them myself. I could comfortably reach them with the stepladder. I lighted them, and in a few minutes they were throwing their reassuring beam of light out across the sea.

I went down to my bedchamber. Senara was there, lying on her pallet with dreams in her eyes.

I was about to mention the lanterns when she said, "They will be going away soon."

"Who?" I asked.

"The Puritans. They want to worship in freedom, and they say the only place where they can do so is in Holland."

"Will Dickon go with them?"

"Yes," she said.

"You will miss him."

She did not answer. I had rarely seen her so subdued.

Then she started to talk about the Puritans. They were people who would die for their beliefs. "Imagine that, Tamsyn. It's noble in its way." She laughed suddenly. "Dickon is greatly tempted. I can see that. He wants to be a Puritan, and his whole being cries out against it. As mine would. It is a continual battle for him. Battles are exciting. *You* want everything to be peaceful. *You* always did. It's not that you lack spirit, but you're not an adventurer, Tamsyn. You're the mother figure, there to love and protect. I'm not like that. I'm the mistress . . . to tempt, to snare and to be unpredictable."

"You are certainly that," I retorted. "Why do you visit these Puritans? I know why. It is because it is dangerous. There are going to be harsher rules against them. They are going to be persecuted. Perhaps people will always want to fight again and kill those who disagree with them. The Catholics on the one hand, the Puritans on the other, and they are both supposed to be enemies of the church!"

"The King hates them. Puritans, witches and Catholics who attempt to blow up his Parliament! The King is a strange man. They say he is very clever and that he is renowned for his wit. He loves pleasure as much as the Puritans hate it. Thomas Grenoble told me that he spends much time at the cockfight and pays his master of cocks two hundred pounds a year which is equal to the salary of his secretaries of state. He is a coward too! His garments are padded to preserve him against the assassin's knife. He is terrified of being assassinated. They talk of these matters at Leyden Hall, and they plan to escape from them. It is not that they are running away exactly. . . . They are brave men and women, for they will face fearful hazards. They care nothing for this. They make wonderful plans. They do not intend to stay in Holland."

Her eyes were brilliant. I could see that she was following them in her thoughts; *she* was facing the hazards, and I knew that all the time she was seeing herself side by side with Dickon.

"It is some years since Sir Walter Raleigh found a fair land which he called after Queen Elizabeth—Virginia. It lies a long way across the ocean. They talk of Virginia."

"It was a colony," I said, "and is now abandoned."

"It is a rich land of fruits and plants and trees. Perhaps it will be there that they will settle. They will build a new country where men shall be free to follow their relig

"Provided," I added, "it does not conflict with that laid down by the Puritans."

Senara looked at me seriously for a few minutes, and then she burst out laughing.

"Oh, it is not for the religion, Tamsyn. It's not whether we shall genuflect twenty times a day or make our knees sore by kneeling on a stone floor. What do I care for that! It's the adventure. It's glorious. That's what I care about."

That, I thought, and Dickon. I was very uneasy, wondering what would become of her when Dickon went away.

The next day the violent storm of the previous night had abated. Two things happened. There was a whipping in the Seaward courtyard.

Merry told us about it, her face distorted with misery. She would, I knew, be remembering the occasion when her own Jan Leward had been so degraded.

He had offended the master, this last victim. It was a terrible occasion. The men of Seaward had been commanded to assemble in the courtyard to watch. The women would not look. They set about preparing ointments and bandages to deal with the sufferer when he was untied from the post and dragged unconscious into the tower.

The whippings took place rarely, which no doubt made them more to be feared than if they were a commonplace occurrence. The last one had been Jan Leward. I knew that Merry had never got over it, and because of this misdemeanor, my father had refused them permission to marry for another year. He had told Jan, so Merry had reported to Senara, that he did not want two disobedient servants, and until Jan had proved his loyalty, he could not marry.

I had watched Merry's face sometimes when my father's name was mentioned, and I saw the bitter hatred there.

All that day there was a hush over the castle and everyone was talking about the whipping. A few days later there was good news. We had a visitor. He wanted to see my father and thank him personally. On the night of the storm he had all but been wrecked on the Devil's Teeth. He had in time seen the warning lights, but for that his ship, battered by the devastating weather, would undoubtedly have foundered. It was like an act of God. He had been making straight for the rocks, and then he saw the warning light in time. He had reason to be grateful to the Casvellyns.

The cargo he carried was one of the richest he had ever handled. Gold, ivory and spices from Africa.

He sat drinking with my father all through the day, and he announced that he was sending several barrels of finest malmsey for the enjoyment of my father's servants.

When I thought about it, I realized that I had been the one to light the lanterns. I couldn't resist telling Senara about it. Merry came in while we were talking.

"It's a wonderful feeling," I said, "to have saved that ship. Someone forgot to light the lanterns that night. I thank God that some instinct sent me up there at the right moment."

Senara and Merry were looking at me intently.

Merry said, "So it was you."

"Why," cried Senara, "the malmsey should be yours." She added, "If you mention it, there would be trouble."

I thought I knew what she meant. Of course there would be trouble. The fact that I had found the lanterns unlit meant that someone had failed in his duty. A slip like that could have cost many lives.

We wanted no more whippings in the courtyard.

A week or so later there was news from Lyon Court. My grandmother was ailing, and it seemed long to her since she had seen me.

My father said I might go to see her, and for once Senara did not insist on accompanying me. I believed this was due to the fact that if she did, she would not be able to pay her now regular visits to Leyden Hall and so miss seeing Dickon.

I found my grandmother frail, but she seemed to revive a great deal when she saw me.

Spring often comes early to Devon, and we were able to sit in the gardens. I was happy to be with her but sad to remember how my mother had loved to feed the peacocks and how they used to come to her with a sort of disdainful air to take the peas she offered them.

She wanted to hear about life at the castle, and I happily told her of how I had found the lanterns unlit in the tower and my action had saved the ship. She thought that was a wonderful story and made me repeat it many times. She asked about my father and my stepmother and whether they seemed happy together.

I supposed they were. My father was not the kind to suffer in silence, and my stepmother was difficult to know, but she was as she had always been.

And Senara?

"Senara is interested in a Puritan family who have come to live nearby."

"Senara and Puritans! That's incongruous."

"Senara is so baffling. Sometimes I feel I don't know her."

"Yet you are fond of each other."

"Yes, as sisters."

"You are closer to her than you are to Connell."

"I suppose it is because Connell is a boy. He and I have never had anything in common."

"And Melanie?"

"I am growing fond of her. She is so kind and gentle always. I hope Connell will be good to her."

"Is he not?"

"They are rarely together. Connell hunts and is with my father a great deal."

"And is there any sign of a child?"

"I have not heard."

"I expect Melanie is hoping. And what of Fenn Landor?"

I was silent.

"Has he not been to the castle?"

I looked beyond my grandmother to the tall hedge which shut in her pond garden.

"No," I said, "he has not been to the castle."

She was frowning. "There must be a reason."

"Oh, I think there was some speculation. He did not like it perhaps."

"Speculation?"

"Yes," I said boldly, "about me. It seemed to be in everyone's mind that we should marry . . . everyone's except Fenn's."

"Something must have happened," said my grandmother. "I'll swear he was in love with you."

I shook my head.

"Let us not speak of it, Grandmother," I said. "I would rather not."

"No good comes of brushing something aside because it is hurtful to look at."

"What is this?" I cried. "It has happened so many times. Two people become friendly, and those around them think they must be going to marry."

"Did you think it, Tamsyn?"

I could not find the words to explain, and it was so hard not to betray my emotion.

My grandmother went on: "I wanted it to happen. To me it would have meant such compensation. I wanted your mother to marry his father, and when young Fenn appeared and you and he seemed so suited. . . ."

I said in a cool voice, "He went away to sea without letting me know. He has come back without seeing me. It's clear, is it not?"

"No," said my grandmother firmly. "There must be a reason."

"It is all clear to me," I said. "Fenn has been deterred by all the hints of marriage."

"I shall send a message to ask him to come to see me," she said.

"If you do," I retorted, "it will be necessary for me to go back to the castle before he arrives here."

She could see I meant that. So we sat and talked of old times. She spoke of my mother when she was a little girl, and when she was very tired, she would doze off. She liked me to sit beside her so that I was there when she woke up, and often in those first moments when she was coming out of her sleep I knew that she confused me with my mother.

I think during my stay she tried to make me interested in other young people. She gave several dinner parties to which she invited eligible young men. One or two of them were engaged in the trading company and knew Fenn. His name was mentioned more than once. It was very clear to me that he was a highly respected member of the company, as I would expect him to be.

There were several older men there, seamen mostly who had worked for my grandfather in his various ships in the days before he had become a trader.

I was amazed how these people enjoyed talking of the old days.

"Life has become tame," said one of them who was seated next to me at dinner. "The days of the old Queen was the time to be alive."

Another of his age put in: "And that was the days before the defeat of the Armada. Every man ready to do his best to ward off the foe. People are not like that now. They're selfish, looking for their own gain."

I could not help commenting that they had always been like that.

They talked with great affection of the old Queen, of her vanities, her temper, her injustice and her greatness.

"There has never been so shrewd a monarch, and there never will be," was the verdict.

It was true that they had not the same respect for our

reigning King. He was dirty in his habits, unkempt in his appearance and ill-mannered at the table. He had the disadvantage of having been brought up by Scotsmen, they said.

"Though his mother," said my old gentleman, "was said to be one of the most elegant and beautiful women the world has ever known."

They started to talk of old times and how the Queen of Scotland had been the center of plots to put her on the throne and our Queen had always been one step ahead of the scheming Mary.

"Mary was an adulteress," said one.

"And a murderess," said the other.

They discussed the murder of her second husband, Lord Darnley.

"He was to have been blown up in Kirk o' Field, and we know who planned that. But it went wrong, and he was found in the grounds . . . dead . . . but without a sign on his body of how he died."

I found I was suddenly listening attentively.

"There was nothing to show. . . ."

I felt my heart begin to beat faster, and I said, "How could that be possible?"

"Oh, it is possible," was the answer. "There is a method and these villains knew it."

"What method?" I asked earnestly.

"I believe that if a wet cloth is placed over the mouth and held firmly there until the victim is suffocated, there will be no signs of violence on his skin."

I felt it hard to concentrate after that. Those words kept dancing about in my brain.

There had been no signs of violence on my mother's body. Nor had there been on Lord Darnley's.

I would have liked to talk to my grandmother, but I dared not. She looked so old and fragile that I did not want to upset her.

I said nothing. I wanted to go back to the castle. I was certain now that my mother had feared something. On the night I had left her alone she had died . . . and there were no marks of violence on her body.

Someone had killed her. Moreover, she had had an inkling that someone was trying to.

If she was writing down the events of her days, she must have written something which she considered secret since she had wanted to hide it.

I had to find those papers.

It was April when I arrived back at the castle. When I went up to our bedchamber, I found that Senara's things were gone.

She came hurrying in and hugged me.

"So you are back. I'll admit it doesn't seem the same without you."

"Where are your things?"

She put her head on one side and regarded me with a smile. "I thought it was time you and I had separate rooms. There are enough and to spare in the castle. It was all very well when we were little and afraid of the dark."

I was a little hurt. I thought of the pleasant manner in which we had always chatted before we slept and how she had clearly not been pleased if I was ever not there as, for instance, when I visited my grandmother.

"I've gone into the Red Room," she said.

"Why that room? There are others."

"I had a fancy for it."

I shrugged.

"You're not angry, are you?" she asked.

"No, but I wonder why you felt it necessary."

She smiled secretly. I knew there was a reason. And why had she chosen the Red Room? I knew how daring and reckless she was. A thought had come into my mind. She was in love with Dickon. I was certain of that. The very fact that marriage with him would be so highly unsuitable would make it attractive to her. And he was going away soon, for when the Deemsters left, he was going with them. He was one of them now. He would go first to Holland and join in that greater project to settle in America if it ever came to pass.

An idea came to me then. Could she have chosen the Red Room because if the servants heard strange noises there, they would say it was a ghost and be afraid to enter?

Did Dickon come to the castle to visit her at night? Not the Puritan surely. But how sincere were they . . . either of them? And I believed that they were passionately in love.

It was a very uneasy situation. I wondered what would happen to Dickon if he were really visiting Senara and if my father or her mother discovered this.

Lord Cartonel was still paying his visits. Senara and her mother took wine with him. I was certain that he was going to ask for Senara's hand, and if he did, then I was sure that she would be obliged to take this very grand gentleman. He was just what I believed her mother had always wanted for her.

As for myself, I started my search for the papers again. But where could I look that I had not looked before?

My thoughts were diverted by the talk of witchcraft which had become rife since my departure. Merry was excited by it.

"They do say, mistress," she told me, "that there be a coven of 'em and 'tis not so far away. Some says some place, some another. Terrible things do happen there. 'Tis anti-Christian. There they do worship the devil himself, and he sits there in their midst in the form of a horned goat."

"It's a lot of nonsense, Merry," I told her.

" 'Tis not so thought to be, mistress, pardon the contradiction. There be terrible goings-on. One serving girl were out late, and she saw them there. She peeped and there they was mother-naked dancing wild like . . . as though they was inciting each other to be criminal like."

"How did the serving girl know they were acting in criminal manner?"

"Oh, 'twere clear to see."

"If she were innocent, how would she recognize these criminal acts?"

"Well, 'twas moonlight, and they threw off their clothes and danced together, and then when they be exhausted, they lie down together, and that's the worst of it."

"I would like to question that serving girl."

"Oh, she wouldn't mind that, mistress, only she bain't one of ours. She be terrible upset about it, for she do think they knew she was watching. They would like, wouldn't 'em, seeing they'm sold to the devil and they say he be powerful . . . like God really, but on the other side."

"Merry," I said severely, "you know that no good can come of this gossip."

" 'Tis said that only good will come when every witch be hanging from a gibbet."

I wanted to leave her, but I felt it was imperative that I knew the truth.

I said, "I think the girl imagined she saw this. What was she doing out at night in any case?"

"She'd been to visit her mother, who'd been took ill, and she had to wait with her till help come. She did see familiar faces there in the coven, mistress. She knows now that some be the devil's own."

"Has she said who?"

"No, she be feared to. Every time she do open her mouth to say she be took with trembling. But they be going to make her say. They be meeting . . . all them that is going to put a stop to witches will take her and make her talk. It must be so, mistress. Mistress Jelling have lost her baby . . . stillborn it were, and a terrible disease have broke out among her husband's cows."

I knew that whatever I said would do no good. It frightened me. I could feel the tension rising.

I knew that the servants were watching my stepmother. In their hearts they believed that she had brought witchcraft into the castle. It was some years now since she had come, but the nature of her coming would never be forgotten.

A terrible thought had struck me. If the people were aroused to look for witches, as I believe they had done in other parts of the country, the first place they would look would be in the castle.

Senara seemed to be possessed by a recklessness. I sensed that she was unhappy and that it was because Dickon was going away.

Surely she could never have imagined there would be a marriage between them. She might have done so, being Senara.

Once she had said, "With me all things are possible," and she had meant it.

She was quieter than usual. I knew that she went often to Leyden Hall, and I was almost certain that Dickon crept into the castle at night.

I loved Senara, maddening as she was at times. I did not understand her, but the bond between us was there.

I deplored this recklessness in her. I wanted to implore her to take care.

That was the last thing she would do. She knew there were whisperings. She knew that as her mother's daughter she was suspected. Yet she seemed to take a delight in whipping up their fears and suspicions.

Once she came in late. I knew she had been to Leyden Hall, for she had about her that look of exultation which was often there after her visits.

I said to her, "You have just ridden in on Betsy."

She flashed at me, "Of course. What did you expect me to ride in on? My broomstick?"

And there were servants listening.

The Devil's Teeth

It was strange that when I was not looking for them, I should find my mother's papers.

I had intended to write a letter to my grandmother, and in my mother's sitting room where I did my writing at that time I opened the sandalwood desk box which I often used. There was paper wedged into the side of the boxlike cavity, and as I tried to dislodge it, I touched a spring. A flap of wood fell down, and the papers started to spill out.

I looked at them in disbelief. I glanced at a page. I could not believe it. My heart began to thud with excitement. That for which I had searched so earnestly had fallen into my hands.

I sorted the papers; there were far more than I would have believed possible in that secret compartment of the sandalwood desk box.

I started to read. There it was—my mother's meeting with Fenn's father, the possibility of their marriage and then with my father at the inn and the consequences. Knowing them, it was so vivid to me, and yet I said to myself as I read on, did I know them? I suppose people are different beings to different people. They change their personalities to suit their background like a chameleon on his tree.

There was the coming of my stepmother. That I knew already. She had come on Halloween and been found by my mother. It was a story which had often been told.

And then . . . my mother's discovery of my father's profession.

I could not bear that. I wished I had never found the papers. So on those nights of storm he lured ships onto the rocks. A flash of understanding came to me. The night I had lighted the lanterns in the tower they had been deliberately put out. It was for that reason that there had been a whipping in the Seaward courtyard. Someone had been blamed for lighting them on that night. Someone who should have seen that they were put out.

What can I do? I asked myself. I cannot stay here. I won't stay here. I must get away. I must put a stop to my father's hideous trade.

How?

I could betray him. To whom? I was so ignorant of what should be done. What if I told Fenn? I could go to him and tell him what was happening and he would stop it. And Fenn's father was in that grave. Murdered October, 1600, and by my own father!

I felt inadequate, alone.

To whom should I turn?

There was my grandmother. I could go to her. She was a wise woman. She would tell me what to do.

Then I thought of her frail and failing, and I asked myself, how could I burden her with this?

I must find a way. I would make sure that always the lanterns shone out their beams on the water. They might turn them out, but I would see that they were lighted. At least I could do that. I had saved a ship once. I would do it again.

They would discover, of course. What would they do to me? What would my father do if he knew that I was aware of his activities? He was a violent man, and if he was capable of letting hundreds drown for the sake of the cargo they carried what else was he capable of?

Murdered, 1600! I kept seeing that stone on my mother's grave. I read on in fascinated horror.

She had been afraid. She had suspected something. She had been comforted by my presence, and on the night I was not there she had died.

I had learned so much through those papers, but not what I had set out to know.

How did my mother die?

In view of all I now knew, I was convinced that she had been murdered.

My knowledge had changed me. Senara noticed it.

"What's happened?" she demanded. "Something has."

I shook my head. "What do you mean?"

"I can see it," she insisted. "I've spoken to you twice, and you haven't answered. You're dreaming half the time. And you're worried, Tamsyn. What is it?"

"You're imagining things," I said.

But she didn't believe me, and she wasn't going to let it rest.

"I believe you've discovered something. What is it? Is it why Fenn doesn't come to see you?"

"I don't need to discover that. Why should he come to see me more than anyone else?"

"Because there was some special understanding between you."

"In other people's imaginations," I said.

"Well, if it's not Fenn, what is it? I know. You've found those papers you were looking for."

I started. I must have betrayed myself.

"So you have," she declared.

"The papers are still in their secret hiding place." This was true. I had put them back in the sandalwood desk. I would keep the desk in the old place so that none might find anything different. That was the safest way.

"I believe you *have* seen them," said Senara. "You've been reading the revelations, and it has made you very thoughtful. You can't keep secrets, Tamsyn. You never could."

"You'd be surprised," I said, "what secrets I can keep."

"If you've found those papers and won't show them to me, I'll never forgive you."

"I daresay I shall get through life without your forgiveness."

"So you have found them."

"I said I could do without your forgiveness."

"You are maddening. But you've found them, I know. Don't imagine that I'm not going to pester you till you tell me where they are."

Merry had come into the room.

I wondered how much she had overheard.

It was amazing how difficult it was to keep a secret in a household of many people. I was well aware that several people believed with Senara that I had found the papers.

During that day the uneasiness came to me.

I was possessed of dangerous knowledge. There were several people involved—my father who gave the orders, all the men of the Seaward Tower who were his helpers in his work of destruction, my stepmother who might have been my father's mistress while my mother was alive and who married him three months after her death.

The biggest guilt rested with my father. It was this thought which horrified me. I could not bear that he should be the murderer of my mother. He was the one with the motive. She had known of his trade, but then she had accepted it. I was surprised that she had, but perhaps I did not understand. She had needed him in her life. Whether she had loved him or not I could not know. I was not sufficiently experienced. I was too young, too idealistic. I knew my grandmother had deplored my grandfather's buccaneering ways. He had often boasted of the Spaniards he had killed. Yet she had loved him, and when he had died, it had seemed that her life had finished with his. How was I to understand the complex emotions between men and women? I had a kind of idealistic love for Fenn Landor, but I was shrewd enough to know that I was only on the threshold of love. He had rejected me, and it might be that one day I would love as my grandmother had loved my grandfather and my mother my father. I could not blame her for turning away from that terrible question. He was her husband and she had promised to obey him.

I was certain, though, that my mother had been murdered. I was equally certain of the method. A famous person died in a certain way, and a method was used. That method would be remembered. I thought of Lord Darnley in that house at Kirk o' Field and how he had escaped when the gunpowder was about to blow it up, how his murderers had caught up with him in the garden and there suffocated him with the damp cloth—not in his bed, as they had planned, but in the garden to which he had escaped. And because of this and because his body was found unmarked by violence, people talked of how he died, and that method would be remembered and repeated. In a way all our lives were linked with one another.

One thing was clear. There was a murderer in the castle, and I was possessed of dangerous knowledge—how dangerous that person was not sure.

The simplest thing to be done would be to get me out of the way.

That was why I felt this fear. It was as though my mother were warning me. I had this strong feeling that she was watching over me.

By a coincidence I had overheard that conversation at my grandmother's house, and it had alerted my senses. It was a possible method . . . in fact the only method, and it had proved so effective. Would it be repeated?

I could picture it all so clearly. Merry would come in the morning. She would see me lying there cold and still as my mother had lain all those years ago.

There would be no mark on my body, no indication of how I had died. They would say, it was a mysterious disease which I must have inherited from her mother, for this is exactly how she died.

I knew my danger was at night.

How had I lived through that day? I wondered. If only there was someone to whom I could turn. Should I go to my grandmother, after all?

Evening shadows fell across the castle. I sat at my window and looked out at the Devil's Teeth. There the masts of broken ships were visible. Was it true that on some nights the ghostly voices of the dead were heard coming from rocks?

I went up to the tower room to make sure the lanterns were lighted. They weren't. Perhaps it wasn't dark enough. So I lighted them.

Jan Leward came up while I was on the ladder.

I started when I heard a noise in the room.

"What be doing, mistress?" he said. "I come to light the lanterns."

"I thought it had been forgotten," I said.

He looked at me oddly. "Nay, mistress, 'twas early yet."

I wondered whether he was thinking that I was the one who had lighted them before and earned a whipping for one of his friends.

I went down to my bedchamber. I had not joined them for supper. I felt I could not sit at the table with my father and stepmother and not betray my feelings. I had pleaded a headache.

Jennet came up with one of her possets. I took it uncomplainingly to get rid of her. And when she had gone, I thought how foolish it was of me to have pleaded indisposition. Wasn't that setting the stage for someone to dispatch me in the same way as my mother had been?

I thought, if it is going to happen to me, it will happen soon, and it will be while I am asleep in my bedchamber. I should have been wise and calm. I should have behaved as though nothing unusual had happened. I should have made it seem that that talk of the papers being discovered was mere servants' gossip.

But I had not been strong enough.

I undressed and went to my bed. I had no intention of sleeping. I could not in any case. I was wide awake. It could be tonight, I thought, for if someone is trying to be rid of me, it will have to be done soon, for every minute I live I could divulge something I have discovered in my mother's papers.

I must not sleep tonight.

I propped myself up with pillows and waited.

There was no moon that night, and it was dark. My eyes were accustomed to the gloom, and I could make out the familiar pieces of furniture in the room.

There I waited, and I went over in my mind everything I had read in my mother's papers. I promised myself that if I lived through this, I would write my own experiences and add them to hers, that I might, as she said, look at myself with complete clarity, for that is important. One must see oneself, one must be true to oneself, for it is only then that one can be faithful to others.

And as I waited there in the gloom of my bedchamber, I heard the clock in the courtyard strike midnight.

Now my lids were becoming heavy; part of me wanted to sleep, but the tension within me saved me from that. I was firmly of the belief that if I slept, I would never wake up. I would never know who it was who had killed my mother.

I must be ready.

And then it came. . . . It must have been a half hour past midnight, the steps in the corridor which paused outside my door. The slow lifting of the latch.

Oh, God, I thought, it has come. And a fervent prayer escaped me. Not my father, I implored.

The door was opening. Someone was in the room—a shadowy figure, coming closer and closer to the bed.

I cried, "Senara!"

"Yes," she said, "it is. I couldn't sleep. I had to come to talk to you."

She looked around. "Where's my pallet?"

"It's been taken away. I think it's behind the ruelle."

I was shaking. It must have been with relief.

She went to the wooden chair and pulled it close to the bed.

"I had to talk to you, Tamsyn. It's easier to talk in the dark."

"A fine time to come," I said, returning to normal. And I thought: There will be two of us if the murderer comes.

"Yes," she said. "It was easier when I slept here, wasn't it? I'd just wake you and make you talk. Now I have to come to you."

"Why did you go?"

"You know."

"Dickon," I said. "So he comes to visit you."

"You're shocked."

"I'm finding out quite a lot that's shocking."

"I can't explain my feelings for Dickon," she said. "He's not much more than a servant, is he?"

"Put that down to ill luck. He has some education, as much as you have. He sings beautifully and dances too."

"He doesn't now. He's a Puritan."

"Yet he visits you at night?"

"He's trying to be a Puritan. He wants me to marry him."

"That's impossible."

"They want me for Lord Cartonel."

"He may not want *you* after the Dickon adventure."

She laughed. "Dickon is going away. They're sailing in a week. Fancy! I shall see him no more. I can't bear it, Tamsyn."

"You'll have to."

"Not if I went with him."

"Senara, you're mad. You'd have to be a Puritan."

"Why shouldn't I?"

"As if you ever could!"

"I could try . . . as Dickon tries. I'd have my lapses . . . but I suspect they all do."

"I should put such nonsense out of your mind."

"I want to be good, Tamsyn."

"I suppose most people do, but they want other things more."

"I have to confess to you, Tamsyn. It's about Fenn Landor."

"What?" I cried.

"I couldn't bear that you should marry and go away. It

was all so right for you, wasn't it? He was approved of
by the family. And he was so good and noble, and you
were to live not so far from here and dear grandmother,
and he would be such a good husband. It wasn't fair."

"What are you trying to tell me, Senara?"

"You're such a fool, Tamsyn. Always believing the best
of everyone. You just don't know what life's about. You're
the eternal mother, and we're all your children. We're a
wicked lot, and you think the best of us. Fenn Landor is
another like you. You go through life blindly innocent of
the world. Look at this place. Look what goes on here."

"You know," I said.

"Of course I know. I've spied out things. I've seen what
goes into Ysella's Tower. I've seen the men go out with
their donkeys when the lights are out in the tower. I know
they lure ships onto the Devil's Teeth and they don't save
the survivors. I'm going to make a guess. You've found
those papers, and your mother knew about this, and she's
written about it, and you know now. And you don't know
what to do. That's it, is it not?"

I was silent. She's right, I thought, I'm an innocent. I
don't see what is happening about me. I do believe in the
goodness of everybody. But not anymore. I know someone
in this house is going to murder me.

"Why didn't you tell me?" I said.

"Oh, no. I wasn't going to do that. I used it, though . . .
that's what I've got to tell you. You see when Jan Leward
was whipped, he hated our father. So did Merry. They
were ready to do anything that would bring harm to him.
I questioned them about what I suspected, and they told
me so much. They told me that the grave next to your
mother's was that of Fenn Landor's father, and they told
me how his ship was wrecked and he washed up on the
coast. We put the stones on the graveyards—it was my
idea. They thought it was revenge on your father, but I
wanted it for Fenn Landor. I wanted a big shock for him
because I felt in my bones that he was going to ask you
to marry him that night. I had to stop it. It was only partly
because I didn't want you to have everything that was right
and proper. I didn't want to lose you either. So that's what
we did. Then we put one on your mother's grave. And
when I found you'd brought the stone in, I took it away
and threw it in the sea. It had served its purpose. Then I
sent Jan to tell Fenn Landor what was going on here. He
thinks you know of it."

"Oh, Senara!"

"Yes, he'll despise you and your father, and he'll do something about it. I know he will. He'll be here when there's a wreck and he'll catch them at it. Then we'll see what will happen. But that's why he's kept away from you. I've sent Jan over to tell him that the grave in the burial ground is that of his father. That'll bring some action, you see."

In spite of everything, I felt a certain pleasure. There was a reason for Fenn's absence. I could understand how shocked he must have been by Jan Leward's revelation. I knew how he would feel because of my own bewilderment. He would be as uncertain how to act as I was.

I could explain to him, and I remembered with a sudden stab of joy that I could prove I had not known of the terrible things that were happening. Had I not saved the ship by lighting the lanterns—one of the ships of his own company!

"You see," Senara was going on, "I stir up trouble as the witches stirred up the sea when the Queen was coming from Norway. I am wicked. You could say that I have given my allegiance to Satan. I have renounced God. It's true, Tamsyn."

"And you are talking of being a Puritan?"

"You know I never would be. I talk a great deal of nonsense, Tamsyn. And then tonight . . . I woke up suddenly in the Red Room, and I knew I had to come to you. I had to tell you. I want Fenn Landor to know the truth too."

"Why this sudden change of front?"

"Because something is going to happen. Nothing is going to be the same again. I am a witch. I know it makes you angry when I say it. I don't ride on broomsticks. I have no familiar, I haven't kissed the horned goat, but I stir up the lives of those around me. That's why I'm a witch. I'm going to give you Fenn Landor, Tamsyn. I'm going to make him believe in you. You're my blood sister, and I'm going to make you happy for the rest of your life."

"That's good of you," I said.

She laughed. "Now you're talking to me as you used to. You've forgiven me. Of course you have. You always forgive. You think I'm reformed, but I'm not. I'll be just as wicked tomorrow. It's only tonight I'm good."

"You must be cold too."

"No," she said, "I'm warm . . . warm in the glow of my own virtue. Soon I shall have to say good-bye to Dickon.

Then I shall marry Lord Cartonel and live dangerously ever after."

She went on talking of what her life would be like, and then she was silent.

Fenn filled my thoughts. I must see him. I thought: He will come to see me, and we will go away together. But what of Castle Paling and the evil things which were done there?

And as I sat there, I thought I heard a noise in the corridor.

"What's that?" I asked.

Senara listened.

She said, "It was the wind."

"I thought I heard footsteps outside."

Footsteps outside the door! Footsteps retreating!

I shivered a little and was thankful that Senara was with me.

She talked of her love for Dickon and how it amazed her and him and how she wondered how she could go on living without him.

It was dawn when she went to her bed and the castle was stirring. Only then did I sleep, and when I awoke, it was late into the morning.

I don't know how I lived through the next day. There was one thought which superseded all others. There was a reason for Fenn's absence. If he could be made to see the truth. . . . He *should* be made to see the truth. What could I do? Could I ride over to him? The distance was too far in one day. I could not just slip away. Or could I?

I might go to my grandmother. Then I thought of the shock it would be to her to learn of these things. The terrible activities of her son-in-law, her daughter's acceptance of it and finally her murder.

Yes, I was convinced that my mother had been murdered. I believed that the noise in the corridor I had heard the previous night had been the footsteps of the murderer, who was coming to my room. Senara had saved me, Senara, who had tried to ruin my life, had saved it.

I would not have died as my mother had. She had been fast asleep—possibly poppy juice had been given to her. Because she was unwell, possets were continually taken to her. It would not have been so easy had she been awake.

I could not bear to stay in Castle Paling. The whole place had taken on a sinister aspect. I went out and walked away from it. Then I looked back at Ysella's Tower, where the goods had been stored and where my mother had once been locked in, and Seaward Tower, where my father's men lived—those who were party to his guilty secret and took a share, I doubted not, of the profits. Then Crows' and Nonna's where I had lived my life.

I would leave the castle very soon. If Fenn did not want me—and how could I be sure that he did?—I would go to my grandmother and live with her.

I would not stay in that castle where so many evil deeds had been done.

I thought of my father. Strangely enough I had a glimmer of affection for him. Why, I could not understand. He had never shown me any. There was about him a strength, a power. He towered above the men I saw around him. He was a leader among them. I knew that he was cruel, that he was capable of evil deeds and yet . . . I could not entirely hate him. I could not inform against him. I just wanted to get away, but if I did, I would always be haunted by what was happening at the castle. And oh, how desperately I wanted my father to be innocent of my mother's death.

Then suddenly I knew that I was going to stay another night in the castle. I was going to discover the truth if I could. The night before I had waited in my bed for someone to come to me, someone with murder in the heart. And Senara had come with her revelations, and because Senara was with me, the murderer had gone away.

But tonight I should be alone. I should be prepared.

I did not go down to supper. I said that I was not feeling well. Whoever was afraid of what I had discovered would be able to use that indisposition to good advantage.

In my room I planned what I would do. I would not go to bed. If I did, there was a danger of my falling asleep, even in my excited state. I would go into the ruelle and be there. Through the curtains I would watch if someone came into the room. But it must appear as though I were sleeping in my bed.

I took two pillows and laid them longways in the bed. I covered them up. In the darkness it would seem as though I were sleeping there.

How long the night seemed in coming. I was ready waiting behind my curtains of the ruelle. I heard the clock strike eleven.

How quiet the castle was! Did my mother have no premonition on that night? I was more fortunate than she was. I had her journal to warn me. When she was writing, was she impelled to do so because it was going to play such an important part in her daughter's life?

I sat on the pallet, and I wondered what the future held. There was a great lifting of my spirits in spite of the dangers I felt all around me. Fenn might love me, after all.

Was that a faint sound in the corridor? Had I imagined it? I felt my limbs begin to tremble. I felt courage sapping away.

No, it was nothing. A mouse perhaps? But it *was* a sound. The latch of my door was being quietly lifted.

Someone was in the room.

I peered through the curtains. The figure was moving stealthily toward my bed.

I drew back the curtains and stepped out.

My stepmother turned sharply to face me. She stared at me blankly. It was the first time I had ever seen her disconcerted.

I took the damp cloth from her hand and said, "You killed my mother."

She didn't answer. In the gloom her face seemed impassive. Her surprise had left her. She was calm as she ever was.

She did not speak at all.

She turned away and walked from the room. I stood there, the damp cloth, her murder weapon, in my hands.

I spent a sleepless night. I must make some plans, and I was not sure what. In the morning I would speak to my stepmother; I would make her confess how she had killed my mother.

I sat on the chair which the night before Senara had occupied. I tried to sort out my thoughts. I had to take some action. If only I knew what.

During the early morning the wind had risen. It sent the sea thundering into the caves along the coast, and it sounded like voices shouting to each other. The wind whined about the castle walls like the complaining voices of those who had lost their lives on the Devil's Teeth, demanding revenge on the men who had sent them there.

I was up early. I dressed and went down to the hall. I could hear the servants bustling about. There was no sign of my stepmother.

All through the morning I could not find her, but I saw

my father. He was alone coming across the courtyard from the Seaward Tower.

I went to him and stood before him, barring his way.

"I have something to say to you," I said.

He stared at me; this was not the manner in which people were accustomed to address him, but I had lost all fear of him, and when he made as though to push me aside, I caught his arm.

"I've discovered something . . . terrible," I said.

He narrowed his eyes, and I thought he was going to strike me. Instead he hesitated, and then he said, "Come inside. We can't talk here."

I led the way to my bedroom. I wanted to tell him there, in that place where last night I had come near to death.

I faced him fearlessly, and perhaps because he had always respected courage, his eyes softened slightly. But his expression changed rapidly when I blurted out, "Last night your wife tried to kill me . . . in the same way as she killed my mother."

It was horrible, for I saw the look in his eyes before he could veil it. He knew that she had killed my mother.

"I suspected her," I went on. I pointed to the ruelle. "I was in there watching and waiting. She killed my mother in the same way as Lord Darnley's murderers killed him. I learned how that was done. A damp cloth pressed over the mouth, leaving no marks . . . no sign. And so my mother died. And you knew it. Perhaps you helped. Perhaps you planned it together."

"No!" he shouted vehemently. I was grateful that I could believe that.

"But you knew she did it," I insisted, and he was silent in his guilt.

"You," I went on. "Her husband . . . my father! Oh, God, my own father."

I had never believed I should see him so shaken, for I had never before seen him anything but in command of a situation. I could see, too, a certain anguish in his eyes, and because I had read my mother's journal and knew of that first meeting between them and the attraction which had sprung up, I was aware of the fact that he was looking back into the past and remembering too. He had not been a happy man since her death, yet I could not pity him.

"I loved her," I said, my voice trembling.

"I loved her too," he answered.

"And yet. . . ."

He was himself again, the softness passed. "You wouldn't understand," he said roughly. "Maria was irresistible . . . a witch if you like. She'd put a spell on me."

"And even though she had murdered my mother and you knew it, you married her."

"It's something you're too young to understand."

"I understand there is such a thing as unbridled lust," I said contemptuously.

" 'Twas more than that. Try to understand, Tamsyn."

"I understand this," I retorted. "You are a murderer, for I hold you guilty with her."

"It was done before I knew it. There was nothing I could do to stop it."

"Only marry her and enjoy the fruits of her infamy."

"You will never understand."

"Alas for me. I understand too well."

"You will cease your insolence, girl, or I'll take you to the courtyard and lash you there myself."

"Yes," I answered, "you are capable of that."

He did not try to stop me as I pushed past him and left him standing in my room.

I did not know what I was going to do. All through the morning I looked for my stepmother, but she was nowhere to be found.

It was afternoon when Fenn rode over.

I heard his voice in the courtyard, and my heart started to beat madly.

I ran out to him.

"Fenn," I said, "at last you have come."

He dismounted.

He took my hands and looked at me steadily. "I've wronged you, Tamsyn," he said; and my heart leaped, and in spite of all my indecisions and the horror which was all about me, I was happy.

"I must talk to you," he said. "Where can we be alone?"

"In the burial ground," I told him.

We went there together.

There he said, "So it is my father who lies there."

"You know," I answered.

He clenched his fists suddenly. "The murderers," he said. "I shall avenge him."

"I was hurt when you didn't come," I told him.

"I was miserable . . . most of all, to think that you had been a party to this."

"I never was."

"I know that now. I know that you saved one of our ships. I have spoken to the captain and he has told me that the Paling light prevented a disaster. And I know now that it was you who lighted the lanterns after they had been put out."

"I did not know of this foul trade. Not until I read my mother's journal. She knew. But he was her husband."

He nodded.

"I love you, Tamsyn," he said.

I said, "It's a strange place in which to be so happy."

"But before I can speak to you of this, I have something to do. Your father is responsible for my father's death. I have sworn that my father's murderer shall not go free. I have come here today to speak not of love, but of hatred. I shall never forget, Tamsyn. I shall kill him. I am going to make him pay for the lives of my father and those innocent sailors."

"Let us go away from here. I never want to see this place again. The sound of the wind howling around the walls, the knowledge of what has been done here nauseates me. Let's go right away from here."

"And if we go away, what then? Shall they be left to carry on their hateful business? How could we go away knowing that they went on luring ships onto the rocks to destroy them?"

"Then what can we do?"

"I am going to stop this forever. He has plundered his last ship."

"How can you stop it?"

"What he does is a crime against humanity."

"He is a powerful man in these parts. I know of none who do not tremble before him. Suppose you inform against him. Where would you inform? What would happen? He is too powerful. You would never stop him. He would have means of evading justice."

He looked beyond me with a faraway look in his eyes, and he said, "There is only one way of making sure that he never does this again. That is by killing him."

"But you are a man of peace," I said.

"This is the way to bring peace. Sometimes it is necessary to remove someone who is corroding the society in which we live. We had to kill Spaniards when we defeated the Armada. I had no remorse for them. We were saving our country from a cruel enemy. We drove off those ships which carried the invader and his instruments of torture. I would fight again and again; I would kill any Spaniard who tried to land in England. This is different. This is a ship full of cargo. The wrecker wants that cargo, so he lures the ship onto the rocks; he sends thousands of men and women to their deaths, for he must make sure that there are no survivors to carry the tale of villainy where it might be acted on. No, there is only one way, I say."

I looked at him fearfully. In his eyes there was a fanatical hatred—so alien to him.

"I am going to kill your father," he said.

"No, Fenn," I cried, and I put my arms about him.

He put them aside; then he looked at me sadly.

"It would always be between us," he said. "He killed my father. I can never forget that or forgive him. And I shall kill yours. You will never forget that either."

He looked down at his father's grave; then he turned away and left me there.

I ran after him. I had to stop him: I knew he meant what he said. He had idolized his father; he had gone on doing so after he was dead. He had refused to believe that he *was* dead and gone on dreaming of his return.

And my father was responsible for his death—he had killed him as certainly as though he had run him through with a cutlass and left him to die.

I heard the shouting voices above the wind.

"He be gone out," said one.

I saw them in the Seaward courtyard. There were about four of the men who worked with my father.

"He be at the Teeth," said Jack Emms, a dark-haired man with battered features.

"Why should he go there?" cried Fenn. "There's no wreck. He's been merciful of late. There has been no disaster there for the last two months to my knowledge."

"There he be gone, master."

Fenn had the man by the throat. I had not known he was capable of such violence. It was born of anger which came from the love of his father. He could not forget that but for my father, his father would have been alive today.

"Tell me where he is. I will know," he said, "or it will be the worse for you."

I saw then that Fenn was a man far stronger than my father. I had thought him gentle, and so he would be— gentle and tender—but he was an idealist as his father had been, and now he was full of righteous anger.

"He be gone, master, with Jan Leward. There always be merchandise that stays in the foundered ships. We go out now and then to recover it."

"I am going out there," said Fenn. "I am going to catch him at his evil trade."

"Nay, master."

"But yes," said Fenn. "Yes, yes!"

I was terrified. I pictured my father out there at the Teeth, with the howling wind whipping the waves to fury. And Fenn there . . . in the midst of his enemies.

I wanted to cry, "Don't go. All these men are your enemies. They will destroy you because you have come among them like an avenging angel. You are trying to destroy their lucrative business. Fenn, don't go."

It would be to plead in vain. He was going to confront my father. He was going to accuse him of the murder of *his* father, and I knew he planned to kill him. He would not take the cowardly way out, to go away with me and live far away from Castle Paling. He was right, for neither of us could do this. I knew too that when the wind howled and the storms raged, we should be thinking of sailors in peril near the Devil's Teeth, and the cries of drowning men would haunt us through the years.

But if he was going out there, I was going with him. I leaped into the boat.

"No, Tamsyn," shouted Fenn.

"If you go," I retorted, "I am coming with you."

Fenn looked at me, and his fear for me overcame his fury against my father.

I said, "My father is a murderer. He has been responsible for the deaths of thousands." I was thinking of my mother. He had not killed her, but he had connived at her murder and married her murderess. And since her death he had not been a happy man. Fenn must not suffer a murderer's remorse. I must save him from that. "Fenn," I went on, "I beg of you, do not have his death on your conscience."

His face hardened. "He killed my father."

"I know . . . I know. But it is not for you to kill him. If you do, the memory will haunt you all your life. Fenn, we have found each other. Let us think of that."

But I could see he was remembering the father whom he had loved—gentle Fennimore Landor, who had never sought to harm anyone and who had dreamed idealistic dreams of bringing prosperity to his country.

We had reached the Devil's Teeth. How malevolent they

looked with a tetchy sea swirling threateningly about them!

A wooden chest with iron bands had been caught in the rocks, and it was this which my father was trying to salvage.

"Colum Casvellyn," shouted Fenn. "You killed my father, and I'm going to kill you."

My father turned sharply to look at us, and as he did so, his boat rocked dangerously. He stared at us for a few seconds in amazement; then he said, "You fools. Go back. There's danger here. What do you know of these rocks?"

"I know this," answered Fenn. "You lured my father to death on them."

"Go away, you oaf! Take yourself out of my affairs."

Fenn had stood up, and I cried out in fear, "Fenn, be careful."

I heard my father's derisive laughter.

"Yes, be careful. Go away, you . . . trader. You don't understand this business. It's too dangerous for you, boy."

At that moment my father's boat tipped suddenly, and he was pitched forward. The boat turned over, and he was in the water. I heard him give a cry of agony as he threw up his hands and sank. He emerged a few seconds later. The water was up to his neck.

"I'll get him," cried Fenn.

"It's too dangerous," I warned, but Fenn was out of our boat, swimming cautiously to that spot where my father was.

"Go away," shouted my father. "I'm caught. The Teeth have got me. Can't pull myself free. You'll kill yourself, you fool."

Fenn ignored him.

Minutes passed while I watched in terror. The water was stained red, and I thought: They will both be lost.

"Fenn, Fenn," I cried. "It's no good. There's nothing you can do."

But he did not listen to me.

It seemed a long time before I helped him pull my father's mangled body into the boat.

He lay on his bed, my bold cruel father. The physician had seen him. Both his legs were injured. He had prided himself that he knew the Devil's Teeth better than any living man, but they had caught him in the end. The eddies about the rocks were notoriously dangerous, and when he had fallen into the sea, he had been immediately sucked under. Strong swimmer that he was, he could do nothing against such odds, for he had fallen between the two rocks known as the Canines, the most dangerous of them all.

And Fenn had saved his life. That is what makes me so proud. He had intended to kill him, and in that moment when my father lay helpless and all Fenn would have had to do was leave him to his fate, he had risked his own life to save that which a short while before he had threatened to take.

So Fenn brought home my father's poor mangled body, and we did not need the physician to tell us that he would never walk again.

Melanie was there, cool and efficient. Dear good Melanie, we all had reason to be grateful that she belonged to our family, then—and more so in the years to come.

So my father lived—not the same man. How could he be? He who had been so active would never walk again. This was retribution. The Devil's Teeth which he had used as his murder weapon on so many were turned against him. And the punishment he must suffer must be greater than death, for he was not a man lightly to endure inactivity.

Fenn came to me when the physician had gone.

We did not speak. We just looked at each other, and then he put his arms around me, and I knew that we should never leave each other again.

It was the next morning when we found my stepmother's cloak on the shore. It was in that very spot where my mother had discovered her. There was nothing else but her cloak.

The inference was that she had walked into the sea.

There was a great deal of talk in the castle. The servants whispered together. Change was everywhere. The master had been struck by avenging providence. He would never stalk through the castle again. And the mistress had gone, the way she had come.

They had always known she was a witch.

Fenn wanted me to go to my grandmother until we could be married, but I said I must stay awhile. I must be with Melanie, who was now pregnant and had taken my father under her care.

My stepmother had gone; my father was crippled. It was a stricken house, but the danger had disappeared.

Senara came to my room, her eyes wild. "Everything has changed, so quickly," she said. "You've got your Fenn, after all. Who would have believed it? He now knows what a fool he was to think that you could ever have stood quietly by and watched your father's business. And you know what a noble gentleman he is. He sets out to kill and then saves. Now, with free conscience and hearts beating as one, you can begin to live happily ever after."

"You may laugh at us, Senara, but we shall be happy."

"And what of me?"

"Let us hope that you too. . . ."

"Dickon is going to Holland. Shall I be happy without him?"

"When we are married," I said, "I shall live at Trystan Priory. You must come there too. I don't think you'll be happy here in the castle."

"My mother has gone now."

"She had to. She killed my mother and would have killed me, but I discovered in time."

"What do you think happened to her?"

"I think she walked into the sea."

Senara laughed aloud. "Oh, Tamsyn, you don't change. Full of remorse, do you think she was?"

"No, she found the position untenable. She was betrayed as a murderess and my father a cripple for the rest of his life. The weight of her sins must have been heavy."

"Never. I knew her well, Tamsyn, better than you ever could. She came of a noble Spanish family. She was traveling in the ship with her husband, my father, when it was caught on the Devil's Teeth. She never forgave that. She told me much. She came here and determined to destroy the household which had changed her life. She ensnared your father. They were lovers from the first. He never tired of her. She left soon after I was born, and he bought a house for her some miles from here in the heart of a wood. He used to visit her, and there she wove her spells. Then she came back, and she sent your mother away so that she could marry your father. And she did. But she was tired of the life. She remembered Spain and the hot sun and the flowers and the gracious manners of courtiers, for she was highly born. Lord Cartonel didn't come to see me, Tamsyn. He came to see her. She has gone with him. They will go to Spain, and we shall never hear from her again."

"Is this truly so, or is it one of your dreams?"

"It is a good story, is it not? You will find that Lord Cartonel has disappeared too. He is a spy for the Spaniards, I doubt not. You will never see either of them again."

"Can she leave you, her daughter, and never see you again?"

"Quite easily. She left me before, did she not? She did

not want children. They do not fit into her scheme of things."
She shrugged her shoulders. "It is hard for you to understand . . . you with your mother and your kind grandmother. We were different. We are not like ordinary folk."

"Senara, once again I must ask you not to talk so. It is
dangerous."

"Life is dangerous, Tamsyn. Even you should have learned
that by now. When you are married to Fenn and your children are playing at your knee, it will still be dangerous."

She was right, of course, but whatever life held for me
I was ready to face it with Fenn.

Melanie wanted me to marry soon, although I had said
I would stay awhile and help her nurse my father. But she
would not hear of it. He was bewildered and could not
believe that this had happened to him, to Colum Casvellyn,
the man who had always had his own way. Oddly enough,
Melanie was the one who could soothe him best. It was a
remarkable discovery that there was such power in this
quiet girl. My brother, Connell, was changing too. He was
the head of the house now, for that poor wreck which my
father had become could scarcely be called that now. It
was as though his new responsibilities gave him sudden
strength. He was regarding Melanie in a new light; she was
no longer the dull little wife whom he had married for con-
venience. Once I had thought he was growing more and
more like our father, but now there was a sudden halt in
that progress. It was as though he had had a revelation and
was taking stock of himself. I was glad for him . . . and
for Melanie.

It was evening, and the light was fading fast. Senara was
with me in my bedchamber, and as we talked, I suddenly
saw from my window that lights were approaching. It was
a party of people, carrying torches, who were wending their
way up the slope toward the castle.

I listened to their chanting voices, and what they said
sent a cold shiver down my spine.

"Give us the witch."

Senara stood beside me, her eyes dilated.

"They are intent on murder," she said, "and they are
coming for my mother."

"Thank God she has gone."

"Yes, she has cheated them."

The torches were now lighting up the scene; the chanting voices were growing louder.

Merry came running into the room.

"They've come for the witch," she said, "the witch from the sea."

"Don't they know she has gone?" I asked.

"They know but. . . ." Merry was looking fearfully at Senara. "If they can't have the witch from the sea, they'll take her daughter. Oh, God help us all. They wouldn't have dared if the master had been himself. But now he be nothing but a wreck broken on the Devil's Teeth, and there be none to stop 'em."

They had always wanted the witch from the sea. They had watched her and blamed her for their ill fortune. They believed she had bewitched my father, but they feared him so much that when he was there to protect her they dared do nothing.

"They will find me, Tamsyn," said Senara. "They will tie me to a stake and burn me alive. Or they will hang me from a gibbet. Poor Dickon, his heart will break."

Connell strode in, Melanie with him.

"The mob is at the gate," he said. "They are calling for the witch."

"She's gone."

He was looking at Senara. "They're greedy for blood," he said. "You must get away. You must never come back here. You'll never be safe. I'll hold them at bay. I'll show them who is the master here."

It might have been my father speaking. I turned to Senara and said, "We'll go out through the Seaward Tower. They won't be around that side of the castle. We'll take two donkeys."

"Where?" asked Connell.

"To Leyden Hall," I answered. "They'll hide her there until she leaves for Holland."

"Go quickly," said Connell.

And we went out. The night air cooled our burning faces as we rode away.

I saw the exultation in Senara's eyes, and I knew it was because she was going to Dickon.

We were on our way to Leyden Hall by the time the torch-lit mob was in the courtyard. Connell would subdue them, I knew. He was now the lord of the castle.

I must say a sad farewell to Senara, but I had the future to think of with Fenn.